MAZURKA

Pagan turned, looked at the man, smiled in a thin way. He didn't answer the question but hoped that his smile, so devoid of mirth, suggested an unspeakable threat. Closing the door, he went out into the corridor and dipped his face into a drinking-fountain, letting a jet of lukewarm water splash against his eyes and forehead. A gun in a left-luggage locker, a nameless man in New York who'd sent Jake all the way to England – maybe it was all very simple, nothing more than a straightforward political assassination . . .

But there was a dark area at the back of Pagan's mind, a room in which assorted problems lay like unlit lightbulbs awaiting a surge of electricity to illuminate them. And in this room there lived Pagan's muse, his own inner policeman, his personal inspector, who was rarely ever satisfied with simplicity and who hated darkness passionately. He loathed puzzles too, such as the plain white envelope, sealed and unaddressed, that Alexsis Romanenko had carried in his briefcase.

About the author

Campbell Armstrong is the pseudonym of
Campbell Black, an acclaimed author in other
spheres, who since writing JIG is now in the
front rank of international thriller writers.

Mazurka

Campbell Armstrong

CORONET BOOKS
Hodder and Stoughton

British Library C.I.P.

Armstrong, Campbell, *1944–*
Mazurka.
I. Title
813'.54[F]

ISBN 0 340 49185 X

Printed and bound in Great Britain
for Hodder and Stoughton
Paperbacks, a division of Hodder and
Stoughton Ltd., Mill Road,
Dunton Green, Sevenoaks, Kent
TN13 2YA. (Editorial Office:
47 Bedford Square, London
WC1B 3DP) by Cox & Wyman Ltd.,
Reading.

For the children – Iain, Stephen, Keiron and Leda

I would like to thank Major R. B. Claybourne (USMCR) for his fine technical help; Mr Bruno Laan for being an indefatigable source of information who patiently answered my questions even when they were on arcane matters; and the Joint Baltic American National Committee for generously providing information that helped with the background to this novel. I would also like to thank Harriette Pine for kindly showing me Brooklyn and Brighton Beach in the dead of winter.

You must take a good look at reality and understand that in future small nations will have to disappear . . . The Baltic nations will have to join the glorious family of the Soviet Union.

– V. M. Molotov,
Soviet Foreign Minister to V. Kreve-Mickevicius,
Deputy Prime Minister of Lithuania, July 1940

The fate of the three Baltic states is unique in human history. Nowhere else in the world are former parliamentary democracies occupied, annexed and colonised by a conquering power.

– The Copenhagen Manifesto, July 1985

The established habits and ideas are disintegrating before our eyes. The disappearance of something customary provokes protest. Conservatism does not want to give way but all this can and must be overcome . . .

– Mikhail Gorbachev, *Perestroika*

Mazurka (n.) A Slavic dance in triple measure.

1

Edinburgh, Scotland

There were too many things wrong with Edinburgh in late August. The crowds that filled Princes Street and spilled over into the old thoroughfares leading up to the Castle, which floated in the drizzling mist like a great galleon, gave Jacob Kiviranna a sense of claustrophobia. He was distressed by crowds, especially those that consisted mainly of American and Japanese tourists, restless as magpies, searching for quaint bargains in stores with none to offer. And then there was the weather, which was wet and joyless. It had been raining in a slow, merciless way ever since he'd arrived in the city the day before and checked into a small hotel behind Hanover Street – and now he couldn't rid himself of the feeling that his lungs were waterlogged.

He looked at his watch, an old Timex, and saw he had thirty minutes until the train arrived at Waverley Station. He moved along Rose Street, Edinburgh's famous street of bars, passing open doorways through which he could see flocks of hurried drinkers. He stepped inside one of the pubs, sat on a stool at the far end of the counter – a solitary spot – and ordered gin.

In the mirror behind the bar he gazed at his reflection. The eyes were deeply set and bright and somehow made people uneasy when they looked into them. The few acquaintances Jacob Kiviranna had made in his lifetime – other than analysts and therapists – had invariably found pretexts for drifting out of his orbit and slipping from sight. There was an intensity about him, an other-worldliness, that deterred friendships. Even as he sat now in the bar his lips moved almost imperceptibly in the way of people who have lived lives of extreme loneliness and who converse, if at all, with the voices they hear in their own skulls.

Stitched to the left shoulder of his khaki combat jacket was a Disneyland legend, the face of Mickey Mouse. On the right sleeve was a small American flag. Kiviranna's ponytail was held tightly in place with a brown rubber band. He wore a wispy beard and looked like a super-annuated hippie, a relic of another place and time. To a casual onlooker, he might have seemed like a raddled casualty of the drug culture, somebody who had taken one trip too many and hadn't quite managed to make it back and who now lived, poor soul, in a crazy world of his own making. And yet there was something more to Kiviranna than just this impression of being out of touch. There was something purposeful in his air of vague bewilderment, the kind of look aspirant saints carried back with them from the wilderness.

He sipped his drink, looked once again at his watch. If British Rail obeyed its own inscrutable timetables there were now twenty-five minutes until the train arrived on platform three at Waverley Station. He reached inside the pocket of his jacket and touched the gun. It was an Argentinian nine-shot Bersa 225. When he'd handled it in his hotel room this morning, he'd liked the icy blue finish of the pistol, the silken, almost fleshy sensation.

Twenty minutes. He left the bar without finishing his drink. It was a mere ten minutes to Waverley Station, hardly any distance at all, but he'd stroll there slowly.

On Princes Street he stared up at the Castle. It reminded him now of a natural artifact, something hacked by nature out of wind and rock and still in some weird process of change. Along the gardens of Princes Street flags fluttered bleakly. Posters advertising this or that Festival event were limp and soggy and indifferent. Avant-garde plays. Mime shows. Mozart. Pipe and drum bands.

Ahead, Kiviranna saw the entrance to the station. He paused, jostled on all sides by people with umbrellas and shopping bags. A group of boys wearing the green and white scarves of a local soccer team went banging past him, singing something unintelligible and irritating. He put his hand against the outline of the gun as he moved closer to the station. There was a familiar pain that had come out of nowhere to take root deep in his head.

He heard the shunting of a locomotive and the shouts of newspaper vendors and the screeching brakes of maroon double-decker buses. For the first time now he felt a sudden fluttering of nerves, something that moved around his heart and made him cold. Something that had nothing to do with the external weather. He adjusted his backpack, stopped to look at the headline on one of the local newspapers, then he moved on.

He took a thin guidebook out of his jeans, pretended to examine it, flipping through the pages but seeing little.

Edinburgh has always been known as the Athens of the North.

The print seemed to slither in front of his eyes. The words might have turned to grey liquid. He put the guidebook away. He went down the steps that led to Waverley Station. He touched the gun once more, a small reassuring gesture. He wiped slicks of rain from his face, ran one hand through his damp beard. And there it was again, that sense of nervousness, of a tremor going through his heart, like some extra pulse added to the rhythms of his body. He'd have to bring that under control. He couldn't afford any rebellion inside himself.

He entered the station, a place of enormous confusion, late trains, loudspeaker announcements, stacks of luggage, discarded newspapers. Porters stood around like impatient gravediggers awaiting the end of a eulogy they'd heard a million times before. Kiviranna wandered through the huge station, scanning the platforms. The loudspeaker announcements bewildered him. Strange place names were uttered in strange accents. *Inverkeithing.*

Kirkcaldy. Kinghorn. He studied the arrivals and departures board.

The pain in his head pulsated now and his jawbone felt locked. He hated the sensation because sometimes in the past it had given rise to the irrational fear, the suffocating fear, that his mouth would one day close and never open again. *Anxiety, Jake, sheer anxiety.* All the shrinks he'd ever encountered in institutions had told him that. And they gave him drugs with mellow names to assuage his fears, and sometimes they worked, sometimes not, and when they failed he'd sit for long, insomniac hours on the edge of his bed, wrapped in a blanket, shivering, imagining all manner of terrible things, hearing all kinds of weird sounds float up from the hostile street below the window of his apartment.

He moved to the gate of platform three. A ticket inspector glanced at him, then looked away. Another Yank. One of the impoverished ones. A middle-aged student doing Europe in five and a half days. The inspector had seen them all in his time. He'd seen fellows who looked exactly like Jacob Kiviranna, 'beatniks' – which was how the ticket inspector thought of them – coming from Amsterdam with marijuana in their shoes, shifty-eyed scruffs who muttered to themselves.

Kiviranna looked along the platform, which was stacked with mail sacks and trunks. He went to a newspaper stand where he browsed for a time. Then he wandered round the concourse of the station and studied the arrivals board again. Seven minutes. Seven minutes that were going to be very slow ones. Seven minutes before he could dispose of the evil that was presently sliding over slick railroad tracks toward Edinburgh.

Despite a bitch of a hangover, Frank Pagan was enjoying the task of escorting Aleksis Romanenko to Scotland. Normally Pagan had no real fondness for trains, for the musty compartments which, even in first class, were extremely uncomfortable. And views from carriage windows were less than breathtaking – the backs of granite houses and sorry little gardens and ramshackle greenhouses. Now and then a face in a rainy window gazed at the passing train as if such an event were the week's highlight.

But today Pagan felt detached from his dislikes. He had spent the previous evening riotously and quite unexpectedly drinking vodka with Romanenko in the Savoy Hotel in London, and now he was numb, and amazed by Romanenko's resilience. The Russian was in his middle fifties and yet he had the ability of a much younger man to bounce back from all the booze he'd drunk the night before.

Pagan, lulled by the rhythm of the train, looked across the compartment at Romanenko, who was holding forth in an exuberant way about the future of the computer industry in the Soviet Union. He demonstrated freely with his strong red hands, he shrugged, rolled his eyes, smiled a great deal – the kind of energetic man who couldn't keep still for very long and whose enthusiasms had a childlike, contagious quality.

Pagan tried to remember where last night had gone. It had begun with a courtesy call, he recollected that much. He'd visited Romanenko's room at the Savoy to discuss the timetable for this trip, and matters relating to security. Romanenko, with that demanding hospitality common to many Russians, produced a bottle of vodka and two glasses and insisted on drinking a toast to 'my new friend from Scotland Yard, my security guard, the very first Brottish policeman I am ever meeting in my life' – a toast that inevitably spawned another, then another, until finally a second bottle was opened and Pagan had the feeling he'd known Romanenko all his life. There had been warm handshakes, embraces, enthusiastic talk about a new purpose, a new spirit, inside the Soviet Union. *You will see differences, Frank Pagan, such as you have never dreamed of. Big changes are coming.* And here Aleksis had looked almost sly, a man privy to information Pagan could not have guessed in a thousand years. Given to winks and nudges and physical contact, he had the manner of somebody bursting to reveal crucial information and yet prohibited from doing so. *Big changes. Big surprises. Wait and see, Frank Pagan.*

Pagan thought he remembered the Russian crying tears of joy somewhere along the way and how the toasts had become more and more fulsome, with references to coexistence and peacefulness and how the 'Rosha' of the future was going to be. *A country, my friend Frank Pagan, for the twentieth century! Yes! Out of the Middle Ages and into the wonderful world of the computer! Yes! A hundred times yes! Let us drink another toast to the new Rosha! And to you and me, Frank Pagan, let us drink to a new friendsheep!* And then they'd gone together down to the bar, because Romanenko had the urge to strike up more *friendsheeps*, this time with women, and all Pagan could remember of the trip was Romanenko's ruddy face surveying the bar with lecherous intent, then the way he'd dragged a reticent young woman out of her chair and danced with her between the tables, his arms thrown around her waist and shoulders and his great laughter sweeping aside her delicate protests.

Pagan had a foggy recollection of making it home in a taxi – but the memory was too dim to fix with any certainty. Now, bright-eyed and irrepressible, Romanenko was laughing as he told some horror story about industrial sloth in the Soviet Union. He had a huge repertoire of jokes on the subject of the inconveniences of Russian life, and he related them with an actor's gusto in an English that was often muddled yet always charming.

Apart from Pagan and Romanenko, there was a third man in the compartment. Danus Oates was a middle level official from the Foreign Office, a young man with a pleasantly bland face and a plummy accent that suggested Eton or Harrow. Oates, whose function was to act as a kind of tour guide for the Russian, wasn't a great conversationalist. His talk was limited to such topics as the weather and some background chat about the history of Edinburgh, which he delivered like somebody who has swallowed a recorded message.

In the corridor of the train there was a man from Special Branch and a sullen character, presumably KGB, from the Soviet Embassy. Security surrounding the Russian wasn't especially tight. There hadn't been any death threats or virulent anti-Soviet propaganda in the newspapers or any outpourings of nationalist sentiment from the rabid groups that despised Russia. And Romanenko, after all, was just one anonymous official from a Russian outpost in the Baltic. The protection afforded him was little more than a courtesy, but it was Frank Pagan's responsibility to make sure that the Russian attended the Festival, heard the music he wanted to hear, Prokofiev's Classical Symphony, and was returned to London the following day in one piece – and Pagan took the job as seriously as he could.

"Are we close to Edinburgh?" Romanenko asked, gazing out of the window with some excitement. Like a boy on his first trip overseas, Pagan thought. The flushed expression, the voice a little too loud.

Danus Oates said that it would be another ten minutes or so. Romanenko smiled, lit a cigarette, a Player's, and fell silent for perhaps the only time since the train had left London.

Pagan stared out of the window. It was one of those leaden Scottish afternoons – drab skies and a low heaven, beneath which the granite houses, stained by rain, looked squat and depressing.

"Wish we'd had a better day," Danus Oates remarked. He had an upper-class Englishman's attitude to Scotland. It was an English colony where there were only two things of conversational significance – grouse-shooting and salmon-fishing.

The Russian shrugged. "Rain is not a problem to me, my friend. In Rosha, finding a good umbrella – that's the problem."

Pagan smiled, closed his eyes, drifted for a time.

Romanenko and Oates were, of all things, discussing roses now, a scarlet clutch of which Romanenko had just noticed in a back yard. Oates didn't know a rose from a rhododendron but he'd been trained in the craft of small talk and he made it with consummate ease. It transpired that Romanenko's hobby was rose-growing and he discussed it with the same enthusiasm he had for everything else, his hands caressing the air around him as if it were a delicate flower. He apparently had quite a garden at his dacha on the shores of the Baltic.

He took a wallet out of his pocket and showed Oates some photographs. Oates went into his head-nodding mode.

Pagan, who needed to stretch his legs and check to see if his hungover circulation was still functioning, excused himself and stepped out into the corridor, where he slid one of the windows open and enjoyed the feel of cold rain on his skin.

The man from Special Branch who stood in the corridor considered Pagan eccentric. To his way of thinking, Pagan didn't belong in the club. His clothes – brown shirt, beige necktie undone, a slightly baggy two-piece tan suit, brown canvas espadrilles – were wrong. His manner was wrong. He didn't have the right attitude. The man from Special Branch, who was called John Downey, resented the idea of Pagan being in charge of the security around Romanenko and so he thought sullen thoughts when it came to Frank.

With the special kind of malice that is often found inside a bureaucracy, certain members of Special Branch had been jubilant when Pagan had returned empty-handed last year from the United States where he'd gone in pursuit of an IRA gunman. There were even a few who had rowdily celebrated the disbandment of Pagan's own anti-terrorist section over drinks in a pub called The Sherlock Holmes. From the accounts Pagan had heard, it was an evening of gloating merriment.

For his own part, Pagan didn't give a damn what his colleagues thought of him. He had never lived his life to please other people and he wasn't about to let the opinions of morons trouble him now.

John Downey's waxed moustache suggested something faintly colonial. He had the face of a man who might have watched the last flag of the British Empire come down from the flagpole at the final outpost. He had the deflated cheeks of an old bugler.

"I had better plans for Saturday than this," Downey said. "Spurs are at home to Arsenal. I wanted to be at White Hart Lane."

Frank Pagan didn't share the great British passion for soccer. He watched the daylight disappear as the train plunged briefly into a tunnel, then the darkness was gone again and Downey's face came back into focus.

Downey peered into the compartment at the Russian. "He's not much to look at for a First Secretary of the Communist Party."

Pagan wondered if Downey would have been more impressed by a hammer and sickle tattoo on Romanenko's forehead. He found himself gazing at a globule of moisture that clung to the impenetrable hairs of Downey's moustache. The sight amused him.

"It's a job, John," Pagan said. "Think of yourself as a delivery boy. One Russian brought to Edinburgh, then hauled back to London again. And everybody's happy."

Downey appeared to consider this, as if he suspected a buried insult in the reference to a delivery boy. Then Downey's face changed to a leer. "At least he's not Irish. Is he, Frank?"

Pagan smiled in a thin way. Men like Downey, when they had the hold of a bone, never quite managed to let it go. For many months now, Downey had brought up the subject of Ireland on any pretext. It was infantile, Pagan knew, but it appeared to feed some deep, ludicrous need inside Downey's heart. What a life Downey had to live, Pagan thought. He had his football games and the task of waxing his bloody moustache and what else – beyond making tasteless remarks at Pagan's expense? It was a life that was difficult to imagine in its entirety. And yet not difficult, perhaps just appallingly easy. Despite himself, despite his resolve never to respond to sorry barbs, Pagan had an urge to slash back at Downey in some way – but that required an energy he hadn't been able to find in himself lately. He was treading water, going through the motions, listless. The death of the IRA gunman had pleased some people inside the hierarchy at Scotland Yard. They could at least claim that the man known as Jig was no longer a menace. And there had been a half-hearted attempt to make Frank Pagan some kind of hero, but it was doomed to failure because it was a role Pagan didn't have the heart for. Besides, credit for the gunman's death – if credit was an appropriate word – had been attributed to the FBI. In the end, there had been nothing remotely heroic in the death of the Irish assassin, and it had left Frank Pagan with a sour taste in his mouth.

Now, following the dissolution of his own Irish section, he'd been doing odd jobs for months, mainly guarding visiting dignitaries from African and Commonwealth countries, or Communist tourists like Aleksis Romanenko, who came to Britain to do a little business and squeeze in some sightseeing in this quaint green land.

He stared at Downey. "As you say, John. He's not Irish."

Downey's smile was like a bruise on his face. He enjoyed scoring points against Pagan, especially when Pagan failed to rise to his own defence. "Because if he was a mick, Frank, they wouldn't let you near him with a ten-foot pole, would they?"

Pagan slid the window open a little further and rain blew into Downey's eyes, making him mutter and blink and reach for a handkerchief in his coat pocket. Such a small triumph, Pagan thought. The trouble with a man like Downey was how he reduced you to his own idiotic level. He watched John Downey rub his face with the handkerchief. Moisture had caused the wax moustache to lose some of its glossy stiffness, and now it curled above Downey's upper lip like a furry caterpillar.

"Sorry about that, John," Pagan said. "I hope you brought your waxing kit with you," and he shut the window quickly, stepping back inside the compartment. The train was already beginning to slow as it approached Waverley Station.

Romanenko looked up expectantly. "Are we there?" he asked.

"A minute or so," Pagan replied.

"Excellent, excellent." Romanenko stood up, clutching his briefcase to his side. He wore a very British Burberry raincoat and shoes of fine Italian leather, soft and gleaming.

"Do we see the Castle soon?" Romanenko asked.

"Very," Danus Oates answered.

Pagan watched the platform loom up. When the train came finally to a halt, Pagan opened the door of the compartment and climbed down. Romanenko came immediately after him and almost at once John Downey fell into step beside the Russian, who was sniffing the air deeply and saying how railway stations smelled the same the world over, an observation with which Oates, whose experience of railways was minimal, readily agreed. The sullen man from the Soviet Embassy walked several feet behind the group looking this way and that, his head, reminiscent of a pumpkin, swivelling on the thick stalk of his neck.

Pagan stared the length of the platform, aware of people disembarking from the train, being met by relatives, little reunions, porters hauling baggage, mail sacks being unloaded – too much activity to follow at one time. Too many people. Pagan, who was walking about five or six feet ahead of the Russian, looked in the direction of the ticket-barrier, some twenty yards away. Beyond the gate there were more crowds. The bloody Festival, he thought. And a local soccer game into the bargain. There was no real control here. The environment wasn't properly sealed. And that made him uneasy. But uneasiness was something that plagued him these days, a sense of groundless anxiety. He supposed it was part of his general mood, his indecision, the feeling that his life and career were a pair of bloody mongrels going nowhere in particular.

"I understand we have a car waiting outside the station," Danus Oates said. "We're to dine at the George Hotel, which is said to be the best in the city. The chef is preparing Tay salmon in an unusual manner in honour of your visit."

Pagan wondered what was meant by 'unusual' in this case. He hoped it wasn't going to be some nouvelle cuisine monstrosity, salmon in raspberry sauce with poached kiwi fruit. He had a sudden longing for plain old fish and chips smothered in malt vinegar and eaten out of a greasy newspaper, preferably *The News of the World* with its lurid tales of child-molesting vicars. He had an urge to whisk Romanenko away from any official arrangements and plunge with him into the side-streets of this city, into the dark little pubs and alleyways and courtyards, into the places where people really lived their lives. This is the way it really is, Aleksis. This is what you don't find in the restaurant of the George Hotel.

"We must visit the Castle after we've eaten," Romanenko said. The eagerness in his voice was unmistakable. He had a thing about the Castle.

"Of course," Oates replied.

Pagan looked towards the ticket-barrier. Crowds were milling around. Loudspeaker announcements reverberated in the air. Through the station exit, some distance beyond the barrier, Pagan saw a square of rainy grey sky. A bleak Saturday afternoon in August in what he considered the most austere of European capitals. Behind him, Romanenko was staring up at the vast glass ceiling of the station.

They reached the ticket-barrier, Pagan still a few feet in front of Romanenko and the others. Which was when it happened.

When Jacob Kiviranna saw the train come to a dead halt, he was standing about six feet beyond the ticket-barrier. He took a few steps forward, pushing his way through the crowd, his hand covering the pocket that contained the gun. It was strange now how utterly detached he felt.

He watched Romanenko's group approach the barrier. There were five in all. Romanenko was talking to a man in a camel-hair coat and pinstriped suit. On Romanenko's left side was a well-built man with a dark moustache. In front of the Russian was a tall short-haired man in a tan suit, who moved with a watchful sense of purpose. And in the rear was the fifth man whose overcoat and haircut identified him as Russian, most likely KGB.

Kiviranna focused on Romanenko as he came through the barrier. Then he stepped closer, squeezing himself between a porter and a group of genteel elderly Scottish women with walking-sticks and umbrellas who were trying to induce the porter to carry their luggage. Kiviranna reached into his pocket and removed the Bersa, concealing it in the palm of his hand. He needed one clear shot, that was all. One clear shot at Romanenko.

Kiviranna brought the gun up. The sound of loud-speaker announcements detonated inside his head and then dissolved in a series of meaningless echoes, because he was conscious now of nothing save the short distance between his pistol and Romanenko's face.

With an expression of horrified disbelief, Romanenko saw the gun and raised his briefcase up in front of his eyes, a futile attempt to protect himself. Kiviranna fired directly into the Russian's heart, and as Romanenko screamed and collapsed on the ground and his briefcase slithered away from him and panicked pigeons flapped out of their roosting places in the high roof, Kiviranna turned and started to run. But the tall man in the tan-coloured suit, who had hesitated only a second in the aftermath of the gunfire, seized him roughly around the waist in the manner of an American football or rugby player and dragged him to the ground.

Frank Pagan, struggling with the gunman, disarming him, clamping cuffs on his wrists, was conscious of old ladies yelping and porters hurrying back and forth and the appearance of two uniformed policemen who immediately began to keep curious onlookers away – including a group of soccer fans who had apparently decided that the violence in Waverley Station was more authentic than any they might see on a soccer field. There was chaos, and that was a state of affairs Pagan did not remotely like. There was chaos and gunfire and he hadn't been able to prevent this awful situation from happening and that galled him as much as anything.

Pagan left the handcuffed gunman face down beneath the watchful eyes of one of the uniformed policemen, then he turned to look at Romanenko, who lay flat on his back with his eyes open, as if it were not death that had paralysed him but a catatonic trance. There was a dreadful wound in Romanenko's chest, and Danus Oates kept saying "Oh my God, my God," as if the killing would mean a demotion for him inside the Foreign Office. John Downey, who at least knew how to behave around a murder scene, was wading into the spectators and cursing as he roughly pushed them back. It was all madness, that special kind of disorganised lunacy which surrounds any scene of blood. It was the way flies were drawn to feed and bloat themselves on a fresh carcass, and in this case the carcass was one Frank Pagan had been supposed to protect. But he'd failed and Romanenko, the ebullient Romanenko, the enthusiast, the new friend, lay dead.

You weren't supposed to let this kind of thing happen, Pagan thought. This was going to be an easy job. The kind of work any nanny should have been able to accomplish without breaking sweat. And now suddenly it was a mess and he felt the muscles of his stomach knot. Oates, like a somnambulist, was reaching down to pick up Romanenko's briefcase, which had fallen alongside Aleksis's body.

The man from the Soviet Embassy, who hadn't uttered a word all the way from London, said, "Please, the case," and he made a move in Oates's direction, stretching out his hand to take the briefcase away from the young Englishman.

Pagan stepped between Oates and the Russian. He seized the case from Oates and held it against his side. "It stays with me," he said.

"On the contrary, Mr Pagan," the Russian said in immaculate English. "It goes back to the Soviet Embassy. It may contain business documents that are the property of the Soviet Union. Private material. Confidential matters."

"I don't care if it contains the Five Year Plan for the whole of bloody Siberia," Pagan said. "It stays with me. A man has been murdered and the case may contain material evidence of some kind. If it doesn't, you'll get it back."

Danus Oates muttered something about the possibility of a diplomatic incident, as if there were no words more blasphemous in his entire vocabulary. Pagan gripped the briefcase fiercely.

The Russian looked at Oates. "Explain to Mr Pagan that the briefcase is Soviet property. Explain international law to him, please."

Oates stammered. His tidy little world had collapsed all about him and he appeared unsure of everything – diplomatic protocol, international law, perhaps even his own identity. He had the expression of a man who suddenly discovers, late in life, that he's adopted. "I'm not sure, it's outside my province," was what he finally blurted out. Pagan almost felt sorry for him. Good breeding and all the proper schools hadn't prepared Danus Oates for violence, other than the kind in which pheasants were despatched by gentlemen with shotguns.

"I keep the case," Pagan snapped. "And that's final."

The Russian wasn't easily appeased. He reached towards Pagan and tried to pull the briefcase away. Pagan placed a hand upon the Russian's shoulder and pushed him back – a moment of unseemly jostling that might quite easily have led to further violence had it not been for the fact that there were policemen everywhere now, plainclothes men from the Edinburgh Criminal Investigation Department, uniformed cops dragged away from soccer duty, sirens whining, ambulances roaring through the rain. Pagan, clutching the briefcase to his side, was suddenly drained by events – and at the same time angered by what he saw as his own delinquency in performing a task that should have been as simple as sucking air.

A tall man with white and rather theatrical side-whiskers appeared at Pagan's side. He introduced himself as Inspector Dalrymple of the Edinburgh CID. He had a melancholy manner and he surveyed the scene with the unhappy expression of a drama critic at an amateur performance. Pagan took out his ID and showed it to the Inspector, who looked suitably impressed.

"I wish this hadn't happened in respectable old Edinburgh, Mr Pagan. Gives the place an awfully bad name." He stared first at the corpse, then at the handcuffed gunman, who lay motionless on the ground. "I'll give you a hand getting the body out of the way. The least I can do. Keep Edinburgh clean, eh? Don't frighten the tourists. After all, this isn't Glasgow," and Dalrymple chuckled briefly, because Glasgow's reputation as a rough, criminal city was something Edinburgh people never tired of gloating over.

The Inspector, stroking his copious whiskers, began to issue orders to various policemen. Ambulance men, those attendants of injury and death, had appeared with a stretcher. Pretty soon there would be nothing left, no traces of the violence that had happened in this place. Pretty soon there would be nothing but dried bloodstains and a memory of murder. Pagan watched the body of Romanenko being raised on to a stretcher with a certain finality. But nothing was final here at all and Frank Pagan knew it.

John Downey had appeared out of the crowd and stood beside him. Crow, Pagan thought.

Downey blew his nose loudly, then studied the centre of his handkerchief, grotesquely fascinated by his own effluence. "Well, Pagan," he said, folding the handkerchief into his pocket. "This is what I'd call a fine kettle of fish."

"One thing I always liked about you, John, is your original turn of phrase."

Downey smiled, and it was a brutal little twist of his lips. "You're up shit creek, Frank. Romanenko was your baby and you let him slip down the plughole with the bathwater. The Commissioner's going to need an extra dose of the old digitalis to cope with this one, chum."

Shit creek, Pagan thought. It was a stagnant waterway he knew intimately. He stared at Downey. There was an urge to strike out suddenly, a longing to stifle the man. He resisted the desire even as he realised that it was the first really passionate yearning he'd felt in many months. There was spirit in him yet, he thought – and despite the chaos around him it warmed his blood and it made his nerves tingle and it kicked his sluggish system into some kind of life. All this might be a mess, but it was his own to straighten out. He had become the proprietor of a bad

17

situation, like a man who has unexpectedly inherited a house he later discovers has been condemned.

The goon from the Soviet Embassy, who had been lingering close to Pagan as if he might still get a chance to snatch the briefcase away, said, "I promise you, Pagan. Unless you hand over the case, you have not heard the last of this."

That promise was the one thing of certainty, Pagan thought, in an uncertain state of affairs. He turned and walked back to the place where the handcuffed gunman lay motionless.

The big man who stood that same night on the ramparts of Edinburgh Castle wore a charcoal suit especially made for him by an exclusive tailor who operated out of basement premises on East 32nd Street in Manhattan. He also wore a matching fedora, pulled down rather firmly over his head. He had a craggy face dominated by a misshapen nose. It was the kind of face one sometimes saw on former boxers but the eyes were clear and had none of that dullness, that dead-dog quality, that afflicts old fighters. He was sixty years old and still muscular and hard the way he'd always been because condition was important to him. In the past, it was condition that had saved his life. He was still proud of his body.

He removed a cigarette from a silver case and lit it with a gold Dunhill lighter on which his initials, M.K., had been engraved in a craftsman's script. He never inhaled smoke. He blew a cloud from his mouth and looked down across rainy Edinburgh, marvelling at the damp nimbi that glowed here and there in the night and the floodlit monuments. The rain, which had been sweeping relentlessly across the city, had slowed now to little more than a drizzle and the night had a quite unexpected beauty, almost a magnificence, that touched the man.

From the distance he could hear a sound of bagpipes and although it was strange music to him, nevertheless the despair in the notes, the unfulfillable longing, moved him. Scotland was not his own country – but very little separated him from his native land. The North Sea, Scandinavia, the Baltic. It was hardly any distance at all. He felt a painful twinge of homesickness. But then he'd grown accustomed to that sensation over the years and whereas it had troubled him deeply in the past, now he was in control of it. But only up to a point, he thought. Because every so often he was still astonished by the way the sensation could creep up on him and, like some wintry vulture, claw his heart.

He crushed his cigarette underfoot. Tonight was not the night for those old predatory birds. Tonight was not the time for remembering that he hadn't seen Estonia since 1949, when he'd been captured by Soviet forces and shipped inside an overcrowded freight car to Siberia, where he'd survived along with other Baltic freedom fighters, along with many thousands of the dispossessed – brave Latvians, valiant Lithuanians, headstrong, determined men who might have lost the battle but would one day win the war, because they had a secret weapon Stalin and all his butchers could never strip away from them. They had hatred.

He moved along the ramparts, wishing – dear God, how he wished – he was strolling along the cobblestones of Pikk Street, past Mustpeade clubhouse, through the Suur Rannavarav and down to Tallinn Harbour to look at the ships. Or passing the medieval Kiek-in-de-Kök cannon tower and the Linda statue to reach Hirve Park where he had walked hand-in-hand many times with his wife Ingrida on those summer nights in June when it seems the sun will never sink in the sky. It had become a dream to him, a dream of a dead city, a beautiful corpse bathed in pearly light.

But he wasn't going to yield to memories. In any event he'd heard how the Tallinn of his recollection had changed with Soviet occupation – the Russians had torn historic buildings down, renamed streets, and erected those dreary blocks of high-rise apartments that were so deadeningly characteristic of Communist architecture.

He checked his wristwatch. It was almost nine. He had been waiting for more than an hour. But what was a mere hour when weighed against the forty-three years that had passed since the Russians had 'liberated' his country? Old men learned one thing. They learned how to sing in the soft voices of patience.

He looked at the young man who stood alongside him. In the young man's blue eyes the lights of the city were reflected.

"He's not coming, Mikhail," the young man said. He was extraordinarily handsome, at times almost angelic, but he had no self-consciousness about the perfection of his looks because external appearances meant very little to him. When he entered a restaurant, or stepped inside a crowded room, he turned heads and fluttered hearts and caused glands to work overtime – he affected people, mainly women, in ways that rarely interested him. This coldness, this seeming indifference, only enhanced his physical desirability. He wasn't merely a handsome young man, he was a challenging presence in the landscape, and difficult to conquer.

Mikhail Kiss looked away from his nephew and made an indeterminate gesture with his enormous hands. He had killed with those hands. He had dug graves with them and buried his dead comrades with them. "If he isn't coming, then he's bound to have a damn good reason."

"Like what?"

Mikhail Kiss shrugged. Who could say? Meetings were hard to arrange, and sometimes things went wrong, timetables became confused, time zones were overlooked, planes were delayed, trains ran late, a hundred accidents could happen. Nothing was perfect in this world anyway – except revenge, which he carried protectively in a special place deep inside his heart. He nurtured revenge, and fed it carefully the way someone might tend an exquisite plant. Vengeance was precious to him, and vows that had been taken long ago were not forgotten. He was a man who still breathed the atmosphere of the past.

He moved closer to the young man, seeing the way a muscle worked tensely in the cheek and how the blond hair, which lay lightly upon the collar of his raincoat, was speckled with drops of very fine rain.

"Something must have gone wrong, Mikhail."

Mikhail Kiss squeezed his nephew's shoulder. He didn't say anything. He never allowed himself to think the very worst until there was no alternative. Leaping to conclusions was a sport for the young and tempestuous.

The young man, whose name was Andres Kiss, leaned upon the stone parapet and looked down through the darkness that rose up around the rock on which the Castle had been built. He restlessly rubbed the rough surface of stone with the palm of one hand. A person with a sense of history might have imagined, even for the briefest time, the touch of the mason who had put the stone in place many centuries ago. He might even have imagined calloused skin, a face, a concentrated expression, and marvelled at how the past created echoes in the present. But Andres Kiss's sense of history went back a mere forty years, and no further.

He turned his face away from the sight of the city spread out beneath him, and he looked at his uncle. "I have a bad feeling in my gut," he said. "I don't think he's going to come."

A gust of wind blew soft rain at Mikhail Kiss's eyes, and he blinked. He felt exactly as his nephew did, that something had gone wrong, that down there in the shadowy pools between lamps and neon signs something altogether unexpected had happened to Aleksis Romanenko.

2

Zavidovo, the Soviet Union

The cottage was a simple three-room building located on the edge of Zavidovo, a one hundred and thirty square mile wilderness some ninety miles from Moscow. The house was surrounded by trees and practically invisible until one was within twenty yards of the place. It was reached by means of a mud track, which was severely rutted. Dimitri Volovich had some trouble holding the car steady on the awful surface, especially in the dark. He parked a hundred feet from the cottage, then stepped out and opened the rear door for Colonel V. G. Epishev, who emerged into a blackness penetrated only by the soft light from one of the cottage windows.

Epishev ran a finger inside his mouth, probing for an annoyingly stubborn particle of the apple he'd eaten on the way from Moscow. He had a pleasant round face, the kind you might associate with a favourite uncle. It wasn't memorable, which suited him very nicely. In the West he could have passed for a stockbroker or a certified public accountant. His manner, which he'd cultivated over years of service in one or other Directorate of the KGB, was indeed avuncular, sometimes kindly in a way that disarmed even people who were his sworn enemies. And he was known among these enemies – a diverse group that included political dissidents he'd imprisoned or practising Christians he'd dissected or errant Jews he'd shipped in the opposite direction from Israel and into a colder climate than they desired – as Uncle Viktor, although no affection was implied by the term.

He turned towards the lighted window, hearing Greshko's music issuing from the house. An incongruous sound in the Russian night. He wondered what it was that the old man found so absorbing in American country songs. It was a weird taste Greshko had acquired in the late 1940s, when he'd spent six months as *rezident* in Washington at the Soviet Embassy.

Epishev, followed by Lieutenant Volovich, entered the cottage. Neither man was at ease in this place. As officers of the KGB, they had no compelling, official reason to visit Greshko, who had been removed a year ago from his position as Chairman of State Security. He was therefore non-existent, *persona non grata* inside ruling circles – even if there were those who feared him still and who awaited news of his death with considerable impatience.

The nurse appeared in the doorway of the bedroom. She was a small black-haired girl from the Yakut, and her oriental features had a plump-cheeked innocence. Epishev was never sure about her. She went about her business briskly, and her Russian was very poor, and she seemed to think it perfectly natural that Greshko would have visitors – but you could never tell. The Colonel, who had lived much of his life promoting a sense of paranoia in others, didn't care to experience the feeling for himself.

"He's awake," the nurse said. Her uniform was unnaturally white, almost phosphorescent in the thin light of the room.

Epishev and Volovich went towards the bedroom door. The music filled the air, a flutter of fiddles, a scratching Epishev found slightly painful. The bedroom was lit only by a pale lamp on the bedside table and the red and green glow of lights from Greshko's sophisticated stereophonic equipment, which the old man had had imported from Denmark.

Greshko's face emerged from the shadows. Once, it had been large and round, reminding Epishev of an angry sun. Now, changed by terminal illness, the skin was transparent and the eyes, still brightly piercing, were

23

the only things that suggested any of Greshko's former fire. Angular and terrible, the features appeared to draw definition from the shallow pools of light in the small room. When he spoke, Greshko's voice was no longer the harsh commanding thing it had been before, a dictatorial instrument, imperious and thrilling. The cancer had spread to his throat and when he said anything he did so laboriously, barely able to raise his voice above a rasping whisper. A length of plastic tubing ran from Greshko's body to a point under the bed. It was transparent and would fill now and then with brown liquid, the wastes of Greshko's stomach. Or what was left of it.

Epishev moved nearer the bed. He tried to ignore the smell of death that hung around the old man. He concentrated on the dreadful music, as if that might help. A man with a nasal condition was singing.

> *As I walk along beside her up the golden stair,*
> *I know they'll never take her love from me.*

"Poor Viktor," Greshko said. "You never liked my music, did you? You made passable attempts at trying, didn't you?"

Epishev was held by Greshko's eyes, as he'd been trapped so many times in the old days. If Epishev had ever had a true friend in a life that was almost entirely solitary, it had to be Vladimir Greshko. Only Greshko's patronage and protection had spared Epishev the whimsical wrath of Stalin, at a time when Stalin was launched on still another crazed purge of Soviet society and Epishev had been a young man of twenty-two, barely at the start of his career. His youthful ambition, so far as he'd ever been able to comprehend, had been his only 'crime'. And Greshko's intervention with The Great Leader had saved Epishev the long one-way trip to Siberia. Epishev remembered this with a gratitude that would never diminish. He had repaid the debt with years of unquestioning loyalty to Greshko.

Greshko made a small gesture with one thin white hand. "Come closer."

Epishev sat on the edge of the bed. This close to Greshko, he thought he could *see* death, as though it were a shadow that fell across Greshko's face. "Listen a moment," the old man said. And his hand, a claw of bone, dropped over Epishev's wrist. "Listen to the music."

Epishev shut his eyes and pretended to concentrate.

> *If tonight the sun should set*
> *On all my hopes and cares*

Greshko said, "Do you hear it, Viktor?"

Epishev looked into the old man's eyes. He wasn't sure what he was supposed to hear.

"Ach," Greshko said impatiently. "You're too young. Too young."

It was an odd thing how Epishev at the age of fifty-five always felt young and inexperienced in Greshko's presence, always the neophyte in the presence of the old master. Nobody knew Greshko's real age, which was somewhere between eighty and eighty-five.

"You never knew what it was like to build the railways in the 1920s, how could you? The great spaces. The sky, Viktor. That endless sky."

Epishev couldn't see the connections here, couldn't tell which way the old man was going. Since his sickness and removal from office, Greshko had increasingly rambled in directions that were hard to follow at times. Epishev had heard how, as a young man caught up in that first dizzying outbreak of Bolshevik success, Greshko had gone into the wilderness beyond Sverdlosk to lay railway tracks. It was a period of his life the old man reminisced about frequently.

"That's the sound of it all," Greshko said. "In that music, there's the sound of the endless sky. And the wind across the plains, Viktor. That's what I always hear. I don't understand all the words, but the feelings – always the feelings. Why does it take an American to capture something so plaintive?''

Epishev glanced at Volovich, thin and motionless and uncomfortable in the doorway. To Volovich's right was a stack of record albums, perhaps a hundred or so in some disarray. Epishev, who had an excellent command of English, could read the names of certain singers. Hank Williams. Johnny Cash. Bill Monroe. Smiling men in cowboy hats. He wondered how they could smile so, when they produced such miserable sounds.

The music came to an end and there was a silence in the bedroom, broken only by the sucking noise created by the plastic tube.

"What has Birthmark Billy been doing recently, Viktor?'' Birthmark Billy was the derogatory way Greshko referred to the new General Secretary of the Party, a man he loathed so much he could never bring himself to use the proper name. "Tell me the latest news. Has he been tearing things apart again?''

"He had the Director of the KGB in Krasnoyarsk arrested on a charge of corruption.''

"Krasnoyarsk? That would be Belenko. Belenko was one of my own.''

"Yes,'' Epishev said.

Greshko was suddenly restless. His hands fluttered in the air. "Soon there won't be a single institution, a single law, a single custom he hasn't attacked and changed. This whole society will have been altered beyond recognition. Don't doubt this, Viktor, but one day in the very near future these changes are going to affect you as well. You'll go into your office as usual and you'll find the furniture has been moved around and a total stranger is sitting where you used to sit. And they'll send you to Gorki where, if you're lucky, you'll find yourself directing traffic. And if you're unlucky, Colonel Epishev . . .'' Greshko's hands dropped to his side and something – some spark of life – seemed to subside inside him. He lay very still.

Epishev had heard this speech before in one form or another, and now he waited for the fire to build in Greshko again, as he knew it would. He was also puzzled why he and Volovich had been ordered to come to this place at such an hour, but he couldn't hurry Greshko, who never volunteered information until he was ready to do so. The old man sighed and turned his face toward the lamp and Epishev could see the scar on his throat where the surgeon had gone in with a knife.

"God damn him," Greshko said quietly. "God damn him and his cronies." The old man stared at Volovich. "Close the door, Dimitri."

Volovich did so. With the door closed, the air in the room was charged with the electricity of conspiracy.

Greshko said, "The Russian people need the whip of authority. They don't need some quack who comes along and drops tantalising hints about how there are going to be some new freedoms. Elections! A free press! More consumer goods in stores! You don't find the Russian spirit in democracy and better nylon stockings and finer toothbrushes and imported French wines! The people don't understand these things. They don't want them because they don't know how to use them. And even if they deceive themselves into thinking they *do* want these things, they're not ready for them." Greshko paused. His breathing was becoming harsh and laboured.

The strange voice was subdued now, almost inaudible. "What the new crowd fails to understand is that the Russian people need a little *fear* in their lives. They need emotional austerity. Stalin understood it. Brezhnev, who was a lazy bastard in many ways, also understood it. And I understood it when I ran the KGB. But this new gang! This new gang thinks they have a magic wand and they can wave it and everything will change overnight. They fail to realise this isn't the West. Democracy isn't our historic destiny.

27

Adversity is the glue that has always held Russia together."

Greshko raised himself up once more with an amazing effort of will and looked towards Volovich.

"Put something on the turntable, Dimitri," he said.

Volovich found an album and played it. It was a man singing about his life in a place called Folsom Prison and it was very maudlin. Epishev wanted to get up from the place where he sat and put a little distance between himself and the wretched plastic tube, but he didn't move. Even as he lay dying, there was a magnetism about Greshko, perhaps less well-defined these days but still a force Epishev knew he couldn't resist.

Greshko licked his dark lips, stared up at the ceiling, seemed to be listening less to the sounds from the speakers than to some inner melody of his own. He moved his face slowly back to Epishev and said, "Romanenko is dead."

So that was the reason for this midnight summons! For a moment Epishev didn't speak. Greshko's sentence, so baldly stated, floated through his mind.

"Dead? How?"

"Shot by a gunman in a railway station in Edinburgh about six hours ago."

"A gunman? Who?"

"I have no more information," Greshko said. "I only learned about the assassination less than two hours ago," and he twisted his neck to peer at the bedside telephone, as if he expected it to ring immediately with more news. So far as Greshko was concerned the phone was both a blessing and a threat. His various contacts and sympathisers around the country could always keep in touch with him, but at the same time they always had to be circumspect when they called, because they were afraid of tapped lines and tape-recorders, and so a curious kind of code had evolved, a sub-language of unfinished sentences, half-phrases, substitutions, a terminology whose caution Greshko disliked. He had always preferred forthright speech and down-to-earth images and now it seemed to him that more than his exalted position had been stripped from him – they'd taken his language away from him too.

Epishev asked, "How does this affect us?"

Greshko smiled, a weird little expression, lopsided, like that of a man recovering from a severe stroke. And then suddenly he looked bright, more like the Greshko of old, the one who had regarded the delegation of authority as a fatal weakness. This was Greshko the ringmaster, the man who guarded the computer access codes of the State Security organs with all the jealousy of an alchemist protecting his recipe for gold, a man as cold as the tundra and whose only love – and it *was* love – was for his precious KGB, which was slowly having the life sucked out of it by the new vampires of the Kremlin. Epishev imagined he could hear the brain working now, whirring and ticking, then taking flight.

Greshko said, "Our main concern is whether Romanenko's message has fallen into the wrong hands or whether it reached its intended goal. If it *was* intercepted, then by whom? And what did the message mean to the interceptor? The problem we have is that we were never able fully to ascertain the *content* of the message. The only way we might have done that would have aroused Romanenko's suspicions, and that wasn't worth the risk . . ." Greshko drew the cuff of his pyjama sleeve across his mouth and went on, "We know Romanenko had planned to pass it along in Edinburgh to his collaborators, we also know the message was an indication that all the elements of the scheme were successfully in place – but we don't know the *extent* of the information it contained. Was it some vaguely-worded thing? Or was it more specific? Could a total stranger read it and understand *exactly* what events are planned inside the Soviet Union a few days from now? Was it written in some kind of code? You see the threat, of course, Viktor. In the wrong hands, this information could be disastrous for all of us."

Epishev was silent. From his long association with Greshko, he knew that the old man's questions were not intended to be simply rhetorical. Greshko had no time for verbal sophistry. When he asked questions, he wanted answers. The correct answers. It was really that simple. Romanenko had gone to Edinburgh to deliver a message. Greshko needed to know what had happened to it. A great deal depended on finding out. Epishev placed his palms together, rubbed them. There must have been a look of some uncertainty on his face because Greshko said, "You still haven't overcome your fear, have you, Viktor? You're still unconvinced, aren't you?"

Greshko reached for a small bottle on the bedside table. He opened it and held it up to his mouth. It contained Brezhnev's old remedy for all illnesses, valerian root and vodka flavoured with *zubravka* grass. Greshko was convinced that it was the only thing that kept him alive.

"I'm not afraid, General," Epishev replied. But he wasn't absolutely sure.

"Everybody feels fear at some time or other, Viktor. There's no shame in saying so. I know you, Viktor, and I know what runs through your mind. Romanenko was an enemy of the State. He was involved in a conspiracy against our beloved country. Right? And since you are being asked to take part in this same conspiracy against a State you've served so faithfully for most of your life, the words treachery and sedition pop into your mind, don't they, Viktor? But that's muddled thinking! The State you served no longer exists, Colonel. The Russia you love is being dismantled in front of our eyes – and if something isn't done quickly, it will cease to exist in any recognisable way." Greshko paused and snatched a couple of deep breaths, his shrunken lungs filling to their inadequate capacity.

"Viktor," Greshko said, and his hand went out once more to touch the back of Epishev's wrist, a chill connection of flesh that made Epishev want to shudder. "Any major blow against this new regime has a damned good chance of destroying it and that should be a cause for rejoicing. Romanenko's conspiracy can only hasten the end of those charlatans who've seized power. They've encouraged certain freedoms. They've told those ethnic minorities that their rights are to be respected, haven't they? They've manufactured a climate in which every dissident moron feels it his duty to argue and squabble with the State. So let them suffer the consequences of what they've created in this country. The quicker they're booted out of office, the better. The means don't matter a damn."

Greshko paused a moment. "And the beauty of it is that there are no files on Romanenko in any KGB office! There's nothing on any of the computers! There's absolutely no trace of Romanenko's association with this conspiracy! We've been watching Romanenko for years, and we've known what he's been planning because he lived in our damned pockets and never suspected a thing because we were always careful . . ." And he laughed, because his own foresight delighted him. When he'd seen the changes coming after the death of Brezhnev, and then later the demise of the hapless Chernenko, he'd taken the trouble to remove all kinds of information from the KGB, knowing a day would come when it would be useful to him. And that day, Epishev thought, had arrived with a vengeance.

"Are you with me, Viktor? Are you still loyal to me?"

Epishev replied, "I've never been disloyal to you, have I?"

"There's a first time for everything, Colonel."

"Not where you and I are concerned, General." The idea of disloyalty would never have entered Epishev's mind. It was more than just the fact of his gratitude to the old man and the years of their alliance, it was a question of shared beliefs. Like Greshko, Epishev thought that the Soviet Union was heading hurriedly toward disintegration. As if it were some massive star whose course has been suddenly changed, the republic was doomed to explode from internal pressure. Those fresh winds everyone said were blowing through the country were as poisonous as radioactive clouds. And Epishev, like Greshko, had absolutely no desire to breathe them.

"Then we're agreed, Viktor. Romanenko's plan must be carried through to the end. Regardless. We may not like the idea, but we have no choice except to go along with it if we want to see our country restored to what it was. In other words – *the plan must succeed*."

Epishev knew what was coming now. He had known it ever since Greshko had announced Romanenko's murder.

"When you go back to Moscow tonight, you'll see the Printer," Greshko said.

It might have been routine, except for the fact that Greshko had absolutely no authority any more, save for what he bestowed on himself. It might have been standard operating procedure. But it wasn't. Greshko though, like a great actor, was able to create the illusion of all his old power.

"When the Printer has your papers ready, you leave the country." Greshko was buzzing now, barely able to keep his hands still. "You have that authority. You don't need a written order. You'll find out what has happened to Romanenko's message. If it fell into the right hands, then we have nothing to worry about. If it's in the possession of the wrong party, and the outcome of the whole scheme is threatened, you will eliminate that threat. It's simple, Viktor. There are no ambiguities."

Eliminate that threat. Epishev wondered if he still had the heart for that kind of task. When he was younger, it had come easily to him. Now, even though he enjoyed such tasks as interrogation, even if he didn't object to rubber-stamping papers that condemned people to imprisonment or death, he wasn't sure about killing somebody directly, somebody whose breathing you could hear, whose eyes you could look into, whose fear you could smell. He hoped it wouldn't come to that. Perhaps Romanenko's paper had arrived at the appropriate destination. Perhaps everything was already in its rightful place and Greshko's precautions were, although understandable, nevertheless unnecessary.

He stood up, stepped away from the bed. He looked a moment at Volovich, but it was impossible to tell what Dimitri was thinking. After all the years together, he still couldn't read Volovich with any ease. Was Dimitri going along with this? Greshko, with all his old arrogance, had obviously assumed so, otherwise he wouldn't have been so open. Dimitri hadn't been made privy to everything because Greshko had insisted on limiting the Lieutenant's knowledge as a matter of routine security, but he knew enough to understand what he was involved in.

"We're not alone, you know," Greshko said. "There are hundreds of us, Viktor. Thousands. I'm in daily contact with men, some of them in positions of great authority, who feel exactly as we do. And these men are ready to take over the reins of power at a moment's notice. Some of these men are known to you by name. Some of them you can call on for help overseas. You know who I mean. Others prefer to remain anonymously in the background. I mention all this to make you feel less . . . solitary, shall we say? We're all dedicated to the same thing. We're all patriots."

Epishev went a little closer to Dimitri Volovich. He caught the sickly citric scent of Volovich's Italian hair oil. It was awful, but anything was better than the odour surrounding Greshko's bed.

"This is the most patriotic thing you have ever been asked to do," Greshko said. "If it helps, think of yourself as a loyal officer of a small, elite KGB that operates secretly inside the larger one. Think, too, of how this elite KGB is connected to some of the most powerful

33

figures in the country, men who are just as discontented as ourselves."

Epishev was already thinking of the drive through darkness back to Moscow and the visit to the Printer. He was thinking of identification papers, a passport, airline tickets.

"Remember this," Greshko said. "If there are complications and you're delayed outside the country, I want to be informed. I want news, no matter how trivial it may seem. Don't call me directly on my telephone. Volovich here will be the liaison. Every day, Viktor. I expect that much. But let's be optimistic. Let's hope the business is straightforward and our worries needless."

There was a sound from the bedroom door. The nurse stepped into the room, carrying a tray which held small medicine bottles. "I need my patient back," she said, and she smiled cheerfully.

"It's feeding time at the zoo," Greshko remarked. He winked at Epishev, who turned away and, without looking back, left the bedroom.

On the road to Moscow a fog rolled out of the fields, clinging to the windshield of the car. Volovich drove very slowly even when he'd turned on the yellow foglamps. Epishev sat hunched in the passenger seat. He blinked at the layers of fog, which parted every now and then in the severe glare of the yellow lights, only to come rushing in again.

"Does it constitute treason, Dimitri?"

Volovich stared straight ahead, looking grimly into the fog. "I never think about words like that."

"I'm asking you to think about them now."

Volovich shrugged. "I take my orders directly from you. Always have done. I'm a creature of habit, and I'm not about to change at this stage of my life. If you're asking whether I'm loyal, the answer is yes. Besides, I never think about politics."

Epishev leaned back in his seat. He closed his eyes.

Politics. This was no mere matter of politics. If Volovich chose to simplify it for himself, that was fine. But it came down to something that was far beyond the ordinary course of Party personalities and rituals. What was going on here was a struggle between the old ways and the new, and Epishev – who loved his country as fiercely as Greshko – knew where his own heart lay. There were flaws in the old ways, but it was a system that worked in its own fashion, one that people had come to accept. And if there were failings, they were temporary, and inevitable, because the road to Communism wasn't exactly smooth – or even straight. The Revolution had never promised an easy path. Epishev, who had been a Party member for more than thirty years, and before that a dedicated child of the Komsomol, knew what the Revolution had intended. Like an ardent suitor with a faithful passion, he had committed his life to this one mistress. He tolerated all her failings and loved all her glories. And sometimes, when he thought about the Revolution – which he saw as an ongoing process, unlimited, as demanding as it was endless – he experienced an extraordinary sense of iron purpose. He was in the slipstream of history. Everything he did, every task he carried out, no matter how distasteful, had been shaped by the historic forces that had overthrown the Romanovs in 1917.

But to toss all this away! To open windows and throw the old system out! To change the purpose of the Revolution! And to do all this with such indecent haste! Heresy was hardly the word.

Epishev stared into the fog and sighed. He had absolutely no choice but to go along with Greshko. Anything else would have been complete hypocrisy. It didn't matter if Greshko was motivated by pure patriotism, or the promptings of a dying man's monumental ego, because Epishev knew his own reasons were good. He was, as Greshko had correctly pointed out, a patriot. He knew no other way to be.

The fog was thinning now. Epishev glanced at Volovich. "When I need to telephone, I'll contact you at your home. I'll use the East Berlin link. It's safer."

Volovich switched off the foglamps. The car began to gather speed. Between thin pine trees, a half-moon had appeared, suspended in a way that struck Epishev as forlorn. He was thinking now of Romanenko, the First Secretary of the Communist Party in the Estonian Soviet Republic, and trying to imagine a shadowy gunman in a railway station. When he'd first heard Greshko speak of the organisation that called itself the Brotherhood of the Forest and how this old association of Baltic freedom fighters had been the driving-force behind Romanenko's plan, when Greshko had patiently explained the merits of the conspiracy and how it might be used against Birthmark Billy and his cronies, Epishev's first instinct had been to distrust the entire undertaking. Romanenko was an Estonian, a Balt, and Epishev trusted absolutely *nothing* that originated in any of the Baltic countries.

More than fifteen years ago he had spent nine months in Tallinn, the capital of Estonia, where he'd been sent from Moscow to purge the city of Estonian nationals with suspect sympathies. The Balts were a clannish crew, annoyingly supercilious at times, and they tended to protect one another from the common enemy, which they saw as Russia. He remembered Viru Street now, and Tsentralnaya Square, and the 5th October Park. A handsome city, a little too Western perhaps and its native population too irreverent, but there was a pleasant atmosphere, at times almost a buoyancy, in the cafés – places like the Gnome and the Pegasus – that one found nowhere else in the Soviet Union.

More than buoyancy, though. There was *defiance* throughout the Baltic. One encountered it in Latvia and Lithuania as well. There were strikes, and well-organised protests, and various groups babbling publicly about their rights and singing forbidden national anthems. It was as if all three Baltic nations still believed themselves to be independent of Russia. So many Baltic nationals even now resisted – and loathed – the absorption of their so-called 'republics' into the Soviet Union. And they were encouraged in their dreams by émigré communities overseas, mainly America. He thought of the social clubs in Los Angeles and Chicago and New York where old men played cards or shuffled dominoes and wrote angry letters to their Congressmen about 'prisoners of conscience' behind the Iron Curtain. All that was harmless enough. All that was empty noise and the fury of frustration. Dominoes and cards and folk-festivals and national costumes amounted to nothing. Conscience, after all, was cheap.

But now it had gone beyond simple conscience. The Balts had engineered a plot which had been in the planning a long time and, if Greshko had his way, stood every chance of success. And if it did succeed, it would release all kinds of turmoil, all manner of ancient frustrations and ethnic demands for sovereignty and self-determination throughout the Baltic. What Greshko hoped for was an apocalypse – a popular uprising inspired by the success of the plot and unified by its symbolism, mobs in the streets, tanks and soldiers of the Red Army fighting the local populations of Tallinn and Riga and Vilnius, the disintegration of Soviet influence in satellite republics, a decomposition that might spread beyond the Soviet Union itself and into Poland and East Germany and Czechoslovakia, an anarchic state of affairs that would doom the upstart brigade who ruled these days from the Kremlin. What Greshko desired was nothing less than a new Revolution, one that would replace the bastard liberalisation of the Politburo with an older, more reassuring socialism. What Greshko really wanted was yesterday.

Epishev put a finger inside his mouth and finally located the sliver of apple that had been stuck between his back teeth for the past hour or so. He examined it on the tip of his finger. He had a way of staring at things that suggested the concentration of a coroner inspecting an unusual corpse. He wiped the pellet from his fingertip and sighed, looking out at the moon, which had a curiously hollow appearance, as if it were simply an empty sphere. And he had a sense of uneasiness for a moment, because he felt he'd become exactly the kind of person he'd spent most of his life hunting down and destroying. He had become an enemy of the State.

But the uneasiness passed as quickly as it had come, and Epishev watched the fog return, spreading like acid across the face of the moon.

When the nurse had gone Greshko lay alone in the darkened bedroom. On certain nights, his fiery pain was beyond any of the opiates the nurse administered. And then there were other nights – and this was one of them – when he felt free of the burden of his cancer. There was calm and stillness and even the prospect of a future to anticipate.

He stared at the window. Outside, the night was completely quiet, and the quiet was that of his own death. But he could hold it at bay, he could keep it from entering this bedroom, he was too busy, too curious to die. Besides, his hatred would not allow him to expire. He needed only to live long enough to hear the noises of chaos and destruction. He needed only to live for five short days, if the Baltic scheme ran according to its own timetable. And Viktor would make sure that it did.

He turned his thoughts to Epishev. A good man, a good Communist, if perhaps a little too *ruminative* at times. But there was also an element of brutality to Epishev and he'd go to the ends of the world for Vladimir Greshko. What more could you ask for?

Epishev would probably use a Hungarian or West German passport and leave Eastern Europe through Berlin, perhaps passing himself off as a commercial traveller or, as he'd once done many years ago, as a piano tuner. A piano tuner! Sometimes Epishev could be inventive. And if that wasn't always a desirable quality, there were times when it was admirable, especially when you combined it with a streak of ruthlessness and complete commitment to the class-struggle of Leninism – something Greshko himself had come long ago to regard with utter cynicism.

More important than imagination, though, was the fact of Epishev's bottomless loyalty, which Greshko had bought cheaply years ago with a simple lie about how Joe Stalin wanted to purge Viktor from the KGB and the Party. Stalin hadn't been remotely interested in Epishev. Indeed, the old *vozhd* hadn't even *heard* of the young man. But Greshko had dreamed up the fiction, thus presenting himself as Epishev's saviour, as the man who had intervened *personally* on Epishev's behalf. From that time on, Viktor had never questioned a single order issued by his deliverer. A lie, but justifiable within a system where power depended on a network of unquestioning loyalties you forged in any way you could.

Greshko smiled. The idea of setting in motion events that would alter the self-destructive course of this great empire delighted him. He shut his eyes and stuck his hand out to touch the surface of the bedside telephone. He knew he hadn't been given the privilege of a phone out of charity or kindness. He had a telephone for one reason only – so that his conversations could be eavesdropped, his intentions monitored. But Greshko also knew that only a token attempt was made to record his messages because he had called in an old debt from a certain I. F. Martynov, Chief of the Internal Security Directorate, who also happened to be a closet homosexual with a dangerous liking for those lean and lovely teenage boys of the Bolshoi School of Ballet. There were choice tidbits about Martynov's life in Greshko's possession, unsavoury items that Martynov, a married man with overwhelming political ambitions, could not afford to have made public. A little mutual backscratching, a couple of unspecified threats, and Martynov had agreed that only a small proportion of

Greshko's conversations would be monitored *strictly for appearance's sake*, and that even these would be sanitised by Martynov himself.

So Greshko used the telephone freely, though not without some caution. He might have a lock on Martynov, but such locks could stand only so much pressure. His callers, on the other hand, who knew nothing of Martynov's editorial wizardry, were always wary. A retired admiral in Minsk, a former UN ambassador in Kharkov, a Party boss ingloriously ousted in Perm, a retired Minister of Foreign Affairs who called from his *dacha* in Stavropol, a former Deputy of the Supreme Soviet from Moldavia, and many others – Greshko's callers were men who had previously been in power and who were now living reclusive lives filled with bitterness and a desperate yearning for what they had lost. But there were other supporters too, the kind who wished to remain anonymous because they were men who still had prominent positions they wanted to keep. A Deputy Chairman on the Council of Ministers, a dozen or so members of the All-Russian Congress of Soviets, a Vice President of the Supreme Soviet, several KGB *residents* overseas, and a variety of personnel in five different Directorates who owed their promotions to Greshko's patronage in the past.

These men did not risk telephone calls. They smuggled notes to Greshko, messages brought by visitors, terse words of support, commitments, promises for the future, loosely-worded statements that, read carefully, left no doubt about their feelings concerning Birthmark Billy and his gang. It was a subterranean network, an amorphous one in need of strong organisation, but nevertheless huge, and what gave it strength was its resistance to change, its longing for the way things had been before. It was growing daily, drawing recruits from the ranks of the dissatisfied, or from those whose power-bases had been eroded or whose privileges had been removed. It was growing quietly and in secret, pulling in politicans, army officers, bureaucrats, ordinary workers, and it would continue to do so, just as long as things continued their decline inside Russia.

Greshko suddenly perceived the vastness of the Soviet Union, the great plains, the mountain ranges, the lakes and rivers, the *taiga*, in a flash of illumination and love. What was that line the Americans used in one of their songs? *From sea to shining sea* . . .

They were such apt songwriters, the Americans.

3

Martin Burr, the Commissioner of Scotland Yard, had spent several years of his life in the Royal Navy and had lost his right eye during a vicious skirmish with a Nazi U-boat at Scapa Flow in 1943. He wore a black eyepatch which gave him a jaunty, seasoned appearance. The one good eye, green and bloodshot, surveyed the world with weary intelligence.

Pagan respected the Commissioner. At least he wasn't a politician. He was first and foremost a policeman and loyal to those he commanded. And if sometimes he was imperiously paternal, then that was almost forgivable in view of his enormous responsibility, which was to keep the peace among the thousands of men – some of them highly-strung – whose careers and destinies he controlled.

Now, as he hobbled around his large office with his walnut cane supporting his bulk, he kept glancing sideways at Pagan, and there was just a hint of explosiveness in the good eye. Pagan, who had returned from Edinburgh by plane only a few short hours ago, still wore the suit that had been made grubby during his scuffle with Romanenko's killer.

"There will be some form of protest," said the Commissioner. "No doubt there's some damned First Secretary from the Russian Embassy already brow-beating the Foreign Minister. They'll bitch every chance they get, Frank. Bloody Bolsheviks."

Bolsheviks, Pagan thought. That was a quaint one.

He noticed that the Commissioner's office was without windows. The light in this room was always artificial, issuing from recessed tubes of fluorescence that made objects seem ghostly.

The Commissioner sat down and looked gloomy. He rapped the carpet with his cane and for a second he reminded Frank Pagan of an English country squire. It was deceptive. There was nothing sleepily bucolic in Martin Burr's character. And his public-school speech patterns concealed a sharp brain and a streak of ruthless determination. "Let's see what we've got here, Frank, before I come up with some bland yarn to feed to the wolfhounds of Fleet Street."

Pagan longed for a window, a view, a sight of the city. This office oppressed him, despite the collection of sailing ships in wine-bottles and the small models of British destroyers that littered a shelf, the only items of a personal nature in the whole place.

"Romanenko gets himself shot. And I'm not blaming you because a man can't have eyes in the back of his head, after all. But a lot of people, and I include the press as well as the Russians, are going to think us incompetent idiots. Be warned, laddie – some people are going to say you might have been more vigilant." The Commissioner looked at Pagan and shrugged. "Some people are already saying it, Frank. When the Yard isn't solving crimes, it's doing the thing it does best. I'm talking about gossip. I'm telling you I sit atop a pyramid of bitchery like some bloody pharaoh who's got nothing better to do than listen to the whining of his courtiers and the moaning of his soothsayers."

The Commissioner smiled and Pagan wondered if there was some sympathy to be detected in the expression. Sometimes, when he didn't want you to observe his true expression, the Commissioner had the habit of turning his face to one side so that only the inscrutable eyepatch was visible, which gave him the crafty demeanour of a pirate who possesses one half of the map to the secret place where the doubloons are buried.

"Now the briefcase, Frank. According to the wallahs along Whitehall, it's theoretically the property of the Soviet Union because Romanenko was a representative of that country. Therefore it has to be returned. However, I'm not in any great hurry to oblige. One doesn't want to be scurrying around doing the Russians favours, does one?"

Pagan stared at the briefcase, which was propped against the wall. Alongside the case, there lay the contents of Jacob Kiviranna's backpack and the weapon, the Bersa, that had been used to kill Romanenko. It was a sorry little collection of items and Pagan had some difficulty in associating these things with the violence that had happened only a few short hours ago in Edinburgh. There was a harsh dreamlike quality to the experience now, and yet he could still hear the sound of the gun being fired as if it were trapped inside the echo-chamber of his skull.

"But first," the Commissioner said, "before you talk to this fellow Kiviranna, let's examine his cargo." He hobbled toward the backpack, staring at a couple of shirts, a pair of jeans, socks, underwear, a guidebook to Edinburgh, a rail ticket, two hundred and seven dollars, a prescription bottle that contained several capsules of Seconal, and Kiviranna's American passport.

Pagan picked up the document and stared at the photograph. It showed a man with a rather sulky expression, a petulant set to the lips, hair drawn back tightly against the sides of the head. The ponytail couldn't be seen because of the direct angle of the shot.

"He entered London at Heathrow three days ago. It's the only stamp." Pagan flipped through the blank pages in the manner of a man scanning a murder mystery to reach the denouement without having to wade through the locked rooms and the poisoned sherry and all the other red herrings. "And somewhere along the way he acquired the Bersa."

The Commissioner said, "And since it's damned near impossible to smuggle a weapon into any country these days, it stands to reason he had an accomplice who provided him with the weapon. So what are we dealing with, Frank? And who the hell is Jacob Kiviranna anyway? Is he part of some bloody mad right-wing cult? And did he *really* expect to shoot our Soviet friend in broad daylight and make an escape? These are questions we need to have answered, Frank. And I'm tossing it all, lock stock and bloody barrel, into your court."

Where else could it be tossed? Pagan wondered.

The Commissioner continued. "Besides, what was so important about Romanenko that he deserved to be shot? As I understand it, he was nothing more than the First Secretary of the Communist Party in some Baltic Soviet Republic, which is not exactly a place where hot-shot Party comrades make a name for themselves. And all he came here for was to discuss some humdrum business proposition pertaining to computers, for heaven's sake. It isn't quite the kind of thing that marks a man out for assassination."

Frank Pagan replaced the passport alongside Kiviranna's other possessions. It was Romanenko's briefcase that absorbed his attention now. He wanted to open it, but he realised he was going to have to wait for the Commissioner to give him permission. The Commissioner seemed to be savouring the closed briefcase, wandering around it, and once actually prodding it with his walnut stick.

"I wonder if there's anything in this case that might suggest a reason why Romanenko was shot," Burr said.

"I've been wondering myself."

Burr paused a second, then said, "Do the honours, Frank."

Pagan picked up the case, which was of good brown leather. It was locked, but he easily forced it open with the use of the Commissioner's sharp brass letter-knife. He dumped the contents on the desk. Papers, files, documents in Russian, a schematic diagram of a computer which looked like a maze in a child's book of fun. There was a packet of Player's cigarettes, a disposable razor, a hairbrush, and a shirt, purchased in the Burlington Arcade in London, that was still enclosed in its original cellophane wrapping. There was also a sealed envelope with no address on it.

The Commissioner sifted through the papers. "It's a pathetic assortment, Frank. Apart from what looks to me like business documents, it's just the kind of stuff a man might carry if he plans a quick overnight stay in another city."

Pagan spread the papers on the desk. He knew no Russian at all and he felt, as he always did when he encountered a language with which he was unfamiliar, that he'd been stripped of a vital cognitive sense. He might have been staring at a complicated code. He was also touched a little by sadness, because he'd liked Romanenko. Pagan had always had an affinity for people who courted excess.

The Commissioner, whose own Russian was limited to the word *nyet*, looked perplexed. "We're going to have to call in one of the smart boys from the Foreign Office. Otherwise, this is gobbledygook. And I'd personally like it translated before we turn it over to the Soviets." The Commissioner sniffed. "I'd like to know what's inside that sealed envelope, though."

Pagan picked up the envelope and held it up to the light. He longed to tear it open.

The Commissioner asked, "Do we use a steam kettle? Or do we simply slice the thing with a knife?"

Frank Pagan grinned. "Go for broke," he said, and he ripped the envelope open. It contained a single sheet of yellowing paper covered in a language completely alien to him. Disappointed, he stared at the strange words, written in faded blue ink, as if they might be made to yield up some kind of sense simply by an act of concentration. The Commissioner peered at the sheet with a look of frustration on his face. He even pressed his nose close to it, sniffing the old sheet of paper which smelled musty, like something stored for many years in a damp attic.

"What language is that?" the Commissioner asked.

"I haven't got a clue," Pagan said. He glanced at a couple of words – *Kalev, Eesti, tooma*. The handwriting wasn't very good. "Danus Oates is something of a linguist."

"Then let's fetch the lad," said the Commissioner.

"He's somewhere in the building," Pagan said. "Last time I saw him he was swallowing Valium in the canteen. Events in Edinburgh unsettled his delicate constitution." As they had unsettled his own, Pagan thought, which was a lot less sensitive than Danus Oates's.

"Fat lot of good Valium's going to do him," said the Commissioner. "In the meantime, you ought to have a word with our American friends in Grosvenor Square, Frank. See if they've got anything on this Jacob Kiviranna. The fellow to contact over there is a chap called Teddy Gunther. See what you can get from Kiviranna first, although from what I hear he's either rather surly or two bricks shy of a load."

Pagan arranged Aleksis's papers in a neat pile.

The Commissioner said, "So far as Romanenko is concerned, if you want to find out if there's anything that made him a suitable candidate for assassination, the man to see is Tommy Witherspoon. He's got something to do with the Foreign Office, though if you ask me that's only a cover. I think Tommy really liaises between the FO and some of our intelligence agencies. Tommy lives and breathes Russia. I'll give him a call and tell you might have a question or two for him."

Pagan looked down at Romanenko's papers a second. The dead man's effects. The bits and pieces of a life. A life that had been blown away right in front of his own

47

eyes. He felt acutely depressed, as if he might have done something to prevent the catastrophe. It was too late for regrets – but then when were regrets ever timely? He remembered the hours he'd spent drinking with Romanenko, how the Russian's booming laughter filled the hotel room, the conspiratorial way Aleksis had said *You will see differences, Frank Pagan, such as you have never dreamed of. Big changes are coming.* The biggest change so far had been Aleksis's murder, which was surely the last thing Romanenko had had in mind.

"By the way, if the press gets on your arse, you've got nothing to tell them. Keep that in mind." The Commissioner paused a moment. "Whole thing's a bit of a bloody mess. But you've had worse, haven't you, Frank?"

Frank Pagan looked up at one of the fluorescent tubes which, slightly flawed, blinked now and again. "Maybe," he answered. He moved towards the door. "Don't you want to sit in on my interview with Kiviranna?"

The Commissioner shook his head. "As I said, Frank, I'm leaving it entirely to you. In any case, I'm sure to have some Russians to deal with very shortly." He adjusted his eyepatch. "One last thing. Change your suit first chance you get. You look like something the cat dragged in."

Jacob Kiviranna was being held in an interrogation room on the second floor, a bare chamber with no windows, a table, a couple of uncomfortable chairs. He chain-smoked, tilting his chair back against the wall and blowing rings up at the ceiling. He'd undone the ponytail and now his long brown hair fell around his shoulders. He had a glum expression on his face, disturbed only by the occasional tic of a pulse beneath his right eye. Pagan's impression was of a man whose life was a closed book which, once you opened it, would contain a drab little story of childhood neglect, lonely adolescence and fruitless adulthood, a serial of failures and pitiful vignettes.

He glanced at the young uniformed policeman who stood, arms folded, in the corner of the room, then sat down facing Kiviranna and tossed the US passport on the table. It fell open at the photograph. Pagan wondered about the ethnic origin of the name Kiviranna.

"Jake or Jacob?" he asked.

"I don't care," Kiviranna replied. He had a flat, lifeless voice, like that of a man whose verbal interplay with others has been strictly limited.

"Let's start with the biggie, Jake. Why did you kill Romanenko?"

Kiviranna didn't answer. He dropped a cigarette on the floor, crushed it with his ragged sneaker.

"It's going to make my life a whole lot easier if you answer my questions, Jake," Pagan said.

Kiviranna shut his eyes, placed his arms on the table, then lowered his face. His mouth hung open and he made exaggerated snoring noises. Bloody comedian, Pagan thought. He glanced again at the cop who stood in the corner. The young man looked about nine years of age. Every year's influx of new recruits seemed younger than ever and they made Pagan, at forty-one, feel old and weatherbeaten.

"Let's try another question," Pagan said. "Where did you get the gun?"

Kiviranna opened one eye. He smiled at Pagan but remained silent. He had brown teeth misaligned in his dark gums. Pagan studied the man's combat jacket, the Mickey Mouse patch on one sleeve, the small US flag on the other. He gazed at the beard, which was shapeless. He had the feeling he was peering into the past, confronting a species that, if not extinct, was at the very least threatened. You rarely encountered hippies these days. Now and then an old DayGlo van would chug past you on the street and it would be plastered with faded peace signs and weathered bumper-stickers bearing mellow messages, or you'd see some clapped-out forty-year-old flower-child sliding quietly along the sidewalk – but they didn't seem to come in bunches any more. Pagan remembered a time when he'd admired the lifestyle, before it became ugly and drugged.

He wandered around the room, pausing when he reached the door. "I wish you'd talk to me, Jake," he said. "If it's something simple, if it's just that you don't like Russians and you think the only good Commie's a dead one, I wish you'd say so."

Kiviranna sucked on a cigarette. There was some tiny response just then when Pagan had mentioned the Russians, a very slight thing, a small change in the man's expression.

Pagan decided to pursue the opening. "By the way, Jake, they want you. Did I mention that already? They'd like to talk to you. In the circumstances, I can't say I blame them."

"Who wants me?"

Pagan went back to the table and sat down. "The Soviets. They'd like me to turn you over to them. They're being pretty persistent about it. And I'm not sure I can prevent it."

"You're out of your mind," Kiviranna said. "No way would you hand me over."

Pagan shrugged. Sometimes when you interviewed a person you got lucky very quickly and you managed to touch a little nerve of fear. And it was apprehension that showed now on Kiviranna's gaunt face.

"I don't know, Jake. You shot one of their own. They're not happy with you. Come to think of it, I'm not exactly delirious about you either. Take your pick. Either you talk to me, or you take a short car ride to the Soviet Embassy, where you get to sit in a dark room and they shine lights in your eyes and smoking isn't allowed. You'll meet some men whose coats seem just a little too tight and who make loud noises with their fists."

Kiviranna sat upright now. "I killed the guy on British soil. I know the law, man."

"You *think* you know the law, Jake. But when it comes

down to tricky stuff like the death of a Russian, it starts to get pretty complicated. Diplomatic considerations raise their ugly little heads, chum. Her Majesty's Government might owe the Soviets a favour, let's say, and that favour might just turn out to be you."

Kiviranna leaned back against the wall. "I set one foot inside that Embassy and I'm history. I'm past tense."

"Right, Jake. It's not a healthy prospect."

"It's a fucking political game. And I get shuffled like a pawn."

"Pawns don't get shuffled, Jake. You're thinking about cards." Pagan smiled, and leaned across the table so that his face was a mere six inches away from the other man's. "Let's just talk, okay? No more rubbish. Let's start with motive."

"Motive?"

"Why did you kill Romanenko? Money? Political conviction? Or was it something else?"

"He was a fucking asshole, man."

Breathtaking. Pagan had expected some high-flown political cant, the kind of platitude assassins and terrorists so enjoy, that overblown rhetoric which was ultimately meaningless. *He was a fucking asshole, man* wasn't the kind of thing he'd anticipated at all. He stared at Jacob Kiviranna for a while before he said, "If that was sufficient cause to blow a man away, the streets would be practically empty."

"Okay. He sold out to the Russians. Is that enough for you?"

"Exactly how did he do that?"

"You name it. He carried out Kremlin policies in Estonia. He kissed all the Russian ass going. Guy was never off his fucking knees. An order came down from Moscow, Romanenko was the first to implement it. Didn't matter what it was. He'd get the job done. He was the Kremlin's rubber stamp. It didn't matter he was born in Estonia, he was the Kremlin's boy through and through. Which made him a goddam traitor."

Pagan listened to the man's toneless voice, then picked up the US passport, flipped the pages. "You're an American citizen, Jake. How come you give a damn about Romanenko anyway? I don't see how he could have affected your life."

"I got family left over there," Kiviranna said. "Cousins, a couple of uncles, aunts."

Revenge, Pagan wondered. Did it come down to a motive as basic as that? "Had Romanenko threatened your family? Had he done something to them?"

Kiviranna didn't say anything for a time. He smoked another cigarette and the small windowless chamber clouded up and the young cop by the door coughed a couple of times. Kiviranna gestured with the cigarette and looked very serious. "He didn't *have* to do anything *personal* to them, man. He was a Communist and a traitor to his own people. That's enough. We're talking about evil. I eliminated evil. That's the only thing that matters. You see evil, man, you wipe it out. The more evil you get rid of, the more good there is in the world. That's what it's all about. It's logical."

Evil – now there was a fine melodramatic word you didn't hear a great deal these days unless you frequented certain extreme religious sects or moved in mad terrorist circles, where it was used to describe anyone who didn't believe in either your choice of a God or your cause. Pagan studied Kiviranna's face again, wondered about his background. Had this wild-eyed character, who impressed Pagan as the kind of man you saw speaking to himself in the reading-rooms of public libraries, come three thousand miles to commit a murder because he believed that Aleksis Romanenko was *evil*? Was he driven by a missionary sense of bringing goodness and light into the world? Had he planned this killing all alone? Had he walked around with a dream of death in his head for weeks, perhaps months on end? An obsessive, a sociopath, the kind of guy who suddenly pops up with a handgun and makes a name for himself by killing a person of some standing in a political system he thought deplorable. *I eliminated evil.* Jake the avenger, the equaliser, the mad angel of light.

"So wiping out this evil was your own idea, Jake? Is that what you're telling me?"

"You got it."

Pagan was unhappy with this reply. It didn't answer the question of how Kiviranna had come into possession of the gun. Somebody had presumably passed the weapon to him after his arrival in Britain, and when you had two people you had a conspiracy, and so much for a lone killer theory. For another, Pagan had the feeling, which he couldn't readily explain and which surfaced in his mind at the end of a chain of unanalysable instincts, that Jake, albeit lonely and out of touch, was basically a gullible soul, and that the killing of Romanenko was an idea that had been *encouraged* in him. It wasn't a conclusion he'd reached without some kind of assistance, some kind of *persuasion*.

"How did you know Romanenko was going to be in Edinburgh, Jake?"

"I read it in a paper, I guess."

"An American paper?"

"I guess so, I don't remember."

Pagan's eyes were watering in the smoky room. It was hardly likely that Romanenko's visit to Britain had been mentioned in any US newspaper. It wasn't entirely newsworthy in America to print a story about an obscure Communist Party official making a quick business trip to the United Kingdom. It was even less likely that any press item would mention something so utterly unimportant as the side-trip to the Edinburgh Festival. So here was another question: *how had Jake come across his information?* There was only one answer – it had come from the same person or persons who provided the gun.

Pagan got up from his chair and walked round the room.

"Let's go back to the weapon. How did you get it, Jake?"

"I bought it here in London. I don't remember the store."

Pagan wheeled around quickly and strode back to the table. "You don't just walk into a shop and buy a gun in this country, Jake. You fill in forms, there's a waiting-period, the police run a thorough check on applicants. You haven't been in England long enough to acquire a weapon legally."

Kiviranna looked down at the surface of the table. His hands shook, and he pressed his palms together to keep them steady. "I need a favour," he said.

"Let's hear it."

"I had some medication in my backpack. I'd like it."

Pagan nodded at the young policeman, who went out of the room to fetch Kiviranna's medicine.

"Nerves trouble you, Jake?"

"I have some problems, man. I'm getting over them."

Pagan looked sympathetic. "Back to the gun, Jake."

Kiviranna shut his eyes and rocked his body back and forth for a time. "Okay. I got it in Soho. I went into a club, I asked around, guy sold me the gun. It was easy."

"You're trying my patience, Jake. You don't walk inside some club in Soho, a complete stranger, an outsider, and find somebody to sell you a gun. It doesn't happen that way. You need an inside track. Think again."

Kiviranna was silent. He stroked his beard. "I got a real bad headache."

The door of the room opened and the young policeman stepped inside, handing the brown prescription bottle to Pagan, who laid it on the table and rolled it back and forth as he studied Jake's anxious face.

"Tell me about the gun and you get one of your pills."

Kiviranna was silent a moment. "Okay. The gun was in a luggage locker at that station – what's it called?

King's Cross?'' He stuck a hand out towards the bottle, but Pagan covered it quickly with a palm.

"How did you know the gun was going to be there, Jake? Who told you? Who gave you the key to the locker?''

Kiviranna didn't take his eyes away from the bottle in Frank Pagan's fist. The look on his face was one of subdued desperation and Pagan, clutching the pills Jake was aching for, felt a surge of sympathy for the man and a slight disapproval of his own cruelty.

"He was an old guy I met in New York.''

"Did he just walk up to you on the street? Did he say here's a key, fly to England, fetch the gun, shoot Romanenko?''

Kiviranna shook his head. "He got my name from somewhere, he called me. We met a few times. I never knew his name, and that's the truth.''

"How come he approached you, Jake? What made him choose you?''

"I guess he heard I had certain sympathies.''

"Were you offered money?''

"Expenses, that's all. I wasn't going to take money for ridding the world of a guy like Romanenko.'' Kiviranna sounded a little offended by the suggestion. "We met a few times, we talked, I agreed to do the job.''

"Where did your meetings take place?''

Kiviranna was speaking more frankly now. "Different places, man. Sometimes Manhattan. Sometimes Brooklyn. One time we met at Coney Island, next to the old parachute jump. Another time the boardwalk at Brighton Beach.''

"Tell me the man's name, Jake.''

"I don't know it, I swear. He wasn't anxious for me to know, and I wasn't anxious to find out.''

Pagan took the cap off the bottle. "Why did he want you to kill Romanenko?''

"Because he felt the same way I did.''

"Tell me more about this mystery man.''

Kiviranna's forehead glistened with sweat. "What's

to tell? He was maybe seventy, in there somewhere. He spoke with a thick accent. Shabby clothes. He didn't look like he had two nickels to rub together. But I guess he got money from somewhere, enough for my expenses anyway. I don't remember much more."

"And even if you could remember more, you wouldn't tell me," Pagan said. He tilted the bottle and a few capsules slid on to the table. He examined them carefully, checking the name of the manufacturer, Lilley, imprinted on the side of each one.

"I've told you everything," Kiviranna said.

"I don't think so, Jake." Pagan pushed one of the pills across the table to Kiviranna, who picked it up quickly and tossed it into his mouth. "Enjoy. We'll talk again tomorrow. Maybe you'll find your memory has improved after a good night's sleep."

Pagan put the medicine bottle in his pocket together with Kiviranna's passport, stood up, walked towards the door. He was struck by fatigue but he knew that it was something he was going to have to carry around with him for some hours yet.

"What if I don't have anything new to tell you in the morning?" Kiviranna asked. "What then?"

Pagan turned, looked at the man, smiled in a thin way. He didn't answer the question but hoped that his smile, so devoid of mirth, suggested an unspeakable threat. Closing the door, he went out into the corridor and dipped his face into a drinking-fountain, letting a jet of lukewarm water splash against his eyes and forehead. A gun in a left-luggage locker, a nameless man in New York who'd sent Jake all the way to England – maybe it was all very simple, nothing more than a straightforward political assassination planned by Jake's anonymous acquaintance and carried out by Kiviranna who, through his own strange filter, saw the world in terms of black and white, evil and good. Maybe that's all there was to the affair.

But there was a dark area at the back of Pagan's

mind, a room in which assorted problems lay like unlit lightbulbs awaiting a surge of electricity to illuminate them. And in this room there lived Pagan's muse, his own inner policeman, his personal inspector, who was rarely satisfied with simplicity and who hated darkness passionately. He loathed puzzles too, such as the plain white envelope, sealed and unaddressed, that Aleksis Romanenko had carried in his briefcase.

4

London

Thomas Maclehose Witherspoon, who had a first-class degree in Political Science from St John's College, Oxford, was walking his cocker spaniels in Green Park when Pagan met him shortly after eight-thirty. He was a tall man with an adam's apple that suggested something stuck in his windpipe. He wore a navy blue blazer with some kind of crest on the pocket and white flannels, as if he were a fugitive from a cricket game. Witherspoon's thin hair was combed flat across the enormous dome of his head. The pedigree spaniels, named Lord Acton and Gladstone, were romping in the distance, and ignoring Tommy Witherspoon when he called their names.

When Witherspoon spoke, in a voice that might have been sharpened by razor blades, there was a scent of port on his breath. Pagan wondered if he'd dragged Tommy away from some polite little dinner party, causing the man a terrible inconvenience.

Witherspoon picked up a fallen branch and called after his dogs again. "Highly-strung buggers," he said.

Pagan thought a good kick in the arse might have induced in the creatures a sense of obedience, but he didn't say so. Witherspoon tossed the branch in the air and watched it fall.

"So you're the notorious Frank Pagan, eh? Heard about your Irish business."

Pagan, wondering when his name would cease to be associated with Ireland, made no reply. He studied the sky a moment, watching the August sun slide down between trees of an impossible greenness. London could still amaze him at times with its verdancy.

"So you lost Romanenko," Tommy Witherspoon said, in a weary way, as if Pagan's problems were a total bore. "I must say I thought it damned careless of you."

Pagan, irked by Witherspoon's manner, wanted to come back with a barbed comment, but resisted the temptation. He sniffed the air instead. There was a smell of diesel, ruining all this summer greenery and presumably pumping toxic materials into the bodies of nightingales.

Tommy Witherspoon asked, "What can I do for you anyhow?"

"What do you know about Romanenko?" Pagan asked.

"Isn't that an irrelevant question, Pagan? The fellow's dead and I understand you have the assassin in custody, and I don't see how any further knowledge of Romanenko could possibly be of assistance to you."

What an unbearable toad, Pagan thought. "There are some things I want clarified, that's all," he said.

"Ah, clarified," Witherspoon said. "You're on a personal quest, are you, Pagan? A man with a burning mission?"

"Personal?"

"The old ego. The policeman's pride. Can't stand the idea of being involved in a royal fuck-up, so you've got to start poking around to make yourself look somewhat less useless, eh?" There was raw snideness in Witherspoon's tone.

Pagan had a sense of something chill coiled around his heart. Maybe all it came down to was the inescapable fact that – as John Downey had so cruelly and succinctly put it, and as Tommy Witherspoon had echoed it – he'd fucked up. And maybe he was doing nothing more than turning over stones and trying to look busy because the more conscientious he appeared the better he'd feel. It was a sorry little insight and he hoped there was no truth to it. What came back to him again were Aleksis's

59

drunken words – *big changes, big surprises*. He supposed the big changes referred to the reconstruction of Soviet society, but what were the big surprises? What had Aleksis, with his sly winks and nudges, intended to suggest with that expression? *Wait and see, Frank Pagan,* Romanenko had said. Wait for what? It was one of the problems of death – it left silences and unanswered questions behind.

"Look, Romanenko was shot and I want some background," he said. He put a little steel into his voice now, a cop's impatience.

Witherspoon yawned. "Well, Pagan, if it's going to calm you down, I'll give you the quick tour. Romanenko was First Secretary of the Communist Party in Estonia. Estonian national, in fact. Don't be too impressed with his grandiose title, though. It's common practice for Russians to put nationals in charge in their colonies, but the real power always lies with the Second Secretary of the Party, who's invariably a Central Russian, a Soviet, handpicked by the Kremlin. Romanenko was just another titular head, a symbol, a sop. You find people like Romanenko all over the Russian Empire. Latvia. Lithuania. Georgia. Armenia. You'll find them in every one of the fifteen so-called autonomous republics – which is a laughable name for colonies – of the Soviet Union. It's designed to keep the natives restful and the dissidents asleep at night if one of their own is nominally the boss. It's a bloody sham, of course. Chaps like Romanenko don't have much in the way of real power. And they can't blow their own noses unless they get a direct order from the Kremlin – provided the Five Year Plan has manufactured enough hankies to go around." Witherspoon smiled at his own little joke.

"If Romanenko was so unimportant, why would anybody want to shoot him?" Pagan asked.

"Now that's hardly a taxing mystery," Tommy Witherspoon said in an offhand way. "Consider this. There are certain parties outside the Soviet Union, let's call them exiled malcontents, who have very long memories and carry grudges the depths of which would astonish you. Romanenko would be an obvious target for any Baltic exile loony fringe, because he was so clearly in cahoots with the Russian lords and masters. Ergo, the fellow's perceived as being a first-rate rotter, selling his own country out to Moscow. Do you see?"

Witherspoon, in his own aloof way, was echoing what Kiviranna had already told Pagan, which was something of a disappointment because Pagan had somehow expected a different answer, one with more substance, a little more meat on the bones of the affair.

"Now," Witherspoon said, "I'll throw a little extra fuel on the general bonfire, Pagan. Given the current changes inside the Soviet Union – which may or may not turn out to be window-dressing and only time will tell – there has been something of an upsurge of nationalism in the Soviet colonies. Lithuanians demonstrate for independence. Latvians collect signatures on petitions. Kazakhs gather in Red Square to wave their flag. Given this perception of some freedom, which may be merely an illusion, certain exiled parties feel the time is right to throw some external support behind the nationalist movements inside the Soviet Union. Are you with me?"

Pagan saw Witherspoon's dogs come bounding back, pink tongues flapping. Witherspoon patted them, fed them some kind of tidbits from a cellophane bag. "Good lads," he said to the eager creatures in the kind of voice a man might have reserved for his two very young sons.

"You're saying that the killing of Romanenko might be a message for the boys back home that they're not alone in their quest for independence. That there's support in the West."

Witherspoon arched an eyebrow. "Quite. And that's all there is to this business, Pagan. In your shoes, I wouldn't start looking for skeletons in closets. If it amuses you to dig for little mysteries where none exist, be my guest. But if I were you, I'd put aside your policeman's pride, admit you were less than vigilant, thank your lucky stars that the assassin was sufficiently an amateur to be so easily caught, and sit down in some quiet corner to compose your report."

Pagan ignored Tommy's patronising tone. Amateur was a fair description of the manner in which Kiviranna had shot Romanenko. No telescopic rifle fired from a concealed place, no attempt at diversionary tactics, no planned route of escape. A passionate amateur, someone with at least *one* oar out of the water, who considered Romanenko a stain to be wiped out. Was Witherspoon right? Was Pagan being dictated to by his bruised ego, his failure in Edinburgh to protect a man he'd felt a certain fondness for? Was it on so flimsy an edifice as his own injured vanity that he was playing detective?

"Must be off," Witherspoon said, leashing his spaniels. "Trust I've been of some help," and he walked away from Pagan without looking back, straining to keep his mutts in line.

Alone in the centre of Green Park, Frank Pagan continued to watch the sun as it slid inexorably down into darkness, and it was the kind of nightfall in which leaves cease to rustle, and the stillness suggests all kinds of impenetrable secrets. When the sun had finally gone, leaving a brassy layer of thin light over London, Pagan walked in the direction of Mayfair. He wondered about the identity of the person in New York who'd sent Jacob Kiviranna on his mission – if indeed such a man existed or was simply a figment of the killer's imagination. And the feeling hit him again that there was more to this whole business than the easy surfaces of things suggested, but he was damned if he could pin it down.

It was completely dark by the time Pagan reached the American Embassy in Grosvenor Square. He'd walked all the way from Green Park and up through the streets of Mayfair, lost in the kind of aimless speculation that turns a man's mind to blancmange. There were a couple of lights in the American fortress but, apart from a Marine guard and a few clerks on the upper floors presumably performing nocturnal tasks of a clandestine nature – probably the cipher boys of the CIA – the place was lifeless and almost ghostly. The guard, a handsome black with an accent that suggested Alabama, had been expecting Pagan and escorted him inside the building where the man known as Theodore Gunther was waiting in the lobby.

Ted Gunther was a short man with a crewcut. He wore thick-lensed glasses and a striped seersucker suit that hung on him rather badly, crumpled by the humidity of the night. He shook Pagan's hand, glanced at the grubby jacket, but was apparently too well-mannered to mention Pagan's sartorial condition. Frank Pagan sat down and as soon as he did so an exhaustion coursed through him and he could feel the demon of sleep hover on the edges of his mind.

"Bad business in Edinburgh," Gunther said.

Pagan agreed. A very bad business.

"Martin Burr mentioned something about a passport I might check out for you."

Pagan took the document from his pocket. Gunther flipped quickly through the pages, looking for God knows what. He stared at Jacob Kiviranna's photograph then, like a connoisseur sniffing a wine, held the document up to his nose and smelled the binding. He held the passport between thumb and forefinger and bent it slightly, a bibliophile assessing the authenticity of a first edition.

"It seems one hundred per cent the genuine article," Gunther said. "It hasn't been tampered with. It even smells good. Sometimes the paper smells wrong when it's a fake. I doubt it's a forgery. But if you don't mind, I'll hold on to it in the meantime and take a more clinical look-see."

"Be my guest," Pagan said, gazing across the lobby where a dim light burned.

"I guess you want a little more from me than verification of Kiviranna's passport. You'd like to know something about his background, if he belonged to any organisations, whether the FBI has anything on file. A radical association. A crime or two."

"Anything you can turn up," Pagan said. "He claims he has an accomplice in the United States. I'd like to know if you can shed a little light on the identity of the mysterious associate. Maybe there's even more than one. I can't get a handle on whether Kiviranna's telling me the truth or whether he's making up stories as he goes along."

Theodore Gunther took off his glasses and rubbed his eyes. "I'll help you all I can, of course. Always glad to be of some use to our allies, Frank. You can count on it." And Gunther smiled for the first time. It was one of those open American smiles that suggest placing each and every relationship on an easy first-name basis because formalities have no place in friendships between historic partners.

"Tell me, Frank. What kind of fellow is this Kiviranna anyhow? How does he strike you?"

Frank Pagan shrugged. "He wouldn't be on anybody's guest-list for an intimate dinner-party, I'll say that much. And I'm not going to be astonished if you find a background of mental illness and/or drug problems. He looks more harmless than vicious, but that's not a compliment. I get the distinct impression he's out to lunch more often than he's home."

Pagan tilted his head back in his chair. He was reluctant to get up and return to the streets of Mayfair. Ted Gunther took a packet of mints from the pocket of his limp jacket and placed one on his tongue. He said, "It's a sorry fact, but there are all kinds of fringe outfits back home who see Communism as the numero uno enemy of the free world. Most of them are harmless, thank God, but every now and then some weird fish slips through the net. Perhaps that's all Kiviranna will turn out to be. A weird fish who wriggled through a hole."

Pagan rose from his comfortable chair. He saw the Marine guard from the corner of his eye, the stiff uniform, the boots that shone like two black mirrors, the glossy visor of the cap pulled down flat against the nose.

"I'll get back to you as quickly as I can," Gunther said.

"I'd appreciate it." Pagan walked across the lobby and Gunther, who had a funny little stride, like a man with artificial hip sockets, came after him. Together, both men went out of the Embassy and stood on the steps.

Pagan looked across Grosvenor Square, that corner of London that had virtually become an American colony. He wasn't sure, at the time or much later, why his attention was so suddenly drawn to a dirty yellow Volkswagen beetle which was turning left on the Square even as he watched it. Perhaps it was the pall of exhaust smoke that hung behind it like a dark shroud. Perhaps it was the rattling sound made by the loose exhaust pipe or the horrible squeal of faulty brakes. Or perhaps it was the face of the pretty young woman at the wheel – who glanced at him briefly as the grubby little car passed out of sight, leaving nothing behind but the odious perfume of its passing.

Gunther held out a hand to be shaken. Pagan took it, thinking it was slack and pawlike and, despite the humidity of the evening, a little too damp just the same.

"I'll make some calls right away," Gunther said. "Rouse some folks out of bed."

"Which will make you popular," Pagan remarked.

"I'm more interested in answers than winning any popularity contest, Frank," and Gunther smiled again, the very essence of Anglo-American friendship.

Pagan walked down the steps away from the Embassy, crossed Grosvenor Square, searched the traffic for a taxi. When he reached the other side of the Square he looked back at the darkened Embassy and saw Theodore

Gunther go inside the building, the glass doors swinging shut behind him.

Moments later, just as Pagan successfully hailed a cab and was about to step into it, a light went on in a second-floor window. Pagan glanced up and saw Gunther's silhouette pass briefly in front of the glass.

Panicked, Jacob Kiviranna woke in the dark holding-cell, his body drenched in sweat, yet he was cold and his teeth rattled together and he couldn't keep his hands still. He sat on the edge of his bunk, his blanket wrapped round his body. He was afraid, more afraid than he could remember having been in his life before. Was it this sense of terror that made him so fucking cold? He wished he had more downers because the first one had worn off and now he was frazzled and disoriented and it was only with a great effort that he could remember where he was.

He shut his eyes and rocked his body back and forth and remembered the face of the old guy who'd given him the key to the luggage locker and the airline ticket and an envelope that contained five hundred dollars for expenses. He remembered the tiny glasses the guy wore, and the way they were perched on the end of his long nose, and how frayed the cuffs of his jacket were – but that was all he could bring to mind. And when the cop called Pagan came back in the morning to ask for the old guy's name, he wasn't going to believe it when Kiviranna told him once again that he didn't know it, that he'd never known it, never asked. He could point out the places where he'd met the old guy, he could take him to the boardwalk or show him the apartment building in Manhattan where the guy lived or where they'd walked at Coney Island, or even his own coldwater apartment in the Village where the old guy had come one time. But when it came to a name, forget it. There were some situations when you just didn't want to know names, when secrecy was everything.

And Pagan wasn't going to believe that.

Without batting a fucking eyelid, Pagan would turn him over to the Russians. And the Russians would stick him on board an Aeroflot flight to Moscow, and that would be the end of it. Kiviranna opened his eyes and looked around the dark little cell, vaguely making out the door, the unlit lightbulb overhead. There was no way he was going to Russia. Under no circumstances. Never. What they'd do to him over there – they'd interrogate him and beat him and then finally prop him up against a stone wall and shoot him. His perceptions of the Soviets had been shaped by stories he'd heard from older relatives in the USA, men and women who'd survived Stalin's various holocausts and who remembered wholesale executions and famine and even rumours of cannibalism during the 1930s and who told horror stories about how, to this very day, immigrants sometimes disappeared from their homes in New York City and were smuggled back to Russia by the KGB. And they were never heard from again.

He got to his feet and, still draped in the blanket, wandered up and down the cell. In the corner of the room was a porcelain washbasin and a paper-towel holder. Kiviranna ran the hot water faucet until it scalded his palms. That was one kind of pain, and he could just about stand it, but he knew the Soviets had ways of inflicting unthinkable agonies. No, he wasn't going to Russia to be executed for the murder of Romanenko – which wasn't murder at all, but a justifiable act, a moral act. That's what the old guy had drummed into him every time they met. *Romanenko doesn't deserve to live. Look what's he done to our people. He's scum, he's not human. There's a good word for him. And that's evil. He sold us down the goddam river. You kill him, your name's going to be legend. A hero.*

Kiviranna, who had been attracted by the possibility of heroism, went back to the bunk. He pulled the mattress to the side, revealing the metal frame, the springs. He touched the frame, his hands trembling. Sweat ran from his forehead into his eyes and he blinked because the salt stung. He stepped back from the bed, stared up at the lightbulb. The thought that came into his head just then seemed totally logical to him. He bent over the bed, laid a hand on the interlocking pieces of thin wire. Totally logical. He was surprised he hadn't thought about it before.

In a life that had often been puzzling, and lonely, and brutally drab, in a cold world where most people inexplicably shunned or avoided him, he understood he'd reached a pinnacle by killing the monster known as Romanenko. A summit. It was as if he stood on the crest of a hill and could see his whole past stretched out below him, a sequence of worthless menial jobs, a couple of jail stretches for petty offences, months of hospitalisation in institutions without windows where he was given injections and subjected to all kinds of humiliating tests, a clumsy infatuation with a woman who despised and ridiculed him. He could see all of this vanishing towards the horizon and he knew that his existence had amounted to a total waste of goddam time. Until the killing of Romanenko.

What was the rest of his life going to be like after that high? He shivered under the blanket. He went down on his knees and began to unhook the metal springs attached to the frame of the bed.

He wasn't going to Russia. He was sure of that.

5

Fredericksburg, Virginia

The large white house, built in neo-colonial style,
was located in a narrow leafy street on the edge of
Fredericksburg. Its former owner, an Australian who
had made a vast fortune publishing a horse-racing sheet,
had sold the property in 1985 to a man who said his name
was Galbraith and who hinted vaguely that he had retired
from a lucrative career in the aerospace industry. Both the
name and the career were fabrications. The property, all
seven wooded acres of it, changed hands for one million
dollars in a transaction so smooth and quick it surprised
the Australian handicapper, who took the money and
moved to Boca Raton.

The house, set some distance from its closest neighbour, had undergone considerable changes under the
direction of the new owner. Steel shutters were hung
on the windows, an elaborate security system installed,
and several new phonelines added – although not by
technicians employed by the Bell telephone company.
A huge mainframe computer was hooked up in a room
on the second floor, which had been remodelled for
just that purpose. The interior walls were painted a
uniform oyster-shell colour. Mature trees were planted
all around the property and, as if these did not quite
satisfy the owner's lust for privacy, a ten-foot brick
wall, electrified along the top, was also constructed.
Galbraith, an enormously fat man with an addiction to
things English – such as croquet, crumpets and Craven
A cigarettes – was rarely seen in the neighbourhood,

perhaps only occasionally glimpsed as he went past in a stately Bentley with darkly tinted windows.

At two a.m. US Eastern District time, two hours after Frank Pagan had left the American Embassy in London, a beige BMW drew up at the gates of the dark house, which slid open to admit the vehicle. The car moved up the circular driveway, then parked directly in front of the house. The driver, a man called Iverson, emerged from the German automobile and climbed the steps to the front door. Iverson inserted a laminated card into a slot, and was admitted after a moment. Inside, he headed at once for the door that led to the basement.

Iverson had bright blue eyes which were heavily lidded and his chin appeared to have been carved in stone. His blond hair had been cut so close to the skull that the scalp seemed blue-tinted. He was in his late forties, but the lack of lines and creases, the lack of *animation* in the face, made it impossible to guess. It wasn't the kind of face that accommodated expressions with any ease. There was severity and a sense of singlemindedness about the man. He descended the stairs to the basement in the stiff-backed manner of someone who has been for most of his life associated with one or other arm of the military.

Galbraith, dressed in the kind of loose, monklike robe he found very comfortable, his feet bare, sat on a brown leather sofa in the basement. He sipped espresso from a demi-tasse, then set the cup down on a smoked-glass table and raised one hand, which resembled a small plucked chicken, in a rather weary greeting.

"Sit," Galbraith said in an accent that was Boston, but had been tempered to suggest the other side of the Atlantic. "Welcome to *As The World Turns*."

Iverson sat. He stared at the various consoles on the wall, some of which depicted the darkened garden outside, while others flashed a variety of data transmitted from the mainframe on the second floor. Some of this information, which was coded, concerned the flight-plans of American fighter aircraft on NATO assignments in various parts of Europe. Other data, which constantly changed, listed such things as troop manoeuvres in Eastern Europe and the Soviet Union, the movement of ships and submarines in the Soviet Baltic fleet, the orbits of Russian spy satellites, the location of Russian radar installations, and a whole lot more besides, much of it irrelevant in global terms.

Galbraith had a whole world brought into the basement by the consoles. He was like some fat spider in the dead centre of an intricate electronic web whose strands stretch around the globe. He sat sometimes for hours, observing the relentless flow of information that travelled from space satellites and other complex computer links at great speeds along the filaments of his web. Iverson studied the consoles in silence, glancing now and again at Galbraith's face in which the eyes were mere slits surrounded by ravioli-like pillows of white flesh.

Galbraith, who weighed two hundred and eighty pounds, breathed noisily as if sucking enough air for three men. His laboured breathing had been one of the arguments he'd used when he'd first gone before a secret session of the Congressional Select Committee on Intelligence Operations to demand funds for the purchase of this property in Fredericksburg. *The air in DC, gentlemen, is becoming increasingly hard to live on. It dulls the senses and clouds the mind. Fresh air means increased alertness, and a happier, healthier crew. And cost-effective, too, a lower tax base, cheaper utilities, less expensive housing.*

Galbraith was as persuasive in argument as he was imposing in girth. Few politicians ever liked to contend with him, and fewer still demanded a reckoning, although there were always a couple who longed for his blood, small-minded men who called themselves – proudly, mind you – 'moralists', and who waited a chance to pounce on the fat man, catching him in some ugly covert operation with blood on his palms. These were men, usually from states where the electorate was corn-fed, who had a smell of old bibles and damp pulpits about them, and who drew their constituencies from the same people who donated money to TV ministries. They were stupid men, and narrow-minded, but they were not to be underestimated because they wielded the kind of power that could punish intelligence efforts where it really hurt – in the old pocketbook. And they waited, with withdrawn fangs, for Galbraith to commit a public faux pas, or fall into an espionage scandal. But not even these critics realised that Galbraith was effectively separating himself from the DIA – the Defense Intelligence Agency – to establish an autonomous branch, an inner sanctum, in the tranquil countryside of Virginia. The operation became known, to those who knew such things, as the GIA, Galbraith's Intelligence Agency.

The funds were approved and Galbraith moved the computer operation out of the capital, although he left most of his staff behind in the old quarters. He took with him only a handful of specialists, men and women trained to interpret the data provided by the computer. These were people he'd hired personally and who tended to see the world through the same prism as Galbraith himself did, which was one of self-preservation and what the fat man thought of as 'sophisticated' patriotism – to differentiate it from 'frontier' patriotism, which he considered a mindless kind of thing, a redneck instinct, a mere wormlike reflex. Galbraith's version was grounded in the simple assumption, which needed no drum-rolls to accompany it, no National Rifle Association to maintain it, that the continued existence of the United States as the primary power in the world guaranteed the continued existence of the world itself.

"Good of you to come at this hour, Gary. Smoke?" And he pushed a box of Craven A across the glass surface of the coffee table. Iverson declined. With a remote control device, Galbraith switched off the consoles. Iverson noticed the absence of electronic humming in the room now.

Galbraith said, "Here's a fine illustration of the limits of modern technology, Gary. While we sit in this lovely house and can keep track, say, of a couple of penguins merrily fornicating in Antarctica, we still haven't reached a situation where we can do a damn thing to predict human behaviour. In other words, just as we think we have matters under control, up pops some human idiot to scramble the whole equation."

"Which human idiot do you have in mind, sir?"

Galbraith stood up. His huge robe flowed around him like a collapsing tent. He went to a closet, opened it, took out a packet of English chocolate digestive biscuits and nibbled on one. Then, disgusted by his own needs, he tossed the half-eaten biscuit into a waste-basket. "They've ordered me to diet again, Gary. Which makes me cranky as hell. It came down from no less an authority than the White House physician, who speaks in a voice like God's. Galbraith, he says, there's a svelte person inside you, and he's dying to get out. Either you let him out, or you die. Svelte, I ask you. Do I look like there's a thin bugger inside me pining for freedom?"

Iverson said nothing because he'd never known how to make small talk. Years of military service and discipline had robbed him of most social graces. He was all business. He smiled uneasily as he looked at the fat man, knowing full well that Galbraith's obesity was his trademark as much as Aunt Jemima's face on a packet of pancake mix. On the Washington dinner-party circuit, at least along that inner track where the real power-brokers wined and dined, several people had perfected an imitation of the Galbraith waddle, which the fat man responded to in a good-natured fashion. None of his impersonators knew for sure what he did for a living, an ignorance Galbraith fostered by behaving in a self-deprecating way. He made fat jokes at his own expense. My obesity, he'd once told Iverson, is my cover – in more ways than one.

Iverson said, "You were talking about a human idiot, sir."

"Yes, so I was." Galbraith returned to the sofa and plumped himself down. Iverson's presence was comforting to him because Gary was a man without hidden emotions. No neuroses, no festering depths. Galbraith sometimes thought that Iverson was a relic from the Eisenhower years, when no shadows disturbed the American psyche, a time when the boy next door was exactly that, not some secret cock-flasher or dope fiend or peeping-tom. Iverson made Galbraith positively *nostalgic* for the simpler days of the Cold War, the apple-pie days.

"I'm talking about an idiot who has scuppered our friend Vabadus, and has thus threatened White Light."

"Scuppered?"

Galbraith looked wan suddenly. "Vabadus is dead, Gary. He was shot by someone unknown to us."

Iverson went straight to the only point that mattered to him. "Before or after the connection?"

"Before, alas. It wouldn't have mattered had it happened after. Then we'd know everything was secured." Galbraith made a fist out of one of his plump hands in a rare gesture of irritation. "It's my understanding that dear old Scotland Yard has become involved, which may pose problems for us."

"Of course," Iverson said.

"With luck, they may miss the point. They may simply overlook it. On the other hand . . ."

"On the other hand the Yard may become a little too alert," Iverson said.

"Precisely, Gary. And we can hardly tell our British allies what's going on, can we? Nobody tells them anything these days in any event, so why awaken them from their well-deserved slumber now and talk to them about White Light?" Galbraith sat back and sighed. He turned the name White Light around in his head for a moment. It was the in-house code for the Baltic project. Galbraith, who had grown up in intelligence agencies at a time when code-names were bestowed on anything that moved, had christened this project White Light in memory of his one trip through the Baltic countries at the height of the so-called Khrushchev 'thaw'. What the fat man most remembered, aside from a rather depressing socialist shabbiness in the capital cities of the Baltic, was the extraordinary length of summer nights and how the sky was suffused by an odd white clarity.

"So what do we do?" Iverson asked.

Galbraith stared at the younger man. "I think the only reasonable thing is to keep a very close eye on the situation in London and if it gets out of hand – if, say, certain persons at the Yard get a little too alert – then we may have to do a dark deed."

Iverson, who knew what was meant by the phrase dark deed, nodded his head slowly. "What do we know about the killer?"

Galbraith took a folded sheet of paper from the pocket of his huge robe and passed it to Iverson. "So far only a name, which I've written down for you."

Iverson stared at the name. "You want me to look into his background?"

"I think it's essential." Galbraith picked up the remote device and pressed a button and all two dozen screens flickered back to life. He stared at one screen in particular, which showed a list of all fighter planes, mainly F-16s, allotted to NATO, and their schedule for that day. "At least I don't see any problem with this aspect of the matter," and he waved a hand at the screen.

"That's the easy part," Iverson agreed.

"I love smooth sailing, Gary. I love it when the parts click nicely together. It's like solving Rubik's Cube by sound alone." Galbraith tapped the remote device on the surface of the table. "But I just hate unexpected problems. And I especially hate the idea of anything unfortunate happening to Scotland Yard personnel, God knows. Sometimes, though, self-interest takes precedence over sentiment, Gary. It's that kind of world these days. I wish it were otherwise. But we're all realists in this neck of the woods."

Iverson agreed again. It was another thing Galbraith liked about Gary. He was such an agreeable fellow. Galbraith dismissed him, heard him go back up the stairs, then there was the sound of the door closing. Alone, the fat man stared at his black and white electronic universe in an absent manner. He was thinking about Vabadus again. He felt he'd lost a friend, even though he'd never met the man. Vabadus, in Estonian, meant freedom. Galbraith thought it a very appropriate choice for the late Aleksis Romanenko.

London

Frank Pagan's flat in Holland Park had more than a touch of squalor about it. It was the kind of place in which a man clearly lived a solitary life. Somehow, Pagan had the feeling that it was always late in this apartment, always dark, as if sunlight never managed to find its way through the curtains. When he stepped into the living-room, the first thing he did was to pour himself a glass of Glenlivet. He surveyed the chaos of things like a stranger who finds himself suddenly tossed into another man's world. There was a milk bottle with curdled contents and three slices of hardened toast and a glass of orange-juice that had alchemised into an antibiotic. Pagan shut his eyes and savoured the drink.

In Roxanne's day, of course, everything had been different. But there was an abyss of self-pity here Pagan didn't want to encounter. Recollections of a dead wife were at best numbing, at worst excruciating. Loneliness had a gravity all its own and it pulled you down into its bleak centre. He stepped into the bedroom and wondered how long it had been since he'd laid flowers on Roxanne's grave. Weeks now, he supposed. There had been a time when he'd gone daily to that terrible fucking place and stared at the headstone as if, through the sheer mystic effort of will, he might conjure the dead woman up out of the cold earth and love her again.

He sat on the edge of the unmade bed and stared into his drink. He wondered if he was somehow getting better, if he was finding a quiet place to put his grief, like some safe-deposit box of the heart where it could be left locked and hidden. He'd removed Roxanne's photograph from the bedside table three months ago but in some odd way it was still there and he imagined it always would be. He closed his eyes again and sipped his drink and tried not to think about his wife and the way she'd died that Christmas because of the festive activities of a mad Irish bomber who'd detonated a killing device on a crowded London street. All he knew was that the planet without her was not exactly a better place. And perhaps this was the loneliest and most dreadful realisation of all – the world was reduced, diminished, by her absence.

These painful recognitions dismayed him. He rose, wandered to his stereo, found a record and set it on the turntable. It was an old Bo Diddley tune named *Mona*, with the kind of hard, driving rhythm that was almost a form of anaesthetic. He turned up the volume and let the noise crowd the room. Pure therapy, raucous and uncomplicated. Then, as if compelled to move by the music, he strolled around the room.

Consider simpler things that are not connected to love and grief. Consider the violence that had taken place at Waverley Station – when? Had it only been ten hours ago? The music had stopped now and the apartment was eerily quiet and he poured himself a second Glenlivet.

Perhaps it was more than his injured ego that made him want to impose a mystery on the event in Edinburgh, that made him want to look for hidden depths where Tommy Witherspoon claimed there were none. Perhaps it was the fact that his life, which had been about as exciting as that of a guppy mooning around inside an aquarium, had taken an interesting turn. It might be nothing but a brief illusion of mystery – even that was more intriguing than the blunted way things had been before.

He turned his thoughts once more to the contents of Romanenko's briefcase and as he was wondering whether Danus Oates had translated the material, he was surprised to hear the sound of his doorbell ringing. He went to the intercom and turned it on.

A woman's voice, distorted by the outmoded electrical system, said, "Mr Pagan?"

"Speaking," was all Pagan could think to reply.

"I know it's late, but I'd like to see you."

The accent was American. Pagan looked quickly around the apartment. How in the name of God could he have a visitor in a dump like this, especially a woman?

"My name's Kristina Vaska," the woman said. "I realise we don't know each other, Mr Pagan."

"Can it wait?" Pagan asked. "It's been a long day and I'm tired."

"I appreciate that. But it's very important I see you. It concerns Aleksis Romanenko."

"You better come up. I'm on the second floor."

He pressed the buzzer that unlocked the front door. Immediately he began to clear some of the mess from the dining-room table, a futile effort because no sooner had he carried the glass of penicillin and the milk bottle into the kitchen than he heard the woman knocking lightly on his door.

She was in her late twenties, possibly early thirties, and as soon as he looked at her Pagan realised it was the person he'd seen driving the yellow VW around Grosvenor Square. He was struck at once by the intensity of her eyes, which were that shade of brown that comes close to blackness, the absence of light. And yet there *were* lights, tiny flecks that seemed almost silver to Pagan. She had a wonderful square jaw that suggested tenacity. Her dark hair, cut very short, was curled tightly against her head. There was no makeup on her face. She wore a white linen jacket and blue jeans, all very casual, and she carried a bulky shoulderbag. She was lovely in the effortless way some women seem to be, as if by pure chance, a happy collision of disparate elements. The word Pagan wanted was serendipity.

"My humble abode," he said, thinking he might make some excuse about how his cleaning lady had the pox and couldn't come, poor old dear, and he was sorry about the shambles.

Pagan stared at breadcrumbs on the soiled table linen and cursed the odd nervousness that had afflicted him suddenly, the unease. It was almost as if the ghost of Roxanne Pagan sat in the bedroom, resentful at the intrusion of a woman into the apartment. Pagan underwent a mild sense of guilt. It was pure bloody nonsense, he thought. It was something a man had to grow out of. The spirits had their own lives to lead. And the living had living to do. But why was it so *difficult*?

The woman held out her hand and Pagan shook it a little too quickly. Her skin was cool against his own.

"I'm sorry it's this late," she said.

Pagan was too restless for sleep anyway. He gestured towards a chair and Kristina Vaska sat down. He noticed she was very slender in the way dancers sometimes are, that she moved as if her body were an instrument she played unconsciously. Pagan was so unaccustomed to company in this place that he didn't think to offer her a drink. Besides, now that she had impressed him with her appearance, now that he'd looked carefully at her, he had a more important question to ask.

"Do you usually follow people around?"

Kristina Vaska smiled. "Would you believe I was in Grosvenor Square at the same time as you by pure chance?"

"I've been known to entertain a few weird beliefs in my time," he answered. "That wouldn't be one of them."

"I wanted to talk to you."

"And so you followed me."

She nodded her head, still smiling. It was the smile that did it, he thought. He'd always been a sucker for a mischievous grin, for that certain elfin quality. He saw at once that Kristina Vaska was the kind of woman with whom you couldn't be angry for very long, which put him at an emotional disadvantage because he'd lost one of his more potent weapons – the forceful annoyance, the irritated flash of the eyes, which sometimes made people very wary of Frank Pagan because they sensed dangerous levels inside him.

"I've been following you ever since you left Scotland Yard. I trailed you all the way here. Then I got nervous. So I drove around for a while. After that, what the hell," and she shrugged. "I just pulled out the old courage and rang your doorbell. I figured I had nothing to lose."

The quality of persistence, Pagan thought, and a suspicion formed in his mind that he didn't much like. "Let me guess," he said. "You want a story. You want Frank Pagan's eyewitness account of murder in Edinburgh. Sorry to disappoint you, love, but I don't talk to the press."

Kristina Vaska gazed at him, and her look was as cool as her hand had been a moment before. "I don't have any association with the press, Mr Pagan."

Pagan said nothing for a moment. He had a sense of sheer awkwardness. He fussed with the tablecloth, moving crumbs around. Empty gestures. He wished he could find something terrific to do with his hands. "You mentioned Romanenko," he said finally. "Is there something you want to tell me?"

"Let me ask you a question first," she said. "What do *you* know about him?"

Pagan had an interrogator's dislike of having questions directed against him. "Not much," he replied.

"What do you know about the country he came from?"

"Russia?"

Kristina Vaska shook her head. "Estonia, Mr Pagan."

"I only know it's part of the Soviet Union – "

"*According to whom?*" The tone of her question was as sharp as the point of a needle.

Pagan saw it coming. He knew what he was in for and he felt himself cringe. She was going to be one of those slightly cracked ladies, all spit and intensity, who had a firm political stand she shouted about at every opportunity, a portable platform she could assemble in no time at all out of the carpentry of her convictions. Apolitical himself, despite some left-wing leanings that had been stronger in his twenties, Pagan was very uncomfortable with zealots. In his personal experience they were either dangerous or deranged, and sometimes both at once. They had a habit of shaping the world to meet their own political requirements. To Pagan's way of thinking, zealots were first cousins to terrorists. It was just a matter of degree.

"The United States doesn't recognise Estonia as Soviet territory," Kristina Vaska said. "Nor does your own country. So far as the US and the UK are concerned, the Soviet Union illegally seized all three Baltic nations in 1940, after they'd been independent for twenty years."

Pagan started to interrupt, but it was impossible.

"The pretext – and the Russians aren't exactly subtle when it comes to such matters – was that the Baltic had to be defended against the Nazi menace. When World War II started, the Germans drove the Russians out of the Baltic, which was only a temporary condition. The Russians came back in 1944 to take up where they'd left off – as the great liberators of Estonia, Latvia and Lithuania." Kristina Vaska paused a moment and what Pagan saw in those dark eyes was more than anger, it was a deeply-held resentment, the kind that lodges unshakably in the soul. She stood up and walked around the room now and Pagan, entranced by her movements, that indefinable harmony of motion called grace, watched her.

"The point is, Mr Pagan, the people of the world are very familiar with Nazi atrocities. They know about what happened to the Jews of Europe. But when it comes to Soviet atrocities in the Baltic, there's a kind of ignorance that frustrates the hell out of me. I'm talking about the mass deportations of Baltic nationals to Siberia. I'm talking about hundreds of thousands of people from three separate nations with their own language and cultures who were uprooted and shipped out of their homelands and if they were lucky enough to survive inconceivable journeys in railroad cars, they found themselves in labour camps, where most of them died anyway. This is a horror story, Mr Pagan. This is genocide, plain and simple. And it's going on to this very day. It's going on, perhaps in more subtle ways, but it's still happening because the KGB sees to that. The KGB makes sure, at every level of Baltic society, that the native peoples of the Baltic countries are being Russified – which is just a polite fucking word for extermination."

She stopped moving and stared at him. He had the feeling he'd been hit across the skull with a stout wooden plank. She went on about how native languages were falling into disuse, cultures dying, how TV stations broadcast only in Russian, how young people were being conscripted into the Soviet Army and shipped to Afghanistan to fight a war they didn't care about on behalf of a system they despised, and Baltic peoples were being dispersed to other parts of the Soviet Union, and anybody who raised his voice to complain had the nasty habit of disappearing from view.

There was an aura of energy about her, almost a force-field. Pagan, who could think of nothing to say because she'd somehow managed to make him feel a little ashamed of his own neglect of recent history and uncomfortable with what she surely perceived in him as insensitivity, wondered about her background.

She talked with an American accent, but what was her family history?

"I'm sorry," she said.

"Sorry?"

"Sorry you don't know more about it. And sorry I went on at you. I hate to lecture."

"And I hate being lectured," Pagan said. But he was intrigued just the same. He had run into many of the disenfranchised persons of Europe in his life. The Poles, the Hungarians, the sad exiles who formed social clubs in London suburbs and held dances and sometimes wrote letters to newspapers. It was just that he hadn't considered the Baltic nations as countries with identities as singular as those of Poland or Hungary or Czechoslovakia. He'd always thoughtlessly assumed they were indivisibly a part of the Soviet Union and if he ever considered them at all it was a process that took place on some far edge of his awareness, a subject that never troubled him, never came into focus in a place where he could see it clearly. Every now and then he'd read about a student riot in Latvia or some form of protest by the Catholic Church in Lithuania, every now and then he'd absently read about petitions delivered to the United Nations by people with strange, unpronounceable names – but there was a distance to these things, as if he were seeing them down the wrong end of a telescope. It was, he realised, unforgivably parochial of him. And it was no real justification to tell himself that cops weren't exactly famous for their interest in affairs beyond their own particular parish, which was usually small and well-defined, a tidy little patch where you knew all the scams that were going on.

"People forget," Kristina Vaska said. "That's the problem. When a wrong isn't righted immediately, it becomes the status quo, and people just don't think about it any more. It's easy, you see. It's the complacent way."

"And I'm complacent," Pagan said.

"And ignorant. Which pisses me off." She looked around the room. "And you also live like a pig, which pisses me off even more."

Pagan smiled. Her earnestness had suddenly gone and there was levity in her expression and he could see, behind the features that had become so damned stern a moment before, a sense of humour, a warmth. "I'm not here a great deal," he said feebly.

"I can't say I blame you." She glanced through the kitchen door, which unfortunately Pagan had left open. "Now there's a room where some bodies might be buried. I bet you lie awake at nights and hear things moving about inside the refrigerator."

Frank Pagan closed the kitchen door. "I thought you came here to talk about Romanenko," he said.

"You needed a little edification first."

"Which you provided."

"I'm not exactly through with the background yet, Mr Pagan."

"I had the feeling," he said. The education of Frank Pagan, he thought. And so we grow.

Kristina Vaska wandered to the window and ran the palm of one hand down the edge of the curtain. Then she let her hand fall to her side and turned to face Pagan. "I don't know how serious you are, Mr Pagan. And I don't know how seriously you take me. Sometimes you seem just a bit flippant. Maybe it's something in your manner."

"I'm listening," Pagan said. "Seriously."

"I don't suppose you've ever heard of a man called Norbert Vaska?"

Pagan shook his head. "A relative of yours?"

"My father."

There was a silence in the room suddenly. Pagan was aware of the quietness of the night pressing against the house, the darkness laying a still film upon the window. And Kristina Vaska, who could go from impassioned enthusiast to bantering domestic critic in a matter of seconds, had changed yet again. Her eyes were directed into herself and Pagan knew that whatever she was looking at it wasn't anything in this room.

"My father taught engineering at the Tallinn Polytechnical Institute in Estonia," she said. "He was a good engineer. At least he was a better engineer than he was a Communist. He didn't believe in the system. He had status, you understand, and materially his life was fine. A car. A good apartment. A refrigerator. Things we take for granted in the West. Unlike some people, though, my father couldn't continue living under a system he considered malignant just because he happened to be one of the privileged ones. In 1966 he joined a group called the Estonian Movement for Democracy which developed ties with similar groups in Latvia and Lithuania."

She glanced at Pagan, as if she wanted to be absolutely sure of his attention. He thought how grave she looked now.

"He became an editor of an underground newspaper, the *Estonian Independent Voice*. This involved considerable risk to himself. Maybe you can imagine that. Aside from writing articles and distributing the newspaper furtively, he often had to make trips to Riga in Latvia, or he'd go to Vilnius in Lithuania. I've tried to imagine how terrifying it must have been for him – attending underground meetings in the dead of night in somebody's apartment . . . a group of men whispering about how to fight the Soviet occupation of their countries. I've often tried to picture that scene and I always feel the same cold fear. Here was a man with a position, prepared to risk it all for his personal beliefs."

She looked at Pagan, almost as if she wanted to be sure he was listening. "He was arrested by the KGB on April 14, 1972. I remember it clearly. There was a knock on the door after midnight. Now there's a simple little phrase that's utterly terrifying, Mr Pagan. There's something people like you and me don't have to live with. *A knock on the door after midnight.* Three men took my father away. They had no warrant. Who needs a goddam warrant if they're KGB anyhow? They ransacked the apartment. They trashed the place. They left my mother and me behind. We heard nothing more about my father for three months. He'd been put in what's called 'special confinement'. That's a goddam awful phrase. You see nobody. You talk to nobody. You get nothing to read. You sit in a windowless room and you know nothing because nobody tells you anything. After three months, we heard he'd been sentenced to life imprisonment in the city of Perm in the Soviet Union. It was one of those places that pretend to be psychiatric institutes. You've heard of them, no doubt.''

Frank Pagan said he had and that he was sorry to hear about her father. But he wondered where this was going, how the dots were going to be connected, what the relationship was between Romanenko and Kristina Vaska's narrative.

"After, we heard he'd been transferred to a labour camp in the Arctic Circle. Then, without any warning, my mother and I were expelled from the country and flown to Helsinki. All this was done, you understand, without one single word of explanation. Nothing. A car came to fetch us. We were told to pack as much as two suitcases would hold. We were given passports. We were handed expulsion papers, which meant we were stripped of Soviet citizenship – although that didn't exactly cause a great gnashing of teeth. After a month in Helsinki we went to the United States. On September 12, 1972, we arrived in New York City. I'm good with dates, Mr Pagan. Certain dates just seem to stick in my mind. For example, I haven't seen my father since April, 1972. It's a long time. It's too long.''

She moved across the room. She came very close to Pagan as she passed. He was aware of something stirring in the air around him. Call it electricity, he thought. Whatever it was, it took him by surprise. It was an unexpected reaction and he wasn't sure how to deal with it.

"I know it's brave of me," she said. "But I'm going to risk your kitchen. I'm dry. I need water."

She opened the kitchen door. Pagan heard her rinse a glass, then there was the sound of ice-cubes being pried loose from the freezer. When she came back she smiled at him. "There's a process known as defrosting a freezer, Mr Pagan. A polar bear could live in yours." She sat down, sipped her water, stared at him.

"I was never very good at science at school. I don't understand the principles of freezers."

"I don't think it takes an Einstein," she said, shaking the slightly furry, opaque cubes in her glass.

Pagan turned the subject away from his embarrassing domestic life. "Have you heard from your father?"

"He's not exactly in a place served by a postman, Mr Pagan. As for his location, I'm not sure. The last time I heard any news about him he was in a labour camp near Murmansk in Siberia. That was more than a year ago. According to my source, he was very ill. He had pneumonia and he wasn't getting the right kind of medication. There's no such thing as a malpractice suit in a Siberian labour camp."

Frank Pagan said, "I keep reading in the papers that things are supposed to be getting better for political prisoners in the Soviet Union."

"Sure, if you're a famous physicist or you've got influential friends in the West. But not if you're simply a former professor of engineering at the Polytechnic in Tallinn. Norbert Vaska doesn't have clout. He's just another forgotten prisoner, another number among thousands. It's going to take years and years if men like my father are ever going to be released under some general amnesty programme. It takes a long time for *anything* to change in Russia. There are too many people with a vested interest in the system. People who don't like change at any price." She drained her glass, set it down on the table. "Which brings me – finally – to Aleksis Romanenko. You were probably wondering."

"It had crossed my mind," Pagan said. And for some reason he couldn't name he felt an odd little tension go through him. He had the feeling that whatever conclusion Kristina Vaska was approaching, it was somehow going to complicate his life. He saw her reach inside her large purse. As she did so, the telephone rang and Pagan put out his hand towards it, annoyed by the sudden intrusion of the world outside, irritated by any interference at the crucial point of the woman's story. He had an unhappy rapport with phones at the best of times. Now it was a sheer bloody nuisance and he was tempted just to ignore it and go on listening to Kristina Vaska. But he didn't.

The urgent voice he heard was the Commissioner's.

"Young Oates has turned up something that might pique your interest, Frank. I suggest you drop whatever – or whoever – you're doing, and get your arse over here on the double. I'm keeping a very unhappy Russian diplomat at bay, and I don't know how long I can stall him before the Third World War breaks out."

"I'll be there," Pagan said. When Martin Burr used the phrase 'I suggest', it was always a command meant to be obeyed immediately.

"Come in that fast American car of yours and pretend we've just abolished the speed limit, would you?"

"Give me ten minutes," Pagan said.

"Make it nine. And I'm not joking. There's been another development here, quite apart from Oates's translation, that might come as something of a surprise."

Pagan put the telephone down. *Shit.* How could Martin Burr's timing be so damned bad? He looked at Kristina Vaska, who was watching him expectantly. He wondered what kind of surprise Burr had in mind.

"I'm sorry," he said. "I've just been summoned by the Commissioner. It's like getting a message from God."

"Then you don't want to keep God waiting," she said. "I'll put the end of my story on hold, Mr Pagan."

"How do I get in touch with you?"

Kristina Vaska shrugged. "I haven't made a hotel reservation." There it was again – that smile which changed her entire face and made her eyes light up and dissolved all the gravity of her expression. "I could easily wait here. I mean, if you don't mind. If you don't think I'll be in the way."

"I don't know when I'll be back," Pagan said.

"I'm not in any hurry."

Pagan, who was seized by a feeling of total discomfort, gestured toward the sofa. "It opens out into a bed," he said. "You'll find blankets in the bedroom if you need them." He thought of this woman stepping inside his bedroom, and the image was an odd one, like a picture hanging aslant on a wall.

"I'll be okay. Don't worry about me, Mr Pagan."

He hesitated a moment in the doorway. It was obvious that she sensed his awkwardness and found it amusing.

"Just don't go anywhere," he said. "I'm anxious to hear the rest of your story."

"I promise you'll find it very interesting."

Pagan opened the door. But he was still hesitant. It was all very strange to him. A woman in his apartment, an attractive woman waiting for his return. Somebody with an unfinished narrative that was connected to the disaster in Edinburgh. Why hadn't Martin Burr waited just a few minutes more before telephoning? Pagan hated interrupted stories.

"Don't worry. It's perfectly safe to leave me here," she said. "Cross my heart I won't steal the silverware. It's probably lying in the sink anyway, too dirty to steal."

Pagan smiled. "I wasn't thinking about the silverware."

Kristina Vaska said, "I bet you don't have any anyhow. You look like a man who uses disposable plastic cutlery, Mr Pagan."

"Call me Frank," he said. "And if you want to know the *real* truth, I eat with my hands."

Saaremaa Island, the Baltic Sea

It was almost dawn when Colonel Yevgenni Uvarov stepped out of his quarters and walked quietly across the concrete compound. He passed under the shadows of the radar scanners, which turned silently, ominously, in the early light. Anything that moved out there on the Baltic would send a signal back to the scanners, which would then feed the signal into the one-storey building Uvarov now entered. There was a row of small green screens that received the radar transmissions. They were largely inactive and the technicians who stared at them were bored in the manner of men who spend their days in expectant vigilance that more often than not fails to produce excitement. They watched the screens and their eyesight invariably became bad over a period of time. Uvarov had the thought that the men under his command were prisoners of the green screens, hopelessly addicted to studying radar signals.

Uvarov crossed the large room, pausing every now and then to examine one of the screens, or to check the progress of a trainee operator. He reached his desk, located at the back of the room, and he sat down. His chair was hideously uncomfortable. The surface of his desk was clear. There was nothing of a personal nature to be seen anywhere. He kept a photograph of his wife and children inside the desk. Every now and then, as if to remind himself of the reason for his decision, he'd open the drawer and glance at the photograph – and what filled him was a sense of devotion and gratitude and love. He had only to look at the photograph, which was a stiff studio shot done in slightly unreal colours, to make himself believe that his course of action was the correct one. Just the same, he often felt a fear so great he was convinced it showed on his face, that other people couldn't fail to notice it. And sometimes the fear yielded to a kind of despair – he had spent fifteen years of his life in the Army and within the next few days he was going to throw it all away. The whole thing had the texture of a bad dream, a nightmare in which he was trapped as surely as a fly in the jaws of a spider.

His wife and two teenage children lived in Moscow. Uvarov only saw his family whenever he was granted leave. It didn't happen often. Last year, when his wife had fallen ill, he'd requested compassionate leave, and he'd been denied. The refusal galled him. The service to which he'd devoted so much of his adult life should not have denied him such a simple plea. But it was the system, it was the way the system worked, with a lack of understanding for human needs. Uvarov felt he'd been denied more than compassionate leave. He'd been denied his humanity. And his family had suffered needlessly.

A year ago. How much had changed in that short time, he thought. He yawned because he'd slept badly. He always slept badly these days. He stood up, walked around the room, observed the operators at their screens. Then he went outside.

He could hear the slow Baltic tide that came and went upon the beach beyond the wire perimeter. A few gulls, scavenging the shoreline, flapped in the dawn light. This depressing island, thick with military installations, rocket-bases and airfields and anti-ballistic missile interceptors, was another factor in his sense of general disappointment. Now and then an opportunity arose for brief leave on the mainland, which meant perhaps a twelve-hour visit to Tallinn – certainly never enough time to travel to where his family lived. Whenever he returned from Tallinn, a pleasant medieval city, a place with a sense of life and colour, it took days before he could suppress his restlessness and discontent.

He raised his face to the sky. Overhead, six MIG-27s

flew in formation, breaking the cloud cover and then vanishing in the direction of the mainland. An impressive display, he thought. A show of force and strength. Suddenly Uvarov felt small and insignificant and the task he'd agree to do struck him as overwhelming. He wouldn't go through with it, he couldn't, he didn't have the nerve. But then he wasn't alone in the undertaking, there were others involved, officers like himself who were ready to act at the appointed time – or so he'd been told by the man he'd met several times in Tallinn. What if it was a lie, a kind of sadistic ploy to test his loyalty? What if the man in Tallinn was some kind of inspector of internal affairs whose job it was to detect the potentially disloyal, the weak, those who had no commitment to the system?

Uvarov felt a tightness in his heart. He moved back in the direction of the low, grey-stone building, passing once again under the radar scanners. He sometimes had the feeling he was doomed to spend his whole life in this wretched place, forever commanding the men who endlessly studied the green screens and waited for the sky to reveal signs of danger. It was an awful prospect, one he couldn't tolerate.

He opened the door, crossed the room, returned to his desk. He sat down, studied the reports of NATO activities that had been recorded in yesterday's logs, the usual harmless catalogue of flights, the practice bombs dropped beyond Russian territorial waters, the idle strafing of the Baltic, nothing out of the ordinary. Then he pushed his chair back from his desk and thought of the photograph in the drawer – which reminded him of the very thing he didn't want to think about, the brown envelope concealed under the floorboards of his family's apartment in Moscow, the package that contained three US passports and fifty thousand American dollars in small bills that had been given to him by the man in Tallinn, the man he knew only as Aleksis.

6

London

The surprise Martin Burr had mentioned turned out to be depressing and sickening. Frank Pagan stood motionless in the doorway of Kiviranna's cell while the Commissioner hobbled around inside the small chamber, his cane making quiet ticking sounds on the floor.

Burr said, "Have to hand it to him. He was an ingenious bugger."

Pagan crossed the threshold, thinking how the cell was too small to contain three men, even if one of them was dead. Jacob Kiviranna lay across his bunk. The mattress had been removed and was propped up against the wall. A long length of wire, one end of which lay close to Kiviranna's lips, was attached to the light-fixture in the ceiling. The bulb had been unscrewed and lay on the floor. Kiviranna's eyes were closed and there were black burn marks around his lips and nostrils. Urine soaked the blanket he'd wrapped himself in. The cell, poorly-ventilated, smelled of scorched flesh.

"He unhooked the bedsprings from the frame, patiently straightened out a length of wire, stuck one end into his mouth then the other into the electric socket," Burr said, and peered up at the wire that dangled from the ceiling.

Pagan looked down at the corpse, then turned away, went out into the corridor. Martin Burr followed. Pagan peered the length of the corridor for a time, saying nothing, trying to imagine Jake placing the wire between his lips, laying it over his moist tongue, then standing up on the bed-frame to unscrew the lightbulb and twist the free end of the wire into the socket. He felt a fleeting nausea. Suicide always struck him the same way – a sheer bloody waste. What had prompted it, what madness, what fears had come to Jake in the darkness of the cell and driven him to such an act?

Both men were quiet for a moment before Burr said, "Let's go back up to my office. We'll have a glass of something, then look at what young Oates has produced."

Frank Pagan hesitated a second before he followed Martin Burr in the direction of the lifts. He was thinking how tidy it all seemed now. Too tidy. Both assassin and victim were dead, which – if Jake had been telling the truth – left only an enigmatic accomplice in the United States, somebody who might already have disappeared into the shadows from which he'd first namelessly emerged. Somebody who, if Ted Gunther failed to turn anything up, might always remain an anonymous mystery.

Pagan stepped inside the lift, beset by an unexpected sense of anger at Jacob Kiviranna. He closed his eyes as the cage climbed in the shaft. Whatever answers Jake might personally have been able to provide were forever lost now.

It seemed more stuffy than usual in Burr's uncluttered office. Pagan picked up the sheet of paper the Commissioner had laid on the desk. For a second all he saw as he stared at it was the sight of Kiviranna, an after-image dishearteningly impressed upon his retina. He drained the shot of Drambuie Burr had poured for him, then set the glass down. He knew you were supposed to savour the stuff, but he wasn't exactly in a sipping frame of mind.

"Poetry, Frank. Why would Romanenko carry around a piece of poetry inside a sealed envelope? I can understand a man travelling with a *volume* of poems, let's say, if he wants to while away some boring hours on a trip or if he needs to read himself to sleep. But what I *don't* understand is sealing a few lines of the stuff inside an envelope.''

Pagan studied the sheet of paper that was covered with Danus Oates's cramped, scholarly handwriting. Here and there words had been crossed out and alternatives written carefully in the margin, indicating how Oates must have struggled over an exact translation. He'd also provided alternative words in parentheses.

But the day will (tomorrow?) soon be breaking/When all the torches will be burning/Throwing flames in widening circles/Which will free (untie? lit: cut the cord of) the arm embedded/In the mighty chains of rock./Kalev will be coming home/To bring happiness (contentment/freedom?) to the people/Of a new Estonia.

He placed the sheet on the Commissioner's desk. He didn't consider himself a judge of poetry, but he thought he knew enough to recognise bad verse when he saw it. "I assume something's been lost in the translation," he said.

"I agree it's somewhat overstated, but it sounds to me like a patriotic poem, and that kind of thing has a tendency to be bloated," the Commissioner said, plucking at the edge of his eyepatch. "The point is, who the hell is Kalev? And why was Romanenko carrying this particular poem around, Frank? It looks as if he'd had it in his case for half a bloody century too. The paper's practically falling to pieces. And here's another odd thing – Oates tells me it was written in a language I'd never heard of before, something called Livonian, which is almost extinct. According to Oates, it's related to modern Estonian, and to some elements of Latvian.''

Pagan looked at the poem again. He had difficulty concentrating. "It could be a message Romanenko intended to deliver before he was killed. Maybe he was supposed to make contact with somebody in Edinburgh, somebody who'd understand the significance of those lines. Why carry something around in an envelope if you don't mean to deliver it?"

"A possibility," the Commissioner remarked.

"It could also be a code of some kind."

"I thought about that. If it's a code, where does one start? Codes are a bit out of our province."

Frank Pagan had a moment in which he felt sleep flutter somewhere at the back of his head. "What else did Danus Oates translate?" he asked.

The Commissioner indicated a small stack of papers at the side of the desk. "That poem's the only unusual thing. There's some technical stuff as well as correspondence between Romanenko and a man called George Newby, the director of a microchip company in Basingstoke that was apparently tendering a bid for Romanenko's business."

Pagan said, "If Romanenko was supposed to meet somebody in Edinburgh, who was he? And what exactly did this individual do when Romanenko didn't show up? Did he just shrug his shoulders and walk away? The more I think about Aleksis, the more he slips between my fingers."

He set the poem down on the desk, although he continued to stare at it. Kalev, he thought. It was the kind of name given to extraterrestrial characters in the comic books of his youth. *Kalev! Emperor of Saturn! Master of Cosmic Wisdom!* Pagan could have used a little of that cosmic wisdom himself right then. He took his eyes away from the poem because staring wasn't bringing him any answers.

The Commissioner rolled his walnut cane back and forth on the surface of his desk. "To make matters somewhat more intricate, there's an impatient little sod called Malik from the Soviet Embassy waiting downstairs for me. He's come to collect the briefcase. According to the Foreign Office, the case and its contents go back to the Russians. *Immediately*. I've been stalling Malik as best I could until I talked to you about this enigmatic poem.

But if I don't return the material sharply, Malik's going to lodge an official protest with the Foreign Secretary, which would be a bore."

Pagan stood up and walked around the windowless room. "Do you intend to return the poem?" he asked.

The Commissioner smiled. It was the expression of a man who was no stranger to mischief. "My feeling is that the Russians have got enough on their plate without having to worry about a bit of bad verse. And if anybody ever asks, we've never even heard of the bloody poem."

Pagan saw something enjoyably conspiratorial in his superior's face. It was an aspect of the Commissioner's personality he liked – this sneaky way he had of taking risks, of defying authorities even higher than himself.

Pagan carefully placed Oates's translation of the poem, and the brittle original, back in the envelope, and stuck it in the inside pocket of his jacket. The Commissioner swept Danus Oates's other translations into a drawer, picked up a telephone, said something to whoever was on the other end of the line.

After a minute, Malik entered the room. He was a short man with enormous eyebrows and a face that suggested a rocky promontory. Pagan observed that the Russian, who wore a lightweight Aquascutum overcoat of a decidedly bourgeois nature, had a certain self-righteous expression on his face. He was the offended party, the victim of the tactics of capitalist law-enforcement officers, and consequently of monstrous capitalism itself, and nothing was going to change that. If need be, he'd play this injured role to the hilt. His eyebrows quivered as he spotted the briefcase.

"Are you ready to hand it over?" he demanded. His English was excellent.

"We've come to our senses at long last," Pagan said.

Malik stared at Frank Pagan, obviously unsure of Pagan's tone, which was sarcastic. The Commissioner said, "What Frank Pagan means is that you can take the briefcase. It's all yours, Mr Malik."

Unceremoniously, Malik grabbed the case and held it against his chest. "Your methods leave much to be desired, gentlemen," he said. "It's not enough that you fail to protect the life of a high Soviet official – you then confiscate the property of the Soviet Union, which you keep in your possession, without good reason, for twelve hours."

The Commissioner made a soothing noise, although it was clear to Pagan that his heart wasn't in it. He was going through the motions of commiseration. Pagan leaned against the wall and folded his arms.

Malik patted the case. "We are also going to make an official request to interrogate the killer of Romanenko. This will be done through the proper channels, of course."

Both Pagan and Martin Burr were silent. Then Burr said, "I'm afraid that won't be possible."

"You're going to refuse the request?"

"I don't have a choice," the Commissioner replied.

"And why is that?"

Martin Burr explained. Malik shook his head in disbelief. He said, "First you allow Romanenko to be assassinated. Then you make it possible for the criminal to escape justice by committing suicide. What kind of organisation are you running?"

"I resent your tone," Burr said. "We hardly made it possible, as you put it, for Kiviranna to take his own life."

"A suicide," Malik remarked. "How utterly convenient for you. Now the killer is no longer around to answer questions that might be embarrassing to you. Are you *certain* he took his own life?"

"What are you suggesting?" Burr asked. His face had turned the colour of a plum.

"His death spares you the need for a public trial, Commissioner. It spares you the awkwardness of putting the man in the witness-box, where he becomes the perfect symbol of your inadequacy to secure the life of a Soviet official. Who knows? Perhaps you even encouraged the unfortunate man's demise."

"You're an outrageous twit," Burr said, and thrust the tip of his cane into the rug, a wonderful little gesture of restrained savagery. His sense of fair play had been insulted but what else could he have expected from a Bolshevik anyway? They had their own rules and sometimes they defied the understanding of a decent men.

Malik moved toward the door. He clutched the briefcase at his side. "Goodnight, Commissioner."

The Commissioner harumphed. If the Russian was going to flaunt good sense, then he, Martin Burr, was most assuredly not going to observe good manners. So far as he was concerned, the Bolshevik didn't deserve common courtesies.

The door closed behind Malik.

"Little shit," Burr said. "Have you ever heard such balderdash in your life? The sheer *gall* of the man is appalling."

The Commissioner sat down and sighed. He looked rather depressed all at once. "What have we *really* got, Frank, when all is said and done?"

"We've still got Kalev."

"Whoever he is," Martin Burr remarked dismally.

Pagan was thinking of Kristina Vaska. He was thinking how he wanted to hear the rest of her narrative.

"I may have a way of finding out," he said.

The Commissioner stared at his desk lamp. "Let's hope so, Frank. I hate being in the dark."

Frank Pagan agreed. The dark, with all its secrets, all its inaccessible corners, was not his place of choice. He thought about Aleksis – drunk, laughing, joking, dancing with a reluctant partner, an embarrassed English rose, in the subdued bar of the Savoy, a man of mirth and boundless energies. But it was clear now that there had been other sides to the man as well – secretive, submerged, hidden from view. And whatever they were they'd led to his own murder, a suicide, and the arrival of a woman, with an unfinished story, in Pagan's apartment.

Aleksis, Pagan thought, you may have been an insignificant Communist Party leader in some minor Soviet colony – *but what were you really up to?*

Zavidovo, the Soviet Union

Vladimir Greshko heard the sound of a car and turned his face to the window of his bedroom, seeing the first yellow light of dawn press upon the glass. He was always a little surprised to have lived through another night. Death, with all its dark finality, had been much on his mind during the last couple of weeks. He didn't believe in an afterlife. What would a man do with eternity anyhow, except scheme against his fellows? To form Marxist action committees and provoke Revolution in heaven? To convert angels to Engels and replace God with Communism?

He raised his face, rearranged his pillows, covered the plastic tube with the edge of his bedsheet. The obscene sucking sound of the device filled him with disgust.

He saw the bedroom door open. The Yakut nurse stepped in, nervously wiping her tiny hands in the folds of her white uniform. Behind her stood General Olsky. *Olsky – of all people!* The sight of the new Chairman of the KGB quickened Greshko's tired blood. He wondered what had brought Stefan Olsky all the way from Moscow to this godforsaken place.

Olsky wore a dark pinstriped suit. Greshko considered him a pencil-pusher, a clerk, a man without an ounce of flair in his soul, a colourless bureaucrat so typical of the new breed. He was Birthmark Billy's protégé and therefore a member of the Politburo's inner sanctum. When Greshko had run the organs of State Security, Olsky had been a mere Deputy in the Third Directorate. His rise, engineered by the General Secretary, had been spectacular. At the age of forty-one he was the youngest man in Soviet history to be Chairman of the KGB, which was another source of resentment for Greshko, who hadn't assumed control himself until his sixty-first birthday.

"You look well," Stefan Olsky said.

Greshko said nothing for a moment. He seethed whenever he imagined Olsky occupying *his* office, sitting in *his* chair. He knew Olsky had had the office redecorated, that all the old paintings had been returned to storage and replaced by charts – charts, sweet Christ! – that the old phone system had been renovated and the six phones Greshko had enjoyed supplanted by a single device that allowed Olsky to hold what were known as 'conference' calls. Every day new changes. Every day something else swept away.

"I look as well as a dying man can," Greshko said. "You're trying to be kind, Stefan."

Stefan Olsky approached the bed. This was his first visit to Greshko's cottage, and he'd heard about the old man's condition, but he hadn't been prepared for the smell that hung in this room – this commingling of human waste and disinfectant, this deathly odour.

Olsky stepped to the window, looked out. He had recently taken to shaving his head, as if to make himself look older, more experienced. He ran a palm self-consciously over his skull. His wife had pleaded with him to let the hair grow back. She said she didn't want to wake each morning and find an egg on the pillow next to her.

"It's pleasant here," Olsky said. "Greenery. Fresh air. Very nice."

What had Olsky really come here for? And why so early in the day? Greshko surveyed the Chairman's face. Unmarked by experience, the old man thought. How could such a face frighten anybody? To run the organs you needed *presence*, you needed to be able to instil awe in other men. If Olsky had presence, if he had charisma, it was of a kind Greshko couldn't possibly understand. He was even a *teetotaller*, for God's sake, which fitted very nicely with Birthmark Billy's anti-vodka crusade. But what the General Secretary didn't realise was that vodka was the *fuel* of Mother Russia. To take vodka away, to reduce its production and price it beyond the means of a worker, was a natural disgrace, like yanking an infant from its mother's tit. But none of the new gang had any affinity for the heart of the country, at least not the way Vladimir Greshko, a poor peasant boy from the Stavropol Territory, perceived it. What did they know about the unending struggle against the bitter climate and a countryside racked by famine in the 1930s? They were all college boys, chicken-hearted, cologne in their armpits, educated by the benefits of a Revolution they were now attempting to dismantle. *Ingrates!*

Thoughts of Olsky provoked rage. What made things worse was that Greshko, at the time of his abrupt removal from office, had come into possession of information which alleged that Olsky had investments in Western European money-markets held, of course, in fictional names, dummy corporations and the like – but if the allegations were true, what kind of Communist did that make Stefan Olsky?

Greshko wished he'd been able to present this information to the Politburo, which would have been distressed by the furtive capitalism of Comrade Stefan, but by the time he decided to do so it was too damned late. All the doors had been slammed shut in his face with a finality that even now sounded through his brain. Too slow, old man, he thought. And perhaps just a little too complacent. But he still had the information, and a time might come when it would prove useful. One of the lessons of his long life was that you never threw *anything* away.

Olsky turned from the window and smiled. He had dark eyes and high cheekbones and a wide mouth that was rather pleasant and generous. "I imagine it could get lonely here," he said. "You're lucky to have a great many friends, Vladimir."

"I've been blessed," Greshko remarked. What was Olsky driving at? "I'm not completely forgotten by my old comrades."

"Some of whom are very dedicated to you. Some of whom travel considerable distances to visit you," Olsky said.

"Only to pay their last respects, Stefan."

Olsky had always found Greshko to be slippery and devious. There was a certain charm about the old fart, which Olsky acknowledged rather grudgingly, although he'd never been a fan of Greshko's way of running the organs – autocratic, secretive, possessive. Olsky had heard Greshko referred to within the Politburo as King Vladimir, and not always jokingly.

Like a monarch, Greshko had ruled the KGB as if it were a court, with courtiers who curried favours and engineered palace intrigues in an atmosphere of distrust and malice. What underlay this regal technique of management was paranoia and fear – which had also forged durable loyalties between Greshko and many of his former subordinates, a fact that troubled Stefan Olsky. He didn't intend to run the organs the way Greshko had done. He believed in inter-departmental cooperation and an open-door policy – concepts that were not readily grasped by the old guard, who grumbled and complained at every little change and sometimes even reminisced openly, brazenly, about how things had been different under the control of General Greshko. It was going to be difficult and slow, and very demanding, to change the KGB.

"Is that why you've come, Stefan?" Greshko asked. "To pay *your* last respects?"

"Not entirely. The fact is, some of your visitors . . . disturb me, Vladimir."

Greshko smiled. "Don't tell me you *spy* on me?" he asked in mock horror. He knew that some of the foresters who worked around Zavidovo sent information back to Moscow about who had been seen in the vicinity, what they'd done, where they'd gone. During his own tenure he'd received information from the same men who nowadays provided the service for Olsky.

"Reports have a way of reaching me," Olsky said. "Rumours are like homing pigeons."

"And what do you hear, General?"

"Some of your friends have nostalgic longings. Some of them belong to certain organisations, Vladimir, that call themselves by such names as 'Memories' or 'Yesteryear' – consisting of men who have a dangerous yearning for the way things were. War veterans. Factory managers. Party members. And they have some sympathetic ears inside the Central Committee. Obstructionists, Vladimir. People who cling to the past."

"I can't be held responsible for the sympathies of my friends," Greshko said. "People are slow to change their ways, Stefan. Give them time. Sooner or later, they'll get used to this new Russia you're building." *This new Russia*. Greshko had uttered these words in a way that was almost sarcastic.

"What about you?" Olsky asked. "Are you getting used to it?"

"I'm dying," Greshko answered. "I don't have time to get used to anything."

Olsky was quiet a moment. The old boy could put on a good act, he could smile and look altogether innocent, but Olsky was wary. "There's talk of a conspiracy, Vladimir. I hear rumours in Moscow. I hear them too often."

"Conspiracy!" Greshko laughed, a rich, hearty sound. "Listen to me, Stefan. A few old friends get together here and there. They talk about the old days. They drink vodka, get sentimental, they weep a little. Where's the conspiracy in that? One of the first lessons you must learn is that Moscow has a hidden rumour factory. My advice to you, comrade, is not to listen. Or if you must listen, be selective."

Olsky walked back to the window. He had been Chairman for only five months now and the last thing he needed as he reorganised State Security was a conspiracy of hard-liners, diehards, old reactionaries whose imaginations could carry them no further than the idea that the greatest of all Russian leaders had been the murderer Stalin. Rumours, whispers, shadows – sometimes Olsky had the feeling he was listening to voices inside a closed room, voices that fell silent as he approached the door. He turned his face once more to Greshko. Even sick and dying, the old man managed to give off a glow that suggested residual power. What you had to remember about Greshko was that he still had friends in high places, that when you approached him you did so cautiously.

"Is that why you came here?" Greshko asked. "To warn me about the company I keep?"

The atmosphere in this room was cloying. Olsky was anxious to go, to get inside the car and have his driver return him to Moscow. That night he'd promised to take his wife, an amorous woman called Sabina, to a new drama at the Sovremennik Theatre. For some reason, perhaps because of their air of freedom and licence, experimental plays always excited her, an excitement she brought back home to the bedroom. Olsky never tired of his wife's advances.

"There's one other thing," he said.

"Go ahead."

"I've been conducting an inventory, Vladimir. Of files. Computer data. Current cases."

An inventory. Greshko thought how sadly typical it was of Olsky to make the organs sound like a damned haberdashery. "And?"

"A certain file is unaccounted for, Vladimir. I don't have to remind you of how serious that is."

"You don't have to remind me of anything." Greshko

thought of the documentation he'd removed and he felt a quick little shiver of tension. "Clerks and computer operators are notoriously slipshod. They've probably made some kind of idiotic mistake."

Olsky was silent a moment. "We were able to establish that the missing file was that of somebody called Aleksis Romanenko, First Party Secretary in Tallinn. Whoever removed the file forgot to delete the name and number from the central directory."

Damned computers, Greshko thought. He'd never really grasped all this new technology. He wondered if this was something that should worry him. Did it matter that Olsky knew Romanenko's file had been removed? Probably not. So long as he didn't know what was in the file, then it wasn't worth bothering about.

"What makes you so sure that the file was *removed*, Stefan? Sometimes there are glitches, and computers destroy their own data. Or so I've heard."

"True," Olsky said. "But in this particular instance there was a date when the file disappeared. The computer recorded the date automatically, which it would not have done if the program were malfunctioning. So I'm led to believe the material was *deliberately* taken."

"By whom?" Greshko asked.

Olsky shook his head. "I have no idea. I thought perhaps you might be able to throw a little light on the matter. You had charge of the files at the time when this particular data was taken."

"One file among hundreds of thousands? Are you serious? I've never even heard of this fellow – what did you say his name was?"

"Romanenko."

Greshko looked incredulous. "Really, Stefan. What's so damned important about one missing file in any case? What's such a big deal that the Chairman himself has to worry about a trifle like this?"

Olsky went to the door, which he opened. He looked across the kitchen at the Yakut woman, who was stirring food in a saucepan over the wood stove. She turned her face, regarded him briefly, then looked away again.

Olsky said, "Normally, it might mean nothing. But Romanenko was assassinated yesterday."

"*Assassinated?*"

"In the circumstances, the missing file struck me as an odd coincidence."

Greshko placed his hands together on the surface of his quilt. "Ah, now I understand your puzzlement." He tapped the side of his skull. "The name means nothing to me, but if I remember anything, I'll be sure to get in touch with you. The trouble is, my memory's like some damned dog that won't come when I call it. I'll try, though. I promise you. I'll try."

"I'd be grateful," Olsky said. There was a long pause before Olsky looked at his watch. "I have to return to Moscow."

"Of course," Greshko said.

"Goodbye, Vladimir."

As he stepped out, Olsky watched Greshko's face, which in shadow appeared enigmatic. But perhaps not. Perhaps there was some other expression barely apparent in the shadows, a hint of amusement, of pleasure, like that of a man enjoying some hugely private joke.

Olsky had no illusions about the way Greshko despised him. He left the house and stood for a moment under a large oak, which shielded him from the morning sun. He listened to the drone of flies, the cawing of rooks, the sound of a horse whinnying in the distance. Then he looked in the direction of his car, wondering if it had been a mistake to come here in the first place. Simple vanity – was that it? Had he wanted the old man to see that the organs of State Security were at last in strong young hands? That the dried-out old ways were inevitably passing and a new generation was changing things? To impress and perhaps worry a sick old man – was that why he'd mentioned conspiracy and his knowledge of Greshko's friendships? If so, he'd underestimated the former Chairman, who wasn't likely to be in the least concerned by references to intrigues and acquaintances of dubious loyalties. A dying man was beyond ordinary fears.

Olsky moved out from under the tree. When he reached his car, he looked back at the cottage. No, he thought. It was the missing file that had really brought him here from Moscow, a file whose removal could have been achieved only by Vladimir Greshko himself or by somebody who'd been given that authority by the old man.

It was strange, he thought, how the old man hadn't asked a single question about Romanenko's assassination – no interest in place and time, no interest in detail, the means the assassin had used or if he'd been apprehended. Absolutely nothing.

Either Greshko didn't give a damn about the killing or else he'd already learned the details of Romanenko's murder from another source. If the latter was true, then he'd been lying when he'd denied ever having heard of Romanenko.

Olsky got inside the car, settled back in his seat and closed his eyes, unable to shake the feeling that Greshko, in his wily way, had been playing a game with him for the past thirty minutes, a game based on subterfuge and concealment. And Olsky felt the frustration of a man trying to introduce new rules when certain players stubbornly prefer sticking, no matter what, to the old ones.

Ten minutes after Olsky's departure, Greshko spoke into the telephone. "Has Epishev gone?"

"He left five hours ago, General," Volovich replied. "On the first available flight."

Greshko set the receiver down. He looked at the calendar on the wall. There were now four days left. Sighing, longing to smoke one of the cigars his physician had denied him, he tried to content himself with squeezing a small rubber ball he kept in the bedside table. It was a poor substitute for drawing rich tobacco smoke deep into one's lungs. By God, how he would have loved to light one! He tossed the stupid ball aside in a gesture of contempt, then he opened the flask that contained the special mixture.

He sipped, thought of Olsky, smiled. It was fascinating to watch the new Chairman fish in waters too deep for him ever to penetrate. *You're keeping the wrong kind of company, General Greshko. A certain file is missing, General Greshko. Wipe my arse for me, General Greshko.*

Greshko laughed aloud. He would love to nail Olsky, to crucify that shaven-headed upstart, to see him hung out to dry like a bundle of wet kindling.

Four days. He corked his flask, knowing he could live that long.

7

London

Kristina Vaska was amused by Pagan's apartment. She wandered through the rooms slowly, thinking disorder was almost a law of nature here, from the untidiness of the bedroom to the flaky state of the bathroom, where towels and discarded socks formed a small, lopsided pyramid. But Jesus, there was something touching in all this mess, something that, in spite of herself, provoked a maternal response. It was an easy reaction and she didn't trust it. If Pagan couldn't look after his domestic life by himself, why should she even think of doing it for him? She'd long ago given up the notion that there was something engaging about men who needed to be looked after. Like careless boys, they couldn't fend for themselves – but she was damned if she was going to find such helplessness attractive. Pagan was already appealing enough in his own hesitant way. He didn't need the assistance of charming ineptitude.

In the bedroom she came across a silver locket that hung from the lampshade by a thin silver chain. On the back of the ornament were the initials R.P. She fingered the item for a time, wondering about the initials. Somebody P. Somebody Pagan.

In the drawer of the bedside table she solved the problem. She found a framed photograph of a woman, a lovely woman with an intelligent face. Across the bottom of the picture were the words *With all my love, Roxanne, September 83. Our Third Anniversary*. Kristina Vaska put the photograph back and wondered what had become of

Pagan's wife that she was nothing more than a picture stuffed in a drawer and a locket hung from a lampshade.

She crossed the bedroom and opened a closet, where several suits and sports coats hung on a rack. This was obviously Frank Pagan's neat corner, his tidy place. The suits and jackets were enclosed in transparent plastic bags, set aside from the general chaos of the apartment. An island of order. The suits were good ones, well-tailored in a modern way, and some of the sports coats were, well, slightly ostentatious. There were also several shirts whose patterns might have been designed by a coven of drunken Cubists. Frank Pagan was clearly a man of some vanity who tried to keep in touch with sartorial trends. On the bottom of the closet were shoes, most of them casual slip-ons, all neatly aligned.

She shut the closet and sat on the edge of the bed, staring through the open bedroom door into the living-room, where a stack of long-playing records was arranged against one wall. The first thing she'd done when Pagan had left was to go through the collection of albums, because she believed you could learn about a person from his or her choice of music – a theory tested by Pagan's collection, which consisted entirely of what she considered noise. Every record was early rock and roll, ranging from well-known stuff like Little Richard and Jerry Lee Lewis, to material she found obscure, Thurston Harris and the Sharps, Freddy Bell and the Bellboys. What could she learn about Pagan from this assortment except that he liked loud simplicity and indulged in massive, possibly lethal, overdoses of nostalgia?

She rose, wandered back into the living-room. Clues to a man's life, she thought. The music. The prints on the walls which were mainly old concert posters – The Rolling Stones at Wembley Stadium, Fats Domino at the London Palladium. As if they'd been hung by a hand other than Pagan's, perhaps that of the absent Roxanne, there were also delicately faded prints depicting scenes of 19th century English country life. It was quite a contrast between the rowdy and the bucolic.

She walked to the window, where she parted the curtains and looked down into the street. Across the way was one of those quiet squares that proliferate in London, a dark area of trees beyond the reach of streetlamps. Branches stirred very slightly in the soft night breeze. She imagined incongruous animals foraging for food out there – a badger, a field mouse, creatures disenfranchised by the city. Then she moved toward the sofa and lay down, closing her eyes.

When she heard the sound of Pagan climbing the stairs, then the twisting of the key in the lock, she sat upright. He came inside the living-room with a vaguely unsettled expression on his face, like that of a man who suspects he's stepped inside the wrong apartment. She was amused by his awkwardness, by the way her presence in his territory affected him.

"How was God?" she asked.

"Flustered," Pagan said.

"I thought Gods were unflappable by definition."

"They get anxious when something's not quite right in their domain."

Like Martin Burr, Pagan was also flustered. Like Martin Burr, Pagan had the feeling that something was not quite right in his domain. Part of it was due to this woman's sudden entry into his life. He looked around the room as if he expected to see changes, small rearrangements she might have made in his absence. But everything was the same as before. What would she move anyway? The bloody furniture? It was a ridiculous notion. She probably hadn't even risen from the sofa all the time he'd been gone. He was entertaining some silly thoughts, and he wasn't quite sure why.

"Are you too tired for the rest of my story?" she asked.

"I want you to take a look at this first." He removed the poem from his pocket and handed it to her. There was a tiny connection of flesh as his hand encountered hers. "Tell me if it means anything to you."

She read it, looking solemn. "I know it better in the original," she said, and there was a catch in her voice. *"Küll siis Kalev jõuab koju, Oma lastel õnne tooma, Eesti põlve uueks looma.* It's been a long time since I recited anything in Estonian. And it's been a long time since I read those lines."

Pagan had never heard Estonian spoken before. What it reminded him of was Finnish, which he'd heard once or twice, finding it a little too arctic to be mellifluous. He looked at Kristina Vaska. She had her eyes shut very tightly and two thin tears slithered down her cheeks. He felt suddenly helpless – what was he supposed to do? Go to her, put his arms round her, comfort her? He wasn't sure how to behave.

"I'm sorry," she said.

"It's okay."

"It's not okay. I don't like to cry. I don't like feeling homesick and I can't stand being weepy." She opened her eyes and forced a tense smile. Then she dipped into her purse and took out a paper tissue, which she pressed against her eyelids. Pagan watched in silence. He had a longing to hold her hands.

"Can I get you a drink?" he asked.

"I'm okay."

"You're sure?"

"I'm sure." She smiled again, a pale effort, and gazed at the poem. "I haven't read *Kalevipoeg* since I was a kid."

"Can you explain the poem to me?"

"It's from an old legend. Kalevipoeg was the son of Kalev. Kalev, who founded the kingdom of Estonia, was the son of the god Taara. According to the story, Kalevipoeg impressed the gods with his upright character, so they severed his legs at the knees then they embedded his fist in the stone surrounding the gateway to hell. Which is where he is to this day – preventing the return of the Evil One, the Devil."

113

"The gods have a strange way of showing their appreciation," Pagan said, wondering if a little half-arsed levity was even remotely appropriate. "So Kalevipoeg is some kind of local hero."

"A symbol of goodness."

"And he's expected back when things get really rough?"

Kristina Vaska said, "Yeah, but I doubt if he's ever going to return. He's had plenty of opportunities. And if he hasn't come back by this time, I'd say he's simply not going to show. Gods are notoriously unreliable."

"They have their own timetables, that's all."

Kristina Vaska scanned the poem again, her hand trembling slightly. "I assume Romanenko had this in his possession, Frank?" she asked. It was the first time she'd used his name and she did so almost coyly, in a way Pagan found appealing – as if she were speaking a very private word.

Pagan nodded. "The question is, why was he carrying it around with him? It was written in something called Livonian and stuck inside a sealed envelope."

"Maybe I can shed a little light on why Romanenko would have this poem with him."

"How?"

"By telling you something about the man, which is the reason I'm here anyhow," she said. "As I recall, I was getting to the end of my tale when I was rudely interrupted. Shall I continue?"

"I'm listening." Pagan was impatient now.

Kristina Vaska took a deep breath. "Okay. I was up to the part where Romanenko was about to make an appearance. First, a question. Have you ever heard of an organisation called the Brotherhood of the Forest?"

Pagan, sensing an unwelcome detour, shook his head.

Kristina Vaska said, "The Brotherhood fought the Soviet occupation until 1952, maybe 1953. Mainly they had nothing but rifles and guts. But what really finished them off were Soviet reprisals against the farmers who supplied the Brotherhood with food and shelter. So they disbanded. Some were executed, others imprisoned. A few fled from the Baltic. My father, who was a member of the Brotherhood when he was sixteen years old, threw his rifle away and managed to slip back into society, which wasn't easy for him – given his views. I suppose he thought he could continue the struggle by political means. It wasn't a period of his life he talked about, you understand. He let one or two things slip when he was in an expansive mood or if he'd been drinking, but never anything of substance and *only* in front of the immediate family."

Frank Pagan watched her. The darkness of the eyes, the mouth that was a little too large for the face and yet somehow absolutely right, the soft curl of eyelashes – a skilled portrait artist or a poet might have done justice to her idiosyncratic beauty. Pagan, neither artist nor poet, was content to look and appreciate.

"I want to show you something, Frank."

She opened her purse. She took out a small, cracked photograph, an old black and white affair with a scalloped edge. She handed it to him. Pagan saw two young men, boys – one neatly bisected by the crack in the picture – standing in shirtsleeves under the branches of a tree. They both held rifles. Their faces were misty with that nebulous quality old photographs often have and their expressions weren't easy to read. There was toughness in them, and grimness, but they were both grinning in a stiff fashion as if the photographer had bullied them into smiling when neither of them felt like it.

"The man on the left is my father," she said.

Pagan looked at the face of Norbert Vaska, seeing no resemblance between the man and his daughter.

"The man on the right," she said, then paused.

Pagan raised his face from the picture and waited.

"Don't you recognise him, Frank?"

Pagan, puzzled by her question, looked at the picture again. How could he possibly recognise a Baltic rebel in a photograph that had to be forty years old, a soldier in a forgotten war fought when Frank Pagan had been barely five years old?

"Look closer," Kristina Vaska said.

Pagan did so. There was something, the foggy edge of recognition, but then it slipped away from him. "I give up," he said.

"The man on the right is Aleksis Romanenko."

"Romanenko?" Pagan stared at the photograph. Time had eroded the resemblance between the man with the rifle and the one who'd been assassinated in Edinburgh. There was some mild similarity, nothing more. "Are you sure?"

Kristina Vaska was emphatic. "Beyond any doubt."

"I'm having a hard time with this, Kristina," he said. "You're telling me that Romanenko, the First Secretary of the Communist Party in Estonia, was once a guerilla who fought *against* the Soviets? That he was a member of this Brotherhood?"

"That's what I'm saying."

Pagan laid the photograph on the rug. Romanenko's face gazed up at him – and now Pagan thought he saw another quality there, a certain defiance, a challenge from the past. "I need more," he said quietly.

Kristina Vaska stood up and walked to the window. She parted the curtains and gazed out at the park in the square. "Aleksis Romanenko was one of my father's best friends. Even when he began his climb in the Party, he was still Norbert Vaska's friend. Until the early 1970s he would visit our house. The visits stopped after my father's arrest in 1972."

Pagan caught something here, a slight stress in her voice. He asked, "How was Romanenko able to rise in the Party?"

She turned from the window. "He obliterated his past, Frank. He recreated his own history by falsifying records. You've got to remember how the war scattered people all over the Soviet Union. The deportations alone accounted for millions of people uprooted and shipped elsewhere. Think of the confusion. Wholesale turmoil. Badly kept records, documents destroyed in air-raids, birth-certificates and identity papers burned. An ingenious man like Romanenko could take advantage of the situation."

She paused, looked distant, even a little forlorn. There was at times, Pagan thought, a certain delicacy to her features. "He must have lived with the constant fear of being found out. Which is the way my father lived. In the end Norbert Vaska couldn't work within the system any longer. But Romanenko did."

"Worked within or worked against?" Pagan asked.

"Both. The phrase we want is a double life. Aleksis may have been the Party Secretary, but he believed in the independence of the Baltic countries. And secretly, he did everything he could to support that goal."

Pagan remembered the way Romanenko had held his briefcase against his chest in the railroad station, the way his face had looked when the gun was fired. Contorted, horrified, a man stepping suddenly into a nightmare and seeing all his fears, which he has nurtured for thirty years or more, suddenly rear up at him in the form of an assassin's gun. A double life, he thought. So that was Aleksis's secret world, his hidden depths. The idea that Aleksis had worked against the Soviet system gave Pagan a small glow of pleasure.

"Then we can assume the KGB found out about Romanenko and killed him." But as soon as he'd said this Pagan thought how trite it was. How pat. Simplicity had a certain elegance, but in his experience simple things often turned out to be deceptive, layers yielding to other layers, each revealing a fresh complexity.

There was Jacob Kiviranna, for example, an American who had travelled three thousand miles to shoot Romanenko, and there was the mysterious associate who'd arranged for the gun to be made available in London. Could Kiviranna and his accomplice be a part of some devious Soviet solution to the problem of what to do with the two-faced Romanenko? A hired gunman fetched from overseas to kill Romanenko in Edinburgh, which at least had the merit of complying with the old axiom that you never shit on your own doorstep?

Pagan dismissed this and not simply on the grounds of its simplicity. The idea of Jake Kiviranna being recruited by the KGB didn't ring any bells for him. Jake hadn't impressed him as the type on whom *any* clandestine organisation would take a chance. It was possible that Jake *might* have been used unwittingly by the KGB, but that raised another question Pagan found puzzling.

He looked at the woman and said, "The problem I have when I blame the KGB for Romanenko's death is this – why was he allowed to leave the Soviet Union in the first place? If the KGB intended to kill him, it would have been less messy to do it quietly at home. A lonely road, a car accident, something out of the public eye. Why go to all the trouble of shooting him in a railway station in Edinburgh? But then if it wasn't the KGB who organised his murder, who did?"

Kristina didn't answer. She stared at the window and saw dawn, the colour of a cloudy pearl, in the London sky. Pagan watched the same quiet light, enjoying the silence in the room for a while before turning back to her.

He said, "Maybe Romanenko had changed his views over the years. Maybe he'd become tired of the deception involved and settled down as a loyal servant of the Party. In which case, he might have been killed by some people he'd let down badly." It was a frail little kite, but Pagan, mired in possibilities and speculation, flew it anyhow.

Kristina Vaska said, "I doubt Romanenko would have changed his loyalty. You have to keep in mind the fact that Aleksis belonged to the Brotherhood. And the bonds of the Brotherhood just don't go away. These are men who simply won't forgive the Soviets for murdering their nation. They kept in touch with each other over the years, Frank."

The Brotherhood, Pagan thought. If it existed now, what else could it possibly be but a band of ageing men thriving on dreams? How could it be anything other than a harmless kind of social club, games of bridge or gin-rummy interspersed with patriotic songs and some bilious grumbling and toasts of loyalty made with wizened hands?

"Okay. Even if this outfit is alive and kicking, what makes you so damned *sure* Romanenko still had anything to do with it?"

Kristina Vaska said, "Because of the poem."

"Ah, our old mate Kalev."

"Exactly."

"Enlighten me, Kristina. Make it as clear as you can."

She smiled. "It's very simple. The poem had very special meaning for my father's cell of the Brotherhood. Aside from its obvious patriotic content, the poem was used when they wanted to send a message secretly. Anybody reading it would understand its meaning immediately. Anybody who received these lines always knew what they stood for. They're a green light, Frank. They mean go. They mean everything is in place and it's okay to go ahead."

"Go ahead with *what*?"

"With whatever the plan happens to be."

"What plan?"

"I don't know in this case. The only assumption I can make is that it's something directed against the Soviets. Given the background of the Brotherhood, knowing how they feel about the Russians, what else could it possibly be?"

Something directed against the Soviets. Pagan stared into his empty glass. Bafflement was a tiring business. Even as she explained some things, Kristina Vaska made others even more obscure. Was it part of this mysterious plan for Aleksis to pass the envelope to a contact in Edinburgh, as Pagan had thought before? Was the connection to be made at the Castle? Was that why Aleksis had expressed such an interest in visiting the place – because somebody had been waiting for him up there in the dark fortress? And would this man, this spectre, read the lines, inspiring lines resonant with nostalgic echoes of an old guerilla war, and know precisely what he was supposed to do?

Pagan had the feeling he was being moved further and further away from the core of things. Like some object on a fretful tide, he was being sucked back from the safety of the shoreline. Deep waters, he thought. And growing darker as he trod them.

He asked, "If the poem's a message, and Aleksis was the messenger, who was the intended recipient?"

Kristina Vaska had no answer to this question. Pagan rubbed his eyes. What he needed was the light of a fresh morning, a new day, a brain that didn't feel like a leaden mass locked in his skull. He looked towards the half-open bedroom door and wondered if he could find sleep.

He shrugged. "Maybe we can talk again at breakfast." *Breakfast*. He wasn't sure if he had anything more to offer than some stale Rice Krispies floating in milk of a dubious vintage.

"Is that an invitation to stay?" Kristina Vaska asked.

"If you don't mind the sofa."

"The sofa's fine, Frank," and she seemed to linger over his name, as if she were inviting Pagan to read something into her tone of voice.

"I'll get you some blankets." He stepped into the bedroom, foraged inside a closet, then carried a couple of blankets back to the living-room, where the woman had already taken off her shoes and was lightly massaging her toes. He set the blankets down, watching how she smoothed her flesh with long, supple fingers.

She raised her face to him and smiled. "I appreciate your hospitality. Really."

Pagan went back into his bedroom and closed the door. He could hear her move around. He wondered if she slept naked, a disturbing speculation.

He stared at the ceiling. Sometimes he could sleep on a

problem and then, as if he were visited in the dark by his muse, he'd wake with some kind of answer. He didn't feel optimistic this time, though. He suspected that his muse, normally fond of cryptic problems, had vacated the premises with the haste of an unhappy tenant.

He reached out, killed the light. But he couldn't put the idea of the woman out of his mind. The more he contemplated her, the more irksome questions and doubts arose. It would have been comforting to accept Kristina Vaska at face value, to be certain that she was no more than she claimed to be – the angry daughter of a man imprisoned and destroyed by a brutal system, somebody who had simply entered Pagan's life because she wanted to help.

But Pagan took very little at face value, no matter that the face in question happened to be bewitching, and lovely, the kind that might plunder and pirate your heart and simply sail away with it.

He kicked off his shoes, and shut his brain down – although it continued to murmur still, like some busy river he could hear in the distance.

It was twenty-five minutes past noon when V. G. Epishev stepped inside the Roman Catholic church in the Fulham district of London. The humid air in the church had the texture of flannel. He sat down at the rear and looked absently at the altar. A dolorous clay Virgin peered off into the middle distance. Behind her, concealed in shadow, a large crucifix hung on the back wall. Rows of candles in glass jars created small flickering islands of light. Here and there, supplicants kneeled in front of the jars and crossed themselves, or else genuflected as they passed the altar.

The whole effect, Epishev decided, was tawdry and sentimental. The mystery of Christianity distilled in cheap candles and icons – was this all there was to it? Did people actually find hope and sustenance here? He wondered if the appeal lay in the fundamental simplicity of it all, the easy cycle of sin and redemption.

He sat back in the pew. His forehead was sticky. Even the slight draught that cavorted through the candles was thick and warm. He wasn't altogether uneasy in this place, rather more puzzled. Years of interrogating believers, years of exploring their hearts, hadn't brought him any closer to an understanding of their faith. He knew that faith, which transcended the limits of reason, was a great leap they all claimed to have made. And, like the curator of a museum in possession of an interesting artifact he cannot identify, Epishev was mystified, and fascinated, by the nature of this commitment.

He wiped sweat from his forehead. As he did so, he was aware of Alexei Malik slipping into the pew beside him. Epishev took off his glasses quickly and put them in his pocket.

"Why did you choose this place?" Malik asked.

"I have a warped sense of humour." Epishev, who wanted to get down to business immediately, noticed the briefcase Malik was holding. "I assume that's Romanenko's?"

Malik nodded. "It's Romanenko's." A short pause, then, "But the message is gone."

Epishev was silent for a long time, fanning the heavy air with a hand. "Who removed it?"

Malik's voice dropped to a whisper, like that of a man whose words are constantly monitored, constantly eavesdropped upon. "I think we can be certain it was done at Scotland Yard, either by the Commissioner or a policeman called Frank Pagan. It's very likely that the Commissioner delegated the entire matter to Pagan. A man by the name of Danus Oates was also present in Edinburgh. Oates is something of a linguist and if Romanenko's message had to be translated he'd be the man to do it."

Epishev massaged his eyelids. The flight from Moscow to Berlin, then from Germany to London, had tired him.

Some kind of spiced-up eggs had been served on board the second plane and he could feel them burning a hole in his stomach. "We must find out what the damned message said. The General wants to be one hundred per cent certain that the plot is not about to be derailed, Alexei."

Epishev watched a middle-aged woman kneel quickly before the altar. A priest emerged from shadows and engaged her in conversation, hovering over her like a large black bat.

"What about the assassin?" Epishev asked. "What do we know about him?"

Malik stuffed his handkerchief away. What he disliked about Colonel Epishev, with whom he'd worked in the past, was the way the man asked questions. They were always phrased directly, always posed in a tone that made you feel as if you were taking an oral examination, and that every question could be answered in only one acceptable way.

Malik said, "The assassin somehow managed to take his own life a few hours ago."

This item of news surprised Epishev. "In custody?"

"In custody," Malik replied.

"How careless of the custodians," Epishev said and returned his gaze to the front of the church, noticing for the first time a stained-glass window depicting Christ in his last agony. "What have you learned about him?"

"Very little," Malik answered. "His name was Jacob Kiviranna, an American."

"With a Baltic name," Epishev said. "Was he acting alone?"

Malik said, "We think so. According to the Soviet Mission in Manhattan, the killer didn't belong to any dissident groups in the United States. And he certainly had no known affiliations here."

Malik, whose official function was to serve as assistant to the Ambassador (a liberal recently installed by the new regime in Moscow), had a whole network of informants throughout the United Kingdom, a varied crew of alcoholics, homosexuals, loners, sociopaths, blackmail victims, fellow travellers, exiles, and fantasists numbed by the Welfare State who needed the romance of thinking themselves spies. He'd spent a long time building this network, and much of the intelligence that reached him was reliable. If he said Kiviranna had no allegiance with any organisation inside the UK, he was offering an assessment that was reasonably accurate.

"These might be useful," and Malik took a sheet of paper and a photograph from his pocket, passing both items to Epishev. "I was unable to get a photograph of Danus Oates, only an address. However, I did acquire a picture of Frank Pagan. His address is on the back."

Epishev stuck the paper inside his wallet, then studied the photograph briefly. The likeness of the man called Pagan was blurry, but what Epishev saw was a lean, determined face. The picture appeared to have been taken without the subject's knowledge because Pagan was looking off into the distance, away from the camera, and his expression had no self-consciousness about it. It was a hard face in some respects, but there was a slight suggestion of humour around the eyes, as if this man took himself seriously only to a point.

Epishev put the picture away. He was impatient to be out of this church now. It had begun to affect him adversely. It was a place where people came to share a common belief, and Epishev, who had shared very little with anyone in his life, felt a quiet little ache of unease. He stood up. "Did you bring me the other thing I wanted?"

Malik said that it was outside in the car. Both men left the church. The early afternoon sky was overcast, the air suffocating. Malik's car was an unexceptional Subaru, a rental. A car with diplomatic plates might have been more than a little obtrusive parked outside a Catholic Church in a working-class district of Fulham.

When both men were seated in the Subaru Malik reached across and opened the glove compartment.

Epishev took out the gun, which was a brand-new Randall Service Model with a silencer. He held it in his palm, admiring it a moment before placing it in the pocket of his coat.

He put a hand on Malik's shoulder. "You've been very helpful, Alexei."

Malik smiled. "We're on the same side, Viktor. We want the same goal. The kind of things happening in Russia . . ." Malik paused, searching for the correct expression. "They're not Russian."

Epishev stepped out of the car, feeling the gun's weight drag at his coat pocket. "You're right, Alexei. Whatever else they might be, they're not Russian."

He didn't look back at Malik as he moved away from the car and along the pavement. *The same side, Viktor. The same goal.* The restoration of the Revolution's credentials.

He stopped on a street corner outside a small grocery store. He took Malik's slip of paper from his wallet, memorised the address written there, then tore the sheet into fragments. He turned Frank Pagan's photograph over, committed the address on the back to memory, then ripped the picture into four pieces. He placed all this litter, rather fastidiously, in a waste-basket affixed to a lamp-post.

Moscow

General Stefan Ivanovich Olsky and his wife lived in a large apartment in the Lenin Hills on the outskirts of Moscow. It was a modern home, filled with Western appliances and decorated in the kind of blond wood surfaces one associates with Scandinavian houses. It was located on a street that was off-limits to most Muscovites, guarded at each end by uniformed militia men.

Unlike most Russian women married to powerful men, Sabina Olskaya kept herself informed about her husband's work and discussed it with him. But mainly she listened, because she knew her real strength came from her sympathetic ear. She was also ambitious on her husband's behalf, imagining a day when he might ascend from the Chairmanship of the KGB to General Secretary of the Party.

She lay in the bedroom, listening to the sound of her husband running water in the bathroom. It was early evening, and they'd taken a light meal together, and now they were going to make love, which was something they invariably did at this time every Sunday. The General's demanding schedule meant that their time together was both precious and sacrosanct, and Sabina guarded it jealously. She was a slim woman with long black hair and a wide mouth and front teeth which protruded slightly – a flaw in her appearance Stefan Olsky found very attractive.

He came out of the bathroom wearing a silk robe. As he approached the bed, Sabina rolled on her side, reaching out to slickly untie the cord, so that his robe fell open. She could tell from the expression on his face that he was preoccupied and she knew from experience that when he was absorbed in something he was as distant from her as a man walking on the surface of the moon.

She sat with her back against the pillows, her legs crossed. She had wonderful thighs. Before her marriage, she'd been a ballet dancer in the corps of the Kirov, and she still exercised every day. Now Olsky stroked her thigh absent-mindedly, unconscious of the years of training that had gone into creating such fine muscle tone.

She reached for an apple that lay in a bowl on the bedside table and bit into it loudly.

"So," she said. "You let that old fart Greshko upset you?"

"Am I upset?"

"Let's say you're distracted, shall we? He's a sick old man, he lies buried in the countryside, why should he worry the Chairman of the KGB?"

Stefan Olsky closed his eyes. Inside the bedroom there was a caged bird, a small yellow canary that sang in a tuneful way. The General listened a moment, aware of a warm breeze blowing in through the open window, stirring the long curtains. His beloved wife, the playful breeze, the songbird – all the elements were present for happiness, for contentment. Why then was it so unattainable? He opened his eyes, ran the palm of his hand across his shaved skull. At his side, Sabina practised turn-outs with her feet, then raised her long legs in glorious extensions.

Stefan Olsky said, "Fact. Greshko removes Romanenko's file. (Or authorises its removal, the same difference.) Fact. Romanenko is killed by an assassin. Fact. Greshko associates with people known to be unsympathetic to the General Secretary and his programme."

Sabina, who knew just the kind of people her husband was referring to – and especially their wives, those shapeless, tight-lipped spouses, those unfashionable old biddies who lived like wraiths in their husbands' shadows – made an expression of disgust and said, "They're toothless decrepit shits."

"They can still bite with their gums, dear heart." He had a strong feeling he was missing something, something that kept slipping between his fingers, some gap in a logical sequence, except he wasn't sure what. He had three separate facts, but they didn't provide him with a syllogism.

He thought of how he'd taken over the KGB during this period of enormous social reconstruction, and how the General Secretary made excellent speeches about infusing Soviet society with a new dynamic – but the actuality was difficult, the practical implications complicated. Inside the KGB, for example, the old guard, some of them Greshko loyalists, went to great lengths to make pernickety complaints. It was as if the very word *new* had the same effect on

127

those thick-skulled old-timers as sunlight on vampires.

Change was struggle, an uphill struggle. Sometimes it couldn't be forced, it couldn't be pressured, it had to be coaxed along. Sometimes it only happened through attrition – and you needed patience while the old guard died or retired. Patience, persistence, these were the qualities in himself that Stefan Olsky most admired.

He clasped his wife's hand and held it to his lips. He nuzzled her knuckles, but he was still behaving absent-mindedly.

Sabina Olskaya watched her husband's face. She was very much in love with him and proud of the role he was playing in re-training this cumbersome elephant that was Russia to her. During her career with the Kirov she'd travelled to the West a score of times, and she'd adored it for more than the great stores and the elegant restaurants and the fashionable people walking on the splendid boulevards. What she'd become enamoured of was a certain *spirit* – she could think of no other word – that existed in the West. It was something she discovered in newspapers and books, in cinemas and theatres, in late-night conversations she had with friends in those countries – an exhilarating freedom, a giddiness which at times left her breathless, a world of choices, a world seemingly without limits. The Soviet Union she always came back to depressed her, a lumbering beast in drab colours. But now it was being turned around, a dash of colour added here, a touch of spice there, and Stefan – *her* husband – was one of the men helping to make the alterations. She kissed his forehead just then, more from gratitude than lust. She wanted to live in a new Russia, not the one typified by those old dodos who made Stefan's life so difficult at times with their underhand ways, and their outmoded dogma.

The telephone was ringing on the bedside table. Olsky picked it up. He heard the voice of his personal assistant, Colonel Chebrikov, a stuffy young man whose principal attributes were unqualified loyalty and an ambition that was not markedly acute.

"A man known as Yevenko was arrested a couple of hours ago, General," the Colonel said. "He was in possession of counterfeit currency."

"Yevenko?" Olsky asked. "Should the name mean anything to me?"

"Perhaps not, sir. He's been involved in various currency scandals in the past. In more recent years, his speciality has been forged documents. Sometimes he's known as the Printer."

"And?" Olsky watched his wife rise from the bed and walk to the window, where she stood balanced on one leg. The gown she wore caught the breeze and blew away from her thighs.

"Well, sir, he has information."

"What kind of information, Colonel?"

"He'll only tell it to you. And then only on the condition that you . . . that you are lenient with him. The information concerns a man you asked me to make a report on recently with a view to retirement or reassignment. One of Greshko's people. Colonel Viktor Epishev."

Olsky said, "I'll meet you in twenty minutes, Colonel." He hung up the receiver quickly. He got up from the bed and crossed the floor, catching Sabina by the shoulders, kissing her on the mouth. Then he stepped back from her.

She asked, "Will I stay awake for you?"

Even though Stefan Olsky said yes, yes she should stay awake for him, he wondered how many hours of his time would be absorbed by his other wife, the one infinitely more demanding and more complex than Sabina, the one called Mother Russia.

8

Brooklyn, New York

Andres Kiss, his blond hair moved by the breeze, hurried along the boardwalk at Brighton Beach. Even in his haste he walked with grace. People who noticed him, and many did, were impressed by his poise. There was nothing clumsy, nothing angular, in the way he hurried. If he suggested a blur, it was a streamlined one. He wore a three-piece suit of dark brown silk. His white shirt was open at the collar because he hated the restriction of neck-ties. He paused once, scanning the Sunday afternoon crowds that had come out to promenade and sniff the ozone.

Old Russians, many of them Jews, sat in the doorways of shops and jabbered or played cards. There was loud music coming from various sources, a clash of sounds – balalaikas on somebody's tape-deck, rock and roll from a ghetto-blaster hoisted on the shoulder of a passing skateboarder, the drone of some 1950s Soviet crooner limping out of battered speakers that had been set up on a vendor's table where you could buy tapes bootlegged from the original Russian records. Here and there people were huddled in earnest political discussions about the direction of Soviet society or in serious debate about the inadequacies of Blue Cross and Blue Shield. Old ladies walked dogs through the salted air and sometimes paused to let their pets poop.

Andres Kiss knew this scene so well he didn't analyse it, didn't think about the mix of cultures or the way foreign languages and dialects filled the air around him.

He walked until he reached the closed door of what had once been a hot-dog shop during the golden age of the boardwalk, that halcyon time when nearby Coney Island, now a haven for druggers and muggers, had been a safe place for family outings.

The window of the shop was filthy and the faded lettering on the glass barely legible. Andres Kiss reached deftly into the pocket of his pants and removed the key the old man had reluctantly consented to give him only a few weeks ago.

He glanced up and down the boardwalk before inserting the key into the lock. You couldn't be too careful. Brighton Beach, with its enormous immigrant community from Soviet Europe, was a hotbed of gossip. Stooped old women with shopping-bags babbled on street corners, eyes hooded and lips flapping. They were as efficient as any telegraph system. Then there were the scum from the so-called Russian diplomatic mission in Manhattan who infiltrated the neighbourhood so they could collect information on who was saying what, data they shipped back to Russia where it was used to put pressure on families still over there. Andres hated the KGB with a passion so profound it rendered him speechless.

He turned the key, then stepped inside the bleak room beyond, closing the door at his back and smelling the dank scent of the place, a fusion of sawdust and mildew. Sunlight hardly penetrated here. His eyes slowly became attuned to the dimness and he made out the old refrigerator, a prehistoric job which had no door. Then a couple of battered chairs. There was an ancient menu on the wall. Hot dogs were 15 cents. Soda cost a nickel.

"You call this punctual? For this you wear a fancy wristwatch?"

The voice that came out of the gloom was thickly accented. Andres saw Carl Sundbach emerge from behind the refrigerator. In what little sunlight filtered through the grubby window, Sundbach appeared fragile.

131

He wore an antique raccoon coat, the way he always did from the first of September to the last day of March, regardless of the temperature. His face was thin and angular and there were glasses attached for safekeeping to a threadbare string that hung round his scrawny neck. He was one of the richest men in the whole of Brooklyn, probably in all New York State, but he was so frugal he made Scrooge seem like a charitable foundation.

Sundbach came a little nearer. He scanned Andres's face a moment, his little eyes flicking back and forth.

"You don't know time, huh?" And he seized Andres's wrist in his hand, tapping his fingernails on the dial of the Rolex. "Thirty-two years old and still you don't know time. Even when we got a calamity going on."

Andres took his hand away and said, "I'm ten minutes late. So what?"

"So what? Maybe the world is falling to pieces and you want to know so what?"

"Nothing's falling to pieces, Carl," Andres said.

"I hear different, sonny. I hear bad news. You get to my age, you trust your instincts. And what they're saying isn't good. You know what I think? It's all over. It's finished. The whole thing's going to be cancelled. Which maybe isn't such a bad idea."

"It's a goddam stupid idea," Andres said. "Nothing's going to be cancelled. No way, Carl. Not now."

"A terrible thing happened in Scotland. A man is dead, for God's sake."

"I know, Carl. I just got back from Edinburgh. Remember?" Andres was always made impatient by Sundbach. It was tough to practise the composure Mikhail Kiss advocated. *Give him respect, Andres. He's an old man now, but he used to be a real fighter.* Andres forced his mouth into a smile, which brightened his handsomely sullen face. He looked quite angelic right then, the cherubic boy who'd been the joy of the boardwalk as a baby, clucked over by *babushkas*, stroked by teenage girls overwhelmed that anything could be so beautiful, a golden little heartbreaker who always held on tightly to Uncle Mikhail's hand.

"We didn't reckon on *murder*, Andres." Carl Sundbach, whose raccoon coat reeked of mothballs, peered in the direction of the window where he could make out, barely, the old gilt letters on the glass. Some of the letters were missing now, scratched out by weather and vandals. *Brook yns Best H t Dogs. Roo Beer.* Once, he'd fantasised about reopening his shop when the boardwalk returned to its former glory, but in recent years he'd become disenchanted. It wasn't going to happen. Now now. Not ever. All the good days were gone. What you had now were kids guzzling beer and humping under the boardwalk, leaving their battered cans and discarded condoms, which looked like hollowed-out snails, all over the place.

Nevertheless, he kept this place, and he came here sometimes, usually on Sundays when Andres picked him up, riding by train all the way down from Manhattan, where he had a rent-controlled apartment on the lower East side. He'd sit in the space behind the refrigerator and he'd reminisce about the days when Sundbach's had been a going concern and sometimes he even imagined he heard the ringing of the cash-register.

Sundbach shivered. He was perpetually cold, even in sunlight. Andres went to the door and opened it, glad of the sea air. He clutched the old man's spindly elbow as they moved along the boardwalk. Every now and then Carl would nod his head at an acquaintance or he'd tip his ancient hat at a passing female who caught his eye. He still fancied himself something of a lady's man, a *seelikukütt*, a hunter of skirts.

They walked slowly to the side-street where Andres had parked his Jaguar. He opened the passenger door for Carl Sundbach and watched him climb in.

"You ought to drive an American car," the old man said when Andres had the Jaguar going along Brighton Beach Avenue, past the Russian delicatessens and the pharmacies and under the shadow of the El. "The English don't know how to make cars no more."

It was always this way. Always the complaints, always something to whine about. Andres glanced at the front of the Black Sea Bookstore where a couple of guys leaned against their bicycles and argued. Politics, Andres thought. What else would they argue around here? He was of the opinion that such arguments were finally pointless. Talk achieved nothing. What you really needed was another kind of vocabulary – one of action.

Andres rolled his window down. The stench of camphor was clogging his nostrils.

Sundbach said, "I had a British car, a Rover, in Tallinn. Before the Russians came into the Baltic. After the *tiblad* arrived, you couldn't get parts. You couldn't get gasoline. The English knew how to build cars in those days. I must have driven that Rover thousands of miles. Kahula to Narva. Tartu. *Mu jumal*, Tartu was beautiful then." Sundbach sighed. "I used to have this feeling I'd see the old country again one day. Now," and he made a small fluttering gesture with his hand, "I know better."

Carl Sundbach could go on and on, rambling, reminiscing. Pretty soon he'd be remembering the time he ate the rancid *heeringas hapukoorega* – herring with sour cream – at a roadside restaurant in Jogeva and came down with food-poisoning bad enough to kill a dozen weaker men, or the day the Brotherhood blew up a Soviet munitions dump outside Haapsalu in 1949. He had one of those memories that resurrect every small detail of the past, every trifle, the kind of clouds that were in the sky on such and such a day or the colour of a guy's eyes. When he told a story, Carl Sundbach digressed encyclopaedically, feasting on a sumptuous banquet of recollections.

What the hell, Andres Kiss thought, when you'd hauled yourself up from being a poor Baltic immigrant to one of the wealthiest men in the state, when you owned a chain of motels and fast-food restaurants, when you had property all over Brighton Beach, maybe you deserved the luxury of indulgent nostalgia. Andres had often heard the story of Carl's financial success, the sheer toughness involved, the ambition, the way business enemies had been bulldozed. There was still this suggestion of flint to the old man.

Andres said, "You'll see it again, Carl."

Sundbach shook his head. "I'm trying to be a realist, boy."

"You sound more like a defeatist."

"There's a difference?" Sundbach asked.

The younger man never tried to answer Carl's rhetorical questions. He took the Jaguar on to the Interborough Parkway, heading out to the Island. He stared through the window at a sign for the Harry S. Truman Expressway. Overhead, in a cloudless, sunny sky, a small silvery twin-engined Piper flashed. Andres Kiss, filled with a longing to be up there at the controls of the craft, watched it until it went out of sight.

He took a pair of dark shades from the visor, where they'd been clipped in place. He put them on. He liked the way the sun was dulled now. Too much unfiltered brightness could damage your eyes. When he'd been in the Air Force he'd known men who were grounded because of poor eyesight. Andres wasn't going to run the risk of hurting his vision because there wasn't a thing in the world like soaring up there – not sex, not drugs, nothing. It was undiluted freedom when you were twenty or thirty thousand feet high and rolling through cloudbanks. What thrilled him was the idea of defying gravity, of being suspended in a frail craft that could, if the engine stalled, come crashing down through space. And sometimes, as if he were locked in a delicious place between life and death, Andres imagined that fall and was fascinated by the prospect. To smack the earth at eight hundred miles per hour seemed to him an appropriate way to check out, the flyer's way.

In Glen Cove he travelled leafy back roads until he

reached the house, which occupied several acres of prime Long Island real estate. Grey and huge, with turrets and cupolas, and a lawn so immaculate it might have been groomed by a hairdresser, it was situated at the end of a gravel driveway. He parked the Jaguar alongside a black Mercedes. Then he opened the door of his car and looked up at the front of the house. A lime-green awning hung over the porch. Sundbach, who'd dozed for much of the journey the way he usually did, opened his eyes.

"We're here?" he asked hoarsely.

"We're here," Andres Kiss replied.

In the sun-room at the back of the house, where glass walls overlooked prolific rose gardens that blazed with colour, Mikhail Kiss poured tea from a silver pot into dainty china cups. His big hands made the china seem like something plundered out of a doll's house but he poured almost tenderly, a man engrossed in a ritual he respects.

He looked up when Carl Sundbach and Andres came into the room. He thought of the contrast between the young man and the old warrior, the present and the past, strength and frailty. It was important to remember how closely linked past and present were, how much they owed to each other. Without that sense of history, everything they were involved in, everything they'd planned, would be no more than an act of vandalism, a mindless terrorism of the kind that so appalled him.

Carl Sundbach reached for a tea-cup, poured a shot of cognac into it, and sniffed the steam. Andres, declining the offer of tea, stared out into the garden. Through the open doorway a faint gust of wind blew the seductive scent of roses into the room.

Mikhail Kiss, who believed in coming straight to the point, asked, "This tragic event in Edinburgh – is it going to influence us?"

Carl Sundbach made a windy little noise of surprise. "You have a habit of asking questions in the wrong order. What you're asking now isn't what I'd ask myself first. The most important question is obvious. Why was Romanenko killed? Then comes the next question. Who shot him?"

Mikhail Kiss, weary after the long sleepless flight back from Britain, regarded Sundbach's questions as irrelevant. But Carl had poured thousands of dollars into this whole affair and felt he'd purchased the right to ask any questions he wanted.

"Your priorities are wrong, Carl," he said.

"*My* priorities are wrong?" Sundbach asked. "Tell me, tell me how you figure that."

"Carl, does it make any difference who killed Aleksis, or why? It was probably some dangerous oddball with a crazy notion and a gun. What would you have me do? Stop everything? Send out messages saying everything has to be halted? Have you any idea how complicated that would be?"

"I hate complicated," Carl Sundbach said. "Give me simple every time."

"Nothing's simple," Mikhail Kiss said. "All this has taken a very long time to stitch together, and I can't undo the whole embroidery now, even if I wanted to."

Sundbach took off his raccoon coat. His concave chest gave the impression of a man in the throes of malnutrition. He was sweating slightly. "Suppose this killer knew what Aleksis was up to. Let's say this killer knew *everything* there is to know. Imagine that. Just try. Tell me you don't see the consequences."

Mikhail Kiss said, "Only a scared man worries about consequences he can't possibly predict, Carl."

"One thing I hate is a man sounds like he just read a fortune-cookie," Sundbach replied. "This is my point – if Aleksis was killed, then it was because *somebody knew what he was involved in*. Which makes it likely the whole damn scheme's blown. Forgive me, but that's too risky for me. This was supposed to be a big secret – but I told you all along it was too complicated to keep quiet. I kept saying. Make it simple. Short and simple. No, you knew better, didn't you? You had to have grand plans."

Mikhail Kiss stood up and looked out into the garden, turning his back to the room. The way sunlight struck roses always touched him. He remembered how Aleksis Romanenko had been proud of his flower garden around his house on the bank of the Pirita River. *My peasant instincts*, Aleksis used to say. *If I don't grow things I betray my heart and I die a little* – the theatrical kind of thing Aleksis was given to saying.

In the late 1940s and early 1950s both Kiss and Romanenko had been active in the armed struggle against the Russians in the Baltic. There had been some of the predictable differences between two strong-willed men locked in a useless struggle, but they had common bonds – a passion for the land, and a profound attachment to the Brotherhood of the Forest.

Kiss remembered how, during the cold spring of 1951, Aleksis had planted marigold seeds on a wooded hillside north of Kuusiku. Grubby, lice-ridden, undernourished, facing the prospect of annihilation at the hands of Soviet patrols, Aleksis had planted his precious seeds with all the poignant care of a man who expects eventually to see the flowers grow. He also remembered Carl Sundbach, at that time a gaunt man in his late thirties, saying that if seeds could grow to be rifles, he'd be sowing them himself day and night. But since war was not a horticultural event, why bother?

Derision hadn't fazed Aleksis. It was almost as if he'd wanted to bring some flourish of his own, some form of hope, into a situation of despair. And it had been despair, because daily the Russians were burning farms and shooting farmers who'd supported the fight of the Brotherhood. And they'd been increasing the ferocity of their patrols, pouring more men and more arms into the fight so that the only possible outcome for the Brotherhood was starvation and defeat. In the midst of this turmoil Romanenko had planted his seeds, an act of optimism and grace that Mikhail Kiss remembered, all these years later, with great clarity.

It was odd to think of Aleksis dead now. It was like trying to imagine the inside of a vacuum. He had been closer to Aleksis than to any other member of the old Brotherhood. And now another memory touched him, and his eyes moistened, and he felt a tightness at the back of his throat. He remembered the *Kalevipoeg* and how, on the day when they'd parted company, when their cell had disbanded – hungry, lacking weapons, crushed by a weariness no amount of courage could overcome, numbed by an impossible struggle – he'd given Romanenko a handwritten sheet of paper with four lines of verse on it, written in Livonian, a Finno-Ugric language Kiss had once studied as a student at the university in Tartu. A secret souvenir of a doomed freemasonry, a reminder in an almost extinct tongue, a cryptic memento of a struggle that was dying around them.

When we rise again, Aleksis had said, *this paper will be the one true sign*. And so Romanenko had kept the sheet for years, more a symbol of a resurrection than a souvenir of a lost cause. It was this same paper that Kiss was supposed to receive on the ramparts of Edinburgh Castle on the night of Aleksis's death – the same four lines of the old patriotic poem that would indicate the time had come for the re-birth. It was a seal to be embossed on the plan, a guarantee from Romanenko that everything was finally in place for the assault, an imprimatur.

Now Kiss recalled the cold shock, the grief, of hearing about Romanenko's murder on British television and the sudden dilemma the murder posed. To proceed or – as Carl Sundbach was advocating – to forget the whole thing. His first reaction had been to abort, but then he knew that if he were to cancel the operation now, he'd live the rest of his life with regret – and what was more appalling than sinking embittered into old age? The architecture of the scheme was too careful, too intricate and lovely, for it to be shelved and forgotten.

He barely listened to the way Sundbach was whining. Carl's trouble was simple. He'd used up all his guts and stamina in his drive to become rich in America. And with riches had come a cautious, conservative way of looking at things.

Kiss looked at Carl who was going on about this grandiose – pronounced *grandyoose* – plan, wondering aloud why he'd gone along with it in the first place, pouring in money, then more money, and still more money, greasing palms and arranging passports for those who'd have to find a way of fleeing the Soviet Union after the event. Why wouldn't a simple assassination have been enough? Why hadn't they just decided to kill somebody, some Russian high-up, and been content with that? Depleted, finally speechless, Sundbach wiped flecks of spit from the corners of his mouth.

Kiss, who had invested money of his own in the scheme, who had spent freely on arms, money he'd earned on the stock markets of the world, said, "Assassinations mean nothing these days. Any crackpot with a gun can go out and shoot anybody he likes. They don't even make the front-page, for God's sake. Never at any time did we seriously consider assassination."

Sundbach clasped his skinny white hands on the surface of the table. "Listen, if you go ahead now, if you ignore the danger signs, you might be signing the death warrants of everybody involved, including our friends inside the Soviet Union and maybe even ourselves if those KGB scum at the Russian mission also learn about us."

In a quiet voice, one of restrained impatience, Andres Kiss said, "What Mikhail's saying is that the game is too far along for anything to be changed. All the pieces are in position. Everything is ready. And if we go with the plan, we have to go now. Otherwise, forget it."

Carl Sundbach said, "I disagree, Andres. The pieces

are not all in position. There is one vital piece we don't have and we all know what that is. I'm talking about Romanenko. I'm talking about the very big fact that we don't know if Romanenko was going to tell us to play our hand or throw in our cards. And since we don't know this, it's my opinion we take the loss. All the wasted time. We say it was quite an experience, quite a dream, and we back away."

Andres Kiss smiled his most brilliant smile. "It's not a dream for me, Carl," he said. And it wasn't. He had anticipated the conclusion of the scheme so many times that it had come to have something of the texture of an event already past, already history. In a sense, Andres Kiss had lived his own future.

Sundbach fingered the string to which his eyeglasses were attached. "I say we get out now. If it fails, too many people may die. Listen to me. Maybe Aleksis was going to tell us to wash our hands of the whole business. Maybe he was going to tell us that something had gone wrong. How can we know *anything* for sure?"

Andres Kiss stood up. "It's a pity you're not a gambling man, Carl. Then you'd realise there's a fifty-fifty chance Aleksis was going to give us the okay to proceed."

"And you'd take that chance?" Sundbach asked.

Andres nodded confidently. "I'd take it."

Sundbach looked at Mikhail Kiss. "And you?"

"Without hesitation," Kiss replied.

"You're both crazy," Sundbach said. "Both *hullud*. What is it with you pair? You both in love with tragedy? Personally, I don't like the feeling of putting my goddam head under a guillotine. I figure suicide isn't one of my options. And I don't want to be responsible for the deaths of other people either."

There was an awkward silence in the room. Then Sundbach sighed. It was an old man's sigh, filled with sorrow and disbelief. He stared out into the roses, thinking how their bright colours seemed suddenly gloomy, like flowers round a sick-bed when the patient is terminal. He had the feeling his was the only voice of reason here.

"So," Sundbach said. "This is the way it goes. Aleksis is dead in Scotland, you don't know who killed him, you don't know if he was carrying the message, *but you're going ahead anyway*."

Neither Mikhail Kiss nor his nephew said anything. Their silence was eloquent, and united, a combination against which Sundbach couldn't compete.

Sundbach put out one thin hand and laid it on the back of Andres Kiss's wrist. "What if they're waiting for you? Bang! You fall out of the sky. No more Andres Kiss."

The young man said, "I'll take the chance, Carl."

Carl Sundbach poured himself a little tea. His hand trembled. He sipped quietly, then looked over the rim of his cup at Mikhail Kiss. "I never made a bad investment before. I never lost a dollar on anything. You know why? Because I never gambled. That's why. Except for this," and he made a sweeping gesture. His eyes were suddenly moist. "Forgive this little display. I was remembering how you came to me years ago, Mikhail. You said you had a plan. I listened. I was the only one who believed in the chance of your success. The others – I'm thinking of Charlie Parming and Ernie Juurman, all the rest of them – they didn't even want to know. They turned their backs on you, Mikhail. Your own countrymen, fellow *patrioots*, they turned their backs. Alone, I supported you. But now . . ."

Carl Sundbach drew the sleeve of his shirt across his face. "I wish you luck. Myself, I'm too old for a doomed adventure. I'm out."

"Reconsider, Carl," Mikhail Kiss said, though not with any enthusiasm. In the last analysis, Sundbach was like Charlie Parming and the others. They had all grown old badly. They spoke easily about vengeance when they'd been putting vodka away, or when they got together for reunions that were invariably boastful in the beginning then finally tearful, but when it came down to action they had no iron left in their hearts. America had made them prosperous and soft. Sundbach was a scared old man who'd gotten in over his head, that was all.

Sundbach said, "Reconsider? No. What I want is a situation I can leave with no regrets. I want Andres to drive me back to the boardwalk. Then I can get on with my life."

Sundbach rose slowly, grabbing his raccoon coat, struggling into it. He thought how the death of Aleksis hadn't changed a thing. Maybe there was still a chance Mikhail Kiss would come to his senses, maybe he'd be able to look at things clearly and understand that his scheme had been only a gorgeous dream. For a while, for too long, he'd believed in Kiss's plan himself – but what was he except an old man with too much money, too much time, somebody who wasn't listening to the way the heartbeat of the world was changing? Then he'd started to listen, he'd started to take the pulse of things, and now he understood that Kiss's way was the way of doom. There was another way, and it didn't involve such destruction, only patience.

He looked at Andres Kiss. "I'll wait for you in the car."

A few minutes after Sundbach had stepped out of the house, Mikhail Kiss and his nephew went upstairs to the room Kiss called his office. It was stacked with books and pamphlets of the kind issued by the various Baltic Independence societies in Western countries. *The Committee for a Free Estonia. The World Legion of Lithuanian Liberation. The Baltic World Conference.* Kiss considered all these organisations well-intentioned but powerless, feeble groups of people who did nothing more than release a flood of unwanted paper, diatribes against Russian activities in the Baltic that nobody wanted to read – petitions to the United Nations for recognition of the sovereignty of the Baltic states, telegrams to world leaders, letters to United States congressmen and Australian senators and British MPs, who sent polite supportive replies marked more by impotent indignation at the plight of the Baltic than anything honest and practical. But what did all this verbiage amount to in the end? The answer was, alas, zero.

Kiss had belonged to a number of freedom organisations in the past, but he'd always resigned from them out of a sense of frustration. Endless talk and petition-signing and the drudgery of committees served the purposes of some people – but not those of Mikhail Kiss, who was tired of how the whole Baltic tragedy had been ignored by world opinion, relegated to the backwaters of old men's memories, a dead issue.

Did nobody care that cultures and languages were being deliberately destroyed and that a completely illegal form of government had been forced upon three nations? That the Baltic was now little more than an arsenal where the Soviets had installed a vast array of weapons and rockets? What Kiss remembered – and this was where the hurt and pain still lay – was the way the three Baltic nations had flourished in that gorgeous period between the wars, a time of economic progress and honest political experiment, of literature and art, a golden age of self-determination, a time for hope and optimism when for twenty short, brilliant years freedom, not fear, had been in people's hearts. Gone now, all of it, down the slipstream of history.

He stared at a framed photograph on the wall. It showed him in 1974 presenting a petition to President Gerald Ford outside the White House. Ford had made a brave little speech that day about how America would always support the integrity and rights of the Baltic states, a nice speech, but one with all the significance of a *munakook*, a sponge cake. And then Ford had vanished inside the White House and the petition disappeared into the attaché-case of a Presidential aide, where it would lie forgotten the way all such idiotic papers did. Even then, on the day of Ford's speech, Mikhail Kiss had already surrendered any belief he'd ever had in the usefulness of paper protests. Even on that fall afternoon he'd understood that the plan, first considered between himself and Romanenko in the middle of the 1960s, was the only possible direction to take.

Kiss moved to his desk where he sat down, picking up a paperweight in the form of a miniature Edinburgh Castle, a recent acquisition whose significance struck him as gruesome now.

"Do you trust him not to talk?" Andres Kiss asked.

Mikhail Kiss looked surprised. "What kind of question is that? If Carl wants out, we let him leave. It's that simple."

The young man said, "I don't like the idea of Carl walking around with the kind of information he has."

Kiss didn't care for the clipped coldness in his nephew's voice. "I've known him a long time. Say what you like about his faults, he can keep his mouth shut. Besides, who's he going to talk to? The nice men at the Soviet Mission in Manhattan?"

Kiss put the small bronze castle down and looked at his nephew. He'd raised Andres from the moment he'd been born, immediately after the death of his widowed sister Augusta in childbirth. It was a responsibility for which Kiss, accustomed to a life of solitude, a life devoted to making money for himself and his Wall Street clients, wasn't prepared. He often wondered if he'd discharged his obligation in the best way, if he'd done everything he might have to raise Andres.

He shut his eyes against the sunlight streaming into the room. He sometimes thought he'd placed too much emphasis on old stories of the Brotherhood, instilled in Andres too much of his own hatred of the Soviets. He'd told him tales of what it felt like to lie on a forest floor while Soviet warplanes bombed the place where you were hiding. He'd told sad stories about farms burning and farmers being dragged into fields and shot, about the sorrow of having to bury a dead comrade or the elation when the Brotherhood successfully destroyed a Russian convoy. He'd told him of the time he came across an abandoned farmhouse in the attic of which four small children, with piano wire round their necks, hung from the rafters and the way their blackened blood stained the floor beneath them and how he'd never managed to rid his mind of this image, which chilled him still and made his loathing of the Soviets even more intense, if that were possible.

Andres had absorbed all his uncle's hatred of the Soviets and their system, but there were certain things he couldn't grasp. He heard war stories and thought only of revenge. He had no insight into the spirit that had existed in the Brotherhood, no idea of the fellowship. How could he have? What could Mikhail Kiss have told him about the compassion between men, the bonds forged in the crucible of a hopeless war? How could this young man, born and raised in America, have understood the kind of camaraderie nurtured by conditions that had never existed within the United States?

Kiss thought that there was a very real sense in which he hadn't been a good teacher because he'd failed to make the young man's understanding complete, with the result that some element was missing from Andres's personality, an elusive quality Kiss wanted to call 'heart' or 'humanity'. As a human being Andres was all angles and abrasive edges, tightly-focused, somebody whose physical beauty concealed his tough-mindedness. He had, at times, a certain charm, but there was something borrowed about it, as if he were a man trying to speak in a foreign language he hadn't properly learned. He'd never formed close relationships with women, preferring the quick and the casual, simple encounters in dark places. He'd entered the US Air Force at the age of nineteen, ascended through the ranks with chill brilliance, a Major at the age of thirty-one who flew F-16s on NATO missions. On his thirty-second birthday he resigned his commission, because he'd drained the Air Force of all the information he needed to have. It had nothing else to offer him.

The young man's life was an equation in which his military career was one factor, his inherited hatred of the Soviets another. An equation made in steel, Mikhail Kiss thought, durable and unchanging. It was this steel that made him important in the Brotherhood's plan, but it was the same alloy that would prevent him from being the kind of man who loved and inspired love in others. And Mikhail Kiss felt at times a little guilty because of the way, inadvertently or otherwise, he'd moulded his nephew – not into a rounded human being, not into a person with compassion and understanding, but into the destructive instrument of the Brotherhood.

Now Kiss rose from the desk. "Carl's waiting for you," he said.

Andres stood in the window, and the sun made his hair gold. Although he was used to obeying his uncle, he thought Mikhail too trusting. He wanted to say that Carl shouldn't be dismissed this way, that an old man who'd turned his back on the Brotherhood shouldn't be allowed to walk away unconditionally – but he knew Mikhail would counter with a sentimental argument about the history he shared with Sundbach. So he didn't argue. He never quarrelled with Mikhail. He kept his objections quietly to himself. Men like Mikhail and Carl Sundbach, with their old attachments, their facile nostalgia, made him impatient. He walked to the door, opened it, gazed across the landing towards the stairs. There he paused.

Seeing the young man's hesitation, Mikhail Kiss said, "Trust me. Carl won't speak to anybody."

Andres Kiss looked about as relaxed as he ever did. He stepped out of the room, drawing the door shut behind him. He went down the stairs and out on to the porch. Sundbach sat in the passenger seat of the Jaguar. His glasses glinted in the sunlight. He turned his head impatiently and said, "What kept you? I was going to send a search-party."

Andres Kiss moved in the direction of his car. He clenched his fists at his side as he moved, his fine hands turning an angry white colour.

Fredericksburg, Virginia

Galbraith said, "I love the way they shape the world according to how they think it ought to be. They refuse to contemplate disagreeable alternatives. Kiss and Kiss are going ahead *no matter what!* They want to make a statement about that diddlyshit corner of Europe the Soviets stole and half the world hasn't heard about and the other half can only do some pooh-poohing over because it's a goddam *fait accompli* anyhow. I love their dedication."

The fat man, who wore a small acupuncture stud in his right ear – placed there only that morning by a Filipino practitioner everyone in DC swore by – reached up to rub the little globe of metal, which was said to curb the craving for food. With growing exasperation he rubbed for about thirty seconds, then dipped his hand inside a box of Black Magic chocolates by Rowntree Mackintosh, and said, "So much for the ancient healing arts of the goddam East."

He stuffed a chocolate into his mouth, then he reached out to the tape-recorder and rewound the reel to the part where Andres Kiss could be heard to say *It's not a dream for me, Carl.*

"There," Galbraith said. "That's probably my favourite part. You can hear the kid gloat when he says that. His voice practically drips. Frankly, I'm glad Sundbach dropped out. I was never convinced he had the right stuff. A little too fond of the cherry brandy. I always felt he'd come undone eventually."

Iverson, seated beneath the banks of video consoles, heard old Carl say *I don't like the feeling of putting my goddam head under a guillotine.* The meetings in the house in Glen Cove had been taped for more than a year now, and Galbraith had come to regard them as regular Sunday afternoon listening.

"Does he worry you, Gary?" Galbraith asked.

"Sundbach?" Iverson frowned, gave a little shrug.

Galbraith nodded. This morning he was dressed in a dark suit instead of the robes he usually favoured. He wore a blue carnation in his lapel. "He worries young Andres. You can tell that much."

"Andres worries about everything, sir," Iverson said. "When he was in the Air Force he worried about making the grade. Nothing was more important to him than learning to fly. He spent more hours in an F-16 simulator than any man in the history of the Force. He worried about his physical exams. He worried about his eyesight. The clue to Andres is his compulsive personality. He's a perfectionist."

"Which is why we have him," Galbraith said. He had discovered one of his favourite chocolates, a dimpled, strawberry-centred rectangle that he popped into his mouth before closing the box and shoving it across the glass-topped table. At least he was *trying*. "The trouble is, Sundbach worries *me*. I don't like the idea of the old fellow walking out at this stage of the game."

Galbraith killed the tape-recorder just as Mikhail Kiss was saying, *Trust me. Carl won't speak to anybody*. He wandered around the room for a while. Iverson watched him. For a fat man he moved smoothly, seeming to glide at times, like a hydrofoil on a cushion of air. He finally returned to the sofa where he sat down, glanced at his watch.

"I have an afternoon tea affair on the roof in about five minutes, Gary. Do we have anything to discuss before I leave?"

Iverson took out a small notebook, flipped the pages. "One, there's nothing new from London. A cop called Frank Pagan's in charge of the affair, but I haven't heard anything more."

Galbraith said, "Keep on that one just the same."

Iverson said, "Two. I don't have anything new on Jacob Kiviranna except for sketchy details. Where he went to school, where he was born, the fact he spent a couple of years in jail for offences ranging from public nuisance to aggravated assault. We should know more any moment."

"Aggravated assault? That's promising. I think we need to know if Vabadus's killer was a psycho or something else. So keep pressing on that one. Make sure any information we get on Kiviranna reaches Scotland Yard too. It ought to keep this Pagan busy around the edges of things in the meantime. Clear the material with me first, though, won't you?" Galbraith stood up. "We might also do ourselves a small favour by keeping an eye on Carl Sundbach. I'm only thinking aloud now, you understand, but I'm also wondering if it might be necessary to do a dark deed where Sundbach's concerned. Call it a feasibility study, that's all. I don't want you coming in here with blood on *your* hands, Gary."

Galbraith looked thoughtful. Ever since a DIA employee – they were never known to Galbraith as agents, a term he considered theatrical – had been apprehended last year carrying a case containing one point three million dollars into Cuba, money earmarked for certain persons who were anxious to see Fidel unseated and who needed weaponry, ever since this embarrassing little fiasco had been hinted at in a variety of newspapers and periodicals, Galbraith had become hypercautious and overprotective when it came to his department of the agency. He had devised a new policy, which was to use only outsiders, if possible, when it came to the truly dirty deeds. Doing something nefarious wasn't the problem. Being found out was.

"You might want to probe Andres," Galbraith said. "You might want to take his temperature, see if he *really* thinks Sundbach's a danger. After all, we don't want to jump in and do something irrevocable if the old fellow's simply harmless, do we?"

Iverson agreed.

On his way to the door, Galbraith stopped. "Do you think Andres ever suspects anything?" he asked.

Iverson considered this, then shook his head firmly. "I really don't think he's gifted in the area of peripheral vision, sir."

Galbraith looked thoughtful a moment. He stroked his little acupuncture stud and said, "The one thing I wish is that these Balts weren't so goddam sentimental. It's the only problem I have with them. I was never very happy with the sealed envelope business and the poem. To them it's like some holy relic. To me it's unadulterated nostalgia and inefficient to boot. I can see the Brother-hood getting off on using their old call sign – but I keep thinking it would have been so much more damn simple if Romanenko had just telephoned Kiss when they were both in London." Here Galbraith stared morosely at the chocolate box, his expression that of an addict pondering a cure. "Still, who am I to interfere with the rituals of men whose purpose I support and admire wholeheartedly? If that's the way they felt they had to do things, who am I to criticise their habits, Gary? Anyhow, I hate to give you the impression I'm ungrateful to the Balts, because that's far from the truth. On the contrary, I regard their cause as sacred. Without it, where would White Light be?"

Galbraith, smiling, climbed out of the basement. The effort made him short of breath. He rode in the private lift to the roof, which had been transformed into a garden, surrounded on all sides by bulletproof glass. Three satellite dishes scanned the skies silently. There was a view of the countryside around Fredericksburg, a secretive, green landscape. Galbraith walked to the centre of the roof, pushing aside a variety of shrubs and flowers – dense, spreading acacia, red bougainvillaea, dwarf pomegranate bearing inedible dwarf fruit, bro-meliads. It was all a little too much, Galbraith thought.

When he'd asked for a garden up here, some greenery to give the roof aesthetic appeal, he hadn't taken into consideration the ego of the gardener, a man who considered himself no mere potter of shrub and fern but a 'landscape architect'. It had become a world in which ratcatchers were rodent-control agents, and plumbers sanitation consultants.

In the centre of the roof a table had been set up for afternoon tea in the English style. Silver teapot, china plates, scones and assorted jams, small cucumber sandwiches. Two men in dark suits sat at the table. One was Senator Crowe, a Texan, the other Senator Holly from Iowa, both senior members of the Senate Committee on Foreign Relations. John Crowe had been in Washington so long that it was said he'd been consulted on the original plan for the White House. He was an emaciated man with the demeanour of an undertaker. His face, which consisted of hundreds of tiny squares of wrinkled flesh, a parchment patchwork, always made Galbraith think of the Dead Sea Scrolls. Holly, on the other hand, was younger, pot-bellied, a man with a smile that apparently left his face only when he slept. Galbraith thought of him as Jolly Holly, even thought there was something vaguely sinister in the fixed grin.

"These sandwiches have no damned crusts," John Crowe snarled in the throaty voice that made him famous and widely impersonated.

Galbraith sat down, thinking how Crowe always had a vaguely depressing effect on him. Access to the kind of power Crowe had – in the intelligence community, the Foreign Relations Committee, and the Senate Committee on Military Expenditure – had made him a grave, gloomy figure, and wraithlike. He reminded Galbraith of a satirical, spectral version he'd seen of the figure of Uncle Sam in a rabid left-wing movie on the Vietnam War some years ago.

"It's an English affectation," Galbraith said.

Crowe, nodding his head in acknowledgement of

this information, put his sandwich back on his plate as Galbraith poured tea. Galbraith noticed there was a slight tremor over the old fellow's upper lip and a waxiness to Crowe's complexion, as if he'd been dipped in a melted candle.

Senator Joseph Holly picked up a knife, neatly dissected a scone and opened it. He spread the surface of one of the halves with Dundee marmalade. When he spoke he did so in a nasal manner, his voice seeming to emerge from the cavities behind his eyes. "So this is where the taxpayer's money goes," he said.

"This is window-dressing," Galbraith replied. "Where the money really goes is elsewhere, Senator."

Holly kept on smiling. "You spooks know how to spend."

"Keeping the world safe for democracy is no Macy's basement, gentlemen," Galbraith said in a cordial way. He hated fiscal matters, pennypinching, keeping accounts, all the tedious chores involved in his relationship with official Washington.

John Crowe said, "The cost is goddam high, and getting higher."

"By the minute," Galbraith agreed cheerfully.

Joseph Holly ate a small mouthful of scone. A bee floated close to the open jar of marmalade and the Senator swatted it away. It promptly returned, clinging to the underside of Holly's saucer. Holly asked, "Are we being recorded right now?"

"This is the one place where I don't allow recordings," Galbraith replied. It was true that he wasn't taping any of this conversation. He might have done so by activating a small button located on the underside of the table. But this wasn't the kind of talk Galbraith wanted to have any record of – quite the opposite.

"Good," Holly said. "Senator Crowe and myself – we're not interfering, keep that in mind, Galbraith – we want to know if this operation is still go on the scheduled date. We hadn't heard from you – "

" – And I consider your silence arrogant, Galbraith," Crowe said. "You don't bite the goddam hand that feeds you. You don't misinterpret the freedom we give you as a goddam licence to do whatever the hell you like. You keep us posted, for Christ's sake."

Galbraith raised his eyebrows. "I can only plead pressures of office. No excuse, I know, gentlemen." He twiddled his fingers and watched the slow movement of the satellite dishes. He understood Crowe and Holly had come down to Fredericksburg to throw a little weight around because they'd been pressured by their allies – a group that included two generals, three congressmen, and a smattering of anonymous industrialists – to find out what the hell was going on. Besides, Crowe was the nominal Director of the DIA and Holly his titular assistant, although neither man was involved in the daily business of the agency.

Was the bird going to fly? That was the question they wanted answered. That was why they were really here in Fredericksburg. Galbraith smiled. He looked plumply reassuring. "Senators, everything is going according to schedule. There are no snags, no snafus, no unexpected scenarios. The clockwork ticks even as we sit here surrounded by all this pleasing greenery."

Crowe leaned across the table, blocking the sunlight. "I'm happy to hear you say that, Galbraith. I'm very happy. I haven't been sleeping lately. Worry, I guess. I liked the world the way it was, Galbraith. I liked the old world better. The way things are going now . . ." Crowe didn't sustain his line of thought. He faded out into a dark silence, his mottled fingers playing with a disc of cucumber that had fallen out of his sandwich.

Galbraith said, "We *all* liked that world better, Senator. It had a certain predictability about it, which was extremely comforting."

"It surely was," Holly said.

"And well-balanced," Galbraith added.

Crowe suddenly picked up his unfinished thought and

added, "We're going to hell in a goddam handbasket. That's where we're headed."

Galbraith watched the bee slide out from under Senator Holly's saucer. He said, "I think that trip to hell is something we intend to stop, Senator Crowe."

John Crowe raised his waxy face. Galbraith noticed a film of membranous material covering one of the old man's eyes.

Crowe said, "One of the problems is the quality of the people these days. Men who aren't big enough for their jobs. Dwarves and midgets, Galbraith."

Galbraith made a sound of agreement.

Crowe went on, "And I'm not just talking about Washington, no sir. I'm talking about the other side as well. I'm talking about how difficult it is to replace a Brezhnev. Even an Andropov. When we had the Chernenko interregnum I really thought we were in hog heaven. And Christ, we had such goddam high hopes for Vladimir Greshko until he fell ill and they gave him the boot. He was a mean sonofabitch and you couldn't trust him further than you could spit, but he knew his goddam place. I'll tell you this, if he was running the show over there we'd be in a damn sight better position. All this hanky-panky we get nowadays wouldn't be going on. Greshko never had the time for that bullshit."

Galbraith plucked a gooseberry-tart from a plate and nibbled it. Its sourness made him wrinkle his face a moment. He said, "What I liked about Greshko was how you couldn't trust him, but you could always count on him."

"Damn right," Crowe said. "How is the old bastard anyhow?"

"Alive, so I believe," Galbraith replied.

Neither Crowe nor Holly needed to know more than that. The secret of success as Galbraith perceived it lay in controlling the spigot of information, knowing how much to release, how much to hold back. When it came to politicians, who traded in the currency of gossip, you withheld the maximum amount possible and doled out a mere trickle. You slaked a thirst, you didn't release a flood.

Galbraith finished his tea, wiped his fingers in the folds of his napkin. "I think we can safely say, Senators, that the status quo will be restored before the week is out."

Crowe looked happy. Holly smiled his unchanging smile – at least until he stood upright suddenly and slapped the palm of his hand upon his neck.

"Shit," Holly exclaimed. There was a squashed bee, still living, fluttering, in the dead centre of his hand. "Bastard stung me."

Galbraith clucked sympathetically. "At least you have the certain pleasure of knowing your assailant is mortally wounded, Senator. Wouldn't it be wonderful if politics worked with such admirable symmetry?"

9

London

Danus Oates lived alone in a three-room flat in Knightsbridge, not far from Sloane Square. The other tenants of the house were a pair of elderly sisters, both quite mad, who kept macaws in enormous cages, and a retired coffee plantation manager from Kenya whose face had the texture of cowhide left too long in direct sunlight. It was a quiet house and Oates moved about it with stealthy consideration. He was well-bred and well-mannered and, until the horror yesterday in Edinburgh, had always considered his life rather humdrum. He had a future in the Foreign Service, so he was told, and he hoped one day to emulate his father – Sir Geoffrey Oates, Her Majesty's Ambassador to Norway. Like many patriotic men dedicated to public service, he was neither greatly ambitious nor overwhelmingly imaginative, but he was pleased, in a general kind of way, with his existence.

His one extraordinary talent was for languages, which came to him with an ease that was inexplicable, all the more so since there was no history of this affinity in his lineage. He spoke not only the usual languages of commerce and diplomacy – French, German, Russian – but he had an excellent knowledge of Greek (ancient and modern), Spanish, Italian and Swedish. He could read and speak two of the three Baltic languages – Estonian and Latvian (in its Upper dialect) – and he understood to a useful degree some of the arcane forms associated with them, Livonian and Low German. He had a smattering of the Carpathian dialect of Ukrainian, more than adequate

Hungarian, and he was fluent in Moldavian, which was really a version of Rumanian. He was presently teaching himself Ottoman Turkish, or Osmanli, from cassette tapes provided by the Foreign Office Library. Quite often Oates dreamed in foreign tongues.

Because he'd spent hours translating the Livonian material at Scotland Yard, he hadn't returned to his apartment until six a.m. that Sunday morning. He'd been made groggy too by the twenty milligrams of Valium he'd taken in an attempt to restore his ruined nerves. Consequently, he fell into a sound sleep as soon as his head hit the pillow, and he dreamed for an odd reason of the Estonian word for 'potato' in some of its various grammatical cases. *Kartul* meant potato, but because prepositions in Estonian were suffixes, *kartuli* meant 'of the potato' and *kartuliga* meant 'with the potato' and *kartulil* 'on the potato'. His long sleep and his strange dream of *kartulid* – potatoes, plural – was interrupted at approximately four o'clock in the afternoon by a hand clamped over his mouth.

Oates woke abruptly, and found himself looking up into a kindly face, that of a man who might generously toss coins in the cup of a blind beggar. Oates couldn't breathe because the hand was forced very hard over his lips. His sleepy mind, shocked into alertness, considered a number of possibilities. He was being burgled. Or he was about to be raped. Or this intruder with the gentle face was in reality a madman who'd slit his throat any second with a razor.

Oates kicked at the bedsheets and tried to twist his head away, but the older man was astonishingly strong.

"The rules are simple, Mr Oates. I ask some questions. You answer them honestly. You understand?"

Oates blinked his eyes furiously. The stranger took his hand away and Oates sucked air into his lungs. With the return of oxygen to his brain came a defiant urge. After all, what the hell was this chap doing in Oates's flat? What gave him the bloody right to come stealing inside another fellow's bedroom? Oates, who wore black and red striped pyjamas, a present last Christmas from his fiancée Fiona, stepped out of bed, brushing past the intruder.

"Where are you going?" the stranger asked in his accented English.

Oates didn't answer, just kept moving. He was thinking of the telephone in the corner of the bedroom. Calling the gendarmes. Getting some law and order established around here. He'd almost reached the phone when he felt it – a searing pain between his shoulderblades. It rocked his spine, settled somewhere in the middle of his skull like a small glowing coal. He collapsed on the floor and moaned. He looked up at the man, who stood directly over him, shaking his head in a gesture of regret.

"Take me seriously, Mr Oates. Don't force me to strike you again."

Danus Oates moved his head very slightly. The idea of violence terrified him. He stammered the way he'd always done when he'd been a schoolboy at Harrow and an object of cruel fun. "What d-d-do you want?"

"Your cooperation," the stranger said. He squatted beside Oates, who felt paralysed, though whether through fear or because the intruder had struck some vital nerve centre he couldn't tell.

"I believe you may have done some translating, Mr Oates."

That bloody Livonian stuff! So that's what all this was about! Oates was a little relieved to discover that the fellow wasn't an escaped lunatic after all. But only a little. He looked up into the sympathetic brown eyes, the concerned expression.

"What precisely was it you translated?"

"Business d-documents, some business c-c-c-correspondence."

"Is that all?"

"There was also a p-poem," Oates said. He saw no harm in admitting this. After all, he was a budding diplomat, and if this was all some kind of cloak and dagger nonsense he wanted no part of it.

"Tell me about it, Mr Oates."

Oates felt a little surge of security. He was on familiar ground now. "There were four lines of verse," he said. "They were written in a form of Livonian, which is rather obscure. Do you know anything about that language?"

The intruder shook his head. "I don't have time for an academic discourse, Mr Oates. The contents of the poem, please. That's all I ask."

Oates said, "I'm simply trying to tell you the poem was written in a language few people speak any more. There were one or two words of modern Estonian mixed in, but mainly the vocabulary was Livonian. So far as I can gather, the poem referred to somebody called Kalev who apparently has the ability to bring joy to Estonia."

"Kalev?"

Oates nodded. He struggled into a sitting position. The pain had diffused itself, and was no longer centralised, but had broken into little tributaries that flickered along his nerve-endings. He rubbed his arms, which for some reason tingled.

"In your opinion was the verse some form of code?"

"Code?" Oates blinked. "That sort of thing is really rather outside my province."

"This poem wasn't returned to the Soviet Embassy by Scotland Yard. Do you know why?"

Oates, remembering how the strange lines of verse had so intrigued the Commissioner, shook his head. "I'm no expert on how Scotland Yard works."

The man pinched the bridge of his nose a moment, sighing as he did so. "Does Frank Pagan have the poem in his possession?"

Danus Oates said he presumed so except he couldn't be sure, all he'd done was to translate the material, then pass it back to the Commissioner, who would have assigned it to Pagan. He thought the Commissioner wouldn't have given it to anyone else because Burr

had said he didn't want the existence of the poem
bruited about, so the circle of those who knew about
the verse was probably very small. But, good Christ,
Oates didn't know *anything* for certain – he hadn't even
understood the damned poem, he said. In fact he wished
he'd never been in Edinburgh in the first place. He had
an unwanted memory of Romanenko mentioning how
railroad stations smelled and then the loud roar of a pistol
and Frank Pagan throwing himself bodily at the assassin.
His brain was like a large box in which everything made
loud rattling noises.

Oates made it up as far as his knees, but he was
unsteady, and swayed a little. The intruder helped him to
his feet, then back to the bed. Oates sat on the edge of the
mattress. He still felt curiously dizzy, at one remove from
himself. The red stripes of his pyjamas seemed to pulsate
at the corner of his vision. The older man had to have the
strength of a damned *ox* to fell him like that. He looked at
the man, who was gazing round the bedroom, which was
decorated with antique furniture and nineteenth-century
equestrian prints, family heirlooms.

Then the stranger walked to the window and looked
out. There was a view of a quiet Sunday street, parked
cars, a pub called The Lord Byron on a far corner.
Oates gnawed on his lower lip. The man's silence was
unnerving, even menacing. Surely, though, this was the
end of the business. Oates had no information to give, he
didn't have a clue about why the poem wasn't returned
to the Russians, he was actually of very little use to this
stranger – who, if he were a reasonable man, would
recognise the fact and simply depart. Oates prayed he
was exactly that: a reasonable man.

"I mean, if I didn't happen to know the language, I
wouldn't have been involved in any of this," and Oates
attempted a nervous little laugh, which emerged as a
girlish giggle, a sound he didn't quite recognise as his
own. "As for the poem, well, it didn't make any damn
sense to me, but I can't speak on Frank Pagan's behalf,

perhaps it means something to him." He babbled on, driven by his nervousness, words streaming out of him. The stranger turned now, and smiled. It was a warm little expression which chilled Danus Oates to the bone. A few spots of rain struck the window and slithered down the glass. Oates's attention was drawn to them momentarily, and he thought how very banal the raindrops seemed, how ordinary – but then *everything* struck him as commonplace all at once, this bedroom, the bed, his striped pyjamas, the things in his room. Everything was sublimely prosaic except for the gun in the intruder's hand which Oates had noticed when the man turned from the window but had refused to register. A delayed reaction – only now it struck him like a tiny comet flashing through the darkness of his head, and the everyday quality of his surroundings was altered beyond recognition, and all the anchors securing him to the familiar were cut loose.

"L-l-look here," Oates said. "You're not going to use that thing." His tongue adhered to the roof of his mouth and he had no control over the sudden tic under his eye.

The stranger moved closer to the bed. He seemed to be turning something over in his mind. Whatever it was, Danus Oates knew it was connected with his own future, a concept that was rushing away from him with the sound of air escaping a punctured balloon.

The man pushed the gun into the soft flesh below Oates's ear. Oates imagined he heard the weapon ticking like some awful clock measuring his frail mortality. He shut his eyes and tried to swallow.

"P-p-p," but the word *please* wouldn't come out at all.

The intruder came so close now that Oates could feel the man's breath upon the side of his cheek, and he could smell the gun, the peculiar metal odour of it, the hint of oil. He opened one eye and thought how vast the weapon seemed from his perspective.

"Are you telling me everything you know, Mr Oates?"

"*Absolutely*," Oates whispered.

The gun was eased away from his neck and for a moment Oates was flooded with a relief so intense he felt light-headed. It was a sensation that lasted only a fraction of a second. The stranger fired the silenced gun once and Danus Oates, who had no more ambition in life than to become the British Ambassador to a civilised country like Austria or Holland, fell from the bed and toppled to the floor.

V.G. Epishev, struck by vague regret, didn't look at the body. He put the gun in his coat pocket, then stepped quietly out of the apartment, hearing from far beneath him the scream of a bird. And he thought of Vladimir Greshko and the way the old man lay like some bird himself, an aged buzzard with wings folded, eyes shut, talons always ready to strike.

He moved down the stairs quickly, let himself out into the street. Thin clouds floated over the wet slate rooftops of Knightsbridge. A dreary Sunday, an afternoon in which autumn could be smelled on the air like lead. An afternoon for death and dying.

He walked until he came to the place where he'd parked his hired car, a Ford, then he drove away, watching rain slide over the windshield. He was certain that Oates, poor doomed Oates, had been telling the truth. What had he been in any case but an innocent bystander, an accident of history? The option to allow Oates to live hadn't really been viable, although Epishev had considered it. As soon as Epishev had left the apartment, the young Englishman would be on the telephone to Scotland Yard, babbling about his mysterious intruder and all the questions he'd asked.

Verse, Epishev thought. A few lines of poetry. If these were a code, then it might be something simple, something a man like Frank Pagan might be able to figure out. Something that contained dates and times and places, the particulars of the Brotherhood's plot.

He parked his car under a damp tree on a quiet side street. He pinched the bridge of his nose, a characteristic gesture of concentration. His instruction from Greshko had been simple. *Eliminate the threat.* Epishev made no distinction between real or imagined threats – they were equally menacing. What did it matter if the poem contained a code or not? The important thing was the idea that it *might*. Uncle Viktor, who had lived for a long time in a world of menace, had a word for this kind of elimination. He called it precautionary.

Frank Pagan and Kristina Vaska left Pagan's flat and walked across the square, through dripping laburnum and under wet laurels, following a narrow path that led past empty wooden benches. Pagan had wakened with a headache and an urge to walk in the rain, to get out of the apartment and away from the telephone calls from the scribblers of Fleet Street, who wanted his eyewitness account of the murder in Edinburgh.

Kristina Vaska had asked to accompany him and now she stepped along at his side wearing a raincoat she'd borrowed from his wardrobe. It was far too large for her. The sleeves hung three inches beyond her hands, the hem trailed the wet grass. She looked frail and childlike in the oversized coat, but Pagan knew this fragility was more apparent than real.

He surveyed the square, pausing at a place where the pathway divided. It was bleak here, and private, his own rain-shrouded enclave in the heart of Holland Park. The path led past a shelter, a simple wooden edifice with benches that was a retreat for the old people of the neighbourhood. Today it was empty and smelled of damp wood and wet moss. Kristina Vaska paused by the shelter.

She asked, "How long have you lived a life of chaotic bachelorhood?"

Pagan said, "I was married once."

"What happened?"

"She died." Two words. *She died*. Pagan wanted to leave it there, simple and terse, unexplored. He didn't want to go into that history of pain. He looked the length of the square. The only other life forms were an elderly woman, an eccentric in plastic raincoat and hat, walking an enormously fat, boisterous dalmatian.

"I'm sorry," Kristina said.

"It's not anything I want to talk about." He moved past the shelter, listening to the tick of rain on leaves. "Let's talk about Kristina Vaska instead."

"I can think of more interesting topics. What do you want to know?"

"Where you live. What you do for a living. The usual stuff."

She smiled. "I live in New York City. I work as a researcher."

"What kind of research?" Pagan was unhappy with vague terminology, and the word 'researcher' fell into a category of occupations that included financial consultants, management analysts and Members of Parliament.

"Let's say a writer or an organisation wants information. They come to me, tell me what they need, and I find out. I spend a lot of time in libraries. Is there anything you need to know about Sargon the Great, King of Akkad? Are you having a problem about the habitat of Leadbeater's possum? Do you have an urgent desire to find out how the Ashanti live and what they worship? Then I'm the person to see." She looked at him with her head tilted a little to one side. "Among other things, I've also done considerable research – unpaid, entirely on my own initiative – into the Brotherhood, which wasn't altogether easy because the literature isn't extensive."

Pagan tried to imagine her hauling heavy volumes from dusty shelves in obscure libraries and somehow couldn't fix a clear image in his head. "What brought you to England?"

"Am I being interrogated, Frank?"

Pagan shook his head. Had it been so long since he'd carried on any ordinary discourse that he'd forgotten how? Was there a tone in his voice that suggested he suspected everybody he met of *something*? "I didn't mean to make it sound that way. Force of habit, I suppose."

"I guess in your line of business you think everyone has ulterior motives. So you don't take anybody on trust. Including me. I sneak into your little world – a mine of information, a source of intrigue, only you don't know exactly who I am or what my motives are. What makes it even more perplexing is the way I turn up at the same time as Romanenko – and wham! You're sitting on one of those really bizarre coincidences cops aren't supposed to swallow. Correct?"

Pagan, thinking how close Kristina Vaska had come to describing his state of mind, picked up a damp stick and tossed it through the air and watched it fall with a mildly expectant look on his face, almost as if he expected an invisible dog to fetch it for him. "When I get information, I like to know as much as I can about the source." He sounded more defensive than he would have liked.

"Makes sense," she said. She walked ahead of him now, leaving the path and pushing through damp shrubbery. He went after her, noticing the way her hair was flattened by rain against her scalp. One of the most provocative images in Pagan's sexual cosmology was the sight of a woman stepping from a shower or coming up out of the ocean after a swim, her hair wet and uncombed and falling carelessly. Something in the randomness, the basic disarray, appealed enormously to him. As she parted damp shrubbery and rain blew across her face and hair, Kristina Vaska was attractive to him in just that way.

She stopped moving, turned to him, grinned. Her whole look teased him. She raised her hands in a gesture of surrender. "Okay. You got me cold, Pagan. I confess. I was the one supposed to meet Romanenko in Edinburgh. I was his contact. He was supposed to pass the poem to me. I'm the Brotherhood's messenger. Please don't send me to the big house, I don't want to grow old and wrinkle in a cell, please find some charity in your heart.''

She clutched the lapel of his coat and shook him slightly and he laughed aloud at her sudden pantomime, thinking how the sound cut through his unease. Then she released him and turned away from him once again and moved between the trees. He walked behind her, blinking against the rain.

She stopped between two elegant willows whose branches trailed the ground. In this location, this secret heart of the park, it was impossible to see the houses around the square. It was an intimate place, a green island afloat on the wet afternoon, and Pagan felt the unexpected impulse to reach out and touch the woman, perhaps something as simple as laying his fingertips against her lips. With some difficulty he resisted the urge.

She wiped raindrops from her eyelashes and smiled at him. ''Actually, the real truth's boringly simple, Frank. I came to London because I hoped I'd get a chance to talk with Romanenko. I read in somewhere that the Soviets were interested in buying computers in the UK, and that Romanenko was being sent. I had a notion he might *just* be able to use his influence to help get my father released. I wasn't sure how I was going to engineer a meeting, because I know the KGB's usually in attendance – but I thought it was worth a shot. Unfortunately, I never got the chance to see him. I went to the Savoy, but he'd already left for Edinburgh. Then I figured I'd wait for him to return. The rest you know.''

Pagan listened in silence. There was still a shadow across his mind. ''Why do you want to help me? Why bother to tell me about Romanenko and the Brotherhood? Altruism? Or am I missing something?''

''You're not missing anything. Your viewpoint's just a little jaded, that's all. You don't expect people to be helpful. I don't have any concealed motives, Frank. I heard about the killing on TV, I thought you might

Mazurka

need information you weren't going to get anywhere else. Here I am. That's it."

He stepped a little closer to the woman. She ran her fingers through her wet hair. Pagan felt an odd sense of longing. The last yearning he'd had like this belonged in quite another lifetime, in the dead seasons of his past. Eroticism in the rain, he thought. A fine sexual fever under the damp trees. She was bewitching in the oversized coat, a child-woman.

She ducked a little too quickly under a branch, moving beyond his reach, heading out of this leafy corner and back in the direction of the path. Pagan was a little startled by his feelings, which Kristina Vaska must have read in his eyes – given the haste with which she'd stepped away from him. Was he supposed to feel foolish now? Embarrassed by his obviousness?

Saying nothing to each other, they walked back along the path. Pagan gazed at the empty lawns, the damp flowerbeds, the low sky that hung above the square and emphasised the desolation, the emptiness, of the place. The fat dalmatian and the elderly woman he'd seen before weren't visible now, even though the barking of a dog could still be heard through the rain.

"Can you remember where you read about Romanenko's visit?" he asked.

She smiled as if his suspicions were a constant source of amusement to her. "You're priceless, Frank. What difference does it make where I read about it?"

"I'm curious, that's all."

She closed her eyes, looked thoughtful. "*The Economist*. US edition. Any more questions?"

Pagan gazed at the small wooden shelter in the centre of the square. "I don't think so," he said.

"Did I pass the test?"

"Was there a test?"

"From the moment I first stepped inside your flat."

They were approaching the shelter now. Pagan stared beyond it, through the trees, seeing the dim windows of

168

his own apartment. The curtains were still drawn from the night before. He could see the narrow street lined with parked cars. Kristina Vaska was perfectly correct, of course. He'd been testing her all along, and he hadn't quite finished yet. He might be attracted to her, but he wasn't going to get downright careless on that account. An earlier version of Pagan, a younger self, might have had a more romantic lack of caution, a willingness to be indiscreet with his heart – but at the age of forty-one Pagan had crossed a demarcation line on one side of which lay blind ardour, on the other wariness.

"Let's go back indoors," he said. "I need a drink."

V.G. Epishev sat inside the parked car, listening to the quiet sound of the engine running. He watched Frank Pagan and the woman crossing the square in the direction of the street. It was the presence of the woman that threw him off balance. He hadn't expected a companion in Pagan's life. For some reason he'd assumed Pagan's life would be as solitary as his own.

His view of Pagan and the woman was impeded for a moment by a shelter in the middle of the park, then they re-emerged, pausing to exchange some words. They inclined their heads towards each other, and Epishev detected intimacy in this gesture. He wondered if Pagan and his companion were lovers. He tried to imagine them that way, but it was like the taste of an exotic food he hadn't sampled in a long time – and yet he could vaguely remember the tantalising flavour.

Something about the woman disturbed him. She provoked a strong sense of familiarity in him. It was the kind of feeling you had when a word lay on the tip of your tongue but you couldn't quite utter it. He thought he'd seen her before somewhere. No, he *knew* he had.

Pagan and the woman were still moving towards the exit. They walked about two feet apart from each other and there was no apparent intimacy now. Epishev put his hand into the pocket of his coat that contained the gun. He rested the other hand on the door handle, looked along the quiet, rainy street.

It kept coming back to nag him, this feeling that somewhere in the distant past there had been an encounter with the woman. He was sure of it now. He gazed across the grass at her face, which was partly hidden by the upturned collar of her outsized raincoat. A lovely face, but tantalising. She made a gesture with her hand, threw her head back, laughed at something Pagan said. Epishev turned the handle of the door.

Pagan and the woman were about a hundred yards from the low stone wall that surrounded the square. Now the woman was staring almost directly at the car and Epishev brought his hand up to his lips and coughed into it, a reflex action, a gesture to conceal himself from her attention.

Who was she? And where had he seen her before?

He had a little memory trick he sometimes used. It was to envisage the environment in which he'd seen a particular face. It was to recall physical details – dress, weather, the colour of wallpaper, the curtains – and then set the remembered face against these recollections.

Tallinn, he thought. He had the feeling it had to be Tallinn. He recalled a flight of stairs, a bicycle propped against the wall on the landing, an open doorway that led inside a large apartment, a well-furnished set of rooms.

He almost had it then. But the memory was like a badly-tuned television station, a picture that fluttered, blemished by static. Damn. Now Pagan and the woman were a mere fifty yards away and they were walking more briskly than before. They wanted to get out of the rain, of course. To dry themselves off. Epishev undid the safety catch on the gun, and ran the tips of his fingers over the surface of the weapon. He'd step out of the car, approach Pagan with the gun, and the rest would be easy, a matter of getting back Romanenko's mysterious verse, which was presumably inside Pagan's apartment or even on his person, and then he'd dispose of both the

Englishman and the woman, right here on this street if
he had to –

*A young girl in braided hair, a yellow print dress, bare feet
in sandals, a child sobbing . . .*

Pagan and the woman were approaching the stone wall
now, the exit, the pavement. For a second they were lost
behind a clutch of dense trees, then they reappeared.

A child sobbing . . .

And that was when it came to him, reaching across
the years, echoing out of the past, it came to him with
sudden clarity. He could see a young girl's face and
the way her hair was braided and how she'd cried and
scratched viciously at his hands as her father was being
led out of the apartment in Tallinn on a cold morning
more than fifteen years ago. Fifteen long years ago – how
had Frank Pagan come into the orbit of the daughter of
Norbert Vaska, the child called Kristina?

She turned her face towards the car then, for some
reason. She turned, looking damp and pale, her black
hair plastered across her scalp, her mouth a dark circle.
Epishev wasn't sure whether it was recognition that
crossed her face, whether his appearance provoked
memories inside her of that same chill morning so long
ago, when she'd been twelve, perhaps thirteen. He saw
something in her features change, and then she was
reaching for Pagan's arm and pulling it, and hurrying him
across the street to the house. Pagan, running alongside
her, his overcoat billowing around him, looked puzzled
and reluctant as if the woman had drawn him suddenly
into a game he couldn't follow.

Epishev, his sense of timing skewed by the sudden
movement of the couple, tightened his grip on the gun
and was about to step out of the car when he was aware
of the enormous black and white dog thumping and
pounding along the pavement towards him, a massive
spotted creature, perhaps two hundred pounds in
weight, pursued by a woman in a plastic raincoat.
This monstrous animal had sighted Epishev stepping

out of the car and now it charged with crazed canine friendliness toward him, a dumb light in its eyes, paws upraised, tail flailing the air like a whip. Epishev drew the car door shut and watched the creature slobber against the glass before losing interest and padding huffily away. The damned English and their damned pets! But he'd lost the initiative, the element of surprise, even before the appearance of the mutt.

Across the street Pagan and Kristina Vaska had vanished inside the house, and the dark brown door was shut behind them. Epishev cursed, stared up at the windows. Had she recognised him? Of course – how else could one explain the speed with which they'd crossed the street and entered the house? How else to explain that urgency?

Epishev drove the Ford along the street, passing the dalmatian, which had its leg cocked against a wall. He glanced once more at Pagan's house, and then he was turning out of the narrow street, wondering what had brought Kristina Vaska into the policeman's world, and what it would mean if indeed she'd recognised him.

Inside the apartment Frank Pagan poured two shots of scotch and gave one to Kristina. She was silent, listening to the rain upon the window. Pagan watched her sip the drink, then he went to her and rubbed one of her cold hands between his own. She trembled. He walked to the window, looked down at the street, saw nothing below but the woman in the plastic raincoat caressing her spotted dog. There was no sign of the stranger who had so suddenly spooked Kristina and made her claw at his coat-sleeve in such a panicked manner that she'd dragged him across the street and inside the house before he'd even had time to register the existence of the man.

Kristina moved to the sofa and sat down. She was motionless for a long time.

"His name's Epishev," she said in a quiet voice, almost a whisper. "Some people call him Uncle Viktor, and they don't use the name fondly."

Pagan sat down beside her. He wanted to reach for her hand again, but he didn't. "How can you be sure it's the same man?"

"Because it's fucking hard to forget the face of the KGB officer who arrested my father in Tallinn."

Pagan didn't doubt her fear. He could read it in her eyes as plainly as bold print. But there was something else here that troubled him, a convergence of more echoes from the past, actors from an old melodrama that might have been revived purely for his personal bewilderment. Uncle Viktor and Norbert Vaska. The KGB and the Brotherhood of the Forest. It was as if a faded photograph had been retouched, making it appear fresh and new. And it had been thrust rudely into his face, forcing him to look directly into it. He had the thought that his life, which had been simpler only recently, was taking strange, complicated detours. The problem with these departures was the feeling that he had no control over any of them.

He stared for a while at the prints on the walls. "Why would the KGB send somebody here?" he asked. "Why send somebody to spy on me?"

"Spy? I don't think Viktor Epishev would have anything as innocent as *spying* in mind, Frank. That's not what he does. Let me put it to you this way. If he's been sent over here because of you, he's got a more sinister purpose than simply *watching* you."

"He wants me out of the way," Pagan said rather flatly, more a statement of fact than a question.

"I'd hazard that guess, Frank."

"Hazard another one and tell me why."

"I don't exactly know. Let's look at what we've got. Romanenko carries a message he doesn't get the chance to deliver. We assume the message was intended for another member or members of the Brotherhood. Let's say the gist of it is to go ahead with a plan, which we believe is a plan against the Soviets. The message, however, falls into your hands."

"And Epishev wants it."

"Presumably."

"And he wants to silence me into the bargain."

"Yes."

"It's not adding up for me," Pagan said. "If the KGB thinks I have knowledge of some anti-Russian business, the logical thing would be for them to ask me directly. *Frank, old comrade, what do you know about this Brotherhood stuff?* That would be the rational approach. The notion of somebody being sent here to kill me – apart from scaring me quite shitless – seems a little extreme."

They were silent for a while. Then Kristina said, "Here's another possible consideration. Maybe the KGB *already know* what the Brotherhood's up to – only they'd prefer it if *you* didn't."

"Which would imply the KGB is in bed with the Brotherhood, wouldn't it?"

Kristina Vaska nodded. "And that's an impossibility. The likelihood of the Brotherhood fornicating with the KGB is about as remote as finding a civil rights lawyer in Moscow."

"Here's a question for you. How would somebody go about finding out exactly what it is the Brotherhood's up to?"

Kristina Vaska shook her head, moved to the window, looked out into the rain. With a fingertip she drew a thin spiral on the glass. Pagan went towards her. He gazed over her shoulder and across the square.

"I wish I knew more," she said.

"When you researched the Brotherhood, what did you find out about them?"

"I researched their *past*, Frank, and that was tough enough. Their present's even more difficult. They don't advertise for new members. They don't put ads in newspapers giving the times and locations of their meetings. They're not in the business of promoting themselves."

"If I wanted to find one of the members, where would I start looking?"

"Jesus, I wish I had a specific answer to that one. The truth is, they ended up all over the place. Australia. New Zealand. Scandinavia. There's probably even a couple of old members right here in London. But mainly they made it to the United States. Chicago. Los Angeles. Mostly they came to New York City, Brooklyn in particular. But since many of them arrived as young men, they presumably married, raised families, and – like all good upwardly mobile Americans – prospered and moved out into the suburbs. Like I said, they don't advertise their whereabouts."

"If you researched them, surely you must know some of their names?"

There was frustration in Kristina Vaska's voice. She looked at Pagan as if he'd asked the one question that had bewildered her for years. "They weren't stupid men, Frank. They didn't fight under their own names. They used pseudonyms. *Noms de guerre* to protect their families if they were captured. They left nothing but dead-ends behind them when they dispersed. I spent a long time trying to track old members down when I was doing my research. Elusive's an understatement when it comes to their identities. I'd keep running into references to men who operated under names like *Rebane*, the Fox. One man called himself *Kotkas*, the Eagle. Another was *Hunt*, the Wolf. I could never pin anything down about the true identities of these characters. Apart from Romanenko, I never learned any real names. And I tried goddam hard, believe me. It's like I said, Frank. Records – even when they exist – are difficult to obtain and after a while you get so frustrated you can't do anything else but give up. If the men of the Brotherhood took such pains to conceal their identities, what right did I have to come along and try to force open old doors anyway? So I stopped looking. I quit."

Pagan was silent. He stared into the trees. He remembered the way he'd yearned for her down there in the square, that brief flare of longing, as if he might find in her an escape hatch from the lonely condition of his life. He looked at the delicate shadow in the nape of her neck. Now now, he thought. Maybe never. He wondered what it would be like to make love to this woman.

There was a long silence broken only by the metronome of the rain. She turned from the window and said, "Epishev scares me. He scared me when I was a kid, and he scares me now. I have this memory of the way he patted me on the head and told me everything was going to be all right. I can see him and his goons take my father out of the apartment. I can still see the way the bastard smiled."

"Do you think he recognised you?"

"I hope not."

Pagan thought of the pistol, the Bernardelli he kept in a shoebox under his bed. He said, "We're safe here."

"For how long, Frank?"

Pagan didn't answer the question. He was thinking of somebody out there in the rain, somebody who'd been sent from the Soviet Union, a man whose purpose only added to a general mystification that Frank Pagan didn't like. He reached inside the pocket of his jacket and removed the poem, the original version, and he stared at the blue writing on the cracked sheet of paper. Dry old words, dry paper, foreign to him in more ways than mere language.

Saaremaa Island, the Baltic Sea

Colonel Yevgenni Uvarov practised the signature, which he'd seen hundreds of times. He wrote slowly, in the manner of an unpractised counterfeiter. Every time he covered a sheet, he studied it then wadded the paper up as tightly as he could. When he had it compressed into a tiny ball, he took it to the bathroom and flushed it. Once, a little tipsy on the Georgian wine he sometimes acquired, he imagined a secret laboratory where all flushed paper was fished from the sewers and dried out and examined by the KGB, a special department of effluence commissars who were puzzled by the fact that somebody kept signing the name *S.F. Tikunov* over and over, and then tossed the papers down the toilet.

His hand became cramped. He capped his pen, rolled the sheet of paper until it was no larger than a walnut, then turned his face away from the lamp beside his bunk. He stood up, put on his jacket, left his quarters. He passed the leisure room, which was a spartan affair containing an old black and white TV and three ancient easy chairs. Once, Uvarov recalled, a technician called Samov had rigged a makeshift antenna for the TV, and for three nights a station from Finland had been visible, tantalisingly so, bringing another world into this drab place. American programmes, Scandinavian ones, even some pornography – these were watched secretly until Samov's aerial was reported and its inventor sent elsewhere.

There was a full moon outside, and the radar antennae were superimposed strangely against it, as if they were odd cracks that had developed on the moon's surface. Uvarov walked to the shoreline, took the paper out of his pocket, threw it into the tide. He gazed for some time across the silvery water, thinking of his wife and children. He saw a Kirov guided missile cruiser, a floating palace of lights, about a half mile from the shore.

He walked back in the direction of the control centre that housed the radar screens and the computers. Two of the computers were inoperative, and had been for days, despite the arrival of a maintenance crew from Moscow, argumentative men who'd tinkered without success, squabbling among themselves, blaming one another for the failure. At any given time two of the four computers failed to function because of flaws in their basic designs – they were bad copies of Japanese originals. They were scheduled to be phased out, and replaced, but the programme was already five weeks late.

Uvarov entered the centre, smelling the dead, stale air of the place, absorbing the green screens, the uniformed men who sat before them. Nothing was happening on the waters of the Baltic. He spoke to a couple of the technicians, pleasantries, little else. In recent months he'd tended to remain aloof. He saw no future in forming friendships.

He walked to his metal desk, sat down. He pretended to work, to study papers, but in reality he was examining a computer manual which had been circulated by the Defence Ministry. It had been printed in a limited edition, and access was restricted to men above the rank of Colonel. The manual detailed the interfacing between the computers at this installation and those located at other Air Defence posts in the Baltic sector of the Soviet Union and in Moscow itself. He read for a while, then closed the manual, placing it for safekeeping in the drawer with his family's photograph.

The timing had to be unerring. He rose from his desk, walked along the banks of consoles, hands clasped behind his back. He paused when he reached the wall. Where a window might have been located, there hung a large portrait of Lenin. Uvarov felt an odd sense of constriction, of being caged in an airless space. The surface of his skin was hot, and there was a dull ache behind his eyes.

Nerves. Nothing more than nerves. He was living so very close to the edge these days that physical reactions were not entirely surprising. He glanced at the face of Lenin, then walked back the way he'd come. The radar screens were lifeless. Everything here was lifeless. Uvarov suddenly longed to hear his children laughing, or the sound of his wife playing her piano.

He reached his desk, leaned against it, folded his arms over his chest. On the wall some yards away was the Orders Board. He turned toward it, gazing at a variety of instructions, orders, revised orders, revisions to those revisions, procedures. They came in batches every day from Moscow, and they were all signed by the same man – the Commander in Chief of Soviet Air Defences, Deputy Minister S. F. Tikunov.

Uvarov breathed very deeply, tried to relax. The sheer magnitude of what he was involved in made his heart pound and his pulses go berserk. A week ago he'd asked the physician for something to help him sleep, but the doctor had been unwilling to prescribe drugs and Uvarov didn't press the matter. Why have *insomniac* on your record? It would be perceived eventually by somebody in records as a weakness and then it might result in a whole battery of those psychiatric tests everybody had become so fond of lately. And Uvarov had neither the time nor the inclination to be the subject of any kind of inquiry.

The telephone rang on his desk and he was startled for a second by the intensity of the sound. It pierced him. He reached for the receiver and held it to his ear. From the amount of static on the line he knew the call was long distance.

A man's voice said, "Colonel Uvarov?"

Uvarov said, "Speaking."

The voice responded, "Aleksis told me to contact you."

10

Moscow

After Lieutenant Dimitri Volovich parked and locked his car and removed the windshield-wipers as a precaution against theft, he looked the length of the quiet street, which was located between the Riga Railway Terminal and the Sadovoye Ring. It was a pleasant street and Volovich's apartment building was new, built from brown brick and flanked by spindles of newly-planted trees. The sixty apartments were allotted to people with *blat*, the influence necessary to live a life of comfort within the Soviet Union.

As a middle-ranking officer of the KGB, one with many years of faithful if unenterprising service, Volovich was entitled to a few perquisites. The two-roomed flat, with its 13.2 square metres of living space – a little more than the average decreed by the State – was one of them. His automobile, a black Zhiguli, was another. In Soviet terms, he was a man of some means. He was also a person with no particular ambitions beyond loyalty to the organs of State Security, which from a practical point of view meant loyalty to his immediate superior, Viktor Epishev. But it was this allegiance that troubled him as he moved towards the entrance to the building. And it troubled him less in terms of any conspiracy against the State, but more at the level of his own survival. His life, he had to admit, wasn't such a bad one. And he wanted to keep it.

As he was about to step inside the building, he was aware of a long dark car approaching the kerb. It was a

Zil with tinted windows and imported whitewall tyres. Volovich stared at the whitewalls. He knew whose car this was. The rear door opened and he moved towards it even as he fought panic down, like something hard in his throat.

"Come in," a voice said from the back of the car.

Volovich stumbled into the dark interior. He couldn't make out any details in the dimness of the big car save for the shadowy outline of somebody who sat tucked in the corner. He knew who it was in any case, and he was overwhelmed.

"Close the door, Dimitri."

Volovich did so. The car, whose driver was invisible beyond a panel of smoked glass, drove away immediately.

"In all Moscow, what is your favourite drive, Dimitri?"

Volovich licked his lips. He couldn't think. He stared at the shadowy figure and said, "I've always enjoyed the ride to Arkhangelskoye Park, sir."

I'm not guilty of anything, he thought. *Keep telling yourself that.* He breathed deeply and quietly, conscious of the way General Olsky was observing him. The General reached forward to flip a switch set into a panel in the door.

"Driver," he said. "Take us to Arkhangelskoye Park. Go by way of Petrovo-Dalniye."

Volovich gazed out through the tinted windows. He saw the Sovietskaya Hotel and the Dynamo Stadium, almost as if he were viewing them through eyes that weren't his own. He was trying hard not to display any kind of uneasiness or fear, but it was difficult. He was conscious of the Aeroflot Hotel, then the Metro station at Alabyan Street, but these impressions belonged in another world. Volovich's world, which had dwindled abruptly, was confined to this car and the man who sat on the seat next to him.

General Olsky said, "It's an ugly building. I always think so."

Volovich stared at the Gidroproekt skyscraper, which was lit even though nightfall wasn't complete. He had no opinion one way or the other, but he agreed with Olsky in any case. The Zil was travelling along an underpass, beyond which was the road to Arkhangelskoye.

"It's good to have an opportunity to talk to you, Dimitri," he said. "Sometimes a man in my position loses touch with the rank and file, you understand."

Volovich craved a drink. Water, vodka, anything. The surface of his tongue was like the skin of a peach.

"How long have you worked with Colonel Epishev?" the General asked.

Volovich was filled with sudden dread. Olsky wouldn't have mentioned Viktor's name unless he was leading towards something disastrous.

"Twenty years, more or less."

"You're very close to him, I assume."

Volovich sat very still. He wondered how he looked to Olsky, whether his panic was visible somehow, whether he'd given himself away – a line of sweat on his upper lip, a nervous tic somewhere. He wasn't sure. "We work together," he managed to say.

"I have a question," the General said.

There was a long pause. Volovich looked through the window. He understood the car was in the vicinity of the Khimki Reservoir, but suddenly he'd lost his bearings.

"Where is Epishev?" the General asked.

It was the question Volovich had expected and feared. He said, "Unfortunately, General, he doesn't always keep me informed of his whereabouts."

"Nobody seems to know where he's gone. It's very odd. I know my predecessor gave Epishev certain freedoms, and I understand they were close . . . a little like teacher and pupil. But the fact remains, I have no way of accounting for Epishev's absence. He's not in his office, he's not at his home, he left no information with his secretary."

Volovich remembered stories he'd heard about the

General's wife, rumours of her sexual prowess when she'd been a ballerina. He'd seen the woman once, waiting for her husband inside a parked limousine. A woman of stunning beauty. "I wish I could help, General," he said.

Olsky changed the subject suddenly. "Reconstruction is taking place in our country, Dimitri. We must remember to keep open minds at all times. We must be alert. We must be strong enough to shed a strong light on our shortcomings. Change of this magnitude is always painful. But many people, even those who basically agree but argue that we're doing things too quickly, are going to have to adapt – or perish."

Olsky said the word 'perish' softly, almost in an undertone. Volovich thought he'd never heard it pronounced in such a menacing way.

"Certain people belong in another era," the General went on. "They're like dinosaurs. For example, my predecessor, a man of undeniable patriotism, outlived his usefulness. He was quite unable to adapt to new thinking. Is Epishev a dinosaur?"

Volovich didn't know what to say. Nor did Olsky appear to expect an answer, because he went on without waiting for one. "We need men who are flexible, Dimitri. Men who can alter their dried-out old attitudes and work for change – as well as their own advancement, of course. Do you see yourself as such a person?"

Their own advancement, Volovich thought. He liked the phrase. "I try to keep an open mind, General."

"That's all we ask." Olsky flipped the switch on the panel and told the driver to stop the car. There were small sailboats floating on the surface of the reservoir. Volovich remembered there was an aquatic sports club nearby.

"To the best of your knowledge, Dimitri, is Epishev still in the country?"

Volovich made a little gesture with his skinny fingers. Since he'd already said he didn't know where Viktor was, what more was he supposed to add?

"He didn't say anything to me about going abroad, General."

"When did you see him last?"

Volovich felt this question eddy around him like a treacherous little whirlpool. "Perhaps a week ago."

"A week." Olsky appeared to think this over. His look was inscrutable, though, an impression exaggerated somehow by the formidable shaved head. "So far as you're aware, Dimitri, does Epishev have any contact these days with General Greshko?"

Another tough one. Something delicate hung in the balance here. Volovich hesitated. "I don't believe so," he chose to say.

Olsky smiled. "Thank you, Dimitri. I've enjoyed our little talk. Would it be inconvenient if I dropped you here?"

Volovich wondered how many miles it was back to his apartment and whether a bus or a metro ran that way. It had been years since he'd travelled by public transportation. "It's no inconvenience, General," he said. After all, what could he have answered? *It's a fucking nuisance, Comrade Chairman*?

He opened the door, stepped on to the pavement. He watched the big black car vanish down the street. He had a sense of unfinished business, realising that his lie wouldn't hold up for long if General Olsky decided to scrutinise it. If General Olsky fine-tuned his microscope and placed Volovich's statement on an examination slide, the lie, fragile tissue as it was, wouldn't hold up *at all*.

When the car was on the Volokolamsk Highway, General Olsky opened the smoked-glass panel that segregated him from his driver, Colonel Chebrikov, and leaned forward.

"He's the same man," the Colonel said, without turning his face.

"Are you absolutely sure?"

"Completely, General. Lieutenant Volovich visited

General Greshko in Zavidovo last night, accompanied by Colonel Epishev. The meeting lasted about an hour."

Olsky sat back in his seat again, staring out at the streets, mulling over Volovich's lies. Here he had the bits and pieces of a puzzle, like one of those twisted metal problems you were supposed to solve by separating the parts. Volovich and his Colonel, the enigmatic Viktor Epishev, visit Greshko late at night. Within three hours of that meeting, Viktor Epishev goes to see a man called Yevenko, a criminal, in Moscow. Yevenko, the Printer, is instructed to make a passport bearing Epishev's likeness though not his name. The passport is West German, the bearer's name Grunwald. Epishev takes the false passport, leaves.

"Do you believe the Printer's story?" Olsky asked.

Chebrikov said, "The man's in a tight spot, General. He needs all the leverage he can get. Currency crime isn't a joke. He's facing twenty years hard labour, perhaps even the firing-squad. Besides, he did have those photographs. And the stamp."

Olsky shut his eyes, remembering how he'd gone to the Printer's place of business only an hour ago, a grubby basement room in a very old building, a windowless space that smelled of strong chemicals and dyes. There, Yevenko, a dirty little man with ink-stained fingers and the blackest nails Olsky had ever seen, had produced copies of passport pictures he said he'd taken of Colonel Epishev very early that day. He'd forged the German passport, put Epishev's photograph inside, then embossed it with the official passport stamp of the Federal Republic of Germany – which he then also produced with a flourish, flashing it under Stefan Olsky's nose, as if to prove something beyond all doubt.

Yevenko's place was a treasure-house of stolen artifacts. Official stamps from various countries, blank passports from such places as Turkey and West Germany and Malta, three blank identification cards from Interpol, one from the US Federal Bureau of Investigation, and another from the Irish Garda. A man could visit Yevenko and walk out within ten minutes with a new identity and even a job in a foreign police force.

"So where did this mysterious Grunwald go?" Olsky asked.

"We're working on an answer to that one, General."

Olsky opened his eyes. "What does Volovich remind you of, Colonel?"

Chebrikov was quiet for a time. Then he said, "A fish."

"I thought he was a little more wormlike, personally."

"An eel, then," said the Colonel.

"Close enough. Now take me home." Stefan Olsky closed the smoked-glass window, enjoying the sense of isolation he had in the back of the limousine. It was a place where a man might be alone to think. He wasn't allowed such a luxury because his telephone rang and he reached for it at once, hearing the voice of the Major in charge of all KGB computer operations.

"I believe we've discovered what you're looking for, Comrade Chairman," the Major said.

Olsky thanked the man, hung up the receiver, then informed his driver that his destination had changed.

London

It was almost dark, and the rain had stopped, and the wind in the square had died finally. Frank Pagan made a phone call to Tommy Witherspoon, who was not in his office. A plummy voice informed Pagan that Mr Witherspoon, in an emergency, might be found in his club on Piccadilly. The voice added a reminder that this was Sunday, the day of Mr Witherspoon's rest, and any interruption of the man would have to be thoroughly justified.

Pagan put the receiver down. He looked inside the bedroom where Kristina Vaska lay on the bed, her back turned to him, a blanket pulled halfway over her body. Earlier, complaining of fatigue, she'd gone to lie down. Pagan wasn't sure if she was sleeping. He stepped quietly inside the bedroom. She turned her face towards him, blinking in the square of light that fell from the living-room. *A woman in my bed*, Pagan thought. *Somebody I hardly know, somebody attractive to me*. It was a novel consideration.

He sat on the edge of the mattress. "I have to go out for a while."

"Do you want me to stay here?" she asked.

"I don't want you to disappear on me."

"I don't like the idea of being alone, Frank. What if Epishev decides to come back?"

Pagan doubted that the Russian would return. By this time, Epishev might have concluded that Pagan's apartment was the last place of all to visit, that if Kristina Vaska had recognised him then Pagan would have taken precautions. Perhaps Epishev even imagined that policemen were cunningly concealed in the neighbourhood, ready for a reappearance.

"I'll arrange for somebody to keep an eye on you," Pagan said. He reached under the bed and took his gun from the shoebox. He stuck it inside a holster, which he strapped to his body so that the gun hung at the base of his spine. "But I really don't think he's going to be careless enough to come here again."

She still looked doubtful. He picked up the bedside phone, punched out the number of the local police station and asked for a certain Sergeant Crowley. When the Sergeant came on the line, Pagan used his intimidating Special Branch voice to ask that a patrol car be placed outside his home. Crowley had an ordinary cop's attitude toward Special Branch, which was the resentment of a commoner for the aristocracy. So far as Crowley, a decent if plodding man, was concerned, the princes of Special Branch thought the sun shone out of their bloody royal arses. But he agreed to Pagan's request anyway.

Pagan put the receiver down. "That takes care of that."

"How long will you be gone?" she asked.

"An hour or two." Pagan gazed down at her. Then he leaned over and kissed her forehead impulsively. She didn't seem at all surprised by the gesture. She caught his hand and held it and looked up into his eyes. There was something troubled in her expression, a guarded quality.

It was wrong here, he thought. This was the room the dead had claimed, and it was damned hard to wrest ownership from a corpse. He stepped away from the bed, releasing himself from her hand.

"Hurry back," she said.

He crossed the living-room floor and stood at the window until he saw the patrol car appear. It parked in the street below. He returned to the bedroom. "When I leave, slide the deadbolt in place."

"Be careful, Frank." She sat upright, brushed hair away from her forehead. She looked just then as lovely as he'd ever seen her, and he was held in place a moment by a sudden enchantment about which there was a frailty, a sense of illusion, as if she might simply vanish were he to go any closer to her. Pagan, unexpectedly touched by his own reaction, stepped out of the flat.

When he reached the foot of the stairs he heard the sound of the deadbolt being slammed firmly into place. He went cautiously out to the street, glancing at the police car, and the faces of the two young cops, as he walked to his Camaro. The dark square across the way, the lit windows of houses, the still trees – all this familiarity, changed by his consciousness of a man called Epishev, pressed uneasily against him.

Tommy Witherspoon had a slow, disdainful laugh, a *hor hor hor* sound Pagan associated with wealth. If it were possible for somebody to laugh down his nose, Tommy Witherspoon was that person. He wore a black blazer and white slacks and an old school tie Pagan was proud not to recognise. Tommy belonged in his club, you could see that. He merged with the antique wood and the soft lamps and the ancient portraits of past members that hung from the walls and the indefinable ambience of old money and yesterday's empires.

"I mention Epishev and you get hysterical," Pagan said, uncomfortable in this whole milieu, which reeked to him of privileges that, in most cases, hadn't been earned, but rather bestowed, passed down from father to son along the infallible circuitry of blood.

Tommy Witherspoon was drinking madeira. His lips were stained, which indicated he'd been imbibing most of the day. Half-drunk like this, he was even more haughty and less charming than he'd been during Pagan's last encounter with him in Green Park. Alcohol brought out all his worst traits – loftiness of manner and a bristling unshakable self-confidence.

Witherspoon said, "I laugh, Pagan. But there's some slight pity in the sound."

"Pity?"

"If your man is really Epishev, as you lay claim, then I'm sorry for you, old chap. He's a tough cookie, if I may venture an Americanism. I wouldn't like to have Eppie poking around in my neck of the woods."

Eppie, Pagan thought. Tommy Witherspoon's way of talking suggested he was *this close* to where all the skeletons were buried. Keeping secrets along Whitehall, striding discreet corridors all day long, did something to a man. It made him smug, and pompous, and insufferably patronising.

"Just tell me what you know, Tommy. I absorb it, get up, shuffle off into the night. Dead simple."

Witherspoon sipped his madeira and frowned. When he spoke he did so off-handedly, like a man accustomed to believing that his utterances were pure pearls and all his listeners swine. "There are those who say, Pagan, that Uncle Viktor is a creation of the Central Committee. Some argue that if he didn't exist in *actuality*, the Central Committee would have invented him. A man with Epishev's set of mind, which one may accurately call neanderthal, could well have been created by the inner members of the former Politburo. If they wanted to bring forth a model of Communist man, a sort of Marxenstein, if you catch my drift, they might have hammered together dear old Uncle, who has bought lock, stock and bloody barrel the whole Marxist-Leninist waffle. With jam on it."

Witherspoon leaned across the small round table. Pagan noticed how he propped an elbow into a faint ring of wine left by the base of his glass. Two old dodderers, relics of Empire, moved past the table, muttering something mean-spirited about women.

Witherspoon said, "Uncle has been kicking around for a good many years, usually performing dirty tasks assigned to him by the soon to be late, if not lamented, General Greshko."

"I read somewhere that Greshko had retired," Pagan remarked, remembering a couple of newspaper articles that had appeared in recent months about the General, who had been something of a survivor, guiding the KGB through several Soviet regimes. Pragmatic, cunning, one of the old guard – these were the words and phrases that had been applied to Greshko.

"Retirement is a euphemism, in Soviet fashion, for being ousted. Epishev was well and truly Greshko's boy. Greshko played the pipes and Uncle danced to any tune going. Some of the melodies were more than a little unpleasant, Pagan."

"Such as?"

Witherspoon caught the waiter's eye and had his glass refilled. "Greshko assigned him the task of rooting out and silencing, usually for all eternity, anyone who raised his or her voice against the system. I understand Uncle carried out his tasks with the zeal of the true believer. Murder, blackmail, deportations to labour camps without possibility of parole – Uncle used everything in his copious bag of tricks to silence the small voices of dissent. He was very very good at this. He's responsible, one way or another, for thousands of deaths. As for imprisonments, well, the figures are beyond computation."

"A butcher," Pagan said.

"Ah, the endearing simplicity of the policeman's mind. My dear Pagan, you can't just hang one of your banal little labels on the fellow. Butchery is only a part of Epishev's repertoire. As I understand it," – and Witherspoon gave the impression that his understanding was the only correct one – "Epishev is something of a chameleon. He blends with backgrounds. He changes colours. He's apparently not without charm, albeit of a deadly nature. He's the sort of chap who smiles apologetically as he tightens the garotte round your adam's apple. More than a butcher, Pagan. He has much blood on his hands, undeniabl*eee*, but he has a system of very hard beliefs that justify anything he does. And when did you last hear of a butcher slaughtering a cow because the animal didn't happen to share the butcher's philosophy?"

Pagan didn't enjoy being talked down to by Tommy Witherspoon. He was being made to feel like a kid learning the alphabet by staring at letters on wooden cubes. "What's his situation since Greshko was put out to pasture?"

"Who can say? Uncle Viktor belongs in the old camp, Pagan. Whether he can survive the new regime is anybody's guess. Maybe the new boys will want to sweep him under the rug because he's a leftover from the past, and therefore embarrassing. But if he's running around *our* green and pleasant land, as you say, then presumably he still has a function to carry out."

Pagan gazed across the large room. The long windows were dark. On Piccadilly streetlamps were lit.

"I must say, though, I find it *awfully* hard to believe Epishev's here."

"You mean you find it hard to believe you didn't *know* about it, Tommy."

Witherspoon fixed Pagan with an inebriated grin that was very cold. "I really can't see anybody sending him overseas *unless* it was Greshko. If the organ-grinders of the KGB wanted somebody to do some dirty work in London, I have the feeling they'd have sent a younger chap, somebody completely unknown to us."

"Is it possible Greshko *did* send him? Is it possible Epishev came here on business that wasn't officially sanctioned by the present leadership of the KGB?"

Witherspoon looked suddenly befuddled, half-gone in an alcoholic haze. "Anything's *possible*, Pagan. Greshko had a vast power base, and that doesn't just simply *disintegrate* in a matter of a few months. A great many people over there aren't enamoured of the new boys in the Kremlin, don't forget. But the general impression I keep getting is that resistance to the new chaps isn't terribly well-organised, more a kind of choral moaning than anything else. But I can't imagine Epishev aligning himself with a dying old man like Greshko."

"If Greshko didn't send him, and if Epishev's an embarrassment to the KGB these days, then who gave him orders to come here? Did he make the trip of his own free will?"

"As I keep trying to intimate, Pagan, Soviet intentions are frequently too murky for our Western minds to fathom. Especially, it would seem, the mind of a policeman. Cops are fine when it comes to handing out speeding tickets, I daresay, but let them loose in the big world of political subtleties and they're quite at a loss."

Pagan stood up. He wondered how much more of Tommy he could take without doing something utterly uncivilised. "Is there a photograph of him?" he asked.

Witherspoon laughed until his eyes watered. "Lord, no. A photograph of Epishev! I know people in the field who'd give a year's salary for a likeness of Uncle Viktor! A photograph of Epishev! Really, Pagan. What do you think this is? Do you think the KGB supplies us with pics and bios of its top people? Dear oh dear oh dear."

Pagan placed his hands on the edge of the small table. He had one more question. He waited until

Witherspoon's derisive laughter had finally subsided before he asked, "Is the name Norbert Vaska familiar to you?"

"Afraid not. Should it be?"

"Just curious, Tommy." Pagan started to turn away. As he did so, he couldn't help yielding to a mischievous temptation. He allowed his hip to collide with the table, spilling Witherspoon's glass and sending a fair amount of madeira into the man's lap.

"*Ooops,*" Pagan said, a little dazzled by his own pettiness. But it was more than just a small strike at Tommy Witherspoon, it was a reflection of his general frustration, the unanswered questions that crowded his head.

Witherspoon stood up quickly. "Oh, really, Pagan. That was frightfully clumsy of you," and he began to dab at his groin with a handkerchief.

"Sorry, Tommy. Really."

Witherspoon glared at him. "Did you do that deliberately?"

"Hardly. What do you take me for?"

Witherspoon let his wine-red handkerchief drop on the table. He looked highly doubtful. "I've got an answer for that, Pagan. I take you for somebody who's completely out of his league. I take you for somebody Uncle Viktor could have for his bloody breakfast and still not be satisfied. I've got a suggestion for you – let intelligence handle all this. Let the big boys cope with Epishev. You're strictly second division, old chap."

Pagan smiled. "Your nastiness is showing, Tommy. If you're not careful, they'll blackball you out of this place for failing to show civility to your guests."

"Guests? I didn't *ask* you here, Pagan."

"If you had, Tommy, I wouldn't have come." And Pagan turned, moving past the nodding heads of dozing old men in the direction of the lobby. When he looked back he saw a waiter hurrying towards Witherspoon's table with a dripping sponge.

Business as usual, Pagan thought. The servant classes cleaning up the mess made by the overlords. Wondering bleakly when this whole calcified system might change, Pagan stepped out into Piccadilly.

Ninety minutes after Frank Pagan had gone, Kristina Vaska lay in the darkened bedroom with her eyes closed. What she was remembering was the way Pagan had looked at her, first in the park, then just before he left the apartment, an unmistakable look, a light in the eye that had all the hard clarity of a gem. Frank Pagan, who liked to think he played his cards close to his chest, who imagined he went through the world with tight-lipped wariness, had dropped his defences – he had become, on both occasions, *obvious*.

There was a quality to Pagan that drew her, a combination of self-confidence and a lack of polish, a sense of rough and smooth coming awkwardly together in the man. He reminded her of a stone she'd once found on the bank of the Pirita River, a curious stone that seemed to have been welded out of two distinct elements – glassy on one side, gritty on the other, an unlikely amalgam, a small paradox of nature. That was how she saw Frank Pagan.

She hadn't intended to like him. She hadn't set out to be drawn to him. She wondered what kind of lover he'd be, and she imagined honesty, an absence of subterfuge, quiet consideration.

She sat upright, looked at the bedside clock. It was ten o'clock. She took off her clothes and dropped them on the floor and headed in the direction of the bathroom. She glanced at the door as she passed, unconsciously checking the security of the deadbolt. She was going to be safe here. Epishev had no means of getting inside. And if Epishev couldn't come through the front door, then her past couldn't gain entrance either, that nightmare that had taken concrete shape in a rainy London street fifteen years and a thousand miles from where it had first begun.

She imagined her father's face, but there were times

when she couldn't see him with any clarity. There were panicked moments when the face wouldn't come to her, but remained in shadow, an ancient ghost she couldn't summon. And then she had a sense of internal slippage, as if her memories had begun to disintegrate. She shut her eyes, imagined Norbert Vaska's hands, strong and firm, the long fingers that brushed a strand of hair from his daughter's face or held her by the waist and drew her up from the ground – the fingers, yes, but the face, she couldn't see the face except in brief glimpses, like a holograph fading.

As she drew back the shower-curtain, turned on the faucet, adjusted the temperature, she heard the telephone. Her first impulse was to ignore it. Then she thought the least she could do was to take a message.

She wrapped herself in a towel, went back into the living-room, lifted the receiver. ''Frank Pagan's residence,'' she said. Residence was too genteel a word for what Pagan had here. It conjured up visions of order, serenity, well-oiled servants going smoothly about their duties.

The man who answered introduced himself as Martin Burr. He said he had an urgent need to talk to Frank Pagan.

11

Riga, Latvia

Three Soviet Army trucks with full headlights burning clattered along Suvorov Street toward the Daugava River. It was dark and the covered vehicles moved with the illusory urgency peculiar to military trucks, a briskness that suggested high speeds to anyone watching. In reality, the trucks were travelling at no more than forty miles an hour. They crossed the river and entered the area of Riga known as the Pardaugava, the industrialised left bank of the sprawling city. They passed an isolated green area, a rather rundown park, and then an old cemetery, beyond which there stretched a district of factories and warehouses.

Some of these factories were new, but there was a general deterioration the farther the vehicles travelled. They left behind the kind of showplace industrial plants so beloved by Intourist officials and Party chairmen and penetrated a darker, less attractive area of early twentieth-century warehouses and factories and sites where old buildings had been gutted. The air smelled of mildew, and the corrosive aroma of rust, and from elsewhere, borne on a breeze, the salty suggestion of the Bay of Riga. The trucks rolled down streets that became progressively more narrow, little more than lanes built in an age when horse-drawn cabs pulled factory owners from one business to the next, and men filled with inchoate hatreds and resentments planned revolution in sweatshops.

Killing their lights, the trucks stopped finally in a

dead-end street, the kind of place city mapmakers conveniently overlook and then ultimately forget and future generations of city planners rediscover with total amazement. For many minutes nobody emerged from the vehicles, which were parked close to a decrepit building that over the years had housed companies manufacturing window-shades, then shoelaces, then tobacco pipes, and most recently camera lenses. It was abandoned now, although four years ago it had been briefly used as a rehearsal studio for an outlawed rock and roll band called Gulag.

A door opened and a man appeared with a flashlight. He blinked it twice, switched it off. The drivers, dressed in the uniforms of the Soviet Army, emerged from the trucks and hurried towards the building. From the rear of each truck, from under canvas, other soldiers appeared. A mixed crew – a couple of corporals, a sergeant, a major, and a colonel.

The interior of the old factory had a basement, reached by descending a staircase that hung on the crumbling wall in a precarious way. The man with the flashlight went down carefully, warning the soldiers to follow him with caution. The basement, lit by a single kerosene lamp, was filled with all the detritus of all the industries that had ever occupied the building – lengths of twine, slivers of broken glass, unfinished pipes and stemless bowls, tassels of the sort that hung to blinds. There were also thirty wooden crates, the only things in the basement that interested the men.

The man with the flashlight kicked aside the lid of one crate and the uniformed men gathered round in the yellow-blue paraffin flare to look. The weapons, American M-16 rifles, Swiss SIG-AMT and Belgian FN auto rifles, lay in no particular order. There were handguns in some of the other crates – Brownings, Colts, Lugers – and ammunition. One crate contained Czech-made grenades, another Uzi pistols. It was as if whoever had purchased this supply of arms had scoured all the darker bazaars of the international weapons market, buying a lot here, another lot there, an oddment in a third place.

The men were thoroughly delighted with the delivery. They knew the number of weapons was comparatively puny, the task ahead of them overwhelming, but the guns represented support from a world beyond the Soviet Union, and that made the men both glad and touched, and less isolated than they'd ever felt before.

The man with the flashlight, who was known only as Marcus, said they had better hurry. He didn't like staying in this basement any longer than he had to, and the crates had to be moved and the sooner the better. His nervousness was contagious. The uniformed men worked quickly and silently, carrying the crates up from the basement and placing them in the trucks, under canvas. The whole operation took about five minutes before the trucks were ready to roll again. One was headed for Tallinn in Estonia, a second for Vilnius in Lithuania, and a third had only a short distance to travel – a concealed place in the forest around Kemeri, some thirty miles from Riga.

The men took only a few moments to part, even though they knew it was highly unlikely they'd ever meet again. There was handshaking, some edgy laughter, some back-slapping, but mainly there was a sense of grim fatalism about them. Their trips were hazardous ones, their ultimate actions bound to be deadly. But they had no qualms about dying. Even so, there was a moment in which the agitated banter stopped, a profound silence of the kind in which people realise, as if for the very first time, the exact nature of their commitment.

And then the trucks left the area, travelling in convoy for several miles until they reached the bank of the river again, the place where each vehicle went its own way. Headlights flashed three times in the dark, a signal that might have meant good luck or farewell. They moved away from one another now through the streets of the city, past the dark windows of closed shops, unlit office towers, silent houses, past the eyes of patrolling militiamen who, if they paid much attention at all, would see only army trucks hurrying on some military task, and the faces of uniformed men in the high cabs.

These same militiamen wouldn't have any way of knowing that the trucks had been stolen weeks ago, that their cargoes were illegal and their registration plates fake, that the transportation dockets carried by the men were forged and that the men themselves were no soldiers – but a collection of assorted dissidents in stolen uniforms, Baltic deserters from the Soviet Army in Afghanistan, some students from the University of Vilnius, a couple of patriots from the last days of the old Brotherhood, and a few men who had spent time in Soviet jails for their democratic beliefs.

Nor could the uninquiring policemen have any idea of how the weapons inside the trucks were to be used or the blood that might be shed a couple of days from now.

Manhattan

Dressed in a grey Italian suit and matching homburg, Mikhail Kiss moved along Fifth Avenue. It was ten o'clock and the night had shed some of the clamminess that had characterised the day. He looked down at his wedding-ring as he headed in the direction of Columbus Circle, which loomed up just before him. He hadn't removed the ring in more than forty years and as he gazed at it he realised he'd come to think of it as a natural part of himself. It was a source of heartbreak, even after so much time had passed. But time didn't erase everything. Quite the opposite. Sometimes, through the years, things grew instead of diminishing. And Ingrida's face floated before him, spectral and lovely, and then he felt it, the old pain, the cutting sorrow, the sharp glass in his heart, and

what he pictured was how she'd died, with a Soviet
bullet buried in her chest.

He squeezed his eyes shut as he paused at a Don't Walk
sign. He hadn't seen Ingrida die, and what he knew was
only what he'd pieced together from rumour and gossip
in the early years of the 1950s. She'd been taken in a
truck, along with other women whose husbands were
suspected of guerilla activity against the great Russian
Empire, to a meadow outside the town of Paide in
central Estonia. There, the women had been made to
stand in a line, and then a machine-gunner, hidden
by trees, had opened fire. Kiss wondered if death
had come as a surprise to her or if somehow she'd
known it was going to happen, if she'd stepped into
that meadow and come face to face with the certainty
of her own end even before the gun had fired. What
the hell did it matter now? He had an image, and it
wouldn't leave him, and it was of Ingrida's face turned
up to a wintry Estonian sky and blood flowing from the
corner of her mouth and a fat fly, waxy and obscene,
alive, landing on her lips. *Ingrida, mu suda, mu hing. Ma
tunnen puudust sinu jarele.* Ingrida, my heart and soul.
I miss you.

For a very long time, even after he'd found his way
to the United States via Germany, he'd had a fantasy in
which he encountered the machine-gunner. Accidentally
– on the street, in a store, anywhere. And what he did in
this murderous hallucination was to tear the man apart,
to rip his limbs from his body, fibre by agonised fibre.
After years had passed, the fantasy started to assume
other forms. The gunman, after all, was only obeying
orders. And the official who issued the orders to the
gunman did so only because he was following policies
set by the Kremlin. Therefore, individuals weren't to
blame. It was the system, evil and corrupt, which
operated from behind the thick walls of the Kremlin
that was to blame. So Mikhail Kiss's fantasy had become
channelled elsewhere.

He passed the Lincoln Center, moving under lit street-lamps. Then he turned into a narrow street where he paused. Perhaps it was nothing more than the absence of lights, perhaps something he thought he detected in the shadows of doorways, but he was suddenly afraid. He looked back the way he'd come. He realised that the feeling didn't lie in the notion that some local KGB agent might be following him – instead, it was buried inside himself, in the coils of his own nerves. What if Carl Sundbach had been right and this whole affair was doomed? What if Romanenko had been carrying a message that was meant to cancel the project because something *had* gone wrong?

You grow old, he thought. You're thinking an old man's thoughts, fearful and silly. The truth of the matter was simple – he just didn't want to ponder the motives behind Aleksis's murder. Some disaffected emigrant, some crackpot with a pistol, a madman with a political axe to grind – Aleksis's killer might have been almost anyone. He didn't want to think, even for a moment, that anything could have gone wrong with the scheme *itself*. It would go ahead as planned. He and Romanenko had spent too long a time welding their network together, joining each link in secrecy, from the Finnish businessman who carried Kiss's letters to Helsinki to the radical human rights activist from Tartu who placed each communication inside an old windmill at the Wooden Buildings Museum on Vabaohumuuseumitee Road about two miles from Tallinn, from which place it would be retrieved by one or other of Aleksis's trusted associates and delivered to Romanenko. Sometimes, in moments of paranoia, Kiss wondered if along the way there might be a weak link, a treacherous coupling, somebody who revealed the letters to the KGB. But since the operation hadn't been stopped, and Romanenko hadn't been arrested, Kiss always assumed the network had never been penetrated.

He came to another narrow street now and the fear

passed as suddenly as it had come. He was in the vicinity of Fordham University, where expensive apartment buildings flourished on side-streets. He might have taken a more direct route to this neighbourhood than he'd done, but he never came here the same way twice. He crossed Amsterdam Avenue and went inside an old building, a former warehouse converted into studios and apartments.

He climbed to the third floor. At the end of the hallway he knocked on a door, which was opened almost at once by a man Kiss knew only as Iverson. He was probably in his late forties, but the lack of lines and creases, the lack of *animation* in the face made it impossible to guess. Kiss couldn't recall Iverson ever smiling or frowning. There was something decidedly spooky about the man, as if he had no inner life whatsoever, and that what you saw on his face was all there was. Kiss always thought of him as a *külm kala*, a cold fish.

The suite of rooms was completely devoid of furniture. There was white fitted carpet throughout and the walls were glossy white, reflecting the recessed lights. It was a strange apartment, Kiss thought, neat and always spotless, and yet without any sign of ever having been lived in. He assumed that Iverson used it only for these meetings. Kiss took off his homburg and wiped his damp forehead with his palm and considered how perfectly this empty apartment matched Iverson's personality.

"Do we go or don't we?" Iverson asked.

Always straight to the point, Kiss thought. For a moment he hesitated. He walked to the windows, which had a view of the dark river. A barge, bright yellow upon the blackness, floated past. *Do we go or don't we?*

Kiss turned and looked at the man. "We go," he said. *There. It was done. And there was no going back.*

"You've had confirmation?" Iverson asked.

"Yes," Kiss lied.

"I never had any doubts."

Kiss smiled now. What he felt was a rush of pure

relief, like a chemical flooding through his body. It was the sensation Americans called 'high'. He had a tangible sense of the network he'd created, an adrenalin flowing out of this building and through the darkness, a powerful vibrancy that went untrammelled across land and sea to stop, finally, in Moscow. He had a sense of all the links he'd spent years hammering into place coming together at last, as if each link had been galvanised suddenly by a surge of lightning.

Iverson leaned stiffly against a wall. Even the pin-striped suit he wore was bland and unremarkable. He was a man who courted the prosaic avidly. "All you have to do is make sure your man is in Norway. We'll take it from there." For the first time in any of their meetings, Kiss thought he detected an emotion in the man.

Iverson said, "Now it's finally happening, I've got this strange feeling in my gut. You ever ride a rollercoaster, Kiss? It's that kind of thing." And he allowed a very small smile to cross his lips. It looked as if it had been airbrushed on to his face.

Kiss had to come to understand that Iverson – who was either an officer in the United States Air Force or had been at one time, an anomaly Iverson deliberately failed to clarify – feared the Russians. But Kiss, whose focus was limited to three countries with an area of some sixty thousand square miles and a population of eight million, had no particular interest in Iverson's motives. Andres, who had maintained all kinds of connections in the armed forces, had brought Iverson in about eighteen months ago, saying he was a completely dependable man who could provide an essential service. And that recommendation was enough. Whether Iverson was acting alone, or whether he represented a consortium of men who shared his views, some shadowy congregation of figures who preferred to stay offstage, Kiss didn't know, even though he sometimes felt that Iverson was merely a spokesman. But without Iverson's help the whole scheme would have been more difficult, perhaps even impossible.

Strange bedfellows, Kiss thought. An old Baltic guerilla fighter and a mysterious figure with military connections who saw a way to undermine a regime he feared.

"Well," Iverson said. "I guess we don't see each other again."

He held his hand forward and Kiss shook it. Iverson's clasp was ice-cold, bloodless.

"*Nägemiseni*," Iverson said. Goodbye.

Kiss was touched by Iverson's effort to learn a word in Estonian, a language totally alien to him.

"I practised it," Iverson said.

"You did fine." Kiss, smiling, went towards the door. There he turned and said, "*Head aega*," which was also goodbye.

Iverson said, "One thing. We never met. We never talked. This apartment ceases to exist as soon as you step out the door. If you ever have any reason to come back to this place, and I hope you don't, you'll find strangers living here. And if anybody *ever* asks, Kiss, I don't know you from Adam."

London

Frank Pagan looked at the corpse of Danus Oates only in a fleeting way, before turning his back. Oates's splendid silk pyjamas were soaked with blood. Martin Burr, who had come up to London by fast car from the depths of Sussex – where on weekends he lived the life of an English country squire – gazed down at the body with sorrow.

"Damned shame," he said to Pagan and he swiped the air with his cane in a gesture of frustrated sadness. "I wish the cleaners would get here and remove the poor lad. Let's go into the living-room."

Frank Pagan followed Burr out of the bedroom. The

Commissioner sat in an armchair, propping his chin on his cane and gazing thoughtfully through the open door of the flat. A uniformed policeman stood on the landing and three neighbours – two emaciated women and a leathery man, the latter having discovered the body while making a social call – were trying to sneak a look inside the place with all the ghoulish enthusiasm of people who consider murder a spectator sport.

"Shut that bloody door, would you?" Burr asked.

Pagan did so. When they'd first come to Oates's flat, Pagan had told the Commissioner what he'd learned about Epishev from Kristina Vaska, and Burr had absorbed the information in silence. Now Pagan said, "The way I see it is Epishev came here because he'd learned Oates had worked on the translation. He wanted to know what Oates had found out. The answer was, of course, very little – a few lines of verse in an obscure language. What else could poor Oates say? Maybe all he could tell Epishev was that I had the thing in my possession – who knows? Epishev, covering his tracks like any dutiful assassin, killed him. And I was the next name on the list, because I'd come in contact with the verse as well."

"The damned poem's like a bloody fatal virus," Burr said angrily. "You touch it, you have a damned good chance of dying." He was genuinely shocked by this murder and the presence of a KGB killer in London, and the fact that his own dominion was tainted by international political intrigue. He liked, if not a calm life, then one of logic and order and watertight compartments.

Pagan stuck his hands in his pockets. "If it's a virus, it acts in very peculiar ways. The thing I haven't been able to figure out is why the KGB would want to come after people like Oates and myself. Obviously, they imagine I know something, and they don't *like* me knowing it, whatever the hell it is. But what's the big secret? If the Brotherhood's working on an act of terrorism against the Russians, let's say, why would the KGB want to destroy the people who might have evidence of it? Unless the KGB is involved in the plot as well – or at the very least doesn't want it to fail."

"And that's a rather odd line of reasoning, Frank."

Pagan agreed. He moved up and down the room in an agitated manner. He was remembering now how Witherspoon had talked about a struggle between the old regime and the new, and how Epishev had belonged in the Greshko camp along with the old power-brokers, those who had been sent scurrying into reluctant redundancy. It was an elusive thought, a sliver of a thing, but perhaps what was unfolding in front of him was some element of that power struggle, some untidy aspect of it, the ragged edges of a Soviet situation that had become inadvertently exported to England. He turned this over in his mind and he was about to mention the thought to Burr when the Commissioner said, "This Vaska lady. Do you think her information is on the level?"

"I had a few doubts at first," Pagan replied.

"But not now?"

"I'm not so sure."

"But you want to believe her."

"I think what she says about this Brotherhood and Romanenko's part in it is true. And I believe her when she says she came here in the hope of seeing Romanenko about her father. I also have the strong feeling she wasn't mistaken when she identified Epishev."

Oates's living-room was cluttered with very tasteful antiques. There was a photograph on one wall that depicted Danus, around the age of fifteen, in the straw-hat of a Harrow schoolboy. Fresh-faced, rather chubby at the cheeks, all innocence. Pagan paused in front of it, shaking his head. You couldn't begin to imagine Oates's doomed future from such a guilelessly plump face. It was all going to be sunshine and a steady if unspectacular climb up the ladder of the Foreign Office.

Martin Burr was quiet for a while. "If what she says about this Epishev chap is correct, I don't think this whole business belongs to us any more, Frank. I really don't think this is anything we can keep. If Epishev is KGB, it's no longer our game."

Pagan felt a flush of sudden irritation. "We give it away? Is that what you're saying?"

Martin Burr frowned. "I don't think we *give* it away, Frank. Rather, it's *taken* from us. There's a certain kind of skulduggery that doesn't come into our patch, Frank. We're not equipped. And you may bitch about it, but sooner or later you have to face the fact that intelligence will want this one. No way round it, I'm afraid. Besides, I understand our friend Witherspoon has already dropped the word about Epishev in the appropriate quarters."

"Good old Tommy."

"He was only doing what he perceived as his duty, no doubt."

"I bet." *Frank, you should have seen that one coming.* What else would Tommy do but run to his pals and gladly confide in them that Uncle Viktor had surfaced in England and that a certain incompetent policeman was handling things? Pagan could hear Witherspoon's voice, a cruel whisper, maybe a snide laugh, as he chatted to his chums in intelligence. *La-di-da, don't you know?*

"You want me to forget Epishev, is that it?"

"Frank," the Commissioner said. "Don't make me raise my voice. I'm trying to tell you how things are. Consider it a lesson in reality."

"I may forget about Epishev, Commissioner, but is he going to forget about me? I've got something he believes he wants. Keep that in mind."

Martin Burr shook his head. "Ah, yes, I'll expect you to turn your translation of the poem and the original over to intelligence when they ask for it – and they surely will – and then wipe the whole damned thing out of your mind."

"Commissioner, if Epishev shot Oates, that makes it murder in my book, and I don't give a damn if Epishev's KGB or an Elizabeth Arden rep, he's a bloody killer. What makes this very personal, *sir*, is the fact that this killer has my number. And you want me to turn him over to some characters who call themselves intelligence – which so far as I'm concerned is a terrible misnomer. Anyway, Epishev's going to believe I've got what he wants whether I turn it over or not."

Martin Burr ran a hand across his face. "Sometimes I see a petulantly stubborn quality in you that appals me."

Pagan knew he was playing this wrongly, that he was coming close to alienating the Commissioner, who was really his only ally at the Yard. He took a couple of deep breaths, in through the nostrils and out through the mouth – a technique that was supposed to relax you, according to a book he'd once read on yoga. But spiritual bliss and all the bloody breathing exercises in the world weren't going to alleviate his frustration.

The Commissioner said, "It upsets me, too. I want you to know that. I wish there was some other way."

"Then let me stay with it."

"There's nothing I can do. I wish it could be otherwise. But sooner or later, Frank, I'm going to feel certain pressures from parties that I don't have to name. And I'll bow to them, because that's the way things are. Those chaps know how to press all the right buttons."

"I could always work with them," Pagan said half-heartedly.

Martin Burr smiled. "The idea of you working with *anyone* is rather amusing."

"I could give it a try."

The Commissioner shook his head. "Damn it all, how many ways can I tell you this? Intelligence doesn't like the common policeman. Let's leave it there."

Pagan opened a decanter of cognac that sat on an antique table. He poured himself a small glass. There had to be some kind of solution to all this, something the Commissioner would accept. But Martin Burr, even though he'd complained about Pagan's stubbornness, could be pretty damned intractable himself. It was a knot, and Pagan couldn't see how to untie it. What he felt was that he was being brushed carelessly aside, and he didn't like the sensation at all.

The Commissioner reached for the decanter now and helped himself to a generous measure. He returned to his armchair and turned the balloon glass slowly around in his hand. He said, "I like you, Frank, perhaps because I think your heart's in the right place. Even at your worst, I've never questioned either your heart or your integrity. But this – " and Martin Burr made a sweeping gesture with his hand – "this tale of a Baltic clique that a young gal weaves and the presence of this Epishev and a dead Communist up in Scotland into the bargain, all *this*, my dear fellow, is not your private property, alas. Do we understand one another?"

"Perhaps," Pagan said, and drained his glass. The cognac had eased only a little of the pressure inside him.

Martin Burr smacked his lips. "Let's take some air, Frank. I don't want to be here when the cleaners and the fingerprint boys come. They tend to reduce death to a business, which I always find unseemly."

Pagan followed the Commissioner out of the flat and down the stairs, past the goggling neighbours and their questions. Outside in the early morning darkness, Martin Burr stood under a streetlamp and leaned on his cane. The neighbourhood was silent and sedate in that way of well-heeled neighbourhoods everywhere.

"Is she pretty?" the Commissioner asked suddenly.

"What's that got to do with anything?"

"Touchy, touchy, Frank. All I'm saying is that human nature, being the general old screw-up it is, sometimes allows a fair face to turn a man's head. Has she turned yours?"

"Hardly," Pagan replied.

"Just watch yourself. Subject closed." The Commissioner smiled like a one-eyed owl. "As for this Brotherhood, how much does the young lady know?"

"Less than I'd like."

"Intriguing, though. The idea of some old fellows plotting against the Russians after all this time. Makes you wonder what they're up to. And then there's the wretch Kiviranna. Who sent him to kill Romanenko? Too many unanswered questions, Frank."

Pagan detected something in Martin Burr, a quality of curiosity that wouldn't leave him. Even if he was about to turn the Epishev affair over to the lords of intelligence, Martin Burr was still intrigued by it all, more so perhaps than he really wanted to admit. The old cop, Pagan thought. The scent in the nostrils. The mysteries. The rush of adrenalin. Martin Burr was animated, perhaps even hooked.

"I'm still thinking aloud, you understand, Frank, but if Epishev is hunting down this piece of paper, then he knew that Romanenko left the Soviet Union with it in his possession – reasonable assumption? Question – if it's *so* damned important that it gets Oates killed, why was Romanenko allowed to leave with the poem in the first place? Answer – because the KGB *wanted* him to make the delivery. Is that also reasonable? It implies that Aleksis, either willingly or unwittingly, was working for the KGB."

"Or at least for certain KGB personnel," Pagan remarked quietly.

With a rather thoughtful look, Martin Burr stared up into the light from the overhead lamp, where a flurry of moths battered themselves to pulp against the bulb. "Are you positing the existence of factions within that venerable organisation, Frank? Can of worms, old chap. Somebody else's can."

"I don't know exactly what I'm positing," Pagan replied. Can of worms, he thought. He kicked a pebble from the pavement and heard it roll across the narrow street. For somebody about to give up a case, Martin Burr was fretting over it more than a little.

"Pity to turn it over, Frank."

"Pity's not strong enough," Pagan said. How could

he conceivably walk away from this? More to the point, how could Martin Burr expect that of him?

The Commissioner glanced at his wristwatch. As he did so, a taxi came along the street, slowing as it approached the lamp-post where Pagan and Burr stood. Ted Gunther, the man from the American Embassy, emerged from the vehicle. He paid the driver and the cab slid away. Gunther, wearing a suit over striped pyjamas that were plainly visible at his cuffs, looked apologetic as he entered the circle of light.

"They said at the Yard I'd find you here." He blinked behind his thick glasses. "I hope I'm not interrupting anything."

"Nothing that can't wait," the Commissioner said in the manner of a man whose weekend has been totally ruined anyhow.

Gunther scratched his head. He'd obviously been roused from his bed and had hurried here. His crewcut was flattened in patches across his skull and there was an excited little light in his large eyes. He was also slightly short of breath. "I just received the information you asked for about Jacob Kiviranna, and I thought you'd want it right away. I pulled a few strings, called some old favours home."

"You got some poor schmucks to work on a Sunday for you," Pagan said.

"More or less. I sent an inquiry out over the wire immediately after we talked and I made a couple of phonecalls." Gunther took a couple of sheets of paper from his coat pocket and tipped them towards the glow of the streetlamp. He reminded Pagan of somebody raised in the dead of night to get up and make an impromptu speech, somebody who has welded together a few odd phrases but hasn't had time to develop a theme.

"Let me just read you what I've got," Gunther said. "Kiviranna lived in Brooklyn – "

"Brooklyn?" Pagan asked. He remembered that Kristina had told him that some members of the

Brotherhood had settled in Brooklyn in the 1950s. He found himself stimulated suddenly, his interest aroused the way it always was when he confronted correspondences and connections, even when they consisted only of thin threads, such as this one.

"Brooklyn," Gunther said in a slightly testy way, as if he resented having his narrative interrupted. "He had no known family – he was apparently smuggled out of the Baltic as a baby by relatives who are now dead. We don't know anything about his parents. He worked as a freelance carpenter, drifting from job to job, making sure he was paid in cash for his labours. Cash is always hard to trace, and it's easy not to declare it, which meant that Kiviranna managed to steer clear of the scrutiny of our Internal Revenue Service. In other words, for all his adult life, Kiviranna paid no taxes. In fact, I'd say he might have avoided all public records of his existence if it hadn't been for his jail sentences. To begin with, he did five days in 1973 for public nuisance."

"Meaning what?" Pagan asked.

Gunther read from his sheets. "He urinated on a diplomatic car registered to the Soviet Mission in Manhattan then he tried to punch his way inside the Mission itself."

"He didn't like Russians," Pagan said drily, and glanced at Martin Burr, whose face was expressionless. But Pagan had the distinct sense that something was churning inside the Commissioner's head, that even as Gunther recited Kiviranna's history Burr was partly elsewhere.

"It's a running theme in his life," Gunther agreed. "In 1974 he attacked a policeman outside the Soviet Embassy in Washington. In 1977, he drove a motorcycle into a limousine occupied by the Soviet Ambassador, causing considerable damage both to himself and the vehicle."

"A kamikaze sort," Pagan remarked.

Gunther swatted a moth away. "He did five months for that little escapade and underwent psychiatric evaluation. Which . . ." Here Gunther shuffled his papers.

"Which revealed that Kiviranna was something of a loner, didn't join clubs, didn't make friends, felt inferior, that kind of thing."

Predictable, Pagan thought. Assassins tended to be loners. They weren't usually renowned for having social graces and joining clubs.

"In 1980 he became involved in narcotics. He was busted for possession of heroin. Probation, more psychiatric evaluation. Then he appears to have behaved himself until 1984, when he formed an attachment with a woman, or thought he did – the lady thought otherwise. Kiviranna became obsessed with her. When she spurned him, he slit his wrists. He was committed for a period to a psychiatric unit in upstate New York and diagnosed as schizophrenic."

Schizophrenic. What else? Pagan felt impatient. Nothing he'd heard here was compelling enough to explain Gunther's appearance after midnight. There was nothing spectacular in any of this. Why hadn't Gunther waited until morning? The eager ally, Pagan thought. Throwing on his suit over his pyjamas, making haste in the darkness. Pagan thought suddenly of Kristina Vaska in his apartment, and the patrol car in the street, and he realised he wanted to be away from this place and back home with the woman. A little twinge he recognised as something akin to panic rose up inside him.

"He was released in 1985, tried to contact the woman in 1986, was rejected a second time, then he attacked the Soviet Ambassador to the United Nations. Somehow, he managed to smuggle himself inside the UN building, waited for the Ambassador to appear, then stabbed him with a flick-knife. The wounds were superficial, thankfully. He got two years for that one. He was released only five months ago."

Gunther folded the sheets. "That's the story, gentlemen."

Pagan sniffed the night air. He knew why the narrative didn't satisfy him. There was a missing element, and that was the shadowy figure who'd been Kiviranna's accomplice, the person who sent Jake overseas to a rainy Scottish city with a gun in his hand. It was like looking upon the bare bones of a life, a bloodless synopsis from which all detail has been omitted and an important character suppressed.

"You've been very helpful," Martin Burr said to Gunther.

Pagan made a small noise of gratitude because he felt he had to, but he still couldn't keep from thinking that this brief history was hardly worth getting up in the middle of the night to deliver. It rang a slightly false note, only he wasn't sure why. It was as if Gunther had been commanded to deliver this scant information by the powers over him. A sop to the Yard from its Americans chums, Pagan thought. Sheer condescension. No, it was his own state of mind, he decided. It was frustration that made him create whole chapters out of thin nuances.

The three men were quiet for a time as a slight wind picked up along the street and blew through greenery. Martin Burr took a small cheroot from his jacket and lit it, cupping one hand against the breeze.

He smiled at Ted Gunther and asked, "Do we know the name of the woman who treated poor Jake so callously?"

"I don't have that information," Gunther answered.

"Is it something you can find out?"

"I guess. I don't see a problem there."

"Mmmm." Martin Burr tossed his cheroot away, barely smoked. He prodded the pavement with the tip of his cane, then he turned to Frank Pagan, who recognised the Commissioner's *mmm* sound. It indicated an emerging decision, a step he was about to take – but only after due consideration of the protocols involved. Pagan was apprehensive all at once, waiting for Martin Burr to continue.

The Commissioner said, "There's a nice American word to describe Kiviranna, and I think it's patsy.

Somebody used him to kill Romanenko. Somebody used Kiviranna's apparently bottomless hatred of the Soviets. Directed him, shall we say, although he clearly needed very little direction. The question I have is this – did the chap who sent Jake all the way to kill Romanenko *know* what Aleksis had in his possession? Was that the reason he wanted Romanenko dead? Did he want the message to go undelivered? And if that was the case, how did he know Romanenko was carrying anything in the first place?"

Burr looked up into the lamp, staring at the suicidal mazurka of moths. Then he said, "Do you see where I'm leading, Frank?"

It was dawning on Pagan, and he wasn't sure he liked the light that was beginning to fill his brain. *You sly old bastard, Martin*, he thought, but he said nothing.

Martin Burr grinned. He glanced at Gunther, as if he'd just remembered the man's presence, then he returned his mischievous one-eyed stare to Pagan. "I may have to hand Epishev over to other parties, Frank. But I don't have to give them Jacob Kiviranna, do I? He's dead, after all. And intelligence isn't likely to give a tinker's curse about him. I rather think Kiviranna, who did commit a murder, is our pigeon, and ours alone. The man wasn't some bloody KGB villain, after all. He was a common killer, exactly the kind we specialise in."

The Commissioner pressed his fingertips against his eyepatch. "We're perfectly entitled to examine Kiviranna's background, Frank. We're perfectly within our sphere of influence to look into his mysterious life. Nobody's going to take that away from us. And who knows? Perhaps something in the fellow's history will clarify certain matters that are baffling us at the moment. Perhaps you'll even learn more about this odd fellowship – what's it called?"

You know damn well what it's called, Pagan thought. "The Brotherhood, Commissioner."

Gunther had discreetly drifted several yards away, and

stood beyond the reach of lamplight, as if he sensed a private conversation he shouldn't be eavesdropping.

Pagan saw it all now, and he wasn't exactly happy with it. "You get me out of the way, which leaves things open for intelligence. And at the same time you're offering me a bone which may just have some meat on it – enough at least for me to chew on for a time."

"You're an insightful fellow," Martin Burr said. "Like I said, Frank, you may turn something up that will surprise us all."

"You want to have your cake and eat it," Pagan said. "You should've been a politician."

"I'd slit my throat first." Martin Burr looked at Gunther. "How's the weather this time of year in New York, Ted?" he asked.

V.G. Epishev stood for a time in the centre of the darkened square. The rain had blown away, leaving the darkness damp. There were few lights in the windows of the houses around the square – but in what he took to be the windows of Pagan's apartment a lamp burned behind a thick curtain. Epishev parted a tangle of shrubbery, hearing his feet squelch in soft black mud. Nearby, a flying creature – bat, bird, he couldn't tell – flapped between branches.

He moved under trees, stepping closer to the street, glancing up at the lit windows, then observing the police car which had been parked in the same place for hours. He made out the shapes of two policemen inside the vehicle. One, smoking a cigarette, let his hand dangle from the open window. Epishev walked close to the low stone wall.

That afternoon, when he'd first seen Pagan with the woman, he'd driven back to his hotel in Bayswater – a greasy room, an anonymous box overlooking an overgrown yard – and he'd lain for a long time on the narrow bed, pondering the presence of Kristina Vaska. The conclusion he came to was simple: if

Pagan had known nothing of the Brotherhood before, he almost certainly knew something now, courtesy of Miss Vaska. Whether the message was coded or not, the fact remained, so far as Epishev was concerned, that Kristina Vaska would have provided Pagan with some insight into the Brotherhood, at least as she understood it. The question that burned Epishev now was the *extent* of the woman's understanding.

Did she know of the plan? If not all of it, did she know any part? Did she know enough to cause the destruction of the scheme? Even if she didn't – could Epishev take that kind of chance?

All such speculation was finally fruitless. How the woman had come into Pagan's life, the nature of her information – he could dwell on these matters to infinity and still solve nothing. The solution didn't lie in further pointless rumination. The answer lay elsewhere – in action.

He skirted the wall. He reached the street, looked up once more at the lit window, then he gazed along the pavement at the police car. He stood very still, merging with the trees behind him, becoming in his stillness just another inanimate shadow. He saw the red glow of a cigarette behind the windshield, then the spark as the butt was flicked away. It was very simple. He'd walk straight towards the car. He wouldn't look extraordinary at all, just a man taking the night air. He moved out from beneath the branches.

He put his hand in the pocket of his raincoat and curled his fingers around the gun. Then he paused, conscious of the flare of a match inside the police vehicle and the sound of a man's voice carrying along the pavement – *I told the missus, I said the last thing we needed was another bleedin' crumbsnatcher*, and then there was silence. Epishev kept going. He was about twenty-five yards from the patrol car now. He took the gun out of his pocket and held it against his side, so that it was concealed by the folds of his coat. Fifteen yards.

217

One of the policemen was staring at him now from the car. Epishev had the impression of a face half-lit by a streetlamp. Cigarette smoke drifted out of the open window. Epishev called out "Maxwell! Maxwell!" and kept moving until he was only a couple of feet from the vehicle. Then he called the name again "Maxwell! Here, Maxwell! Come to me!"

The policeman with the cigarette asked, "Whatsa-matter?"

Epishev stopped at the window of the car, lowered his face, looked inside. *There were only two of them, nobody concealed in the rear seat.*

"I am missing my cat," he said. He wondered if he sounded suitably concerned. "Brown male with white paws. Very distinct markings. Impossible to overlook."

The smoking policeman turned to his partner. "Seen any cats, Alf?"

Alf shook his head. "Sorry, chum."

Epishev shrugged. He smiled apologetically, as if he were ashamed to have wasted the valuable time of these two guardians of law and order, then he brought the silenced pistol up very quickly and fired it twice into the squad car. It was brutally efficient. The policeman closest to Epishev dropped his cigarette and slithered sideways and his head slumped on his partner's chest. Alf, the younger of the two, lowered his face like a man dozing. Blood stained his blue shirt in the region of his heart.

Epishev stepped away from the car and crossed the street swiftly to Pagan's house, climbing the steps, stopping outside the brown door, checking the lock. It was a simple affair and easily forced, nothing more than a little quiet surgery undertaken with a pen-knife – and then he'd be inside, he'd be climbing the stairs to Pagan's apartment, where perhaps both Pagan and the woman were in bed even now, making love. Two quick shots, Epishev thought. The ultimate orgasm.

He took out his knife, selected a short thin blade from the selection of ten or more available to him, forced it into the lock. He turned it gently, listening for the inner mechanism to be released. Then, breathing in the patiently shallow way of the safecracker, he heard the lock click and felt the door move. He nudged it a little way. A darkened hallway faced him, a stairway. He didn't step into the house. He was wary of the silences and the lack of light.

He put his knife away, took out the gun again. The hallway smelled of stale air and a hint of damp. All he had to do was to stride along the hall and rise quietly up the stairs – and yet he hesitated, because his instincts told him something was not quite right here, something was out of joint and he wasn't sure what.

He didn't move. It was only when he heard the sound of the car draw up and he turned his face back to the street and saw the bright headlamps that he knew –

Frank Pagan wasn't at home.

He'd gone out, leaving the woman with the police to guard her, and now he was back. Epishev heard a door slam and he saw Pagan get out of an American car and come quickly along the pavement, then pause in the manner of a man who has forgotten something. Pagan turned away. *He walked back across the street to the police car.*

Epishev saw Pagan incline his face to the window of the police vehicle, then he raised his pistol even as Pagan, stunned by the sight of the dead policemen, turned his face in the direction of the house. Two things occurred to Frank Pagan almost simultaneously – one was the realisation that a man was about to fire a gun at him from a darkened doorway across a narrow street. The other was that this same man might already have been up to the apartment where Kristina was alone –

Pagan threw himself to the ground, rolling as soon as he hit concrete, twisting his body in the manner of a burning person trying to douse flames, sliding for the safety of the underside of the squad car. He saw powdered concrete rise up inches from his face, dug out of the ground by the violent impact of a bullet.

And still he kept twisting, until his body was jammed against the exhaust system. He reached behind him for his own weapon, a manoeuvre that called for a certain double-jointedness in the cramped space between exhaust-pipe and ground. He fumbled the weapon free and fired it twice but his angle was low and useless and his shots struck a garbage-can on the pavement. They were loud though, wonderfully loud, spectacularly so, and they echoed along the street with the intensity of a car backfiring, except worse.

The gunman took another shot from the doorway of the house and Pagan heard the bullet slice into one of the tyres of the patrol car, which immediately deflated so that the vehicle listed to one side, making Pagan's position even more uncomfortable. But it was the last shot of the brief encounter because now windows were being thrown open along the street, and lights were turned on, and cranky voices, disturbed in sleep, were calling out a variety of obscenities.

Pagan squeezed himself out from beneath the car as the gunman, afraid of all the public attention, started to run. Pagan glimpsed the man's sallow face briefly under a dim streetlamp – somebody you wouldn't look at twice in the street. Then the gunman headed for the darkness of the square, jumping the stone wall and vanishing into the trees. Pagan got to his feet and considered the idea of giving chase, but his mind was on Kristina Vaska now, and he hurried towards the house, rushing the stairs, finding the door of the flat locked, pounding on it, then hearing the deadbolt being drawn and seeing Kristina Vaska standing there, bright and freshly-showered, in one of his robes, an old paisley thing that had never been worn with anything like this kind of elegant sexuality –

"I thought," he said. The relief he felt was like a narcotic. He was stoned by it.

"Thought what?" she asked.

Pagan put his arms around her and pulled her towards him and felt her wet hair pressed against his cheek. He wanted her with a ferocity that astounded him. And he knew it was reciprocated, he could feel her heart beat against him and the heat of her breath on his skin, he knew that he would only have to slide a hand between the folds of the robe and touch her lightly on the breasts – he understood he'd have to travel only a very short distance before he'd be lost.

He stepped back from her. He was thinking of the two young cops in the squad car, how they lay so very close together in a position of intimacy that only death had the chilling skill to choreograph. Two young cops – and they'd been murdered because of a situation they knew nothing about, something that should never have touched their lives, events from a history of which neither of those two men would have been aware.

It was waste, bloody waste.

In a frustrated gesture, Pagan pressed his large hands together until the knuckles were white. He walked over to the window. Below, people were milling around the squad car. Gore drew them out. Violence magnetised them.

He was aware of Kristina Vaska standing at his side. He said, "Two young cops are dead down there. Uncle Viktor's handiwork."

Kristina Vaska shut her eyes and bit very gently on her lower lip. Pagan put an arm round her shoulder and thought how this intimacy provided no real defence against the brutality of the street below.

12

In the early 1950s the facility had been an active USAF airfield but now it was used solely for training pilots and mechanics. Three vast hangars, located nineteen miles from downtown Trenton, contained a variety of aircraft in different stages of dismemberment. Young men worked under the guidance of their instructors, welding, soldering, exploring the mysteries of electronic circuitry.

Some distance from the three main hangars a fourth was situated at the place where the field was surrounded by barbed-wire. This construction, smaller than the others, contained an F-16 simulator. Andres Kiss stood with his hands on his hips and a certain arrogant expression on his face – though the look was less one of arrogance than of supreme confidence, that of a man so sure of his abilities he is contemptuous of any attempt to test them. He swept a strand of blond hair from his forehead and smiled at Gary Iverson, who produced a length of black cloth from his pocket and dangled it in the air. He knew Kiss would pass the blindfold test without difficulty, but Galbraith, whom Andres Kiss had never heard of, had to be reassured because the fat man's eye for detail was like that of an eagle for its food supply. Galbraith could spot an overlooked detail or a sloppy piece of business with uncanny accuracy.

Andres Kiss climbed inside the simulator, which was a working cockpit of an F-16 fighter plane. He studied the panel layout, but it was all so familiar he could have sketched it from memory. He took the blindfold from Iverson's hand and pulled it over his eyes, knotting it at the back of his skull. Because there wasn't enough room in the cockpit for two, Iverson had to stand on the platform attached to the simulator, from which position he could verify the results of the blindfold test.

"We don't need to go through this," Kiss said.

"Do it for me, Andres."

Andres Kiss adjusted the blindfold. He perceived Iverson as a necessary conduit for the Brotherhood's plan. Without Iverson, the scheme would have been nothing more than the sentimental yearnings of old men. What Iverson brought to the plan was reality in the shape of an aircraft, which might have been otherwise impossible to obtain.

Kiss and Iverson went back some years together to a time when Andres had first learned how to fly a fighter plane and Gary Iverson had been his instructor. Kiss was the most willing student Iverson had ever had, the most adept. The young man's affinity for flight was unnatural. Earthbound, Andres Kiss wasn't the kind of man you'd want to spend an evening with. Pub-crawling with Kiss became an exercise in profound tedium even for somebody like Gary Iverson, whose own social graces were tepid at best. But when you put Kiss inside an aircraft he was transformed, some miracle of transmutation took place, and Kiss was touched by a radiance, an ease he otherwise didn't have.

Now Kiss rubbed his fingers together like a man about to shuffle a deck of cards. "Go," he said.

"Manual pitch override switch," Iverson said.

Kiss moved a hand to the left console, touched the switch. He did this without hesitation.

"Antenna select panel," Iverson said.

Kiss smiled and reached for the right console, his fingers passing over the engine anti-ice switch to the place Iverson had requested.

"Master caution light."

Andres Kiss reached forward to the instrument panel. With blindness imposed upon him like this, he relied on an inner vision which in its own way was even more clear than ordinary eyesight. It was as if there existed in his brain an illuminated map of the cockpit. He touched the master caution light in the centre of the instrument panel.

"Oil pressure indicator," Iverson commanded.

Kiss found it to the right of the panel. It was all so goddam easy. Iverson asked for the ejection mode handle and Kiss went to the right auxiliary console without thinking. He did the same for the fuel master switch on the left console, the autopilot switch, the cockpit pressure altimeter – everything Iverson asked for Andres Kiss found without hesitation.

"Can I take this goddam thing off now?" Kiss asked.

Iverson said he could. Kiss undid the blindfold, crumpled it in his hand, passed it back to Iverson. Then he climbed out of the simulator. Both men stood in silence for a time, dwarfed by the height of the hangar. There was a very small skylight set in the roof and morning sun shone through. Andres Kiss experienced the same kind of awesome sensation in a hangar that a devout Christian might in a vast cathedral.

Iverson made a fist of his right hand and glanced at the antique Air Force ring he wore on his fourth finger. He'd bought it twenty years ago in a pawn shop. It was at least a half a century old and it gave Iverson a sense of continuity, of belonging to an exclusive club. Now he remembered Galbraith's instruction to probe Andres about Sundbach, to feel him out. He relaxed the fist and smiled at the younger man. "When I saw your uncle last night I got the impression of . . . I want to say uneasiness, Andres."

"He's getting old, Gary. That's all. Old men are apprehensive."

Iverson thought of the meeting yesterday in the house in Glen Cove and the way Carl Sundbach had walked out. "It wasn't apprehension. I got the feeling he was keeping something back from me. I mean, you guys aren't having problems, are you? Is there anything I'm not being told, Andres?"

Andres Kiss said he couldn't think of a thing. He'd never understood how much Iverson knew about the Brotherhood, or how much research he'd done into the nature of the plan. He assumed Iverson wouldn't have made a plane available without doing a deep background check – but how deep was deep? Did he know about Romanenko and the whole Soviet side of the affair? Did he know about the undelivered message? There was guardedness on both sides, and secrecy, and that was only correct. Security sometimes depended on areas of mutual ignorance. But every now and then there was tension because of this need for secrecy. For instance – who did Iverson work for? Kiss knew he'd gone to work at the Pentagon somewhere along the way, but he didn't know if he was still employed there. And why was he so keen to make an F-16 available? There were old loyalties at work, of course, and a shared past in the Air Force, but these were not enough to make somebody give you a present of a very expensive aircraft. Andres Kiss might have pursued these questions if he'd been a different kind of man. Somebody more reflective, somebody more widely focused, might have explored and probed for satisfactory answers. But Kiss didn't have that kind of scope. On the bottom line, Iverson was supplying a plane that Kiss was desperate to fly – did anything else matter?

Kiss recalled now how Iverson had first entered the plan, how a chance encounter with Gary Iverson at an air show in Atlantic City two years ago had revitalised an old friendship, one Iverson pursued with an enthusiasm that surprised Kiss, an ardour that even flattered the younger man. Iverson issued dinner invitations, or asked Kiss to join him for cocktails in midtown hotels, or sometimes even invited him to make up a foursome at which the women were invariably handsome and silent and eager to please. The friendship turned eventually, as friendships do, on an axis of mutual trust. On one inebriated night Kiss had talked openly about Mikhail, about the men of the Brotherhood, of lost causes and resurrections – not in a specific vocabulary but in a general one that caused Iverson to be intrigued. It began like this, in vague ways, and it grew until Iverson's F-16 had become a pivotal piece in the jigsaw, and Iverson himself a mysterious force behind the success of things.

"Let me be straight with you, Andres," Gary Iverson said. "Some of my people – and I can't name names, you know that – are concerned about one of your personnel."

"Who?"

Iverson admired Kiss's cool, his smoothness, his way of failing to mention such major incidents as the rupture at yesterday's meeting in Glen Cove and the assassination of Aleksis Romanenko. "It's Sundbach. We worry about him."

"Sundbach?" Andres Kiss felt a sense of relief. For a moment he imagined Iverson was going to bring up the matter of Romanenko's murder, and say that it was an obstacle, an incident that had made his people unhappy, that support for the mission was beginning to evaporate. But if he hadn't mentioned Romanenko, then it was because he hadn't learned of Aleksis's role in the scheme. Therefore Iverson's knowledge of the plan's groundwork was limited.

"I wasn't aware you'd ever heard of Sundbach, Gary. You've been doing some digging."

"I didn't leap into this business without doing some research, Andres."

"If you'd dug a little deeper, you'd have learned that Sundbach's out."

"Out?"

"As of yesterday."

"Out? Like how?"

"He quit."

"Let me get a handle on this. He just walked *away*. Just left the room? So long, it's been good to know you?"

Kiss was silent for a long time before he said, "That's right."

Iverson examined a slick of oil on the floor. From another hangar came the roar of a plane's engine being pushed through its paces by enthusiastic apprentice mechanics. "I'm a little surprised, Andres. I'm surprised he walked. There's a lot at stake here, friend, and an old guy like Sundbach . . ." Iverson paused. "Let me be right up front with you, Andres. Point one, Sundbach's a little too fond of his drink. Point two, an old guy who drinks can be indiscreet. Point three, we don't need indiscretion at this stage of the game. Point four, he knows a lot . . ."

"Mikhail says he isn't a threat."

"Maybe Mikhail's right. Who knows? Maybe Mikhail knows Sundbach better than anyone else. All I can tell you is some of my people don't like the notion of this old character having so much information, no matter what Mikhail thinks. Some of my people have this affliction called high blood pressure."

Kiss studied the other man's face carefully, wondering if he were meant to read something into the absence of expression, something that couldn't be uttered aloud but was to be understood, between friends, in silence. Was he being tested? Was this mention of Sundbach meant to be some kind of examination of his feelings, the way the simulator had been a test of his knowledge? More than feelings, though. Was he being asked to demonstrate some initiative, to carry out a task Iverson didn't want to spell out directly? It was subtle, and quiet, and the nuances of the situation troubled Kiss. He felt like a man looking into a fogged mirror.

"People who outlive their usefulness can be damned tricky," Iverson remarked. "Sometimes, though, they just don't do diddley. They potter in their gardens and grow things they can't eat. Is Sundbach like that?"

Kiss said, "He doesn't have a garden."

"Doesn't have a garden," Iverson said, more a private little echo than anything meaningful. He moved towards the hangar doors and pushed them open, looking out across the concrete expanse of old runways, cracked now and weeded. "Well, maybe he'll find something else to pass the time."

"Maybe," Andres Kiss said, and some of the fog began to clear from the face of the mirror.

Manhattan

It was one o'clock in the afternoon when Frank Pagan arrived at John F. Kennedy Airport. He had expected to be met by somebody from the New York City Police Department, because Martin Burr had arranged a liaison, but nobody turned up. It was an insufferably humid afternoon. As he rode in a cab towards Manhattan, Pagan sat with his eyes shut and the window open, feeling a feeble little breeze blow upon his sweating face. You could drown in this kind of weather, he thought. Even the prospect of Manhattan, a city he adored, a city whose electricity sent people scurrying around like galvanised particles, didn't take the edge off his sense of brooding isolation – a condition exaggerated by four scotches on the plane and the absence of Kristina Vaska who, stuck with a ticket she hadn't been able to exchange, wasn't scheduled to arrive in New York until tomorrow.

Kristina Vaska. He could still see that uneasy juxtaposition of images, wet-haired Kristina in the old paisley robe and the two dead cops in the street below, and he was caught between the erotic and the dismal, a place that had all the appeal of an occupied mousetrap. He opened his eyes, stared out at suburban streets beyond the highway, neat boxed dwellings surrounded by neat boxed shrubs. And he remembered the horror he'd felt when he'd looked inside the squad car, when he'd put his face to the window and was about to ask something simple like *Anything happening?* and he'd realised that both occupants were dead, one with his face on the other's chest, the driver with his mouth wide open and blood around his lips.

The two dead cops had caused Martin Burr an apoplectic depression. Pagan couldn't remember ever having seen the Commissioner look so grim, all colour drained from his face and all mischief gone from his one good eye. The cops were hurriedly removed, the car towed, but not before the scandalmongers of Fleet Street, alerted by neighbours, had come upon the scene. Martin Burr had been obliged to hold an impromptu press-conference in the course of which his voice had quivered once and he'd gone silent, holding his emotions in check. No, he told the reporters, he had no idea of the identity of the killer. And no, he had no idea why they were parked opposite Frank Pagan's apartment nor what their nightly routine might be – lies, of course, lies that wouldn't slake the scribblers' voracious appetites for too long.

Later, in the privacy of his office, Burr had said *Don't feel bad about it, Frank. Don't blame yourself for those two coppers.* It was a struggle, and Pagan didn't think he'd win it, because obviously the two young men would still be alive if it hadn't been for the fact that he'd called the local police station for a couple of watchdogs. They'd still be alive, and married, and raising their kids. He stared from the window of the cab, feeling as grim now as Martin Burr had looked in London only a few hours ago. Resentful too, because he was being pitched out of the centre of the action, expelled like some truant schoolboy.

I want you on the first available plane, Frank. I want you out of here and far away from this lunatic. Leave him to MI6. Get what you can on Kiviranna and come home again.

Pagan had been unable to resist saying that he was being shuttled off to do something any responsible cop in New York could do. It would've been simpler to use some local cop and have him talk to the woman who'd scorned Jake Kiviranna – a lady, according to information supplied at the last minute by the ever helpful Ted Gunther, called Rose Alexander who lived in Brooklyn.

Simpler and cheaper. Telexes, Commissioner, don't cost much. Burr had chosen to ignore him.

Pagan looked up into the cloudy sky. He was thinking of Brooklyn, a place he'd visited before and had no real desire to see again. Martin Burr had wanted him to rent a hotel room there, but Pagan had firmly drawn a line of his own when it came to his place of residence. The Commissioner might be the great architect, he might be the one who sent men hurtling across oceans in accordance with his own designs, but there was no way he was going to impose a Brooklyn hotel on Frank Pagan. Pagan had booked a room in the Warwick, which wasn't exactly top-notch, but his per diem covered it. Barely. *Very well, Frank. I don't care where you stay, so long as it's out of trouble.*

He thought of Kristina. Before leaving London he'd booked her into a room in a quiet hotel in Kensington, far from his apartment. He'd driven her to the place by a circuitous route, then made certain she went to her room, which was chintzy in a very English way, cosy, guaranteed to soothe. *Look at those curtains*, he'd said. *How could anything bad happen in a room with curtains that look like they'd been designed by Pollyanna?* She'd laughed, but there was a tension in her, and she was just as depressed as Pagan by the deaths of the policemen. She'd be safe in the Stafford Arms Hotel in Kensington for one night, Pagan thought now. Tomorrow she'd be back in New York. He was missing her already – a new sensation in his life. Previously, he'd missed only the dead. Missing the living was filled with all kinds of possibilities.

He escaped from the cab outside the Warwick on West 54th Street, plunging into the air-conditioned lobby, where he checked in smoothly and went up to his room on the sixth floor. He stood for a time at the window, watching the sky above Manhattan. He went over the puzzles again, seeking connections, trying to pull together various conjectures.

He sat on the edge of the bed and scribbled words

on a notepad. *Kiviranna. Epishev. The Brotherhood of the Forest. Romanenko.* Then he drew a series of connecting arrows, linking each name with the other, until the sheet was covered in a maze of lines resembling a complex spiderweb. Faction was the word he came back to, the idea that within the KGB there was some kind of support for Aleksis's Brotherhood, that a group of individuals – large, small, he couldn't possibly know – was actively encouraging the Brotherhood's scheme. The death in Edinburgh and the failure of Aleksis to play the role of postman, these things had created sudden detours for the supporters of the Brotherhood and their plan . . . whatever it was. A rush went through Pagan, the familiar feeling he got when he had a flash, an insight, when he saw hitherto unmapped terrain from a point above. All right, he thought, there's a power struggle inside the KGB, even within the Politburo itself – but so what? If it were true, it provided only a context for those events that touched him personally. Political realities within the Soviet Union were as distant as Mars and had nothing to do with him. It was as if somebody had shaken the tree of the Kremlin and a couple of strangely-marked leaves had fallen in Pagan's lap, that was all. He could examine the leaves, and dissect them, but he could never see the larger picture, the architecture of the tree.

He sighed, pulled the sheet from the pad, tossed it inside the wastebasket. Which was when he heard a sharp knock and he rose, opening the door. The man who appeared in the doorway was about five feet seven inches tall and wore a polka-dot bow-tie that drooped from his collar. He had on a light tweed jacket, the elbows of which were patched in leather. He resembled a scholar, Pagan thought, the kind of gnome you saw behind a stack of books in a library, eyes glazed over with that shellshocked look of too much knowledge. He had uncontrollable feathery red hair which seemed to rise, like puffs of thin, gingery smoke, from his skull.

"Frank Pagan? I'm Klein," the man said. "Max Klein. NYPD."

Pagan closed the door after Max Klein had entered the room. The bow-tie was all wrong, Pagan thought. What kind of NYPD cop wore such a thing for God's sake? And the green leather patches didn't complement the brown material of the jacket. Pagan noticed the leather sandals in which Klein's bony feet were bare. The word *eccentric* floated into Frank Pagan's head. How did this character, with his odd appearance and scholarly face, fit into the macho scheme of things in the NYPD? Did Klein belong to some special department? The Office of Misfits? Pagan had an image of a large room in which sat cops like Max Klein, men who didn't look and feel like policemen, outcasts and dwarves and innocents, errors of recruitment, who had somehow lost their way in the political labyrinth of the police department.

Pagan shook Max Klein's hand. "Glad you could come," he said.

"I was going to meet you at the airport," Klein said. "But things got away from me. Story of my life."

Pagan sat on the edge of the bed, looking at Klein, who was scratching his foot through the strap of a sandal.

Klein said, "I've got an address for you somewhere," and he dipped into the pocket of his jacket, pulling out an assortment of paper, slips, creased notes, a couple of dollar bills, matchbooks, lint. He placed his collection on the floor, then he got down on his knees and started to sift through it.

Organised man, Pagan thought.

Klein said, "I'm filled with good intentions. I keep meaning to buy a wallet and put things inside it in an orderly fashion. I never quite get round to it."

There was a certain childlike quality about Max Klein as he sorted through the detritus on the rug, a *niceness* that showed on his good-natured face.

"Here it is," and Klein brandished a slip of paper. "Rose Alexander."

Pagan took the piece of paper and looked at it. There was an address in Brooklyn and a telephone number. The paper had other scribbles on it, truncated words, dates, a variety of doodles, some of them in the shape of noses, mouths, eyes, all rather skilfully rendered.

Pagan asked, "What do you do in the Department?"

Max Klein stuffed everything into a pocket, then climbed back up into his armchair. "I don't exactly fit any category with ease. Right now I work Fraud in Brooklyn. But I joined the force as an artist – "

"An artist?" *They send me an artist*, Pagan thought.

"I draw faces," Max Klein said and blinked his gingery eyelashes. "I put together drawings from witness descriptions."

Frank Pagan was quiet a moment.

Klein said, "Yeah, I know. I know what you're thinking. You're saying to yourself you've been fobbed off with a guy whose basic skills aren't especially useful."

"Well." Pagan shrugged.

Max Klein fidgeted with his bow-tie. "If it puts your mind at rest, I *do* know my way around Brooklyn. I was raised there, went to school there. It's my territory. So don't write me off just because I'm not some hot-shot investigator who's seven feet three inches in his bare feet."

Pagan smiled. "How much did they tell you?"

"They said a Communist official was killed in Scotland by a guy from Brooklyn. That you were here to check on the assassin's background, which they said was kind of shadowy."

Shadowy, Pagan thought. Max Klein said, "I've got a Department car outside, if you're ready."

Pagan pulled on his jacket, slipped into his shoes. "I'm ready," he said.

Carl Sundbach clutched his grocery sack to his chest and crossed Third Avenue in the direction of Twenty-Ninth Street, where his apartment was located. He skipped nimbly through traffic, thinking he might evade the man following him. He wasn't supposed to know he was being tracked, but the guy wasn't exactly hot-shot at his trade and besides Carl had a nose for such things. His years in the hills and forests of Estonia had honed certain skills he'd never altogether lost, and one of these was an instinct, rather like a small alarm, that told him when he was being watched. He'd turned once, glimpsed the fellow, a medium-sized anonymity in a dark blue suit, then he'd reached the sidewalk and hurried towards Twenty-Ninth Street.

When he unlocked the front door of his building he shut it quickly behind him, peering through glass at the street. But the man was nowhere to be seen. Sundbach climbed the stairs to his apartment, four rooms on the second floor. Out of breath, he let himself in, bolted the door behind him, slumped into a chair in the kitchen and let his groceries – veal, pig's knuckles, celery stalks, onions, all the ingredients for the dish called *sult*, jellied meat – roll from the paper bag in his lap to the floor. He tilted his head back, breathed through his open mouth, shut his eyes.

He'd first seen the man only that morning when he'd gone for his newspaper. Then, minutes ago, he'd been conscious of the same face in the aisles of the supermarket. *Kurat!* The man looked so out of place among the shoppers that Sundbach spotted him at once. He looked like a *lurjas*, a sneak. He'd pretended an interest in the produce section, fingering leeks and pressing zucchini, but it was an unconvincing performance. Sundbach opened his eyes. *Who was having him followed?* That was the big question.

He rose, a little shakily, and walked into the large living-room of the apartment. It was furnished in what one might have called emigré chic, stuffed with chairs and sofas Sundbach had bought from Baltic dealers in New York, old sepia prints of Estonia that depicted the University at Tartu, the steeple of the Oleviste Church, and an aquatint of Tallinn done in 1816 by an artist called A. Schuch. There were also shelves of china, some of it family heirlooms Sundbach had managed to salvage from the old country. There were tea kettles and brass plaques and a collection of Estonian books and underground literature smuggled out of the Baltic over the years. On one wall there hung a gallery of American photographs, each of which showed Carl Sundbach in the company of influential Americans – Sundbach shaking hands with Robert Kennedy during that doomed Presidential campaign to which Sundbach had contributed a small fortune (Carl recalled Kennedy saying he'd make room on his agenda for the whole Baltic issue, only a madman's bullet had put an end to that little dream), Sundbach with then Governor Rockefeller during the groundbreaking for a new Sundbach hotel in Albany, Sundbach with an unhappy-looking Ramsey Clark during the Democratic primary in 1973. There were photographs of Carl in the company of entertainers like Wayne Newton, Liza Minelli, and Robert Goulet, taken at charity luncheons or dedications of hospital wings to which Carl had donated large sums of money. The whole gallery was an immigrant's dream of making good in America, of making not only large sums of money but also of moving in the company of the blessed. Carl was proud of what he'd achieved in his new homeland. By sheer hard work, and equal measures of guts and cold determination, he'd shaped his own dream.

He picked up the telephone that sat on his old roll-top desk. The receiver was an ancient black one, and heavy. He dialled the number of Mikhail Kiss in Glen Cove. Kiss came on the line after the fifth ring.

Carl Sundbach said, "You having me followed, Mikhail?"

"Followed?" Kiss sounded incredulous.

"A man in a blue suit. Everywhere I go, he goes."

Kiss laughed softly. "Why would I send somebody to watch you, Carl?"

Sundbach opened the middle drawer of his desk. Inside lay an old revolver and a photograph album with an ornate leather cover. He flicked the album open, gazed absently at pictures, many of them old black and white shots that belonged in another lifetime. He said, "You want to keep an eye on me. Make sure I give nothing away. Make sure I don't speak to the wrong people or go to the wrong places."

Kiss laughed again. "Take my word for it. I haven't sent anybody to keep an eye on you, Carl. I'm insulted by the suggestion."

"Then who is he? Who sent him?"

Kiss was quiet for a time. "I can only think of the Russian Mission."

"No," Sundbach answered quickly. "A *vanya* I'd smell at five miles. He doesn't dress like a man from the Mission, Carl. He's not Russian, unless the Soviets are starting to wear better suits. So who is he? Who sent him if it wasn't you?"

"Perhaps you're imagining it," Kiss said.

"*Kuradi perse!*" Sundbach slipped into an Estonian curse with the ease of a man who has never left his native country, and who thinks all his thoughts in his native tongue. "I'm imagining nothing, Mikhail."

"Listen to me. You just bought a nice place in Key West, go down there for a few weeks, relax."

"Thanks for the suggestion. I'll keep it in mind," Sundbach said. He hung up and sat for a while with his hand on the receiver. Then he rose, walked to the window, looked down at the street. Across the way a group of teenagers sat on a stoop, passing back and forth a bottle of wine in a brown paper bag. But there was no sign of the man in the blue suit. Florida, for God's sake! He'd bought the Key West condo for tax reasons, he wasn't going to fly down there and sit in the bright sunlight with people who'd lived their lives and had nothing better to do than grow fat and brown.

He was about to turn from the window when he saw

the man in the blue suit pass the stoop where the kids sat drinking. The man said something to the kids, then turned his face up in the general direction of Sundbach's apartment. Carl dropped the lace curtain and moved back from the glass, catching his breath in his throat. If Kiss hadn't sent the man in the blue suit, then who the hell had?

Sundbach sat down, opened the desk drawer, took out the old revolver, weighed it in the palm of his hand. It was a good, secure feeling, the connection of flesh with cold metal. He stuck the gun back, shut the drawer, stood up, looked absently around his living-room.

The thought struck him then, it came out of nowhere like lightning on a calm summery night – the man on the street, the man who was watching him, might have some connection with the murder in Edinburgh. But how could that be?

He pressed his fingertips upon his eyelids and sighed and felt just a little scared. He'd have to sit very still and think it all through, step by step, searching for any small thing he might have overlooked.

Brooklyn

Klein's car was a late-model Dodge, bruised and dented, a sponge on four wheels. Klein drove like a man afraid for his life, his hands tight on the wheel. He had none of the average New Yorker's contempt for pedestrian life-forms and traffic signals, because he slowed at crosswalks and observed the lights cautiously.

It was after six by the time he parked in Brooklyn, and there was a clouded sun hanging in the sky over Sheepshead Bay.

"This is the place, Frank," Klein said. It was a street of old grey tenements. "This used to be an okay neighbourhood, which is hard to believe now. I grew up a couple blocks from here. I used to think this neighbourhood was for very rich people. I always felt dirt poor when I came down this street."

Pagan realised he was disoriented, that he had absolutely no idea of his location because he hadn't been able to follow Klein's route to this place. He stepped out of the car and stood on the sidewalk, watching the small man ease himself from behind the steering-wheel.

"Number 643, apartment seven," Klein said. "That's the joint we want."

Pagan moved toward the entranceway of a tenement. Klein followed nimbly, with a motion that was close to skipping, as if his sandalled feet never quite made contact with the sidewalk.

The hallway smelled of fried food. Two bicycles were elaborately chained to a radiator. Pagan stepped around them, pausing at the foot of the stairs which stretched up through gloom to the next floor. Then he started to climb, and Max Klein followed.

Apartment seven was on the second floor. Pagan waited for Klein to reach the landing, then he knocked on the door. The woman who opened it was about forty, rather appealing, dressed in blue jeans and a peasant blouse. There was a slightly spaced-out expression on her face, as if she'd been interrupted in the lonely act of contemplating her inner landscape. She wore her long brown hair parted in the centre and a metal charm bracelet dangled from her wrist. Pagan had an impression of zodiac signs, Celtic crosses, peace symbols, a whole series of miniatures that shivered as she moved her hand.

Klein flashed his badge and asked, "Rose Alexander?"

The woman nodded, pushing a strand of hair out of her face. "Last time I looked," she said.

"This man" – and here Klein nodded at Pagan – "this man has some questions to ask you."

The woman turned her face to Pagan. "Who are you?"

Pagan told her. He showed her his ID, which she stared at for a long time. She touched the laminated surface of the card and Pagan had the distinct impression she was either stoned or else had done so much dope in her time she'd failed to return from one of her trips. She was caressing Pagan's ID as if it were a lover's poem. Pagan thought there was something anachronistic about a doper caught in middle-age. Rose Alexander was a prisoner of a time-warp, a fugitive from the late 'sixties, the peasant blouse, the blue jeans that he saw now had been patched with little squares of rainbow-coloured material, the peace-symbols hanging from her wrist.

"Scotland Yard," she said. "You've come a long way."

"Mind if we come inside?" Klein asked.

"Be my guest." She held the door open for them.

There were posters on the wall that belonged to the purple age of psychedelia – Jimmi Hendrix in neon three-D, Bob Dylan in an art-nouveau rendering, The Beatles in their Sergeant Pepper finery. Pagan, remembering these times, was plunged back into a world of Nehru jackets, incandescent gurus, scented hand-made candles, and blissed-out songs by Donovan.

On a table in front of an electric fire the inevitable stick of incense smoked in its own little Nepalese brass container, throwing the sickening scent of patchouli into the room. Rose Alexander sat down cross-legged on the floor. She struck a match, lit a cigarette, held the smoke in her lungs a long time in a doper's manner, her small mouth tense.

"Lemme guess," she said. "Since I haven't broken any laws I'm aware of, you must be here to talk about Jake Kiviranna."

Pagan wondered if events in Waverley Station had made it into the newspapers over here. Even if they had, it was doubtful that Rose, ensconced in her own little universe, kept abreast of world affairs. Rose, it appeared, had been expecting news of Kiviranna to surface at some time or other in her life – the bad penny that keeps turning up, as brightly abrasive as ever, no matter how many times you toss it away.

"He shot a man in Scotland," Pagan said.

"It figures."

"You don't seem surprised." Remarkable calm, Pagan thought.

Rose Alexander stared at Pagan coolly. He caught a glimpse of her as she might once have been, young and carefree, even beautiful, strutting the crowded streets of the Haight in San Francisco or getting high at Woodstock, her long hair hanging over her shoulders and her jeans flared above bare feet and zodiac signs painted on her cheeks and forehead.

She said, "If I don't seem surprised it's because I'm not. Do you know Jake?"

"I met him briefly . . ." And here Pagan hesitated. He had half of a sentence still to complete and he was reluctant to do it. "I don't know if you're aware of the fact he committed suicide."

Perhaps a vague flicker crossed her face, Pagan wasn't sure. But she still looked unperturbed. "Don't get the impression I'm a cold bitch. But nothing you've told me so far surprises me at all. I'm not amazed he killed somebody and I'm not exactly blown away by news of his suicide either."

Pagan glanced at Klein, who was fiddling with one of those lamps with a transparent base filled with expanding liquid. Great pink bubbles rose up hypnotically. Rose Alexander lit another cigarette. Pagan sat down in a beanbag chair, which immediately reassembled itself around him like a loose fist.

Rose Alexander said, "I had to get a court order restraining Jake from coming near me. Not once, but twice. He forced his attentions on me when I didn't need them and I didn't ask for them. Jake became a nightmare for me."

Pagan, who wasn't interested in Jake's obsession with this woman, wanted to steer the conversation in the direction of anything Rose might know about Kiviranna's trip to the United Kingdom and the identity of the man who sent him on that fatal voyage. But Rose had other ideas and she wanted to talk about Kiviranna no matter what Frank Pagan desired.

"When I met him first I felt sorry for him," she said. "It was in some bar on Brighton Beach Avenue. He had a lost look. And I've got a thing for lost creatures. I got drunk and Jake got infatuated. For most people, this would be no big deal. Like a slight cold. You sweat it out, it goes away. Not to Jake Kiviranna. Jake's thing for me was colossal. Flowers. Cards. Gifts. Poems. I couldn't turn around without finding Jake in my shadow. It's nice at the beginning. But it gets old real fast, man. I tried to point this out to Jake, I tried to let him down gently, I was kind – but there are some people you can't get through to and Jake Kiviranna was one of them. They hear only what they want to hear. Nothing else makes a dent."

Pagan glanced at Klein, who was going through Rose's collection of record albums. Familiar old names flicked past. The Grateful Dead. Jefferson Airplane. Big Brother and the Holding Company. Names out of a history that seemed more distant than a mere twenty years.

"Jake wouldn't go away. I figured if I couldn't let him down gently, I'd try some reality therapy, so I dated a couple of guys, and I hoped Jake would get the message, but the only message he ever got was the desire to beat me up. Which he did. Two, maybe three times. A couple of broken ribs. Three teeth. A split lip. It might have been worse. He'd beat me, then he'd shower me with flowers. That gets pretty fucking stale. I had to go to court to get a restraining order. The next thing, Jake slashes his wrists. He was a sick sonofabitch. He sent me a poem written in his own blood. Think about that one. Slits his wrists and still finds the time to write verse. Bad verse."

Pagan was quiet for a time, wondering if Rose Alexander had run her course. She stubbed her cigarette out and looked at the rings adorning her fingers, then she tipped back her head and looked at the ceiling and said, "I never wanted to hurt him, you understand."

"I believe you," Pagan said. He struggled up out of the beanbag chair, which made a rasping sound as he rose. "When did you last see Jake?"

"Couple of months ago."

"In what circumstances?"

"He was waiting for me in the street one night. Standard stuff for Jake. He liked to spy on me. He liked to find me with other guys."

"Did he say anything about how he was going away? Did he mention anything about leaving the country?"

Rose Alexander smiled. "One of the problems with Jake was how you could never tell when he was talking bullshit or when he was being on the level. Sometimes he'd talk in this real wild way, sometimes he'd be calm. But you couldn't tell from his manner if he was into fantasy or reality. I don't think I listened, Mr Pagan. I didn't want him around. Even after I got the restraining order, he'd still call me or try to see me. The bottom line is, Jake scared me."

Pagan was quiet for a time. He had a mental image of the way he'd seen Kiviranna in the cell in London. The scorchmarks, the elaborate electrocution carried out with a madman's patience, a death that was both simple and ugly. "What did he talk about the last time you saw him?"

"He was completely out of it," she answered. "He said he was going to make some kind of statement against international Communism – he had this thing about how the Russians had murdered his parents and grandparents in one of those stupid little countries that don't exist any more and how he had to do something about it. I wasn't exactly happy to see him, Mr Pagan. Forgive me if I'm forgetting anything – I wasn't a captive audience. He was talking crazy. I just wanted to get the hell away from him."

"Did he say anything else? Did he talk about friends?"

The woman laughed. "Friends? Jake didn't have any, Mr Pagan. Friendships were off limits to him. How could anybody befriend a guy who was sweet one day, then out of his tree the next? Would you want Charlie Manson for a friend?"

Pagan was frustrated. If this proved to be a dead-end, if Rose Alexander knew nothing about any accomplice, he might as well fold his tent and go home. He said, "Think. Anything at all might be useful."

She was pensive for a time. "Okay. Here's something. The last night I saw him he asked me to give him a ride. He had to be in a certain place at a certain time. The guy he was meeting had a thing about punctuality. Remember, I wanted him out of my life in a hurry, Mr Pagan. So I said I'd drive him where he had to go. Which is exactly what I did. And that was the last I saw of him."

"Where did you take him?"

"To the boardwalk at Brighton Beach." Rose Alexander lit another cigarette, which she held in a hand that fluttered like a small injured bird. It was obvious that any conversation about Kiviranna agitated her.

"Did he say who he was going to meet?"

She shook her head slowly. "He didn't say. It was just somebody he had to meet on the boardwalk, that's all."

Pagan noticed for the first time that she had a collection of freckles around her nose and cheeks. "But no names."

"No names," she said.

Pagan looked across the room at Klein, who had an expression on his face of frustration. "Did he give you any kind of impression of the person he was supposed to meet?"

The woman blew a long stream of smoke and for a moment her face was lost to Pagan. She said, "Sorry. I draw a blank. I guess if he told me anything I must have suppressed it. Or else I never really heard it in the first place."

Pagan was disappointed. He stood very still a moment, looking at a picture on the wall, a sepia-tinted mushroom, a doper's picture, and rather ominous. "If I need to ask anything more, I'll be in touch," he said. "Thanks for your time."

She smiled in an insipid way. "Yeah, sure."

Pagan stepped out of the apartment with Klein. Then he started to go down the stairs. He was aware of Rose Alexander watching from the open doorway.

"I just remembered something," she said, and her voice echoed in the stairwell. "It's not very much, but you never know."

Pagan stopped, turned around, climbed back up to the landing. The woman had her hands in the pockets of her jeans and was leaning against the door frame, her hips thrust forward in a way Pagan found mildly provocative, all the more so for the lack of self-consciousness in her manner.

"Like I said, it might not be much, but here it is." She smiled at Pagan, perhaps a little sadly, as if all she were throwing him was a scrap. "Jake was going to meet the guy in some kind of old shop on the boardwalk. He mentioned that in passing. Maybe it amused him, I don't know. It just came back to me. I didn't ask any questions about it, because I didn't want to know."

Pagan thanked the woman again. Outside in the street he walked toward Klein's car. He got in on the passenger side and Klein climbed behind the wheel. Pagan said, "Suddenly I'm overcome by an urge to get some good sea air into my lungs."

"You got it," Klein said.

Klein drove the Dodge in the direction of Brighton Beach Avenue and the boardwalk. Neither he nor Pagan noticed the pea-green Buick that moved half a block behind them, a stealthy vehicle, the kind of car nobody ever wanted except for people whose need for total anonymity overwhelmed their desire for attention and their good taste. It followed, always half a block behind, all the way to Brighton Beach.

Fredericksburg, Virginia

Galbraith dined in a moody way alone on the roof, consuming a simple Indian meal prepared for him by the chef of a famous Washington restaurant and sent to Virginia by fast car. He ate spinach rice coloured with saffron, tandoori prawns, cucumber raita and mariel mimosas, those delightful little puff pastries that contain grated coconut, sultanas and cardamom seeds. He pushed his plate away, sat back, belched delicately into his napkin, then gazed across the roof at the satellite dishes. He stared beyond, into the mysterious sky the dishes scanned and analysed. He dropped his napkin on his empty plate, rose, crossed the roof and re-entered the house, climbing down and down into the basement.

His digestive juices made rumbling sounds. The Indian meal lay uneasily inside him. He ought never to have eaten in his present mood. And the spicy food he'd just consumed – well, really, he ought to have known better. He moaned as he settled down before the consoles, which he regarded with impatience.

When Iverson came into the room Galbraith didn't turn his face to look. He drummed his stubby fingers on his knees in a gesture Gary Iverson took to be one of exasperation. Iverson also knew, from long experience of Galbraith's behaviour, that the fat man would be the first to speak, that any question on Iverson's part would be utterly ignored.

Galbraith made a plump little fist, misleadingly cherubic in appearance. He spoke in a very flat tone of voice. "I am an anxious man, Gary. Do you want to know *why* I'm such an anxious man, Gary?"

Iverson mumbled something meaningless.

Galbraith smacked the coffee-table with his fist and an ashtray jumped. "Where do I begin? Ah, yes, let's deal with the home front first, shall we? Let's discuss our own shortcomings. A telephone conversation between Carl Sundbach and Mikhail Kiss was logged here two hours ago. It appears that Sundbach has spotted our man. A man of ours, presumably a professional, has been rumbled by an old fellow whose eyesight isn't the best and whose reflexes are arguably threadbare – and yet *he made our man*, Gary."

Iverson looked up briefly at one of the consoles, absently noticing a NATO message, white letters on a black background, a detailed outline of the next day's strategic naval manoeuvres.

"Incompetence, Gary," Galbraith said. "I will not stand for that kind of thing. Now we have Sundbach worrying about who in the name of God is watching him. Do I overreact, Gary? Do I hear you think that? Consider. Sundbach knows he's under surveillance. He can't figure out who's doing the watching. He's an old guy, maybe he gets scared, what does he do?"

Iverson shook his head.

Galbraith hopped up from the sofa, causing vibrations and making motes of dust rise. "I am dealing in possibilities, Gary, which is what I always do. And here's one to stick in your throat. Sundbach, a terrified old man, a man with a gun licence, decides to shoot his pursuer. It's not beyond feasibility, Gary. *The mess! One of our operatives dead in the street!* I am speaking here of shame, Gary. The involvement of the local police. Homicide detectives. *Newspapermen.* Horror!"

Iverson considered this scenario unlikely, but didn't say so. He had seen Galbraith react this way before in situations where he thought the professional reputation of the agency was endangered or where the threat of exposure lurked. He was more than normally sensitive, it seemed, when it came to his beloved White Light project.

There was a silence in the basement. Galbraith, who had the kind of vision that enabled him to see around corners, who had the sort of imagination that allowed him to explore possibilities even as he juggled them, who liked to predict human behaviour as if his brain were a series of actuarial tables or psychological logarithms, returned to the sofa and sat down and his monk's robe flopped open, revealing enormous hairy white thighs.

"Take that useless surveyor out of the street, Gary, and send in the Clowns." Clowns was the in-house term for those highly-skilled and expensively-trained employees whose functions within the Agency were many and various, but always clandestine. Sometimes the Clowns were called upon to erect smokescreens or manufacture diversions when such strategies were needed. They staged car wrecks, set alarm bells off, lit fires, fucked up telephone lines, forged documents, tampered with computer networks, pretended to be insurance salesmen or window-cleaners or Swiss bankers or Italian lawyers or whatever role was required in a given situation. When specialised surveillance was needed, when the ordinary watcher in the street had been exposed, the Clowns were the people you sent for. They were inventive men and sometimes just a little arrogant in the way of all specialists. Galbraith had introduced the concept of the Clowns years ago – a budgetary secret concealed under the vague rubric of Miscellaneous – and they'd been useful on many occasions. They prided themselves on the fact that only rarely had they resorted to real violence. Theirs was a pantomime world, a place of appearances and illusions, flash and noise when needed, or quiet play-acting if that was preferred.

"Did you probe young Andres?" Galbraith asked.

Iverson nodded. "I did."

"And?"

"He quotes Mikhail. Mikhail trusts Sundbach to behave himself."

"And Andres goes along with that?"

"To some extent," Iverson said.

"But not all the way?"

Iverson shrugged. "It's hard to say. He defers to Mikhail, at least on the surface, but I get the feeling he might do something different if Mikhail wasn't around."

"How different? Would he do violence to Carl Sundbach?"

"Maybe. It's hard to tell with Andres. He's like a man completely covered in very tight Saranwrap. You look at his face and you think Prince Charming, and then a kind of glaze goes across his eyes and you know you've lost him. And you don't know where he's gone."

"I want him to stay out of mischief, Gary. That's the only thing that matters. He's got to be on board that plane to Norway at ten o'clock tomorrow night, and it's too close to the end to have a royal fuck-up now." Galbraith rubbed his acupuncture stud. It was said to relieve stress, which so far it hadn't done. "I move now to another matter, perhaps even a little more disconcerting. And that is dear old London, Gary. It appears that Colonel Viktor Epishev of the KGB is running around causing havoc over there, having shot two young policemen on duty. His real target is none other than Frank Pagan, who arrived in New York this very day. (I am having Pagan watched, of course. Let us pray for competence in this instance.) I want to keep Pagan busy diddling round with Kiviranna and out of harm's way, but I really can't have Epishev causing all this grief over in London."

Galbraith paused. He was suddenly conscious of the delicate balance of things, the wheels spinning within wheels, the equilibrium so finely calibrated that even the light touch of a spring breeze might blow it all to kingdom come. He had been given a heavy responsibility, and he was determined to carry it out. The future of mankind, even if mankind were a class among which he found a thousand things despicable, a thousand things grubby, was no small affair. He cleared his throat and surveyed the consoles a moment.

"I really don't know what Vladimir Greshko thinks he's up to by sending his man to London," Galbraith said. "But I believe it's time we found out. Agree?"

"Yes," Iverson said.

Galbraith made a steeple of his fingertips and held it under his lower lip in a contemplative gesture. "I love smooth surfaces, Gary. Porcelains. Silks. Certain kinds of stones. Glass. Mirrors. I like surfaces so smooth you can't feel any kind of seam. What I hate is sandpaper. And what I'm beginning to feel right now is a certain amount of grit forming beneath my fingernails. I don't like the sensation, Gary."

Galbraith dropped his hands to his side. "It's time to make Ted Gunther earn his salary, don't you think?"

13

Zavidovo, the Soviet Union

Because it was a beautiful dawn the Yakut nurse – a firm believer in the benefits of early rising and crisp air, even if the patient was terminal – had helped Vladimir Greshko into a wheelchair and pushed him out into the garden, where he sat in the shade of a very old oak, surrounded by pines and wildflowers and all the rest of what he considered nature's repetitive graffiti. It was, for him, a bucolic nightmare. Despite his rustic origins and the sentimentality he often felt for the land, he had become a city person, somebody made nervous by the racket of birds.

He watched the nurse go back inside the cottage and he glowered at her. To have been detached from his tube, disgusting as the thing was, was like being yanked from an umbilical cord. Twenty minutes, the Yakut bitch had said. Twenty minutes, no more, as if she were bestowing a precious gift on him.

The trouble with nature, Greshko reflected, was its unsanitary condition. Little things chewed on even smaller things. Ants scurried off with disgusting larvae in their jaws. Wild animals and birds crapped where they felt like it. He loved the tundra, those great prairies with their romantic isolation and impenetrable mystery, but when it came to thick trees and the awful green density of this place, he experienced a suffocating claustrophobia.

He closed his eyes, opening them only when he heard the sound of an automobile approaching from the distance. He turned his face to the pathway that led to the cottage, peering through the twisted posts of the old wooden fence. His first thought was that Volovich was coming to say he'd received news from Viktor, but when he made out the shape of the Zil – unmistakable! – he knew his visitor was General Olsky.

He saw Olsky get out of the long black car and come through a space in the fence, where a bramble bush snagged the sleeve of his well-tailored suit. Greshko stared at the bald head as it ducked under the thorns. And then Olsky was crossing the thick grass to the wheelchair in short springing steps. He wore this morning amber-tinted sunglasses, a horrible Western affectation as far as Greshko was concerned. They caught the dawn sunlight and glinted as if two copper coins had been pressed into his eye sockets.

Olsky asked, "How are you today, Vladimir?"

"Unchanged, Stefan. You find me as you found me when you were last here. Two visits in as many days! I feel very honoured."

Olsky circled the wheelchair, pausing immediately behind Greshko. As a technique, Greshko thought it ludicrous. Was he supposed to twist his head round in order to see the little shit? Was this meant to place him at a disadvantage? Greshko wanted to laugh. When it came to technique, when it came to the body language of interviews, he'd written the book.

"Let's walk, Vladimir," Olsky said. "I'll push you."

"As you wish."

Olsky shoved the chair over the thick grass, a shade too quickly perhaps, as if he meant to unnerve Greshko. Olsky wheeled him towards the pines, where the ground was rougher and the chair shook. Then Olsky stopped, catching his breath and sitting down with his back to the trunk of a pine. He snapped a stalk of long grass and placed it against his teeth.

"Do you like it here?" Olsky asked.

"This green prison? What do you think?"

"I can imagine worse places, Vladimir."

"I suppose you can."

Olsky stared in the direction of the small house. "You've got a decent place to live. Your own medical attendant. It could be a whole lot worse. At least the sun is shining and the weather's warm."

Greshko smiled. Just under the surface of Olsky's words, he could hear it – a quietly implied threat, a hint of how the last days of the old man's life could be made utterly dreadful by removing him from this place and sending him in some cramped railroad carriage to the distant north. *Am I supposed to be scared shitless? Am I meant to nod my head and drool with gratitude?* "Why don't you come to the point, Stefan? Dying men don't have time for circumspection."

Olsky was quiet a moment. "Where is Colonel Epishev?"

Epishev, of course. Greshko said, "I assume he's at his desk. Unless you've misplaced him, of course. Which would be damnably careless of you."

Olsky took off his glasses. "Where have you sent him?"

"Sent him? You forget, General, I have absolutely no power in the organs these days."

"He came here. I have that on good authority. He came here with Lieutenant Volovich. I can only assume you issued instructions to him."

Olsky watched a woodpecker as it fastened itself on to a pine trunk and rapped its beak with sublime ferocity of purpose. *Rap rap rap.* Epishev and Volovich had been spotted coming here. Ah, the risks one ran! The trees had ears and eyes and every goddam blade of grass was a potential microphone.

"I receive so many drugs, Stefan. I sleep a lot. Sometimes I have no idea of time. Sometimes people come to see me and I don't remember them ever having visited. And so many people come, I have more friends than I can count."

"I want an answer, Vladimir. Why did Epishev and Volovich come here? And where have you sent Viktor?"

Greshko wondered if somehow Volovich had been made to talk. But if Dimitri had confessed, then Olsky wouldn't be here asking these questions. Things would be different if Olsky *really* knew anything. Things would be rather more straightforward, perhaps even a little brutal. Greshko would have been removed from this place without ceremony. Besides, why should Volovich admit anything that might incriminate himself? The man might be nothing more than Epishev's toady, but he was surely no fool when it came to survival.

Olsky replaced his glasses. "Are you denying you were visited by Epishev and Volovich?"

Greshko smiled in spite of the sudden pain that knifed through his abdomen. Pain like this, you were never prepared for it, it went through your nerve-endings like a dagger through old papers. "How can I deny something I can't remember?"

Olsky felt oddly tense in the old man's presence, even though he knew he had no need to. Sabina was forever reminding him of his own new authority – *Sweet Jesus, you are the Chairman of the KGB, you don't need to be in awe of anyone, my love*. And of course she was right. But there was something in Greshko's demeanour, a quality connected to Greshko's history, the sense of the man's legend that now and then unnerved Olsky. Greshko had walked the same stages, stood on the same platforms as Stalin and Khrushchev and Bulganin and Malenkov, the luminaries of modern Soviet history. Greshko had been at the centre of things for so many years that his absence created a vacuum which, for most Soviet citizens accustomed to seeing his face on state occasions, was almost unnatural – as if the moon had failed to wax.

"First you lose some computer data," Greshko said. "Then you lose one of your Colonels. If I was running the organs – "

"But you're not, General – "

"When I did, *General*, I controlled everything, the tasks of my key personnel, the access codes to the computers, nothing ever slipped away from *me*." With some effort, Greshko raised his voice. "I knew where everything and everybody was, day and goddam night, I lived the organs, *General*, twenty-five hours a day, eight days a goddam week. Don't come here and make accusations that I gave an order to Epishev! You know I don't have *that much* power these days," and here the old man snapped his fingers. "If I did, by God you'd see some iron in the backbone of this country!"

Olsky stood in silence for a time. He had cards to play, but he wanted his timing to be correct. He was prepared to let Greshko rant for a while. He watched globules of white saliva appear on the old man's lips. Then Greshko yielded to a prolonged fit of coughing, doubling over in his wheelchair, wiping his sleeve across his lips. His skeleton seemed to rattle. Olsky, noticing how crystalline mucus clung to the material of the old man's sweater, turned his face away for a moment. The paroxysm passed and Greshko, white-faced, was silent.

Olsky wandered some feet from the wheelchair. With his back to Greshko, he said, "A man called Yevenko was arrested yesterday, General."

Greshko, whose chest felt raw, his lungs on fire, closed his eyes. He had the impression of a thousand wasps buzzing through his brain. *Yevenko*, he thought.

"More commonly known as the Printer," Olsky said. "A criminal type whose speciality is forged papers, passports, and even the occasional rouble. He was arrested on suspicion of currency irregularities. It was a routine kind of arrest, but it had an interesting aspect to it. The Printer, it seems, had a story to tell about recently being called upon to make a West German passport for a man known as Grunwald."

Greshko was sarcastic. "Fascinating. Tell me more."

"Grunwald, according to the Printer, is in reality our comrade Epishev."

"Really," Greshko remarked. He showed absolutely

no emotion on his face. "And you take the word of this criminal?"

"He was in a tight spot. He was ready to barter. People like him usually tell the truth when they face the prospect of lengthy incarceration."

Greshko wheeled his chair a couple of feet. "Let's suppose for just a moment this criminal is telling the truth – although, as you may be aware, General, criminals rarely do. Viktor might have needed a forged passport in the normal line of duty. He works in some very grey areas, after all. He infiltrates underground groups, he may need false ID, a cover of some kind."

"It's possible." Olsky paused. "I'm reliably informed that the man using this passport left the Soviet Union on an Aeroflot flight to East Berlin. He then caught a connecting flight to London."

"London? Why would Viktor travel to London?" Greshko asked. "This is all very thin, General. What evidence do you have that the man called Grunwald is Epishev in any case?"

Olsky said, "The photograph in the forged passport was Epishev's. The Printer assured us of that."

"And you believed him?" Greshko infused scepticism into his voice, the tone of the experienced old master contemptuous of the apprentice's naivety.

Olsky didn't reply to this question. "Did you send Viktor to London, Vladimir?"

"Why would I send him there? Why would I send him anywhere, for God's sake? Besides, I couldn't send him abroad, he'd need clearance from a superior officer."

Olsky, who knew Epishev had the authority to go in and out of the Soviet Union at will, a clearance given him by Greshko years ago, glanced through the trees for a time. There was something just a little pathetic in backing Greshko into a corner. Something almost sad, although that was an emotion Olsky couldn't afford to feel. He wondered why he wasn't savouring this moment. "Comrade General, when I visited you before

I mentioned missing computer data relating to a man called Aleksis Romanenko."

Greshko, like some old parrot, cocked his head and listened. What now? What links was this upstart Olsky trying to make?

Olsky said, "I mentioned that the data had been deliberately removed. But in this particular instance we had a stroke of quite extraordinary good fortune."

"Good fortune?" Greshko asked. There was a lump, like stone, in his throat.

"Indeed. We were able to reproduce the missing data from some back-ups that a clerk took the precaution to make."

"Back-ups?" Greshko asked. *He hadn't thought of this possibility. He hadn't imagined any clerk conscientious enough to make a goddam duplicate of the data.*

Olsky went on, "It's fascinating material. It appears Romanenko had well-developed ties with a subversive organisation both inside and outside the Soviet Union known as the Brotherhood of the Forest. I must make the assumption, Vladimir, that since this data existed when you were Chairman of the organs, you must have known of it."

"I never heard of it. It means nothing to me." Greshko leaned forward in his chair. The damned pain went through him again, making it difficult to concentrate. His eyes watered and he gasped quietly. *Back-ups. Duplicates.* He wondered which wretched clerk was responsible for such a thing. It was his own damned fault because he'd never really understood the intricate ways of the new computer system, he'd always been puzzled by it and overawed, and like any man terrorised by a new technology he'd failed to grasp its potential.

"Come," Olsky said. "A traitor like Romanenko, a man in a high position – and you never knew about him? You with your omniscient knowledge of the organs? Really, General. How can I believe you?"

Greshko spoke quietly, giving the distinct impression of a man surprised by nothing. "Obviously some useless clerk, some slipshod moron, forgot to bring the material to my attention. Or perhaps during the changeover to the present computer system, the data was overlooked."

Olsky laughed quietly in disbelief. "But *you* never overlooked anything, General, did you? And surely you didn't employ morons?"

Greshko listened to the woodpecker again. Rap rap rap. The sharp beak of the creature might have been poking at the timbers of his own brain just then. He became silent in the manner of a man who has unexpectedly just lost a piece in a game of chess, a knight trapped and seized, a bishop ruthlessly snared.

Olsky said, "On the day Romanenko was shot, Epishev came to visit you. Early next morning he vanished using a fake passport. He went to London. Why the sudden rush to visit England? An overwhelming yearning to see Westminister Abbey, General? Or is there some other reason he needs to be there in the wake of Romanenko's murder? And now here's a brand new element – the former Chairman of the KGB, the all-seeing General Greshko, admits he knew nothing of Romanenko's subversion! *And asks me to believe this story.*" Olsky raised a finger to his lips and spoke in a mock whisper filled with comic astonishment. "Or could it be that General Greshko had a good reason of his own to leave Aleksis Romanenko in position as a high Party official? Is that it?"

Greshko waved a hand in the air. "You're full of hot air, Olsky. It's a wonder you aren't floating away over the damned trees."

"I ask myself. Was General Greshko involved with Romanenko in a subversive scheme? Is it that simple? Is this a deeper echo of the sounds of conspiracy I keep hearing?"

"I'd be very careful if I were you, Stefan."

Greshko saw the Yakut woman come out of the house

and approach the wheelchair. She was carrying a tray of medication. He was relieved to see her.

Olsky looked at the nurse as she came striding across the grass. Then he tapped the face of his wristwatch, as if he'd just remembered an appointment. "I'll keep in touch, of course, Vladimir. I know you're interested in the outcome of my investigations." And then he turned and moved toward the parked Zil, sliding through the fence and deftly avoiding the bramble bush that had snagged him before. Greshko watched him step into the large car, then heard the sound of the engine turning over.

"Pill time, General," the nurse said.

Greshko observed the car as it vanished between trees, leaving only a vibration behind. He felt the nurse stick a capsule into his mouth. He swallowed it, listening to the Zil until it became indistinguishable from the drone of insects. Back-ups, he thought. The need for duplicates that sometimes obsessed the petty clerical mind. So be it. He squeezed his eyes shut tightly and concentrated, tracking things through his mind, wondering what *his* next step would be if he were General Smartass Olsky. What would you do next, Stefan? The answer came back at once. *I would put the squeeze on Volovich. I'd twist Volovich like a damp rag until he told me everything he knows.* The question was how much Volovich knew. He hadn't been told the precise extent of the Brotherhood's plan, but he certainly knew enough to cause enormous trouble.

Greshko glared into the sun as if he might stare it down. Back-ups and duplicates, by God! Well, he had a back-up of his own which, like a palmed card, he'd play when the time was ripe. And that ripeness, he felt, was upon him.

He smiled at the nurse and she regarded him in a wary manner. "Why are you smiling?" she asked.

"Why not?"

"You want something. That's when you smile, General. When you need me."

Greshko shrugged, turning his face from the sun, which was the colour now of a blood orange. "Perhaps," was his response to the Yakut woman.

Tallinn, Estonia

Colonel Yevgenni Uvarov disembarked from the launch in Tallinn harbour just after daylight and walked until he reached the Mermaid monument, where he sat on an empty bench beside a clump of shrubbery. He pretended to be interested in the monument, gazing up at the winged woman that stood atop a stone structure, but he couldn't concentrate on it. He read on a plaque that the statue had been erected in memory of the crew of the *Russalka*, which sank in the Gulf of Finland in 1893, but every so often he'd turn and look away, back across the shore to the harbour, where the tall stacks and funnels of ships looked dense and tangled in the dawn sky.

He was unable to still the nervousness he felt. He got up, walked round the green wooden bench, scanned the shoreline, fidgeted. Since he'd taken the phonecall last night on Saaremaa Island he'd been living as if at some distance from himself. He hadn't slept. The idea of sleep was foreign to him. He hadn't eaten breakfast, not even a simple cup of tea. He'd risen in that strangely chill dark just before sunrise and gone down to the fast launch that went back and forth between the island and Tallinn, ferrying mail and supplies, and he'd stepped on board and nobody had asked him any questions even though he'd waited for the captain of the vessel to approach him for ID papers or an official pass. He calculated he could be gone for only six or seven hours before he was missed from the radar base – although in reality his absence might be noticed at any time, especially if there were some unforeseen emergency. But he thought he'd covered himself as well as he possibly could, by informing his adjutant – perhaps the laziest man in the whole command

– that he had to travel on unspecified official business to Kuressaare on the southern part of the island.

He stared at the sea, waited, wondered if he'd done the right thing by coming here, or if he'd just walked into a trap that would cost him his life. He could imagine it – discovery, the disgrace of a court-martial, public humiliation, a death sentence. And what would happen to his wife and children then? Branded, destined to a terrible life, a world in which doors would be closed to them.

Uvarov returned to the bench, sat, waited, smoked a cigarette. The man on the telephone had mentioned Aleksis's name and the importance of meeting – but he hadn't identified himself, and now Uvarov, whose heart would not stop kicking against his ribs, wished he'd never met the man known as Aleksis, that he'd never accepted the US passports and the enormous sum of money, but Aleksis had been persuasive, and convincing, and finally impossible to refuse, with his enchanting pictures of life in a free world, a future for the children, a place where a man might advance through his own merits – Aleksis had painted a portrait of a desirable place that Uvarov's wife Valentina lusted after. *Freedom, Yevgenni. A new life. To bring up our children as we choose, Yevgenni. The risks are worth it.*

Uvarov heard the sound of a car door slam nearby. He stared at the statue, couldn't sit still. He heard footsteps on the cobblestones and he raised his face just as a man came into view.

The voice on the telephone had said, *I read* Sovietskaya Estonia. *I always carry a copy with me.*

Uvarov saw *Sovietskaya Estonia* folded under the man's arm, looked away at once, sucked the sea air into his lungs, felt his eyes smart and begin to water. The man came to the bench, sat down, tapped Uvarov's wrist with the rolled-up newspaper. The Colonel felt a fist close inside his stomach as he looked at the newcomer – who was perhaps in his late forties and wore a thick moustache that covered his upper lip. He was dressed in the uniform of a Major in the KGB, a fact that caused Uvarov to grip the bench tightly.

"Don't believe everything you see, Colonel," the man said. "The uniform is borrowed."

Uvarov pressed his palm to his mouth. The man smiled and reassuringly touched the back of Uvarov's hand. "You don't look so good, Colonel. Let's walk some colour back into your face."

Uvarov rose. The man took him by the arm and they strolled round the monument in the direction of Kadriorg Park. The sun, low over the harbour, cast all manner of strange shadows between the anchored ships.

"Learn to relax, Yevgenni."

Uvarov stopped moving. He stood under a tree, lit another cigarette, tried very hard to smile. Relax, he thought. Tell me how. Show me!

"Call me Marcus."

"Marcus," Uvarov said.

"You suspect a trap. Ask yourself this, my friend. If this were a trap, would I appear in this particular uniform? I'd be in civilian clothes, trying to put you at your ease, wouldn't I? I'd be trying to lull you, no?"

Uvarov made a feeble gesture and the man named Marcus, whose expression was one of weary strength, smiled. "You all suspect you're about to be arrested. Each and every one of you feels the same when I make contact."

Uvarov looked back in the direction of the harbour. A pall of black smoke rose from the funnel of a ship, spiralling slowly upward like a funereal scarf. Each and every one of us, he thought. "How many are involved?" he asked.

"In the armed services of the Soviet Union, less than a score, perhaps less than a dozen," Marcus answered in an enigmatic way. "Outside the services, the number is impossible to estimate. Patriots come and go, Yevgenni. One day you can count thousands, another day hundreds. Mercenaries on the other hand tend to remain stable."

"You're vague," Uvarov said. He didn't like to think of himself as a mercenary. He was going through this nightmare for his family's sake, not because he wanted to accumulate riches in the West.

"I need to be." Marcus looked toward the dark smoke now. He had a face that was pocked and pitted, the result of some childhood disease. It gave him a seasoned appearance, a toughness.

"Why are you making contact? Where is Aleksis?" Uvarov asked.

"Aleksis's part is over, my friend."

Uvarov clutched the man's wrist. "My family – "

"In wonderful health, Yevgenni."

"You're sure?"

Marcus stroked his moustache. "They long to be with you. They long for freedom."

Uvarov felt his anxiety fade, but only a little. He took a handkerchief out of his coat pocket and blew his nose because the mention of his family had choked him and he felt like crying. Marcus, in a gesture of kindness, placed a hand on Uvarov's shoulder.

"Soon, Yevgenni. Very soon," Marcus said. "Now listen to me carefully. I could not give you your final instructions over the telephone, for obvious reasons. As soon as you have performed the function Aleksis hired you for, a small launch will be waiting for you at the jetty that services your installation. It will look like any ordinary military launch except for this one fact – the vessel will not be flying a flag. It will wait for exactly five minutes, no longer. When you get on board, you'll be taken to Hango in Finland."

"And my family?"

"Your family will be in Helsinki many hours before you arrive in Hango. They'll be safe. I promise you."

"They're travelling alone?"

"Of course. But they have passports. They'll leave Russia through Leningrad."

Somehow Uvarov had expected different arrangements, that he'd be going with his wife and children when the time came, but that was fantasy. Obviously, if he wanted to join his family he'd have to go through with Aleksis's task – otherwise, he'd be stranded in Soviet territory while his family was safe in Finland.

"What if something goes wrong?" he asked.

Marcus crossed his fingers and held his hand in front of Uvarov's face. "If we perform our tasks efficiently, nothing can possibly go wrong."

"If is the strangest word in the language," Uvarov said.

Marcus moved a couple of feet away. "Keep your nerve. Don't lose it."

Uvarov wanted to detain Marcus now, because he found comfort in the notion of a fellow conspirator. But he couldn't think of anything else to say.

"In Helsinki, my friend. Your wife and children. And a further fifty thousand American dollars." The man known as Marcus walked between the trees and didn't look back.

Uvarov watched him go. If, the Colonel thought. *If* everything went according to plan. *If* all the nameless conspirators Marcus had mentioned played their roles and adhered to the timetable. If. How many other Army personnel were involved apart from himself? Less than twenty, perhaps less than a dozen, according to Marcus. A small number of men. The smaller the number, the less chance of something going wrong.

Uvarov was slightly cheered by this thought.

The man called Marcus walked to the place where he'd parked his car, an inconspicuous black Moskvich. He took a dark overcoat from the back seat and wore it over the KGB uniform, then he sat behind the wheel. Marcus, whose real name was Anton Sepp, formerly a sergeant in the Soviet Army in Afghanistan, looked back at the figure of Yevgenni Uvarov as he drove away from Tallinn harbour. Then he headed through the streets of the city, passing along Toompea Street in the medieval part of Tallinn, where a network of narrow alleys ran between crooked houses. Already there were a few early tourists moving listlessly, the ubiquitous Japanese with their cameras, a couple of Americans – you could always tell the Americans from the cut of their clothes and the slightly condescending looks on their faces as they studied *quaintness* – and a few Finns who came for riotous weekends of vodka drinking. The tourists would rummage in the souvenir and craft shops or they'd walk to the foreign currency stores on Tehnika or Gagarini Streets. They'd wander the museums and at night, sated by history, they'd sit through a Western-style cabaret of forced cheerfulness in the basement of the Viru Hotel.

Marcus was happy to drive out of the city, past blocks of new high-rise apartments, which were surrounded by mountains of cement and sand and the occasional thin tree. These were depressing areas, and boring – the more so when you contrasted them with the rich medieval architecture of old Tallinn – and yet people were expected to live their lives in such prefabricated tedium. He kept driving until the city was behind him and the sun was rising over the landscape and the countryside around him was rich and green. He turned the car off the highway about thirty-five miles from Tallinn and drove down a narrow track between pine trees. On either side of the track, obscured by thickets of trunks, dark green meadows stretched out and the surface of a narrow lake was visible. The car rocked and swayed over ruts for three or four miles, then the pathway twisted and an old farmhouse came in view.

Whitewalled, shuttered, it appeared at first sight to have been abandoned. But fresh tyre-tracks in the fore-court suggested recent activity and, under a tarpaulin that had been hung across a roofless outbuilding, were three vehicles – a grey Volvo station-wagon, a small

Zaporozhet, and a Soviet Army truck that only a day before had been in Riga in Latvia.

Marcus parked the Moskvich, entered the house, stooping as he did so because the ceiling had been built at a time when human beings were smaller. The room in which he stood was furnished only with a table and four roughly-carpentered chairs. Marcus removed his overcoat. He heard the click of a magazine being inserted into an automatic rifle, a slight echo from another room. A figure appeared in a doorway, a young man with an M-16 rifle held in the firing position.

"Relax, boy." Marcus smiled, sat at the kitchen table, rolled a cigarette from a leather tobacco pouch. He was tired and it showed on his face. He smoked, watched the young man approach the table, saw the automatic weapon being propped very carefully against the leg of a chair.

The young man drummed his fingertips on the table. It was less a sign of nerves than it was of restlessness. He was ready to go into action. He'd dreamed of nothing else for a long time now. Marcus watched the young man, and his thoughts drifted to Aleksis Romanenko. When tasks had been allocated, functions delegated, Aleksis's role had been to make certain that those members of the Soviet armed forces he'd recruited wouldn't fail at the last minute, and that their escape routes were firmly in place. This role had suited Aleksis because it involved travel – both in the Baltic and in Russia itself – and as a ranking official he could go almost anywhere without question. Now, with Aleksis dead – gunned down, or so it was rumoured: hard news was a precious commodity – Marcus had been obliged to assume Aleksis's part, like an understudy stepping in at the last moment. Marcus, a deserter from Afghanistan, didn't have freedom of movement. As a fugitive, his style was cramped. His original role had been to make sure the weapons smuggled into Latvia from the United States were distributed between the Baltic countries, and that the various groups would move in unison when the hour came. But now he was exhausted at having to play Aleksis's nerve-racking part.

Thirty-four hours. He sat back in his chair, enjoyed the cigarette, gazed at the young man, whose rather innocent face concealed a certain ferocity, a dark purpose. The boy, who called himself Anarhist, meaning Anarchist, had spent two years in the Soviet Army in Chabarovsk on the Chinese border and a further two years in a military prison for distributing pamphlets of a nationalist nature, calling for freedom for all the nationalities – the Balts, the Georgians, the Armenians, the Kazakhs, the scores of other races – harnessed by the Russians. There were hundreds like this boy throughout the Baltic, brave and determined and patriotic, and many of them were waiting for the moment.

Marcus crushed his cigarette out. He thought of the trips he had already made – to Riga, Haapsalu on the Baltic coast, Moscow itself – and the final arrangements he had concluded with the people Aleksis had bought. They were all like Uvarov, scared and yet mildly defiant, ambitious to leave a country and a military system that both terrified and stultified. And they were all impatient men too, filled with the belief that the Soviet system was changing but at an intolerably slow pace which couldn't satisfy their needs. A few had indisputably genuine philosophical differences with the system. Others had grievances, complaints that the system was unfair, or uncaring, that it didn't listen to the small if reasonable voices of dissent. Some had grudges that went back years, often to a time before they were born, back to grandparents who'd been purged by Stalin, relatives conjured out of existence by a political programme that could never conceal its inherent barbarism, no matter how much cosmetic surgery was done. Some resented the way their careers had failed to take fire, that their wives were discontented, their homes inadequate, their long separations from family intolerable. A few had material aspirations, their minds filled with pictures from glossy

Western magazines. What they all shared was the belief that they were innocent inmates in a drab prison, and that the only light they could see, if one existed at all, was at the end of a very long tunnel. And none of them knew the nature of the plan, although some might have guessed it, but if so they'd repressed the knowledge, blinded themselves to their own conclusions.

Aleksis had chosen these people masterfully. He had tapped into deeply-rooted discontentments, old grudges and fears, and he'd assembled a team of key personnel, keeping them afloat on money, and passports, and promises. He'd also manipulated them through their families, providing passports to wives and children, making sure the families travelled out of Russia the day before the action was scheduled, thus locking the husbands firmly into the plan. It was, Marcus had often thought, a scheme of quite extraordinary insight, and he could only marvel at the patience with which Aleksis had put it together, the energy involved, the charm and persuasion needed, the clandestine meetings conducted in an atmosphere of fear and distrust and uncertainty.

He rolled another cigarette. A third person stepped into the room now, a girl of about twenty with short yellow hair and light blue eyes. She had just awakened from sleep and she looked bleary. She wore an old American combat jacket, khaki pants, a black t-shirt. Her feet were bare. She sat down at the table and put her feet up on the rough wooden surface, rubbing her eyes as she did so. She was hardly more than a child, Marcus thought, but she had already spent eighteen months in a psychiatric hospital for her role in editing and distributing an underground newspaper critical of Russification. She'd been given electric-shock treatments, the only permanent effect of which had been to leave her with a rather attractive laziness in one eye. Marcus knew her only as Erma. There was an intimacy between them, something that wasn't fully realised as yet, but it was the kind of closeness developed between people with a common cause.

She rolled a cigarette from Marcus's leather pouch, smoked in silence for a time. She was impatient, and anxious. Her spell in the so-called psychiatric hospital hadn't instilled patience into her. Marcus reached out and laid his hand over the girl's.

"You can't hurry time," Marcus said.

The girl stared at him, as if his truism were beneath her dignity. Tucked in the belt of her pants was a Colt automatic. She let her hand drift over the butt of the pistol. Marcus felt it then – the youthful eagerness of this girl, the desire that was in her to fight, something she could barely restrain.

"I had a dream," she said.

"Bad or good?"

"I dreamed the time came and all the streets were empty."

The boy, Anarhist, made a snorting sound. "Dreams don't mean anything," he said.

Marcus stood up, stretched his arms. He would go upstairs now, and try to nap, to settle his mind down in that place where it lay perfectly still. But lately he'd been having a difficult time sleeping. He'd shut his eyes and try to make himself comfortable but then the images would come back in at him the way they always did. He'd be standing on dry, rocky terrain under a terrible yellow sun, his mouth filled with dust and his eyes stinging. Three Afghans kneeled some yards away, their faces turned from him, their hands tethered behind their backs. Marcus noticed – a detail that never escaped him, no matter how many times he played this dreadful movie in his head – how the ropes cut into the skin of the bound men. He blinked his eyes as the wind blew over the rocks and his nostrils filled with dust and somebody on the edge of his vision thrust a revolver into his hand, which he took, understanding what he had to do with it. The wind flapped the headgear the Afghans wore and in the distance was the noise of rockets screaming. *Shoot*, somebody said. And Marcus raised the revolver and fired into the heads of the three men, who fell forward into the dust even as the wind, whistling through the cavities of rocks, still made their clothing flap against their bodies. The same memory, always the same bloody memory, images of a pain he couldn't exorcise. He'd been involved in other things in Afghanistan – the shelling of villages, blowing up bridges and highways, direct combat – but they didn't match the execution of the three guerillas, neither in shame nor in terror.

He climbed upstairs in the old farmhouse, hating his own recollections, but hating the Russians more for having created them in the first place.

London

V.G. Epishev, who operated on the principle that a man in constant motion left a confusion of trails, had checked into a hotel in Earl's Court, a few streets behind the underground station. It was not a great hotel, but it had the merit of obscurity, located as it was at the end of a warren of narrow thoroughfares. He had a room on the top floor, one of the very few rooms in the establishment with its own telephone. *It's extra, you know*, the woman at the desk told him, as if she were pleased by his little touch of extravagance and proud that her hotel could provide the opportunity. *But it's ever such a convenience, dear*.

Epishev lay on the bed, turned his face to the window. It wasn't quite light outside yet. He thought of making a call to Dimitri Volovich, but what did he have to report so far? The prospect of going through the rigmarole of raising the international operator, then being put through to East Berlin, and from there patched to Volovich in Moscow only to speak in terse, uninformative phrases, had no appeal. Greshko could wait. What choice did he have anyway? There was something enjoyable in the idea of exercising a little power over the old man, of being Greshko's eyes and ears, his brain, in a foreign country.

And Epishev was determined to savour the novelty of the feeling.

Besides, he'd been struck once or twice lately by the suspicion that this whole project, this undertaking that had forced him to travel hundreds of miles and had involved him in murder, was less a patriotic task than it was the construction of an epitaph for a sick old man who wanted to be remembered as the saviour of Russia. Perhaps it wasn't the well-being of the nation that primarily interested Greshko, perhaps it was more the prospect of some gratifying words on his tombstone that compelled Vladimir Greshko to sit in Zavidovo like some conniving spider.

Epishev got up, performed some routine exercises, toe-touching, then some brisk sit-ups. He went to the window, opened it, breathed deeply. When the telephone rang, he picked it up on the second ring, understanding it could only be Alexei Malik, since he'd told nobody else of his whereabouts.

"I'm in the lobby," Malik said.

Epishev hung up. He walked down the six flights of stairs to the foyer, which was a threadbare square of a room that smelled of very old carpet and dusty curtains. The desk was unmanned, the foyer empty save for Malik, who stood close to a curtained window. Epishev crossed the floor, noticing a red double-decker bus clatter past in the street. The hotel was shaken a moment by vibrations.

"Let's walk," Malik said. He moved to the door, held it open for Epishev. Outside, there was a slash of milky light in the sky over Earl's Court. Both men moved in silence through the streets, pausing in front of a newsagent's shop which displayed bold headlines concerning the violent slaying of two policemen. Malik paused to survey the tabloids, shaking his head as he read.

"The English don't like it when their policemen are killed, Viktor," he said. "It touches something raw in the British psyche."

Epishev said nothing. He had no interest in Malik's

perceptions of British society. He walked away from the newspaper display, the headlines that shrieked about the murder of policemen and the deterioration of law and order throughout the island in general and how gun-control laws had to have every remaining loophole closed.

Malik fell into step beside him. "I had a meeting with two men from British intelligence, Viktor," Malik said. "They called me at the Embassy, insisted on an urgent conference."

"And?"

"Your name came up several times. They seem to think you're responsible for the killings."

"Preposterous," Epishev said.

"As you say." Malik looked up at the sky in the manner of a man who thinks he feels rain in the air. "I denied all knowledge of your existence, Viktor. What could *I* possibly know about KGB personnel in any case?"

Epishev stopped on the corner of Earl's Court Road. He saw people plunging into the underground station, workers heading towards their places of employment in the half-dark. He turned to look at Malik. "You want to know how they came up with my name, of course."

"I'm curious," Malik said. "Did they pull it out of a hat like a rabbit? Did they conjure it out of nowhere?"

"British intelligence is hardly known for its powers of extrasensory perception, Alexei." Epishev, who didn't like the idea of standing on a main road, moved in the direction of the side-streets again. "The explanation is very simple," and he told Malik about Kristina Vaska, about how she'd recognised him outside Pagan's apartment.

Malik and Epishev turned into a quiet street of trees. From somewhere nearby there was the rumble of an underground train, breaking the silence.

"It's unfortunate," Malik said eventually. "Mistaken identity, of course. Besides, how could this woman recognise you after all this time? When the men from

British intelligence come back, and they're bound to, I'll tell them I made further inquiries and that the only KGB operative by the name of Viktor Epishev is enjoying his retirement in the Crimea, or something to that effect. Therefore, you couldn't possibly be in England."

"That's only going to work so long as they don't start making some inquiries of their own through their network in Moscow. If word gets back to the Chairman that I might be in London . . ." Epishev had no need to finish this sentence. He was conscious of how fragile everything was.

"I shall be completely convincing, Viktor."

Epishev was impatient suddenly. He hadn't accomplished what he'd come all this way to do. He hadn't ensured the security of the Baltic plan. And now there was the disturbing connection between Pagan and Kristina Vaska. He felt exposed, endangered, saddled with complexities he didn't need. His memory of the gunplay in the street last night didn't help his mood much either. Pagan had moved too quickly, squeezing under the car with such alacrity that Epishev hadn't had time for accuracy. It was a good thing to learn for future reference that Pagan's instinct for survival was extremely sharp. It was something to take into account.

Malik looked at his wristwatch. "I need some breakfast. Let's go somewhere for coffee." He clasped Epishev by the elbow and steered him gently back in the direction of Earl's Court Road. Epishev went with reluctance, following Malik into a coffee-bar a few blocks from the underground station, a busy, smoke-filled room run by Turks.

"Why this place?" Epishev asked. He was uncomfortable in this crowded room.

"There's somebody I want you to meet," Malik said.

Feeling vaguely alarmed, Epishev asked, "Meet? Meet who?"

Malik spotted an unoccupied table and headed towards it, drawing Epishev with him. Epishev asked his question again, but Malik was already gazing at the menu, a grease-stained, typewritten sheet, and seemed not to have heard.

"*Who?*" Epishev asked a third time.

"A friend," Malik replied. "Do you want coffee? Toast? Eggs?"

"Friends should have names," Epishev said with some anger in his voice. "I don't like being introduced to people without warning, Alexei. I don't like having things sprung on me."

Malik shook his head in vigorous denial of any underhand behaviour. "I'm talking about an ally, Viktor. An important one."

Epishev was about to say something when Malik stood up and waved an arm in greeting. Epishev turned his face towards the door, seeing the newcomer step in. The man, who wore thick glasses and a lightweight suit, smiled at Malik and came across the room, threading through the clutter of tables and the harried waitresses balancing trays with the agility of circus performers. The man reached the table and pulled up a chair. He shook Malik's hand. Epishev, displeased by what he perceived as subterfuge on Alexei's part, unhappy at the notion that Malik was bringing in an unknown third party, absorbed only a brief impression of the stranger before turning his face to the side.

"Viktor," Malik said.

Epishev looked at the newcomer again. He saw round, rather flabby features, a button-down shirt, a seersucker jacket of pin-striped design, a crewcut.

"Viktor, I want you to meet a very good friend of ours."

The newcomer smiled warmly. "Gunther," the man said. "Ted Gunther."

There was a long silence during which Epishev studied the American's face. There was a certain kind of face which Epishev didn't care for. And Gunther had it – a face as obvious as an open sandwich.

"I think it's time to clarify things," Ted Gunther said,

and he rubbed his hands in the congenially cautious manner of a diplomat about to do some business in détente. "The last thing we want is misunderstandings, right?"

Epishev, still staring at the American, said nothing.

Brighton Beach, Brooklyn

It was dark and the moon was rising on the ocean when Frank Pagan and Max Klein stepped on to the boardwalk at Brighton Beach. The night, hot and close, filled with smells of sweat and the collected suntan lotion of the day and fried foodstuffs, crowded Pagan like some great damp creature risen up from the water. Both men walked slowly to the end of the boardwalk, drifting through the crowds, the roller-skaters and skateboarders, the cyclists, the old couples moving arm-in-arm, the kids popping beercans and jousting for the attention of girls with hairdos fashioned by stylists from other planetary systems – seething activity, clammy heat, the ocean almost motionless. Pagan, sweating, leaned against the handrail and looked out at the water.

"Welcome to Brighton Beach," Klein said, and he waved a hand at the sky, as if the very constellations were a part of Brooklyn.

Pagan studied the storefronts that lined one side of the boardwalk. Here and there a vendor sold soda and hot-dogs, but what really intrigued Pagan were those places that seemed to serve as social clubs, establishments without signs. You could see through open doorways into cavernous rooms where men, mainly old, played cards or studied chessboards. Slavic music drifted out into the darkness, oddly nostalgic, even sorrowful. Though he couldn't understand a word of what was being sung, Pagan found the sound touching anyhow.

Klein said, "These places used to be stores. Some sold tourist trinkets, others greasy foods. But they gradually got taken over by emigrant societies. Mainly the Russians, although you sometimes find Ukrainians or Moldavians or Latvians – you've got to be careful with the distinctions, Frank. Come here some Sundays it's like Babel, guys talking in Russian or Latvian or Georgian. You name it. Odessa Beach, USA."

Pagan started to walk. Klein, nimble in his open sandals, kept up with him. Now and then, like a nautical blessing given in a miserly way, a faint breeze would come up from the ocean and blow aside the humidity for a moment, then the swamplike dark would reassemble itself. Pagan paused in the open door of a clubhouse and saw a middle-aged man in a loose-fitting suit dance with a large woman who wore pink-framed glasses and had her yellow hair up in a beehive. The music was big-band stuff that might have been recorded in the early 1950s.

Klein said, "The people that come to America from the Soviet Union tend to keep to themselves. It's almost a force of habit with them, Frank. They come from countries where everybody was a snoop. Even your next-door neighbour was a potential informer for the KGB. What I'm saying is you can't just walk around here asking questions. If some Balts have organised themselves into a fraternity with a sinister purpose, which is what you tell me, they're not going to be shouting it from the rooftops."

Pagan moved out of the doorway. "Rose Alexander mentioned an old shop."

"Take your pick," Klein remarked. He gestured with a hand, indicating three or four stores that hadn't been occupied in a long time. Some had windows protected by metal grilles, others padlocked doors, one had a faded To Rent sign with a realtor's name bleached by the sunlight. Pagan had a sense of decline here, of an age that had passed, a world receding. There must have been dignity here once, but it had been reduced to the kind of seediness he associated with decrepit English seaside resorts.

He walked a little way, trying to imagine Kiviranna coming along these same slats of wood. It would be dark, and Kiviranna's contact would be waiting for him in the shadows, perhaps inside one of the vacant shops, and Jake would move along the boardwalk in a stealthy manner, taking care that nobody saw him. Pagan conjured up these tiny pictures, almost as if he were forcing himself to see the ghost of Kiviranna appear before him now, leaving a spectral trail for him to follow. He tried to eavesdrop an old conversation. *The man's name is Romanenko. You have to kill him. This is the key to the place where you'll find the gun.*

Would Jake have asked why Romanenko had to be killed? Would he have bothered with a mere detail like that? Suppose he had? What would his contact have answered? *He's carrying something that can't reach its destination, Jake. That's all you need to know.* And Jake might have nodded his head, absorbed the information. But it probably hadn't happened that way at all. Jake's connection would only have to say that the world would be a better place if a treacherous Commie like Romanenko was taken out of it and that would be enough for Kiviranna. Pagan walked to the handrail, leaned there, gazed out over the dark water for a time, seeing the moon that sent a column of shivering silver across the sluggish tide. Then he turned back to the empty stores whose dark windows suggested rich mysteries.

"I suppose it wouldn't be difficult to track the owners of these places down," he said to Klein.

Klein guessed it would be a matter of public record. It would take maybe a phonecall or two, a little legwork. Pagan wanted to know how quickly this could be accomplished and Klein, wondering at the Englishman's dedication, his apparent immunity to jet-lag, figured it might be done first thing in the morning when people with *regular* jobs were at their desks. There was a hint of sarcasm in Klein's speech, nothing objectionable, enough to make Pagan smile to himself.

He continued to stare at the windows. Some had faded signs inscribed on glass, old lettering barely legible in the thin light from the lamps that burned along the boardwalk. *Roo beers. H t dogs. C t on candy* – like half-finished answers in an elaborate crossword puzzle, or words in an alphabet designed to be read only by initiates. Frank Pagan, feeling fatigue creep through him at last, glanced once more at the moon, thought about Kristina Vaska – in whose half of the world this moon would already be fading – then he asked Klein to drive him to his hotel.

They walked back to the place where Klein had parked the Dodge. Once again, either on account of fatigue or darkness, neither man noticed the car that travelled behind them all the way back to Manhattan. It was not this time the pea-green Buick, which had been replaced by a navy blue 1983 Ford Escort, a car unremarkable in every way, and just as anonymous as its predecessor. The pea-green Buick had gone in another direction, back to the apartment building in which Rose Alexander lived.

London

The moon that had taken Frank Pagan's attention had disappeared completely from the sky when Kristina Vaska woke in her hotel in Kensington. She rose at once, went inside the small bathroom, splashed cold water across her face, brushed her teeth. She dressed, packed her suitcase, then she sat for a time on the edge of the narrow bed. She had three hours until her plane left Heathrow. She checked her ticket to be absolutely sure, then put it back in her wallet. She remained motionless on the bed. A morning newspaper had been shoved under the door of her room, one of the hotel's little courtesies, but she couldn't bring herself to pick it up. From where she sat she could read the headline, or at least that half of it which hadn't been folded.

TWO POLICEMEN SHOT IN

That was all she could make out. She turned her face away.

Those men were dead because Frank Pagan had asked them to protect her. It was a world of blood in which men kept dying.

She found it an unbearable thought to get around, an obstacle in the dead centre of her brain. She got up, covered her face with her hands in such a way that an observer might have imagined her to be weeping – but she wasn't, even if she felt like it. She picked up the phone on the bedside table, dialled the hotel operator, asked to be connected with Mrs Evi Vaska at a number in upstate New York. While she waited Kristina imagined the antique phone in her mother's tiny downstairs living-room, the room she called the parlour, she pictured Evi Vaska in her white makeup moving through the small boxlike rooms and down the crooked stairs of the old house, past the shelves of fragile china figures, all the glass reindeer, the crystal ducks, the porcelain gnomes and elves that crowded the little house and that always seemed to be growing in number, as if they bred in the dark. Kristina imagined she heard the lacy gown Evi always wore whispering on the steps as she moved. From her house in the foothills of the Adirondacks, Evi Vaska wrote impassioned letters to Congressmen and Senators and British Members of Parliament concerning Norbert Vaska's incarceration, conducting a relentless campaign she thought would win her husband's freedom.

Relentless, Kristina thought. And doomed.

"Hello?" Evi Vaska's voice was distant.

For a second Kristina was tempted to hang up without saying anything. She hesitated. "Mother."

"Kristina!" Evi Vaska's voice became breathlessly excited. "Are you still in England?"

"Yes," Kristina said. She pictured the house, the hundreds of miniature figures that rendered the place even more claustrophobic than it was, with its narrow passageways and cramped staircase and low ceilings. Even the garden, a wild green riot, pressed in upon

the house as if to isolate it before finally consuming it.
Kristina had the thought that the house and its garden
were like her mother's mind, a place of lifeless figures
and disarray.

"Is there news, Kristina?"

"We'll talk when I come home, mother. I'll drive up to
see you and we'll sit down together and we'll talk."

Kristina pictured her mother's flour-coloured face, the
black eye makeup, the deep red lipstick, the dyed yellow
hair that lay upon her shoulders like the broken strings
of a harpsichord. "In other words there's nothing, is that
what you're saying, Kristina?"

"That's not what I'm saying, mother. Look, I'm flying
back today. At the weekend I'll drive up to you. I'll come
up to the Adirondacks." She tried to keep impatience and
exasperation out of her voice, but she wished she hadn't
called in the first place. She sighed. She didn't have the
heart for this talk. She didn't have the heart for any of it.

"You didn't see Aleksis? Is that what you're trying to
tell me, Kristina? So there's no news of your father? Is
this what you're keeping from me?"

Kristina Vaska put the receiver down. She walked to
the window, pressed her forehead upon the glass, looked
down at the street below. She felt as if she were a victim
suddenly, a casualty of history, wounded by forces from
the past – forces that had killed some people and driven
others, like Evi Vaska who sat in a world of her own
creation, totally out of her mind. And her eyes watered,
but she didn't weep, no matter how tight the constriction
at the back of her throat or the ache around her heart.
She was beyond tears. She needed dignity, which came
through retribution rather than grief.

14

Virginia Beach

There were days when Galbraith needed to get out of
the house in Fredericksburg, when he suffered from a
rarified form of cabin-fever and had to step away from the
consoles and the never-ending flow of data. A man might
choke to death on so many tiny bones of information.
Sometimes he sat in the back of his chauffeured car
and was driven to Cape Hatteras or Williamsburg or
Richmond. On this early Tuesday morning he chose to
go to Virginia Beach, city of soothsayers and palmists,
tea-leaf readers and cosmic masseurs, hitch-hiking gurus
and astral travellers, faith healers and tarot interpreters
and astrologers and other fools. It was a city Galbraith
found refreshingly silly, all the more so since it took
its 'metaphysics' with grave seriousness. On his last
visit here Galbraith had had his chart done by a fey
astrologer – just for the hell of it – who told him that
the heavenly portents were *far* from pleasing. Galbraith
listened to talk about one's moon being in Venus, and
how an absence of earth signs indicated a certain abstract
turn of mind, utter nonsense over which he nodded his
head grimly. He declined the opportunity to have his
past lives revealed for the further paltry sum of twenty
bucks. One incarnation, in Galbraith's mind, was more
than enough. Anything more was arguably masochistic.

He surveyed the ocean from the back of the Daimler, or
at least those stretches of it one might spot between high-
rise hotels. It was a sunny morning and the sea was calm,
and the yachts that floated out towards the Chesapeake

Bay did so with slack sails. Galbraith observed the streets, the summer festivities, people strolling through sunshine, men and women in bermuda shorts, kids in funny hats, the kerbs clogged with Winnebagos from faraway states. The great American vacation, he thought. He wouldn't have minded a vacation himself. He hadn't taken one in fourteen years, unless one considered a trip four years ago to Monaco but that had really been business. And this quick jaunt to Virginia Beach, which had the superficial appearance of a leisurely drive, was still connected to work. Nothing Galbraith did was ever done without purpose. Aimless was not in his vocabulary.

The chauffeur, a black man called Lombardy, turned the big car away from the strip and through streets that quickly became dense with trees. Graceful willows hung over narrow inlets of water. There were expensive homes here, many of them refurbished Victorian affairs filled with brass and stained-glass and heavy with a ponderous sense of the past lovingly restored. Galbraith watched the Daimler plunge down a lane and listened to branches scratch the windows. Lombardy parked the car outside a house which was so well-camouflaged by trees that it couldn't be seen from the road. The black man opened the door and Galbraith slid out of the back seat, puffing as he waddled towards the front of the house.

Galbraith pushed a screen-door, entered a yellow entrance room which led along a yellow hallway to rooms the colour of daffodils. He felt like a man plummeted without warning into a strange monochromatic world, a place of yellow sofas and chairs, yellow lampshades, yellow rugs, a house in which even the mirrors had a faint yellow tint. The effect, he decided, was to make one feel rather jaundiced.

"I liked it better when it was red," Galbraith said.

The small man who appeared at the foot of the stairs wore a saffron kimono. "Red is rage," he said. His black hair, heavily greased, had been flattened on either side of the centre parting.

"And yellow's mellow, I daresay," Galbraith remarked.

"Yellow is springtime and rebirth, Galbraith. Yellow is the colour of pure thought."

"Also yellowjack fever and cowardice."

The man inclined his head. He had some slight oriental lineage that showed in the high cheekbones and the facial colouring. He had exceptionally long fingers.

"Colour and harmony, Galbraith. In your hurried world, you don't take the time to plan your environment. You eat fast and hump fast and read fast and think fast. What an ungodly way to live. The gospel according to Ronald MacDonald."

"When I want to hear about taking time to sniff the goddam flowers, Charlie, I'll read Thoreau. Meantime, I've got other things on my mind." Galbraith wandered to the window and released a blind, which sprung up quickly, altering the monotonous light in the room. "Do you mind?"

"What if I did, Galbraith?"

"I'd ignore you anyhow." Galbraith wandered to a sofa and lay down on his face, closing his eyes. "It hurts here and here," and he pointed to a couple of places at the base of his spine. Charlie tugged Galbraith's shirt out of his pants and probed the spots. Charlie, who had built an expensive clientele among the richly gullible, and employed a hodge-podge of massage techniques together with some oriental mumbo-jumbo, always managed to fix Galbraith for a couple of months or so.

"You're too fat," Charlie said. "No wonder you hurt."

"I didn't drive down here to be abused, Charlie. Mend me. Spare me bullshit about the Seventh Temple of Pleasure and the Six Points of the Dragon and the Jade Doorway to Joy and all that other piffle you fool people with, just fix me."

Charlie pressed his fingertips into the base of Galbraith's spine and the fat man moaned. "You're carrying around an extra person, Galbraith. For that you need two hearts. Do you have two hearts, fat man?"

Galbraith closed his eyes and felt little waves of relaxation spread upward the length of his spine and then ripple through his buttocks as Charlie went to work with his sorcerer's fingers. For a while Galbraith was able to forget his usual worries, drifting into a kind of hypnotic state. There were times in his life when he needed a retreat from the vast panorama of detail that was his to oversee, an escape from the insidious pressures of his world, the network of responsibilities that each year seemed to grow more and more elaborate. Power, he realised, was an ornate construction, delicate membranes imposed one upon another, creating strata that sometimes perplexed him, sometimes made him nervous. He'd realised in recent years that he couldn't carry the weight of his job alone. He had to rely on other people. There was no escape from this fact. The best you could do was make sure you didn't delegate important matters to total idiots. If Galbraith had one dominant fear it was the idea that a dark deed would be traced back to his own outfit, even to his own office, and that some form of public exposure would follow. Sweet Jesus – there were freshfaced youngsters in Congress who fancied themselves investigative officers of the people, *ombudsmen* for the commonfolk, and they were like hounds out of hell if they had the smell of any illicit expenditure of the taxpayer's money, the more so if it were used in a covert manner.

He came suddenly alert when Charlie said, "Your associate is here, Galbraith. I'll leave you now."

Charlie draped an ochre towel across the exposed lower part of Galbraith's body before he left the room. Galbraith twisted his face to see Gary Iverson looking uncomfortable in the middle of the floor. Galbraith had almost managed to forget that he'd arranged to meet Iverson here.

"Pull up a pew, Gary," Galbraith said. If he had more

men like Iverson – reliable, loyal, patriotic, devious –
he might eat less and sleep more. A svelte, well-rested
Galbraith – it was quite a thought.

Iverson dragged a wingbacked chair close to the sofa
where the fat man lay. He'd come directly from New
York, travelling by helicopter to Norfolk and from
Norfolk by car. It seemed to Iverson that he spent
most of his life in motion, like a pinball in Galbraith's
private machine, banging between Fredericksburg and
DC and New Jersey and Manhattan and Norfolk.

"Ever had one of Charlie's specials?" Galbraith asked.

Iverson shook his head.

"Remind me to give you one for Christmas." Galbraith
rolled over on his back. "He issues gift certificates good
for one bath and a rub-down. Highly recommended,
Gary. Besides, this is probably the most discreet place
I know. Charlie appreciates how much some people
treasure privacy."

Iverson looked round the room. Yellow wasn't his
colour. He gazed at the square of window where the
blind had been released. He was very glad to see greenery
brush against the pane. He said, "Early this morning
Frank Pagan and his sidekick Max Klein made inquiries
concerning certain vacant properties on the boardwalk
at Brighton Beach."

"Did they now? Whatever for?" Galbraith sat upright.
He had the feeling he wasn't going to like anything he
heard from Gary.

Iverson said, "They went to the boardwalk last night
after interviewing Rose Alexander."

"Ah, yes, Kiviranna's unwilling friend. I recall her
name from your report. And she sent them scurrying
off to Brighton Beach?"

Iverson nodded. Galbraith closed his eyes a moment.
He had times in which he could literally see trouble as
one might witness thunderheads gathering on a distant
hill. There were connections here that made him very
unhappy indeed.

"Do we know what she told them, Gary?"

"An inquiry was made, sir."

Galbraith frowned. Inquiry was a word that could conceal a multitude of sins. "I trust this inquiry was peaceful?"

"The woman was cooperative. She had nothing to hide. She told us exactly what she'd told Pagan. Shortly before he left for London, Jake Kiviranna had an appointment with somebody on the boardwalk – in one of the old shops."

"Ye gods," the fat man said. "You don't suppose there's coincidence here, do you?" Galbraith asked this question with heavy sarcasm. He thought of coincidence the way an atheist might think of God. Acceptable if you were naive enough to have faith, preposterous if you gave it only a moment's consideration. He stood up, adjusting his pants, discarding the towel. "You understand where this is leading, don't you, Gary?"

Iverson nodded. He had a quick eye for complexity. Galbraith raised a finger in the air and said, "Jake goes to an old shop on the boardwalk. Carl Sundbach just happens to own such an establishment. Carl Sundbach also happens to know that Romanenko is due to arrive in Edinburgh." Galbraith paused, then paced the room, speaking very slowly. "Sundbach tells Kiviranna . . . go to Edinburgh . . . shoot Romanenko . . ."

"Why though?"

"Why indeed? Why participate at considerable expense in the Brotherhood only to make an attempt to scotch the entire goddam operation by using a hired gun? Do you see any sense in that?"

Both men were silent for a time. Galbraith said, "We know Sundbach wasn't happy with the plan. Good Christ, he walked out on it. It's all there on the tape of that last meeting in Glen Cove. But was he so unhappy with it that he decided he'd ruin the goddam thing himself if he could? And then when he realised he couldn't halt the Kiss express, no matter what, he walked away . . ."

"A change of heart," Iverson said.

"Fear maybe. An old man's terror. Old age and terror – there's a combination made in hell. And utterly unpredictable." Galbraith looked thoughtful for a while. "What worries me, you see, is this fellow Pagan getting too close to the flame of the candle. I don't want him singed, Gary, unless it's essential. And if it's essential, I don't want us to be involved. Not even remotely."

In an unhappy voice Iverson said, "It may very well be essential, sir."

"Meaning?"

"I've heard from London."

"And?"

Iverson gathered his thoughts, parading them in an orderly manner in his mind as if they were foot soldiers with a tendency to be unruly. He noticed a pitcher of iced water, rose, poured himself a glass, returned to his chair. "It seems that Frank Pagan has been travelling in some interesting company, sir. The daughter of a former member of the Brotherhood, a man who vanished into Siberia some years ago, has become a companion of Pagan's. The assumption is that this young lady, Kristina Vaska by name, has provided Pagan with some information about the Brotherhood. We're not sure what. But Pagan may be able to come to certain conclusions. He knows something about the Brotherhood, he's about six inches away from Sundbach – it's a situation fraught with danger."

Galbraith loved the *fraught*. He adored the way Iverson spoke in general, with a kind of polite precision. But he worried now over Frank Pagan who was meant to remain on the safer fringes of things and stay well clear of the centre. It really was too bad. He said, "So Viktor Epishev has been running amok over there in an attempt to silence this potential menace." He pulled at his lower lip and looked for all the world like a petulant choirboy who has just been told that his voice is about to break and his singing career is kaput.

"Apparently," Iverson replied. "His initial objective was to make sure that nothing inhibited the scheme, that Romanenko's message wasn't deciphered – "

"*Deciphered?*"

"It seems Greshko told Epishev the message might contain a code of some kind, which in the wrong hands – "

Galbraith interrupted, his jowls quivering with sudden anger and his eyes popping. He was rarely touched by rage but when it happened it was an awesome sight. Iverson was hypnotised by the fat man's volcanic display of temper.

"*Classic Greshko!* No matter what you tell that old fucker, no matter how goddam hard you try to ram something into his head, he runs it through that paranoid brain of his and comes up with something off the goddam wall. He was *told* there wasn't a code. I told him that *personally*. I told him there was nothing hidden in that message, nothing secretive, nothing that needed to be analysed. It's a simple bloody message, I said, and it couldn't mean a damn thing to anyone outside the Brotherhood. But oh no, *oh no!* – that wasn't good enough for *him*. Classic goddam Greshko! Trust nobody, especially your friends, especially your American friends! Always look at the world through the prism of suspicion. Always think the next fellow is trying to put one over on you. He probably thought I was trying to slip a nuclear weapon past him, for Christ's sake! Or drop some fucking bombs on his beloved railroad tracks! Sweet Jesus!" Galbraith shook his head. "The truth of the matter is he didn't need to send Epishev to London at all. He didn't need a man running around over there doing that kind of damage. *All he had to do, Gary, was to leave everything alone.* And that's the one thing he's never been able to do in his entire goddam life. He's never been able to leave anything alone! And that includes White Light!"

Both men were quiet for a few moments. Galbraith walked to the corner of the room where an old-fashioned upright piano was located. It had been lacquered in high-gloss yellow and was almost painful to behold. He sat down and thumped out the first few bars of *St James Infirmary Blues*. He broke off and, feeling a little less tense now, looked at the keys pensively. He was thinking of that summer in Monaco in 1984, the leisurely mornings spent reading on the beach, the splendid dinners at Les Lucioles in Roquebrune or La Couletta in Eze-Village, the magnificent room he had at the Hotel de Paris on the Place du Casino, the white sunlight on a blue ocean. He was remembering evenings in the Grand Casino, walking through the verdant gardens or strolling the gambling rooms, casually playing roulette here, blackjack there, *chemin-de-fer* – rare moments for Galbraith, who hardly ever left anything to pure chance.

He dropped his hands from the keyboard, thinking of how Vladimir Greshko, travelling as incognito as incognito can get, hadn't appeared in Monaco until the third day. Their encounters had all taken place indoors at night – in dark little bars, hotel rooms, secluded restaurants. Their talks at first had been guarded. After all, they had little in common on any superficial level. What could Galbraith, with his Ivy League sophistication and wealthy background, share with the Chairman of the KGB, a rough-edged peasant more cunning than intelligent? The only novel Greshko had ever read, for example, was *Crime and Punishment*. Galbraith on the other hand was a Henry James aficionado. He loved the convoluted sentences and the cultivated world James described what could he possibly feel for a yarn in which the central event was the sordid murder of a moneylender by a broodingly unsympathetic student? All that Russian gloom, dear Christ!

The only true bond between them was a world view, a global vision which, although different in some respects, nevertheless consisted of many common elements – a well-defined balance of power between the two super-nations, an intermittent detente characterised by periods of warm progress and years of arctic chill, a status quo that, precisely because it achieved nothing real other than to promote national anxieties and keep the arms manufacturers of the world on cheerful terms with their shareholders and bankers, was more acceptable than any of the proposed changes both men knew were coming, and both loathed. And their hatred of change, of disruption, of any erosion in their spheres of influence, glued them together with a fastness unusual between men of such different backgrounds.

It wasn't exactly an easy camaraderie. It had its origins in a meeting concerning international terrorism that took place in Geneva in the fall of 1983, when it had seemed to Galbraith that Vladimir Greshko was sending invisible signals across the conference room. An enigmatic note was slipped under a hotel door, a couple of terse phonecalls were made in the ensuing months, and the eventual outcome was the secret meeting in Monte Carlo.

Greshko had said *I am on the way out, Galbraith. Now we will have a world where our much-admired new General Secretary will alter the fabric of things. He wants to create a Russia that neither you nor I will recognise. One we will not understand at all. A dangerous place for me, and for you, Galbraith . . . because you will not know where America stands when Russia changes. And I will not know. And all the people you have become so used to dealing with over the years will be sent to the glue factories like tired old horses. You replace old horses with hardworking young ones, Galbraith. With colts and stallions who have new feeding habits. Think about it . . .*

And Galbraith did think about it, and he cared very little for any of his thoughts. Under the sun of Monte Carlo, both men discussed what might be done to preserve a world both had become accustomed to, a world they considered safe and manageable. Endless talk, demanding and exhausting, two days without sleep, periods of high excitement followed by dismay, too much coffee, too much vodka. What they needed was a plan, something they could remain aloof from and yet somehow take part in, what they needed was a scheme they hadn't themselves designed but one they'd inherited, and could shape to their own ends. Something which, if it happened to go wrong, couldn't possibly be laid on their respective doorsteps. It was two more years before such a situation presented itself in the form of an old friendship between Gary Iverson and Andres Kiss.

And still there existed a mutual lack of trust between Galbraith and Greshko, a situation that would diminish with the years but never entirely dissolve because Vladimir Greshko was programmed never to trust a fat capitalist. Galbraith brought his fingers down on the keys, creating a melancholic minor chord that echoed for a while through the room. With just a little more trust, Greshko might never have sent his man Epishev to London. The old fart must have imagined something was being kept from him, that the devious Americans were up to their usual nefarious nonsense, that the message contained coded details which were to be denied him, and that in the end the Americans wanted to throw a little sand in an old man's eyes. And nobody – *nobody!* – was allowed to make a fool of General Vladimir Greshko.

Galbraith ran off a few more chords, then he played the chorus of *Nobody Knows You When You're Down and Out*. He turned to Iverson. "Epishev is still in London?"

"Yes," Iverson replied.

Galbraith looked contemplative. "I'm thinking aloud, you understand. But he might be useful."

"Useful, sir?"

"He wants Pagan, doesn't he?"

"Yes."

"And Pagan's here, about to make a nuisance of himself . . ."

Gary Iverson nodded his head slowly.

"And Epishev's in London," the fat man said quietly. "Not any great distance as the crow flies."

Glen Cove, Long Island

Mikhail Kiss lay on a deckchair in his sunlit garden. He wore dark glasses and a cotton shirt and khaki shorts that revealed the thick silvery hair covering his muscular legs. He glanced at his watch. It was just after eleven a.m. In eleven hours from now, Andres was going to step on board a Scandinavian Airlines flight from Kennedy. Eleven short hours. Kiss felt nervous suddenly.

He sat upright, looked back at the house, saw the shape of young Andres inside the glass-walled room – he was so damned cool, so cold, you might think the trip that night was no more than a casual tourist affair.

For his own part, Mikhail Kiss couldn't silence his nerves. Maybe it had something to do with the dream, the awful dream that had come to him in the darkness and filled him with dread. In this dream he'd been sitting in a restaurant with Carl Sundbach and Aleksis Romanenko, a very strange place with neither menu nor cutlery, a still room where no waiter ever came to serve. The three men had sat in a silence broken only by a thin music coming from a distance, the unrecognisable music that existed only in dreams, neither melodic nor familiar but shatteringly atonal. And then, from nowhere, a shadow had fallen across the table – but Mikhail Kiss hadn't raised his head to look at the newcomer, at least not immediately.

He got up from the deckchair and he thought *Dreams mean nothing. Dreams are not the harbingers of future happenings.* He walked towards the house, stepped inside the glass-walled room, saw Andres skim through the pages of a news magazine. Mikhail Kiss filled a glass with water and drank quickly. Then he sat down, taking off his dark glasses.

"How are you?" he asked.

"How should I be?"

The older man shrugged. "A big night ahead of you, I thought . . ."

"It's just another night." Andres kept flicking pages.

Just another night. Mikhail Kiss thought how difficult his nephew had been ever since Carl had walked out on Sunday, how distant and aloof, locked inside his own head. *It's not just another night for me, Andres. I've lived a long time with this idea. I've breathed it. I've slept with it and nursed it. I've travelled thousands of miles to make it real. Even when it looked impossible, I still kept going.* He wanted to say these things to Andres, but he couldn't form the words in any way that would give them the hard conviction he felt in his heart.

Andres Kiss smiled, seeing the odd expression on his uncle's face and thinking how old men could be like little kids. He patted the back of Mikhail's hand. "There's nothing to worry about, Mikhail," he said. "Everything will go according to plan." And he thought: *Especially now. Now that he had the idea.*

Mikhail Kiss wondered about the certainty in his nephew's voice. The confidence. Andres had always had that supreme self-assurance that almost seemed at times to be indifference, as if he thought of himself as specially blessed, a magical being, a beautiful young man protected by the gods. Experience hadn't caused him any suffering. What he knew of pain and sorrow he'd learned second hand. Kiss searched the smooth face, the eyes, the perfect mouth, for some sign of uncertainty, some little touch of concern, a feeling, anything – fruitless. Andres Kiss gave nothing away. Mikhail Kiss realised that his nephew scared him sometimes.

Andres closed the magazine and laid it down. The idea had come to him during the conversation with Iverson in Trenton. It had begun like a vapour drifting slowly at the back of his brain, and then it had taken shape and become hard as it floated into the light, and then he'd known with certainty what he had to do with Carl Sundbach. Besides, hadn't Iverson practically *instructed* him to do the thing? Hadn't Gary Iverson done everything but *spell the goddam business out*? To protect himself, to protect his own position, to cover his ass, Iverson obviously couldn't come right out and say *Do it, Andres*. But he'd left Kiss in absolutely no doubt. *Sundbach's a menace, therefore* . . .

Therefore. It was obvious. The young man stood up and looked at his uncle a moment before he said, "I have to go out for a while."

Mikhail Kiss heard something in the young man's voice, only he wasn't sure what. A false note, a distortion. "Out? *Now?*"

Andres Kiss nodded. "I'll be back in plenty of time for you to take me to JFK. Don't worry."

Mikhail stood up. "You shouldn't go anywhere. Not today. You should stay here. You should be relaxing."

Andres turned away, and Mikhail went after him, following him out of the sun-room and into the hallway. "I don't see what's so important you have to go out."

Andres didn't reply. He walked towards the front door.

"What is so damned important you have to go anywhere, especially today, for God's sake?"

Andres opened the door, turned to look at his uncle. "I'll be back, Mikhail."

Mikhail Kiss watched the door close, then heard Andres's car in the driveway. For a long time after the sound of the automobile faded, Kiss stood motionless in the hallway. Then he went back to the sun-room, sat down, lit a cigarette, closed his eyes. He felt a strange little nerve, a cord, flutter in his throat.

And there was the dream again. There was the shadow on white linen, the eerie music. He saw himself raise his head up, saw himself look into the eyes of the fourth man, the one who approached the table, the one who stood over the other three and said nothing. Distanced by the dream, Kiss rose and extended his arm, his hand held out

293

to shake that of the fourth man – who had said nothing and done nothing, except to offer a small, spectral smile.

That smile. That face.

Why had Norbert Vaska come back after all these years to make Mikhail Kiss shudder in the warm morning light?

Manhattan

Of the four properties vacant on the Brighton Beach boardwalk, two belonged to a massive mortgage company in New Jersey, one to a pair of brothers who lived in a retirement home in Manhassett, and the last to a company called Sundbach Incorporated, with corporate offices given as an address in lower Manhattan. On the basis of geographical convenience, Frank Pagan decided that the address in Manhattan was the first one to check, then the retirement home in Manhassett, and finally, if need be, the mortgage company in New Jersey. He had Klein drive him from the Warwick down through the midday sunshine of Manhattan. It was one of those gorgeous late summer days that bless the city all too infrequently, the air marvellously clear, a blustery breeze blowing through the canyons, no humidity, blue skies, skittish little clouds more suggestive of spring than fall.

The address in lower Manhattan turned out to be a rundown brownstone carved into three or four apartments. An assortment of bells were arranged at the side of the door, but the names written on small cards were faded. Pagan squinted at them, locating one that had the name Carl Sundbach on it in very faded blue ink. He glanced at Klein, who said that as corporate edifices went this one was more than a little inauspicious, then pressed the button. After a while the face of a man appeared behind the glass panel set in the door. He stared at Pagan and Klein without opening the door.

"Who is it? What do you want?"

Pagan took out his credentials and pressed them to

the window and the old fellow, putting on spectacles, stepped forward to look. Klein did the same thing with his NYPD badge, but still the old guy didn't open the door.

"What do you want with me?"

"Just a couple of questions," Pagan said.

"Go ahead. Ask!"

Pagan, exasperated by having to shout through a closed door, said, "It's going to be a whole lot easier if you open up and let us come inside."

Carl Sundbach stared at the two cops, whose appearance bewildered him, especially the one with the Scotland Yard ID. He was inclined to panic a little, because if somebody had come all the way from London then it had to be connected with Kiviranna. What else? Now he had the thought that the man who'd been following him in the streets and markets was also a cop. For one dark moment, Sundbach had an urge to throw the damn door open and spill the whole story, keeping nothing back. But he couldn't do that, not even if he lived through a thousand years of torture.

Pagan pressed his face against the pane. "A few questions, that's all. We'll take five minutes of your time at the most."

Sundbach wondered if the failure to open the door was going to be construed as suspicious, if the most reasonable course of action was to admit this pair of jokers, remain extremely cool with them, and send them away satisfied. Cups of tea, perhaps, some quiet hospitality. This was the behaviour of a man with nothing to hide. Lurking behind a locked door, on the other hand, was probably a strategic mistake.

"Okay. Five minutes," and he opened the door, turning towards the stairs even as the cops entered. "This way," he said, leading them up into the gloom. He took a key out of his pocket, opened the door to his apartment, and showed the policemen inside, smiling now and bobbing around them. "You fellows drink on the job? I got some nice Yugoslavian wine somewhere."

Both Pagan and Klein declined. Pagan looked around the apartment, absorbing the sheer quantity of items here, the overstuffed furniture, the heavy curtains, the shelves of books, the scores of old prints that covered everything save for what must have been Sundbach's special wall, reserved for photographs of the old fellow in the company of celebrities. It was a suffocating apartment, overloaded with Sundbach's possessions, many of which must have had nostalgic significance for him. Pagan had the strong feeling of having stepped into another era – back, back to the turn of the century, when people lived around their possessions in rooms where you couldn't breathe and where you just knew a tubercular child lay white and still in a shuttered attic bedroom. There was dust here, and the dampness of old paper, a sense of an unindexed life collected and stored in these rooms.

Carl Sundbach took the stopper from a fine old decanter and poured himself a glass of dark red wine. The glass, he said in a thick accent, had once belonged to the last Tsar's uncle, General Alexei Alexandrovich. He was making conversational noises. Pagan wandered to the bookshelves, glancing at titles, most of them in foreign languages. *L'Entente Baltique. Die Nationalen Minderheiten Estlands.* And pamphlets, scores of them, stacked in bundles, held by string or elastic and stuffed with sheets of notes. They were mainly in languages Pagan couldn't identify. He stepped away from the shelves and gazed at various prints on the walls even as Sundbach was proudly explaining some of his celebrity photographs to an interested Klein.

"This was taken when Bobby came through here on his campaign. A young man, much vigour. I had raised money for him, you understand. You see where he signed the picture? Look there. To my friend Carl, it says. Now this one over here, taken with Perry Como, that came about when he opened the wing of a hospital in Brooklyn. I give a little to charity now and then. America's been good to me."

Pagan found himself looking at a copy of an engraving made by a certain Merian in 1652. It depicted a walled city with steeples and according to the brass plate attached to the frame the city was Tallinn. There were others, views of castles, tall ships in a harbour, churches, all carefully framed and labelled, all pictures of old Estonia. *Bingo*, Pagan thought. He had an equation, a connection between Carl and Jake Kiviranna, an ethnic bond. But it was too easy, too thin. Unless anybody could prove beyond doubt that Sundbach had sent Jake overseas on a mission of murder, unless there was solid evidence of the kind so loved by prosecutors and judges, Carl could fly the Estonian flag from his window day and night and it wouldn't mean a damned thing. It certainly wouldn't connect him to a murder in Edinburgh.

Carl poured himself a second glass of red wine. The New York cop was simple to deal with. He was the kind of American impressed by celebrity. He probably read *People* magazine. The tall *inglane* on the other hand worried Sundbach because he prowled, taking everything in with a quiet, hooded look. And those grey eyes were cold and unreadable. Warmed by the wine, Sundbach felt a flood of confidence. Let them ask their questions and be on their way. He had nothing to hide. He sat down at his desk.

Pagan asked, "What exactly is Sundbach Enterprises?"

Carl Sundbach replied, "A few hotels, a couple of small-town newspapers, a little real estate here and there."

"And you operate this yourself?"

Sundbach smiled. "Nowadays, no. Sundbach Enterprises is part of a big corporation called Van Meer Industries, which is part of something else. IBM for all I know! It's too complicated for me. I got nothing to do with it other than some financial interest."

"You own an old shop on the boardwalk," Pagan said. "Is that yours personally or part of this big corporation?"

Sundbach sipped his wine. The old shop, he thought. They knew about it. So what? It wasn't exactly a secret. "That I keep as my own," he said.

"Any reason?"

Sundbach stood up and, a little flushed, pointed to a framed dollar bill that hung above his desk. "This, my friend. Look carefully. The first dollar I ever made in my own business in this country and I made it on the boardwalk. So I keep the shop. It's sentimental. Do you understand me?"

Pagan nodded. "When did you come to America?"

"Early 1950s," Sundbach said.

"Have you kept up an interest in the politics of the old country?" Pagan asked.

"The old country?"

"Estonia," and Pagan waved a hand at the prints.

"Pardon me, I don't think there's any such place. There used to be, and it was a wonderful country, but now it's called the Estonian Soviet Socialist Republic and soon you won't even see that much on a goddamned map." Sundbach smiled sadly at the Englishman. "You said you had questions, Mr Pagan. Maybe you could come to the point?"

Pagan turned to look at the old man. Shoot from the hip, Frank. "Do you know a man called Jacob Kiviranna?"

Sundbach, whose heart skipped only a little, looked puzzled. "No, I don't."

"Think," Pagan said.

"What's to think?" Sundbach asked.

"Somebody saw you with Kiviranna on the boardwalk."

Sundbach shook his head. He stared at the *inglane*. This was all bluff, it had to be. Even if somebody *had* seen him with Kiviranna, what did that prove? "I don't know the man. Your information's wrong."

Pagan came a little closer to the old man. He smelled the wine on Sundbach's breath. "Kiviranna shot a man named Aleksis Romanenko."

Sundbach turned over the palms of his hands. There was a forced smile on his face. What he wondered was how any kind of connection had been made – had that *perse* Kiviranna talked? But what could Jake have said anyhow? Sundbach had always taken the greatest care to conceal his identity from crazy Jake, who wasn't a man who asked too many questions anyhow. They'd held their very first meeting at the shop on the boardwalk and Sundbach had made a great pretence at forcing entry, as if he wanted to show Jake Kiviranna that he was beyond the law, he broke into abandoned shops, he had a bandit's disregard for other people's property. He was a goddam anarchist, the kind of guy Jake could trust without losing any sleep.

Carl Sundbach cleared his throat. "Aleksis who? You got any more names to throw at me?"

"Just those two," Pagan said.

Carl Sundbach made his chair swivel as he reached for his wine. "I like to help policemen, Mr Pagan. I think they do a great job without much thanks, you understand. But you've given me nothing except puzzlement. I don't know the men you mention. And a shooting – what would I know about a thing like that? I'm a retired businessman, not a gangster."

Pagan said nothing for a time. He studied Sundbach's face in silence. The old man was pouring a third glass of wine in a composed fashion. Pagan wandered round the room, glanced through open doors, saw a bedroom with a vast four-poster bed, an enormous bathroom with an antique tub, a kitchen with an old-fashioned black stove. There was the scent of camphor from somewhere. Pagan imagined closets packed with clothes and mothballs.

Sundbach, he realised, could maintain his innocence until the sun froze over. Perhaps he was telling the truth anyhow, perhaps he knew nothing about the killing in

Edinburgh, but Pagan had one of those niggling little instincts that told him otherwise. He stopped moving, leaned against the wall, folded his arms. *It's all here, Frank. Everything you're looking for is in this room. Crack the bastard open.*

"Talk to me about the Brotherhood, Carl," he said.

The Brotherhood. How did the English policeman know about the *vendlus*? How had he stumbled into that one? Sundbach, the essence of serenity, sipped his wine. "The what?"

"Tell me why you wanted to wreck the Brotherhood's plan, Carl. Why did you send Jake to Edinburgh to murder Romanenko? Are you KGB? Is that it? Did you get an order from Russia? Or straight from the Soviet Mission in New York?"

Sundbach, as if astonished, blew a fine spray of wine through his teeth and laughed. He looked at Klein in the manner of a man appealing to reason. "Is your English friend here on a day-release programme from some kind of institution? Does he have to check back in at six o'clock every night?"

Pagan stepped quickly towards the desk, looming over the figure of Sundbach, who was still seated. "Does the KGB tell you what it needs, Carl? Does it tell you what hoop to jump through – the hoop in this case being the murder of Romanenko? You get poor Jake Kiviranna to do the job because you know there's something loose in his attic, therefore he's a loony, exactly the kind of fellow to pull a political assassination. You don't get any blood on your hands that way. Keep them nice and clean, don't you, Carl?"

Sundbach had an urge to scream at the *inglane* and to tell him how very wrong he was, how his conclusion might be correct but his reasoning was all bent out of shape – but that would have meant telling the truth about the Brotherhood and he wasn't going to do that. The trick was to let the moment pass, let this man's accusations fade into silence, and stay very calm.

"You through, Mr Pagan?"

"I'm through," Pagan said.

"I lost my two brothers between 1945 and 1949," Sundbach said. The anger he felt made it difficult to talk. "The KGB killed them. And you accuse me of working *for* the KGB. I don't want to say any more to you. I don't want you in my house. Go. Go now."

Pagan walked towards the door. He longed for fresh air and sunlight and the breeze scampering along the streets. In this apartment it was hard to draw air into your lungs unless, like Sundbach, the air you breathed was from the past. He opened the door and stepped out on to the landing, and Klein followed.

Sundbach, decanter in one hand, glass in the other, stared across the room at both men. "I would die before I worked for the KGB," he said. "That's the truth."

Pagan drew the door shut and stood for a second on the gloomy landing before turning and going down into the street.

Pagan sat in the passenger seat of Klein's car, which was parked four or five doors from Carl's building. He stared across the street at the windows of Sundbach's apartment. Klein said, "I think I heard one of the old guy's blood vessels pop. You backed the wrong horse there, Frank, when you said the magic letters KGB."

Pagan rolled down his window, let his hand hang out of the car. He didn't question the genuineness of Sundbach's emotional reaction to the mention of the KGB. He said, "I agree. But I've got a feeling he's lying about all the rest of it. He hired Kiviranna, arranged the trip, set everything up. The only thing I got wrong was the KGB connection."

"If that's true, who's he working for?"

Pagan was silent a second, looking up at the apartment as if the curtained windows might be made to yield an answer. "Maybe himself," he said.

"And the motive?"

Pagan pressed his fingertips into his eyelids. "Who knows? Maybe he just didn't agree with the Brotherhood's plan. Which tells us something definite – he knew all about it."

"Which means he's either one of the Brotherhood, or he's got an inside source," Klein said.

"Precisely."

Klein undid his bow-tie, which collapsed and fell in two thin strands across the front of his chest. "What now?"

"I think we let old Carl marinate for a while," Pagan said. "Then we'll go back over there and we'll put some real pressure on him."

Max Klein, who wondered what Pagan meant by 'real pressure' but didn't want to ask, took a pipe from the glove compartment and lit it, filling the car with a richly-perfumed tobacco smoke. Pagan watched the street, noticing a gang of kids outside a corner grocery store, a couple of men passing a bottle back and forth, a TV repairman's van. A young man with blond hair that fell to his shoulders got out of a parked Jaguar on the corner and walked past the clutch of kids and the men drinking. In his white cotton jacket and pants – casual chic, obviously expensive – he had the appearance of somebody who'd made a wrong turning along the way. He looked as if he'd happened upon this drab street purely by chance, which was why Frank Pagan tracked him idly as he came along the pavement.

The man went directly to the building where Sundbach lived, climbed the steps, rang one of the doorbells, waited. Pagan saw Sundbach come to the door, open it, and the young man entered the building after exchanging a couple of words with Carl, who seemed reluctant to let him in. An intriguing pair – the old man in the shabby cardigan and the well-tailored visitor who had the looks of a fashion model. What could they have in common?

Pagan glanced at Klein, who had also seen the young man enter Sundbach's building. "They make an unlikely couple," Klein said. He took a small notebook from his pocket and wrote down the registration of the Jaguar. The notebook was stuffed with loose slips of paper, suggesting the enormous, if finally futile effort of an untidy man to impose order on his world.

Pagan settled back in his seat. "Give it ten more minutes. Then we'll go back for the pipe you just happened to leave behind in Carl's apartment."

"Gotcha," Max Klein said brightly.

Andres Kiss drank a glass of the old man's horrible Yugoslavian wine. This apartment, which he'd visited only once before, was unsufferably cluttered. He put the wineglass on the table, then smiled across the room at Carl, who was sipping quietly. Although there was a sociable grin on the old man's face, he was puzzled, even troubled, by Kiss's presence.

"You go tonight," Sundbach said. "It's still the same?"

Andres Kiss looked at his glass and reminded himself to clean it before he left the apartment. "The plan hasn't changed, Carl."

Sundbach realised he was slightly drunk, that his reactions were coming to him through a series of filters, just like the daylight that fell first through muslin then damask at the window. His head was like the inside of the apartment, murky and overloaded.

"You go be a hero, Andres. Myself, I think there are other options."

Andres Kiss smiled. He put a hand in the pocket of his pants. "Such as?"

Carl Sundbach shrugged. He was remembering the meetings with the madman Kiviranna, the night on the boardwalk, the time they met in Penn Station, or the afternoon they'd walked through the Metropolitan Museum of Art – five, maybe six encounters in all. *You shoot Romanenko, Jake. That's all there is to it. You'll be a goddam hero.* Jake Kiviranna, another asshole, a *tagumik*, with a hero complex, hadn't even asked questions.

Romanenko was a Communist, a turncoat, and that was all there was to the business. He deserved to die. Perfectly logical. Perfectly natural. Jake's mind didn't have compartments that spilled over into each other. There were no complications when it came to Kiviranna. Of course, it would have been a different matter if Jake had known that he was assassinating one of the leading figures in the anti-Soviet underground in the Baltic.

One of the leading figures . . .

Carl Sundbach was suddenly depressed. The murder of Romanenko wasn't a decision he'd taken lightly. He and Aleksis had fought side by side for years, not always liking each other, and not always agreeing, but they'd developed a mutual trust, a dependency. And the Brotherhood's plan had always seemed feasible to Carl, although less so with each passing year. It wasn't just that his memory of his native country was beginning to fade around the edges and had begun to recede in importance to him. It wasn't even the fact that age had depleted his energy, his sense of commitment. It was the idea that fresh new voices were being raised in the Soviet Union which had caused him to stop and think and to debate whether the Brotherhood's way had any merit in the end, or whether it was time to put the scheme under wraps – at least until the new directions in Russia had come into focus. Perhaps the directions would be good, perhaps not. But it was a chance worth taking, especially when the consequences of the Brotherhood's scheme could bring about wholesale slaughter – and not simply inside the Baltic countries.

Carl, who knew Mikhail Kiss was beyond reasonable argument and could *never* be persuaded to give the Kremlin a chance, saw only one way to make the plan grind to a halt. Aleksis had to die. He had to die because nothing short of his murder would make Mikhail Kiss consider abandonment. *And it hadn't worked.* If anything it had backfired, because both Kisses were simply more determined than ever to go ahead. Especially this young one, this terrifying boy with the yellow hair and the face that wouldn't melt *margariini*, this young creature with ice in his veins.

"I asked a question, Carl," Andres Kiss said.

"There are alternatives that are less destructive. That's all I'm saying. I'm talking about reality."

"I'm listening," Andres said. "Reality fascinates me."

"You don't hear the pulse, sonny. You and Mikhail, you're deaf men. You don't want to hear." Sundbach picked up the decanter, but it was empty.

"Tell me about this pulse, Carl. I'm curious."

The old man wandered round the living-room in an unsteady way. "Things are changing over there. The time for this plan has gone, Andres. It's time to put violence in cold storage."

"You really believe what you're saying?"

"Listen to me," and here Sundbach placed a bony hand on the young man's wrist. "We can't get our country back the way it was. But we can get *something* back. We can get some kind of self-determination over there but only so long as we stay inside the system. So maybe it's not independence. Maybe it's not the way it was. But it's the best goddam shot we've got! Your way is doomed, sonny. Your way is pure romantic bullshit – a fart on the wind, Andres. I didn't always see it like that. But I'm prepared to give this new regime a chance."

Andres Kiss shook his head. "You swallow their crap about all these terrific changes?"

"I believe it can happen. Slowly, sure. But it can happen."

"Nothing's so cheap as words. The Russians can talk up some fine intentions. After all they've put us through, you're still ready to trust them?"

"Up to a point – "

"You've grown soft in the head, Carl."

"Listen," Sundbach said. "Try to have patience. Don't go ahead with this foolish scheme. Things will get better in the old country. More freedoms will come. Why not let the new system have a chance? And if it doesn't work out, you can go back to the plan later."

"In your world, Carl, cows will fly."

Sundbach sat down in a very old grey leather armchair. "You're an impossible boy, Andres. What do you know? From where I sit I can smell milk on you."

"You want us to fail, don't you?" Andres asked. "You want the whole fucking thing to fall apart!"

Sundbach said nothing. Why bother to answer the question? It was wasted breath. Tomorrow, over the Baltic, Andres Kiss might have his moment of truth.

"What did you feel when Aleksis was shot, Carl? Glad?"

"Glad isn't the word," Sundbach said.

"What is the word, Carl?"

Sundbach was quiet a moment. "I thought it would be a time for quiet reconsideration. Why rush into violence? Why go ahead with something so drastic if another way could be found?"

Andres Kiss stepped closer to where the old man sat. He saw Sundbach turn his face to the side and look across the room. Andres folded the hand in his pocket around the length of soft, silky material that lay concealed there. It wouldn't take long, he thought. A minute perhaps. A little more. He gazed into Sundbach's discoloured eyes, detecting nervousness in them, something furtive.

Andres touched Sundbach's shoulder very lightly. "You listen to the Russians, you think you're hearing something new. But there's nothing new. It's the same old song only with a new singer. Freedom isn't in the melody, Carl. The words haven't changed. The only thing that's changed is your mental condition."

"All I said was we give it a try. Postpone – "

"Postpone nothing."

Sundbach began to rise from his chair, but Andres gently pushed him back into it. It wasn't a violent gesture, but Sundbach interpreted it that way, as the first trivial skirmish in a situation that would escalate.

He tried to rise again, but again Andres pushed him back down. Carl Sundbach, who had always been a little afraid of this young man, albeit in an abstract sense, was surprised to find how quickly the fear could become a concrete thing.

Andres Kiss said, "With Aleksis dead, you thought the plan would be abandoned, didn't you? That's how you wanted it to be."

Sundbach didn't speak. He sensed violence all around him, the very air of his apartment electrified by it. He saw it in this young man's cold eyes and mirthless smile. So much beauty and no heart.

"You thought if Aleksis was killed, Mikhail would lose his nerve and give up."

Sundbach shut his eyes. The sound of a gun fired in a railroad station echoed through his imagination. He didn't believe he'd been mistaken in arranging for Aleksis to be murdered. But he'd failed to change anything, and it was a failure purchased at a very high price.

Andres Kiss took the soft length of material from his pocket. It weighed nothing in his hand. He let the thing dangle against the old man's lips. Carl opened his eyes quickly.

"What's this?" He pushed it away from his mouth.

"What do you think it is?"

"A stocking, a lady's nylon."

"You got it, Carl."

"Mikhail sent you here," Sundbach said. "Mikhail sent you here to be my goddam assassin!"

Sundbach, panicked into movement, tried to get up out of the chair but Andres struck him quickly on the mouth, knocking him dizzy. Sundbach felt the nylon go around his neck and he kicked vigorously at the young man, striking Andres Kiss on his cheek. The old man got up, rushing across the room to the door. Andres caught him there. He pinned him against the wood and shoved his palm up under Carl's chin and thrust the old man's face back. Sundbach gasped and made a claw of one hand and dug it into Andres's forehead, scratching the flesh, breaking the skin. For a moment, shocked by pain, Andres Kiss released his grip and Carl was able to get a hand on the door-handle. But before he could pull it open Andres struck him on the back of the head with his clenched fist.

Carl slid to the floor and moaned.

Kiss went down on his knees, twisting the nylon stocking around Carl's neck even as the old man flayed at him feebly with his fists.

"For the love of God, Andres."

Andres crossed the ends of the nylon. He pulled them very tightly, hearing Carl groan and feeling Sundbach's hands, which fluttered desperately upwards, pressing against his mouth. Andres held his breath and kept tightening the stocking.

And then Carl was finally silent and his neck, caught in the fatal tourniquet Andres Kiss had applied, hung at an odd angle to his body. Kiss, out of breath, stood up.

"I think it's time," Frank Pagan said, and got out of the car, slamming the passenger door shut. He took a step in the direction of Sundbach's building, conscious of Klein sliding out from behind the wheel, aware at the same time, from the edge of his vision, of the TV repair van pulling away from the pavement.

Later, Pagan might marvel at the gall of the operation, but his first impression was of the van swinging in a squealing arc, making an illegal turn on a one-way street. Then the vehicle clambered up on the kerb and struck a fire-hydrant, which immediately sent a great jet of water rainbowing into the air behind Klein's Dodge. Pagan, halfway across the street, watched the van continue in its destructive path, seeing it plough into the trunk of Klein's car, which crumpled like construction paper. Klein, emerging from the driver's side, was tossed forward by the impact. He fell face down under the glittering cascade of water that rose out of the ruptured hydrant. Pagan hurried back to the sidewalk and leaned over Klein, who was sitting up and dazed, looking at Pagan with the expression of a man on thorazine.

"*Holy shit*," Klein muttered. "Was it lightning?"

The van, which had the logo *Rivoli's TV & Radio Repair* on the side panel, wheeled into reverse and pulled away from the smashed Dodge. It came to an abrupt halt half-on, half-off the sidewalk and then, roaring madly, lunged straight towards Pagan, breaking open plastic garbage sacks and strewing the air with fishbones and potato peels and clouds of feasting, breeding flies. *Dear Christ!* Pagan, half-blinded by water, threw himself to the side as the van rocketed towards him. He slid down a short flight of steps to the door of a basement apartment, twisting his head in time to see the van roar along the street. He rose, raced back up to the pavement. The van was already turning the corner at the end of the street, leaving a pall of blue exhaust like something conjured out of existence by a flamboyant magician.

He walked to where Max Klein sat. "You okay?"

"I'll live," Klein said.

Pagan helped Klein to his feet, then stared through the sunlit water at the empty space where the Jaguar had been. Slick, he thought. The whole thing, dead slick. He looked up at the windows of Sundbach's apartment and something caused him to shiver, and he thought he knew what.

"You want to go after the van?" Klein asked.

Pagan saw the way Klein's feathery red hair had been plastered across his scalp with water. "Let's go back to Carl's."

Saaremaa Island, the Baltic

Colonel Yevgenni Uvarov walked between the computers and the consoles, passing the stern portrait of Lenin, whose eyes seemed to follow one no matter where one moved. The Colonel gazed across the wide expanse of floor towards his desk, then up at the clock on the wall. He couldn't put this moment off for long, not now. He checked his watch, returned his eyes to the clock, as if he were all at once obsessed by time – but he was in reality stalling, delaying the moment from which there was absolutely no return. Burning the bridges, Uvarov thought. Setting them all aflame.

He moved towards his desk. A technician named Agarbekov stepped in front of him. Uvarov was startled by the sudden movement and it must have shown on his face because Agarbekov gazed at him strangely.

"Console eight isn't working, sir," Agarbekov said.

Why was he being bothered by this utterly trifling detail now? Uvarov wondered. "You know the procedures, Agarbekov."

Agarbekov was hesitant. "I followed procedures, comrade Colonel, and nothing was ever done. The repairs were never made. Don't you remember?"

Uvarov put one hand up to the side of his face. He was flustered suddenly, thinking he heard reproach in Agarbekov's voice. He couldn't remember, it was really that simple. For weeks he'd been operating on a level where ordinary things receded, and his memory malfunctioned. He was living – not in the now, the present – but in the immediate future. He looked at Agarbekov, a white-faced twenty-year-old from Kiev with a lock of greasy black hair that fell over his forehead and which he kept pushing away.

"Are you unwell, comrade Colonel?" Agarbekov asked.

Uvarov shook his head. "I'm perfectly fine, Agarbekov. I have so many things on my mind. I can't be expected to concern myself about one small repair. Go through the usual procedures a second time." The sharpness in the voice, the impatience – Uvarov wondered if Agarbekov detected stress in his behaviour. He smiled and tried to appear calm. He placed a hand on Agarbekov's shoulder and made a mild little joke. "Procedures are designed by Moscow with only one purpose, Agarbekov. They weren't written to help you, only to test your ingenuity in getting around them. Didn't you know that?"

"I had my suspicions, comrade Colonel," Agarbekov said.

Uvarov walked to his desk. He sat down, looked at the clock on the wall. He was aware of Agarbekov watching him from across the room. Had the small joke alerted Agarbekov to something? Uvarov wondered. How could it have done? It was innocent, a simple act of sympathy for Agarbekov, who was caught up in the often stupid rules and regulations and procedures that were a part of military life. Uvarov shut his eyes and wondered if Agarbekov was KGB, if he'd been stationed here to observe men in sensitive positions. He opened his eyes, and now there wasn't any sign of Agarbekov. KGB! You see them everywhere. You imagine them all over the place.

He opened the middle drawer of his desk and quietly removed a sheet of typewritten paper. He scanned the words quickly even though he knew them by heart. Then he looked at the top of the page where bold letters read: *From the Office of the Deputy Minister*. Uvarov picked up his pen and his hand shook and he had to work hard to still it. He carefully signed the name S. F. Tikunov across the bottom of the page, then he rose and walked to the Orders Board, where he pinned the sheet up. He could barely breathe. He looked at the sheet hanging on the board and he had the thought that his forgery was utterly childish, anybody could see through it, it would be spotted at once by the operators who religiously took note of all new material on the Orders Board.

His face covered in perspiration, he went unsteadily back to his desk. He passed the computers, two of which were out of order still, and lay exposed to his view – circuit boards, yards of thin wire, the intestinal confusion of broken electronic equipment. He looked at the clock again. At midnight, the message he'd placed on the Orders Board would be routinely transmitted by computer from this installation which – as the major tracking station in the area – was an electronic post office for all pertinent orders issued in Moscow by the Deputy Minister, and relayed to a score of lesser installations along the Baltic coast.

Uvarov sat down. He was conscious of Agarbekov watching from the other side of the enormous room. The young Ukrainian's face was white and expressionless, floating in the bleak fluorescent lighting like a balloon. *Don't stare at me*, Uvarov thought. But then Agarbekov had turned away already and had vanished beyond the banks of screens, leaving Uvarov with a strange sense of unfocused discomfort.

The Colonel looked in the direction of the Orders Board. Even though he couldn't read anything from this distance, he felt that the sheet he'd just pinned there was very distinct, the letters large and bloated. He imagined he could read it plainly. *Routine Electronic Maintenance Order Number 09 06, 1600–1700hrs Wednesday September 6*.

Uvarov got up. For a second he was tempted to remove the notice before anyone had seen it. But he'd made his mind up, and he couldn't cancel now, and besides one of the operators was already standing in front of the board and looking at the faked order pinned there. Uvarov, who expected his forgery to be detected there and then, was filled with relief when the operator turned away from the order without any unusual expression on his face.

Uvarov stepped out of the building. The night air was chilly and he shivered. He listened to the soft sound of the tide, and he thought of the dark waters beyond the range of his vision, and how for one short hour tomorrow the defences of the Baltic coast would be stripped of their eyesight, and in this state of temporary blindness astonishingly vulnerable.

15

Manhattan

Frank Pagan's room had that dreary unlived-in look of hotel rooms all the world over. As soon as he stepped inside, he removed his jacket, still damp from the fire-hydrant, then his shirt. From the inner pocket of the jacket he took out a long brown envelope, which he set on the bedside table. Then he lay across the bed and pondered the ceiling.

He felt the weariness that is an accumulation of things. Travel, frustration, loneliness. And murder. He'd known roughly what he was going to see inside the old man's apartment, he'd guessed it, but even so he hadn't been prepared for the sight of Carl Sundbach with a nylon stocking knotted round his throat. There, surrounded by all his Baltic memorabilia, the old man lay in the middle of the room as if he were himself just another useless, albeit grotesque, keepsake. The broken spectacles, the false teeth scattered over the rug – murder had a way of diminishing a person, of breaking somebody down into his less admirable components. And the killer, assisted by whoever drove the kamikaze van, had slipped neatly away.

Pagan went inside the bathroom, doused his face with cold water, returned to the bedroom, turned on the radio – what this room needed was *noise*. He found a station playing Frankie Ford's classic *Sea Cruise*, and he walked to the window, looking out over mid-afternoon Manhattan. The sun, made hazy by pollution, was the colour of a bruised daffodil. A frolicsome wind flapped

313

along the cross streets and died out in the avenues. Pagan pressed his forehead to the window. Since there existed no such company as Rivoli's TV & Radio Repair – surprise, surprise – the problem now was whether Max Klein could extract some useful information from the registration plate of the Jaguar.

Max had made inquiries just as soon as Sundbach's body was discovered, only to learn that the Jag belonged to an auto-leasing company on Long Island that had leased the car to an entity called Rikkad Inc, with corporate offices in Merrick. It was not apparently leased to any particular individual, but rather to the corporation as a whole, and when Klein had tried to telephone the number of Rikkad Inc he'd received a recorded message saying that Rikkad, a division of something called Piper Industries, was closed for the day and thank you for calling. Piper Industries, with offices in New Platz, had no information to give about Rikkad and suggested Klein try the Merrick number again in the morning.

Pagan turned from the window, suspecting that Klein, if he discovered anything, was going to find himself ensnared in one of those corporate mazes, an auditor's nightmare, where the structure of ownership is complicated and one corporate entity is laid upon another – the point being to obscure responsibility and evade direct culpability in the event of law-suits or tax claims. Klein had decided to look at records in the offices of the Corporation Commission and Pagan, needing some quiet time alone, had walked back to the Warwick.

He wondered what he was left with after the death of Carl Sundbach. Certain facts, certain connections, but they suggested empty railway cars connected to a locomotive going nowhere. He'd hoped that Sundbach was going to be the entryway to the Brotherhood – but that particular little light had been blown out and the entryway was a cul-de-sac in darkness now. And if he was no closer to the Brotherhood, then he was also no nearer to an understanding of their scheme, nor why certain Russians apparently stood in the shadows behind it.

He turned from the window, picked up the envelope on the bedside table, sat on the edge of the mattress. He stood up when he heard the sound of somebody knock lightly. When he opened the door and saw Kristina Vaska there, a small charge of electricity coursed suddenly through him, a voltage almost adolescent in its intensity.

"Frank Pagan?" she asked, smiling.

"The very same."

She stepped inside, closing the door behind her. She sat on the bed. "I wanted to get here sooner, but I went to my apartment to drop off my luggage."

Pagan, filled with the desire to touch her and yet postponing the moment, had ignored the essentials of the woman's life. She lived in this city, therefore she had to have an apartment. Somehow the information surprised him, as if he'd stumbled into a concealed corner of her world. You go in this direction, he thought, and before long you're asking all the old, half-scared questions – is there a boyfriend somewhere? is there somebody else? a rival? even more than one?

"I don't even know where you live," he said.

"Eighty-sixth and Amsterdam."

"How was the flight?" he asked, dismayed by his own question. *How was the flight? Was it raining in England? Did you have the plastic stroganoff for lunch on the plane?* He was staggered by his sudden knack for the inane.

There was a long silence in the room, an abyss into which all sounds were abruptly sucked, as if this narrow hotel bedroom were an island of sheer soundproofed quiet afloat on the turbulence of Manhattan. Pagan stepped towards the bed.

Kristina said, "Oh fuck the flight, Frank. I don't want to talk about airplanes and luggage. That's just stuff. Sit down beside me. I want to forget *stuff.*"

He sat down. He reached for her hand and held it. She

twined her fingers through his and he couldn't recollect any gesture more intimate in years.

"Look at me, Frank. I'm *trembling*, for Christ's sake."

How unlike Roxanne she was, he thought. Roxanne, with a certain coyness, had been passionate in less direct ways. She would have gone at her desire indirectly, using touches, gestures, as if she couldn't quite trust speech to convey her needs. Kristina, less subtle perhaps, was no less exciting. She lay back, curling her legs under her body. There was a lull, a quietness, one of those intolerably enjoyable moments of anticipation. He remembered when he'd walked with her in the park. He remembered the dampness of laurels and laburnum, moisture on old wood, raindrops on a coat. The effusiveness of recollected perfumes. The swift touch of passion he'd felt, the urge to invade this woman's world.

She held one hand out in front of her face and laughed. "I'm shaking like a schoolgirl. I feel idiotic."

Pagan kissed her and the warmth of the kiss, the confident way she returned it, shook him. He undid the buttons of her shirt and slid his hand over a breast and saw how she raised her face back and upwards, her mouth open and her throat in shadow, and it was one of those sublime perceptions he knew would return years later even after this passion had gone, one of those pictures that are immediately luminescent in the memory and against which other encounters are inevitably judged. He was hungry, emptier than he'd ever imagined, driven by an excitement and urgency that surprised him.

Naked, she was perfect. He ran his hand between her breasts and down over the surface of her stomach to her thighs, astonished by the sweet geometry of her body and by his own need to enter her. *Now*, she said. *Do it to me now, Frank.* And her voice was hushed and hoarse, like that of a tantalising stranger. She was a verbal lover, whispering over and over, sometimes his name, sometimes words that might have been vulgar in other situations but now seemed magical to him, sometimes simply making sounds in his ear that drove him to utter distraction. He buried himself in the act of love. He buried himself in a place beyond all the mysteries, beyond Romanenko, beyond the Brotherhood and their secret poetry and old wars, beyond Epishev and gunfire in a railway station. It was a place where all the clamour and the mysteries dissolved and the only truth was this woman and the intimacy he shared with her.

They made love slowly, each trying to be more generous than the other, as if they were exploring each other's limitations only to find none, discovering instead a lovers' world of infinite possibility which Pagan, grown stale in his years of loneliness, had long ago forgotten. When it was over, he propped himself up on an elbow and looked down at her. He realised, with something of a surprise, that he wanted her again. Immediately too, as if he'd discovered untouched realms of stamina and impatient desire in himself.

Moscow

Vladimir Greshko felt death in the back of the car as though it were an invisible passenger. He sometimes studied the darkened landscape, staring across flat fields and through trees and seeing the occasional light of a farmhouse, but mostly he kept his eyes shut and listened to what sounded like death's persistent song – a distant music, a couple of fragmented notes that might have been blown on a wind instrument, seductive and enchanting. He squeezed the small rubber ball he carried in a pocket of his overcoat. *The solace of solid things*, he thought.

The Yakut nurse drove with great caution, easing the car over ruts as gently as she could. Now and again she would make a remark about the folly of this journey, but the General had long ago ceased to listen. Wrapped in a heavy greatcoat which the nurse had demanded he wear,

317

he saw fields give way to construction, to scaffolding and great piles of bricks that littered the landscape. New Soviet housing was going up, those hideous blocks of flats that reminded Greshko of tombstones marking the burial-grounds of a race of giants. There was a thought here he might have pursued at some other time, a symbolism that might have amused him with its irony, something to do with the death of giants – but not now, not tonight.

And then the new construction yielded to finished apartment blocks, drab and lifeless, and the Yakut nurse announced the outskirts of the capital. Greshko felt the rush of energy that Moscow, in her great generosity, always gave him. This was his city. This was where he'd risen to power. He knew the streets, the neighbourhoods, he knew the criminals and informants and spies, he knew where the black-marketeers met to sell currency or buy weapons or dispose of stolen cars. He knew its pimps and whores, ambassadors and bureaucrats, politicians and gangsters. There was nothing he couldn't acquire in Moscow, *nothing* – American dollars, rare works of art, imported cars, automatic rifles, you name it. If you knew where to look, Moscow had everything a man could possibly need or want. From his office on Dzerzhinsky Square he'd once controlled this amazing city, understanding it the way no other man could – especially not a man like General Olsky, who didn't have the rhythms of Moscow in his blood.

But it wasn't *his* Moscow to which he was returning now. It had been taken from him, seized by usurpers, and purged of all his old cronies, who had been shipped to country cottages or seaside villas to rot away the last years of their lives and to dream of how they might regain the power they'd lost. He stared at the buildings, which were old friends. The Central Revolutionary Museum on Gorky Street, the Hotel Minsk, the Yermolova Theatre.

He made the Yakut stop the car a moment. He rolled the window down and sniffed the air, so unlike the countrified stuff he was forced to breathe these days, then he told the woman to drive on. He gave her the address where he wanted to go and settled back in his seat again, restless, animated by his return, which may have begun quietly and was completely unannounced – but which would end differently, if he had his way.

He shut his eyes, reflected on Epishev a moment. Viktor hadn't yet made contact with Volovich, whom Greshko had telephoned only a few hours ago, a nervous Volvovich, terse, talking like a man whose teeth have been welded shut. The conversation had been brief, elliptical. Volovich, undeniably loyal to Viktor, was a rabbit nevertheless, and even if he'd never been told the *entire* extent of the Brotherhood's undertaking, just the same he knew enough to create problems if he came under pressure.

Viktor's failure to make contact troubled Greshko. Either he had no information to impart (a fact he might have relayed by telephone, as a simple courtesy at the least), or else something had happened to him. Whatever, his absence had come under the scrutiny of Olsky. And that was undesirable.

He opened his eyes, peered through the window. The car was travelling along the Komsomolsky Prospekt towards the Lenin Hills.

"Take a right turn here," he said to the nurse.

She did so, swinging the car into a narrow street that was dense with foliage under bright street lamps. The houses here were large, constructed within the last forty years. They had copper roofs and elegant gardens and although they'd been converted to apartments during the past twenty years, they were considered among some of the finest residences in the city. You didn't live in a place like this if you were nobody.

"Here," Greshko said, and he indicated one of the houses that was almost completely concealed by trees.

The nurse turned the car into a driveway, parked it.

Greshko buttoned his greatcoat and stepped out of

the vehicle. The Yakut woman came out to assist him, but he brushed her aside. He had to enter this house unassisted, and pain and frailty and the hole in his stomach be damned. There was dignity in him still, and fire in his blood, and he wasn't going to give anyone the satisfaction of seeing him hobble with the help of a nurse. But he hurt like hell.

"Get back in the car," he told the nurse. "And stay there."

Alone, he went shakily up the steps to the door of the house. He rang a bell, waited. There wasn't an answer. He didn't ring a second time. He opened the unlocked door and found himself in a long, broad hallway with a high ceiling. A staircase led up into darkness.

Nikolai Bragin appeared at the end of the hallway. He wore a baggy three-piece suit and his hair, wild and unruly, sprung from his high skull in uneven tufts. It was the hairstyle of a man who habitually ran his fingers across his scalp. He wore glasses that pinched the end of his nose and he chain-smoked.

"My dear Vladimir," Bragin said. There was a brief embrace. "It's been – what? – two years?"

"It feels like a lifetime," Greshko said.

"Can't stay away from Moscow, eh?"

"I need to get laid," Greshko said, and winked. "One last time."

Bragin laughed. "And you think this is where all the whores are, eh?"

"Indisputably," Greshko said.

Bragin led him into a large drawing-room, which might have been a stage-set for some pre-Revolutionary drama. Both men sat at a sofa by an unlit fire. The fireplace was ornately carved with the figures of eagles alighting on prey. Presumably the piece had been removed from an aristocratic mansion. Greshko thought the place smelled of prosperity, much of it plundered from Russia's history – icons on the walls, old books stacked on the shelves, an ancient silver samovar seated on a gilt-leafed table.

"Tea?" Bragin asked.

"I'm at that stage of my life when only vodka does me any good, Nikolai."

"You shall have some." Bragin rose, took a bottle from a cupboard, and poured two small glasses that Greshko thought were niggardly. Greshko tossed his back immediately, then helped himself to a second, which he also disposed of quickly. It was first-rate stuff and it roared in his blood.

"Now, Vladimir. What brings you all the way to Moscow? You were enigmatic on the telephone."

Greshko poured himself a third vodka and swallowed it in one gulp. Three vodkas and he could hear those American songs in his head! He leaned across the table. *Sweet Christ, how he hurt.* He held the liquid in his mouth before swallowing it. It did what it was meant to – it numbed his nervous system, making the pain seem distant and just tolerable.

He said, "I come here a dying man. Therefore, what I am about to tell you should be seen in the light of detachment, the lack of self-interest common to dying men. I have no personal axe to grind, you understand."

Bragin looked a little embarrassed. Greshko, who wondered if he appeared drunk to the other man, pushed his empty glass away. Too much vodka too quickly was a prescription for disaster. And on an empty stomach that wasn't really a stomach at all these days – merely half of one, or a quarter, he was never very sure what the surgeons had left him of his digestive tract.

"There's a plot," Greshko said quietly. "It involves national security."

"A plot?"

Greshko nodded. "Before I go any further, I want you to know in advance that I can't identify my own sources."

"Of course," Bragin said.

"I know editors and journalists like yourself hear that phrase all the time," Greshko remarked. He paused, looked down inside his vodka glass. Nikolai Bragin, an editor of the daily *Izvestia*, had been a journalist since the mid-1950s and now, at the age of fifty-five, was one of the most prominent newspapermen in the Soviet Union and enjoyed unprecedented access to the highest chambers in the land. For years, Bragin had dutifully toed the Party line. His reputation had been built on dull acquiescence rather than daring. His prose was said to be more effective than any Soviet tranquilliser – of which the Russian pharmaceutical industry had produced few in any event. He printed what the Party wanted him to print. The word 'investigative' was not, in his vocabulary, an adjective used to describe a certain kind of reporting. He had pursued the bland and the inoffensive with a very blunt pencil. And then, in the last two years, lo and behold! a transformation, a small miracle had taken place. Bragin had published a long piece critical of the Government's handling of the pollution of Lake Baikal, and followed it with a three-part series on judicial corruption. Like a lifetime teetotaller introduced regrettably late to the beauties of wine and determined to compensate for the dry years of self-denial, Bragin had been reborn in the journalistic freedoms generously permitted by the Kremlin, trading his blunt pencil for a rapier, and shaking off the blinkers that had restricted his vision for almost thirty years. Nikolai Bragin saw himself as a hero of the press, a protector of the rights of small people against the elephantine clumsiness of central government. He was therefore a natural choice for Greshko. If there was to be some holy new form of openness in Soviet society and in the press, Greshko had asked himself, why not try to make some use of it? Why not test it? Turn it against its adherents? Set it upon itself? Why not give it some ammunition and see if it self-destructs? Everything free, Greshko thought, had also the freedom to destroy itself.

"Certain parties within the organs of State Security are involved in a plan directed against our country, Nikolai."

"Be more specific, please."

"It's my understanding that General Olsky, Chairman

of the KGB – a trusted servant of the state, a man with grave responsibilities – is involved in a scheme with certain dissident factions overseas to perpetrate an outrage against our country."

Bragin was quiet for a second. "And what is the nature of this outrage, Vladimir?"

"That is unknown to me, unfortunately."

"You're being very vague."

The old man reached across the table, laying one hand on Bragin's wrist. "Listen to me, Nikolai. General Olsky, acting against the interests of the State, has sent his emissary Colonel Viktor Epishev out of the country to liaise with a Baltic movement whose primary goal is to achieve independence from the Soviet Union. These forces, as you well know, have existed inside Russia for most of this century. Blackguards and malcontents. Scoundrels. Baltic scum."

Bragin took a pen from his pocket and wrote something down in a tiny notepad. Then he looked at Greshko. "You're making a very serious accusation about the Chairman of the KGB. Can you substantiate any of this?"

"Certain KGB files are missing. These files, which are damning to Olsky because they link him with outlaw elements in the Baltic states, have obviously been destroyed by him in an effort to cover his crimes. Viktor Epishev is also missing. If you were to ask Olsky about Epishev's whereabouts, he'd deny knowledge of them. And that would be incriminating enough. Since when does the Chairman of the KGB *not* know the whereabouts of one of his own Colonels, for God's sake? When I ran the organs, I always knew where all my officers were. Night and day, it didn't matter, I always knew."

Nikolai Bragin lit a cigarette from the butt of one he was already smoking. His fingertips were orange and the front of his waistcoat soiled by spilled ash. His darkly-jowled face was constantly vanishing behind smoke clouds. "It's not enough, Vladimir. If I start asking questions to substantiate your story, people are going to say your personal view of Olsky has caused you to concoct a scheme to discredit the man."

Greshko shook his head. "I expect that, of course. But it might prove enlightening if you were to ask General Olsky why he came all the way from Moscow to see me the other day."

"And why did he?"

Greshko took air into lungs that were barely functioning. "He tried to enlist my support in his scheme. Unsuccessfully, I might add. It's my understanding that he has been secretly trying to muster support from formerly influential people – people, shall we say, that are no longer in power but are ready to rule again if called upon to do so, people whom he thinks might be relied upon to form a new government. Olsky wants to discredit the present regime and replace it with another. With himself, no doubt, in the role of General Secretary. That's his goal. And in collusion with reactionary forces *inside* the country as well as outside, that's just what he intends to do."

Greshko, who had begun to wheeze, took a handkerchief from his pocket and applied it to his lips.

Bragin said, "General Olsky is held in high esteem within the Politburo. You're walking through a minefield."

"I'm used to minefields," Greshko said.

"The trouble is, Vladimir, I only have your word for all this. Who can prove Olsky belongs in a conspiracy? Is there documentation? Is there evidence? I'm sorry to say your word doesn't carry weight these days, Vladimir. For me to consider this story, I'd need more to go on. I can't blunder around asking awkward questions without some foundation."

Greshko sat back in his chair. His heartbeat was monstrous all at once, a frantic drum locked in his chest. He had trouble swallowing and the surface of his skin was clammy. Was this the moment? Was this death coming in? He closed his eyes. How could he exit without nailing that fucker Olsky to a cross? He trembled, concealed his shaking hand under the table.

"Do you need water, Vladimir?" Bragin asked.

Greshko shook his head. He opened his eyes. Steadying his hands, he gripped the edge of the table. "Let me ask you, Nikolai. Is General Olsky a good Communist? Is he ideologically sound?"

"I would imagine so."

"My ass," Greshko said. And he reached for the inside pocket of his greatcoat, which felt heavy and suffocating, removing several photostat sheets. He shoved them disdainfully across the table. *"There's your good Communist, Nikolai. There's your ideologically sound Olsky."*

Bragin picked up the papers and Greshko smiled. It was a good moment, one of the best he'd had in years. He watched Bragin go through the sheets. Bragin made a humming sound between his closed lips as he read. When he'd finished he didn't raise his face up from the papers.

Greshko said, "One hundred and sixteen thousand English pounds in a money-fund organised by Coutts Bank in London. Three hundred and thirty thousand American dollars in a trust run by the Wells Fargo Bank of California. Six million Swiss francs deposited with the Credit Suisse in Zurich. Transaction receipts, records of deposit, all of Comrade Olsky's good Communist activities are right there in front of your very eyes, Nikolai."

Bragin looked up now from the documents.

Greshko said, "I've given you photocopies. If you're interested in the originals they can be found locked in safety deposit box number 1195 in the vault of the Oxford Street branch of the Westminster Bank in London."

Bragin said, "You've done your homework, Vladimir."

"I had excellent sources once," Greshko said.

There was a long silence. Bragin got up. Greshko gathered the sheets together and tapped them on the table.

"This is something of a surprise," Bragin said.

"I imagined it might be," Greshko remarked. "I admit

this documentation in itself doesn't connect Olsky to any seditious movement. But it raises some distressing questions about the General. If he can dabble so freely in capitalist enterprises, and indulge himself in a system he professedly hates – well, who can say what he might or might not be capable of? And how did he amass the money in the first place?"

"Your point is taken," Bragin said, and there was some hesitation in his voice.

Greshko rose. He was no longer unsteady. "What will you do next, Nikolai?"

"One doesn't leap into something so sensitive as this, Vladimir."

"I understood you journalists could come and go as you please these days. I believed you had a mandate to write about dry-rot in the system, Nikolai, no matter where it might be found."

Bragin ran his thick fingers through his hair. "We have some new freedoms, of course. But we haven't been given a licence to kick doors down, Vladimir. We don't destroy reputations in a malicious manner. If Olsky is guilty the matter will come to the surface."

Greshko stepped towards the door, where he stopped, turned around. "You're saying you would need Party authorisation before you could investigate my information, is that it?"

"Hardly," Bragin replied. "However, if I assembled a story with indisputable documentation, the Party would want to examine the evidence before giving its approval to publication – especially in an area such as this one."

"In other words the Party still tells you what you can print?"

Bragin shook his head from side to side. "Vladimir, I have more freedom now than at any other time in my career. But some sensitive matters need to be cleared in advance, that's all."

"Are we talking about censorship?"

"Censorship? I wouldn't use that word. It's out of fashion."

Greshko opened the door. "I'll leave the papers with you. I have copies of my own, of course. I'll see myself out." He paused, turned back. "When you write this story, please be sure you mention the original source of it."

"I won't forget, Vladimir."

Greshko opened the front door. He felt rather jaunty all at once. He paused on the steps, smelling the air. Then he went confidently towards his car, where the Yakut nurse sat behind the wheel. He got in on the passenger side and told the woman to drive him now to the Moskva Hotel on the Karl Marx Prospekt for his second and final appointment of the night. He sang quietly under his breath as the car moved through the dark streets.

He was under no illusion that Bragin could simply write the story as he saw fit. What Greshko had really done was simple. He'd planted a seed to discredit Olsky, certainly. But much more than that. When the Baltic assault took place the very next day, when the extent of the plot became apparent, when those clowns who ran the Politburo were swept away on great tides of discontent and humiliation and public wrath and injured patriotism, Greshko was certain that Nikolai Bragin would remember the man who had forewarned him. Greshko had protected his own reputation. When it came time to analyse his career, when one hundred years from now autopsies were performed on his life and work, he would be remembered as the man who had exposed treachery in the highest echelons of power, who had uncovered corruption in the very heart of State Security. A Soviet saint, canonised by history. And wasn't that what life was all about when you got down to the bitter end of it? Your reputation? Your place in the scheme of things? Your name?

The car halted in front of the Moskva Hotel, and Greshko stepped out. He told the Yakut woman to wait for him. He glanced at the doorman as he entered the hotel. The doorman, touched by a shiver of recognition from the recent past, didn't question the old man muffled in the heavy overcoat as he entered the foyer. Greshko went up to the third floor. The room he entered was dull and a little shabby, the woodwork in need of paint, the wallpaper faded.

A young man sat at a card-table in the middle of the floor. He wore a plaid shirt open at the neck and blue jeans and the cigarettes he smoked were unfiltered Capstans, empty crumpled packets of which were scattered around the room. Greshko smiled at the young man and thought: *My insurance policy*.

The man, whose name was Thomas McLaren, stood up. He appeared a little awed in the presence of the former Chairman of the KGB. He was a ciphers clerk at the British Embassy, somebody Greshko had once caught in what is politely called 'an indiscretion'. A married man, McLaren had been ruthlessly seduced by a female KGB officer called Tamara. A sad affair, really, because McLaren had fallen in love with the woman and she had become fond of him – but permanence was impossible, of course. Photographs were taken of couplings in hotel rooms, meadows, borrowed apartments. McLaren, who understood he'd been manipulated, had been placed on ice for a day when he might be needed. And that day was now.

Greshko sat at the card-table and McLaren fidgeted.

The General said, "I will be quick and to the point. I am going to give you certain documents. You will make sure these fall into the hands of respectable journalists in your country." He took documents from his overcoat, copies of the same papers he'd given to Bragin, and he laid them on the card-table. "They refer to the conduct of General Olsky, Chairman of the KGB."

The young man put a hand out, but Greshko stopped him. "Read them when I leave. There's no time now." Greshko paused because new pain fluttered across his chest and up into his throat and he felt dizzy. He was quiet, waiting for the pain to pass. McLaren, who had black hair and eyes intense with fear of blackmail – a fear he'd carried with him day and night ever since Tamara had been revealed to him as KGB – watched the old man warily.

"General Olsky, handpicked by the General Secretary to run the KGB, is deeply involved in a foreign plot to undermine this Government. A good journalist may ask himself, what kind of human insight does the General Secretary lack that made him appoint this treacherous person? And if Olsky is a traitor, are there others in the present Politburo? Has the General Secretary made other . . . shall we say unfortunate appointments? Is he a man so lacking in insight that he's easily fooled?"

"What kind of plot do you mean, General?" McLaren asked.

"You'll know everything very soon. All I ask is you ensure delivery of these documents to reliable sources. And make absolutely sure you mention my part in bringing you the information. You must also point out to your writers that I made every effort to make our present leadership aware of this corruption, but I was ignored. I tried again and again, always with the same results. Newspapers all over the world will publish the story. The new Russia falls to pieces! All the bold new promises go down in flames of betrayal and treason! Wonderful headlines, eh?"

Greshko, tired now, fell silent. He studied McLaren for a moment. "Please. Try to relax. This room isn't bugged. I still have a little influence, McLaren. I made sure it was safe here before I came."

McLaren looked relieved. He opened the documents Greshko had given him, glanced at them. General Greshko stood up.

"Do as I ask, and all incriminating photographs, as well as negatives, will be destroyed. You understand me?"

McLaren understood.

Greshko walked to the door. For a moment he lost all his strength and had to grip the door-handle to keep from slipping. Then he stepped out into the corridor and walked towards the lifts, stiff-backed, moving with all the dignity he could find. He went down to the lobby, thinking it had been quite an evening, and that if his story failed ever to see the light of day in the Soviet Union, it would at least be published elsewhere in the world, and whispers and rumours, like quicksilver passages of air, would slip back inside Russia, quiet at first, then growing louder, and more shrill, and finally undeniable. After the success of the Baltic plot, Olsky would be removed, and the Politburo purged of Birthmark Billy and his cronies who had tried to fabricate an obscene new Russia, a hybrid society hacked out of half-understood socialism and an uneasy yearning for the stuff of the capitalist world. A bastard place, a nightmare land of varying political beliefs and separate nationalities, Greshko thought as he walked towards his car. But he'd done everything he could to confer legitimacy upon his precious country once again.

Manhattan

Pagan rose from the bed and looked down at Kristina Vaska. She had one knee uplifted, and the other leg stretched flat, so that the pubic shadows, always gorgeous mysteries, were even more inviting. It was a precious moment, and like everything precious fragile, and Pagan wasn't sure what he was supposed to say about what had just happened, or if speech would somehow alter the delicacy of things. He walked across the room to the window, pulling his robe around him as he moved. The afternoon sun was still hazy, slanting through the spires of midtown and yet failing to touch the streets below, which were already locked into that premature twilight characteristic of New York City.

He turned. Kristina was watching him. Pagan went back to the bed and sat down, letting his fingertips rest very lightly on the woman's hand.

"You surprised me, Frank Pagan."

"I surprised myself." And he had, he had.

She stretched in a lazy way, closing her eyes. She hadn't expected to end up in this bed. She hadn't anticipated that rush of feeling, nor had she imagined the extent of his desire, which touched her, filling her with an awareness of how deep his loneliness must have been. At the same time, her own complicity in his release had amazed her, because he'd activated responses in her that, like someone miserly with her emotions, she didn't want to feel.

Pagan inclined his head, let his lips touch the back of her hand, thinking how strange it was to be drawn after all these years into romance, and how much simpler life might have been if he'd relegated this encounter to the bargain basement of uncluttered sex, a one-shot thing, a brief fling, and then silence and amnesia. But it was undeniable – Kristina Vaska, whom he barely knew, had touched him inwardly, in places that hadn't been touched for God knows how long.

He raised his face. "I'm thirsty. Do you want me to call room service?"

"I was under the impression," she said, "that we'd just had room service."

Pagan smiled, reached for the telephone, ordered coffee and sandwiches. He replaced the receiver, remembering the brown envelope that had slipped to the floor during the recent amazing excesses on the bed. He didn't want to touch it, didn't want to be reminded of Carl Sundbach and a world that existed beyond the walls of this room. But he picked it up, even though he didn't open it at once. He held it as a man might hold something contaminated, reluctantly and with great distaste. He was suddenly nervous at the idea of asking Kristina to look at the photographs and wished he didn't have to.

He kissed her, laid a hand flat against the side of her face, and thought how sweetly fragile she seemed right then.

"I want you to look at something," he said quietly.

"Suddenly you've got a grim tone in your voice, Frank. I've heard it before and I don't think I like it. What are you asking me to do?"

"I've got some old photos here," and he opened the flap of the envelope, tipping the contents on to the sheets. "Before you look at these, does the name Sundbach mean anything to you?"

She thought a moment, then shook her head.

Pagan said, "One other thing. Before you pick up these pictures, I want you to be prepared for the fact that your father's in a couple of them."

"My father?"

Pagan nodded. "I found the pictures in the apartment of a man called Carl Sundbach who was just murdered."

She reached for the photographs. There were three in all. Pagan looked over her shoulder as she gazed at them. They were all similar, as if they'd been taken within minutes of each other. Similar and very familiar.

The first depicted three men in shapeless jackets, photographed against a backdrop of wintry trees. The men had rifles, which they held loosely against their sides. One of the men had a bandoleer strapped over his jacket. In the second photograph, there were also three armed men, but one of them was different from the first picture, as if the person he'd replaced had gone behind the camera. In the last photograph there was still another permutation of three men. In each picture the same stark trees formed the background. Taken quickly, Pagan thought. Hasty souvenirs of war snapped by cameramen in rotation. Guns and four tired, grubby men. Guns and weariness. And a sense of camaraderie, as if the men in the photographs were prepared to die together in a common cause.

In two of the photographs Norbert Vaska and Aleksis Romanenko stood side by side, looking exactly the way they had in the snapshot Kristina had shown Pagan days ago. In the third picture Vaska was missing, and Romanenko, who looked impossibly youthful, had been photographed between the other two men. It was this picture that Pagan picked up now.

He said, "The man on the left is Carl Sundbach. The one in the centre is Romanenko. Have you ever seen the big man, the one on the right?"

She shook her head. "Never."

Pity, he thought. There had been a chance that if she'd been able to identify the stranger, she might have presented Pagan with a clue to the Brotherhood, a step closer to the elusive core of things. Since Sundbach and Romanenko were dead, and Norbert Vaska in Siberia, that left only the big man with the broken nose and the high forehead. Was he still alive? If he wasn't, then the Brotherhood would remain what it had always been – a locked room.

"I've never seen Sundbach either," Kristina said. "Who was he?"

Pagan went inside the bathroom, ran a glass of cold water, returned to the bedroom and sat down again. He said, "He was associated with the Brotherhood – but he was also seemingly instrumental in bringing about Romanenko's murder. Presumably this treachery was frowned upon, and it got old Carl eliminated."

"Who killed him?"

Pagan shrugged. "I can give you an eyewitness description of the alleged killer, and I can tell you the make and registration of the car he was driving, but that hasn't helped much so far. A young man with some tricky back-up in the vicinity – which perhaps suggests the Brotherhood is still doing active recruiting."

Kristina ran the palm of her hand over the surface of the old pictures. She touched her father's face with a fingertip, then she gathered the pictures together quickly and put them back in the envelope. "So Sundbach betrayed the Brotherhood," she said.

"It looks that way to me," Pagan remarked.

Betrayal. Kristina got out of bed and went to the bathroom. She closed the door. She sat on the edge of the bathtub, her head tilted slightly to one side. She sat this way for a long time, turning the word *betrayal* over and over in her mind, remembering the very last thing Norbert Vaska had ever said to her, and she saw her father as she'd last seen him and remembered the way he'd whispered to her before they took him away and she heard his grim words again and again. An unchanging litany of whispered echoes. She wondered if she was doomed to listen to those same echoes for the remainder of her life. Or if Frank Pagan was going to provide the means to silence them once and for all.

She opened the door. Pagan came to her and held her very tightly.

"You make me feel good," she said. "I want you to know that, Frank."

"It's one of those reciprocal things," Pagan replied, infusing his words with a flippancy that wasn't remotely appropriate to his feelings. But he was an amateur at the heart's games and he'd lost once before and he didn't think he could stand losing again. And already he was beginning to feel the first soft warmth of seriousness.

There was a knock on the door. He assumed it was room service but when he opened the door he saw Max Klein standing in the hallway, looking a little agitated.

"We should talk," Klein said.

Pagan said, "One moment."

He shut the door, surveyed Kristina Vaska's splendid nakedness. It was almost a crime against nature to cover such wonder up, but he suggested she get dressed. She gathered her clothes together, stepped into the bathroom, and then into the shower. Pagan could hear the sound of her singing *Are You Lonesome Tonight?* over the thunder of falling water as he admitted Max Klein into the room. She had a good strong voice, but she didn't know the words.

Moscow

The telephone rang in Dimitri Volovich's apartment – once, twice, a third time before Volovich answered it. He knew as soon as he lifted the receiver, as soon as he heard interference that sounded like wind whistling through a wet tunnel, that this phonecall was coming from a great distance. He wasn't surprised, then, when Viktor Epishev's voice came across the line.

"I'll be brief," Epishev said.

"I can hardly hear you, Viktor!"

"Tell him this . . ." The voice was swept away for a few seconds. ". . . *reason to believe there may be a threat to the plan* . . ."

"A threat?"

"Just tell the old man that I think I can make things secure in time . . ."

"How bad is the damage?"

". . . *can't hear a thing* . . ."

"Viktor? Viktor?"

The line had gone dead in Volovich's hand. He put the receiver down and stood motionless for a moment. The palm of his hand was damp with sweat. He looked around his living-room, the functional leather armchairs, the table piled with books and newspapers, the old family photographs on the wall. He moved, somewhat listlessly, into the narrow kitchen, made a cup of tea, and considered the prospect of having to deliver Epishev's message to the old man. All the bloody way to Zavidovo with so slim a message, for God's sake! And the risk involved! Exactly what was this threat he'd mentioned? The old man was certain to ask, and Volovich didn't have the answers to give.

He carried his tea into the living-room and made himself comfortable in one of the leather chairs. He loved this apartment, enjoyed the kind of tenants who lived in the other flats. Right now, for example, he could hear the child called Katerina Ogoridnikova practise her piano on the floor above – a sweet sound that drifted gently down, a little Mozart. A talented child, young Katerina, and very pretty, the daughter of a man who operated a chemical plant and a woman who translated foreign journals for one of the ministries. The tenants in this building had a certain social standing, and Volovich appreciated the fact. He had no great desire to go out into the darkness, leaving all this comfort behind, to make the trip to Zavidovo, but he supposed he'd do it in any event since it was his duty to inform Greshko of any communication from the Colonel.

He set his empty tea-cup down on the table. He went inside the bedroom for his overcoat. Sighing, he did up the buttons, placed his key in his pocket, then stepped across the living-room to the door.

He opened the door, went out on to the landing, turned to lock the door. Startled by shadows that moved behind him, he dropped the key and heard it clatter on the floor, a sound that seemed to reach him from a long way down, like a stone dropped in a very deep well. He turned his face in the direction of the shadows.

There were two of them, and they wore the uniforms of corporals in the KGB. Volovich recognised neither of them, but they didn't immediately worry him because of their inferior rank. He glanced down at his key, seeing how it shone under the lamp on the landing.

"Comrade Lieutenant," one of the corporals said. He

was a chubby man with a Stalinesque moustache. "You are ordered to stay in your apartment tonight."

"Ordered? By whom?" Volovich infused his voice with a certain indignation, but he wondered if he succeeded or whether he sounded unconvincing to this pair. *Ordered*, he thought. He didn't like the sound of the word at all.

"We have our instructions, Comrade Lieutenant," the same corporal said.

"And who issued these instructions? Show me paper. Show me documentation. If you don't have it, step out of my way."

There was a sound from the stairs now, the click of heels upon linoleum, and Volovich turned his face in the direction of the noise. A figure loomed up and a face took shape in the light that fell across the landing.

"Let us talk, Dimitri."

Volovich, his heart pounding, stepped back against the wall. He watched General Olsky, in full uniform, bend down to pick up the key, which he then placed in the lock of Volovich's door and twisted. The door creaked open.

"After you," the Chairman said.

16

Manhattan

Gary Iverson stood in the empty apartment in the vicinity of Fordham University, conscious of starkness, white-painted empty rooms and high bright ceilings. The lack of furniture caused a lack of shadow, hence of texture, and he always had the feeling in this place that he was about to be prepped for surgery. He could hear the sound of the other man's voice coming from one of the rooms at the back, and then the voice was silent, and a door opened at the end of the hallway.

Iverson looked at the man who came along the hallway to the living-room. He had an uninteresting face, if somewhat kindly, but it wasn't in any way memorable. Had anyone asked Iverson to close his eyes there and then and describe his companion, he would have found the task difficult.

"Did you get through?" Iverson asked politely.

"Terrible connection. Impossible to hear anything."

"Too bad." Iverson stepped inside the open-plan kitchen, looked in the refrigerator, found a couple of bottles of ginger beer. A recipe on the label informed him that this soda was an ingredient in something called a Moscow Mule – highly appropriate. He took out two bottles and gave one to his companion.

"I wish we had something stronger, Colonel," Iverson said.

Epishev opened the bottle, swallowed, made a face. Then he wandered to the large window that looked out across the river, which had a strange lemon tint in the early evening sun. He had been in the United States on two previous occasions – once to provide security at the Soviet Mission, the second time to investigate the activities of the Soviet Deputy Ambassador to the United Nations, a man suspected of being *soft* on the West, and therefore a possible security risk. Epishev liked the country, or the little he'd seen of it. He understood he wasn't going to see a great deal of it this time either.

Iverson chugged his ginger beer. Then he said, "Welcome to America," and smiled in an artificially charming way. It was also a slightly strained expression because this apartment never failed to make Iverson a touch uneasy – he was forever conscious of Galbraith, ensconced in his basement in Fredericksburg, listening to everything that was said in these rooms. And today he was more than usually sensitive because he knew that Galbraith, having heard of the death of Sundbach at the hands of the unpredictable Andres Kiss, was bound to be wrathful. And when the fat man was angry, it wasn't a pretty sight.

V. G. Epishev turned from the window. He was still dislocated from the trip, the suddenness of it, his own lack of preparation and insight. He'd known about US involvement in the plan all along, of course – where else was an American plane going to come from if not from the Americans? – but it was only when Malik had introduced him in London to the man known as Gunther that he became aware of the *extent* of American interest, how it reached inside the US Embassy and spread, if Malik was to be believed, into the upper reaches of American military circles and God knows where else. *There's more to all this than you and I have ever been told, Victor,* Malik had said. *US involvement doesn't begin and end with an Assistant Ambassador at the US Embassy. It goes higher, and it goes deeper, and some of the most influential men in America are involved . . .*

What was painfully obvious to Epishev was how Greshko had kept a certain amount of information from him, but that fact shouldn't have surprised or irritated him. Greshko had done what he always did so very well. He'd concealed information, and juggled it, doling a little out to one person, some to another, so that the total picture was known only to himself. Devious Greshko, master of deception and legerdemain, creator of his own myth, saviour of Russia. Love and hatred, Epishev thought. Greshko inspired extreme responses in other people, as if any form of relationship with the old man took place on a moving pendulum.

Epishev, who always imagined he occupied a special place in the old man's affections, felt resentful of Greshko just then. The old man had excluded him. Yet – and here lay the hold Greshko had, the true nature of the loyalty Epishev felt – he was no less anxious to please Greshko than before. It was a kind of magic, Epishev thought, a sorcery. At a distance of four thousand miles, Greshko's grip was as strong as it had been at a mere six feet.

He stared at Iverson and said, "Why is there no furniture in this apartment?"

"We keep it for meetings," Iverson said. "Nobody lives here."

Epishev said, "In the Soviet Union, this kind of apartment would be occupied by two families."

Iverson shrugged and drained his ginger beer. He wasn't sure what to say to this. He had a script written for him by Galbraith and he had no desire to deviate from it. He put his empty bottle down on the kitchen counter and said, "Let's talk about Frank Pagan, Colonel."

"And the girl," Epishev said.

"Of course." Iverson walked across the room, putting a little distance between himself and the microphone he knew was planted in the vent above the kitchen stove. It would pick up his voice anyhow, but he enjoyed the idea of Galbraith straining to listen. What he didn't know, but on one level of awareness suspected, was that the entire apartment was one enormous eavesdropping device. The walls had been specially treated with a chemical that amplified any sound and relayed it to a series of hypersensitive pick-ups lodged in the ceiling. A sigh, a whisper, the touch of a handkerchief to a lip, a quiet fart – Galbraith heard it all in Fredericksburg.

Iverson leaned against the wall, arms folded. He had no way of knowing how much he had in common with Viktor Epishev of the KGB, how they both served masters given to authoritarian whim, strong-willed men who guarded their dominions jealously, who resented intrusions and meddlesome outsiders, and who found trust difficult. Iverson and Epishev – both obedient and yet at times capable of some mild straining at the leashes that held them in place, both loyal, both patriots, both pedestrians in the hall of bevelled mirrors that was international political ambition and intrigue.

Iverson said, "According to our information, Pagan and the girl are staying at the Warwick Hotel here in Manhattan. Pagan – presumably because of information given to him by the girl, and because he's come to some understanding of the coded *meaning* in Romanenko's message – has started to drift very close to the Brotherhood. Only this afternoon we were forced to intervene in a situation . . ." *In a situation I might have foreseen but didn't*, he thought.

Gary Iverson, turning the word 'coded' around in his mind, admiring Galbraith's cunning, glanced at his wristwatch and went on, "I don't have to tell you how disastrous it would be at this stage if Pagan and Kristina Vaska interfered with things. There's a third person in the picture as well, a New York policeman called Max Klein, who's been assisting Pagan. It's a sensitive situation, as you can well understand."

Epishev said, "But the solution is very simple, Iverson."

Iverson hesitated. "As you say, Colonel, it's very simple."

"Then what's holding you back?"

Iverson paced the floor, stopping at a place where

sunlight slicing through the windows struck his face and made him blink his eyes. "We need your help, Colonel Epishev."

Epishev was hardly surprised by the request. He hadn't been issued a quick visa and flown first-class to the United States on the first available plane just to play tourist. He'd known his help was needed from the start, from the moment when Gunther had stamped his passport in his offices in the US Embassy and told him that Pagan and the girl were now in New York City – 'pursuing investigations' was how Gunther had phrased it, his face rather mysterious, as if there were more he wanted to say but didn't have the authority to say. Epishev knew what the Americans wanted of him. He wanted the same thing for himself.

"You need to keep your own hands clean," Epishev said.

"The situation's delicate," Iverson replied.

Epishev gazed back out over the river. A tugboat came in view, a small dirty vessel spewing out dark smoke.

Iverson went on, "Killing a New York policeman – to say nothing of a man from Scotland Yard – isn't something we do with great enthusiasm. You, on the other hand, don't have . . ." Iverson let his sentence hang unfinished.

"Killing isn't anything I relish myself," Epishev said quietly.

"Nobody relishes it," Iverson said.

Epishev smiled. "And your superiors have qualms."

"Qualms, sure," Iverson remarked. "But it's more than that. They're afraid of unwanted complications. They don't like the idea of this triple elimination coming back on them, sullying their good name, if you understand what I'm saying."

"They're afraid of ghosts," Epishev said, a slight scoffing note in his voice.

"You might say. Congressional ghosts. Journalistic ghosts. We're a country of inquisitive spectres, Colonel.

It's part of the price we pay for freedom and democracy, you see." Scoring a point, Iverson thought, and why the hell not? He hated Communism. He hated Communists. He didn't like this character Epishev coming to the USA with such ease, and he was unhappy with the idea of any collusion between America and the Soviet Union. But he wasn't the scriptwriter, Galbraith was the creator when it came to situations and scenes, Iverson was merely an actor in the drama. At least he had the advantage of knowing how this particular drama was going to end, and it pleased him to think of the small aircraft floating in darkness with all the density of the Adirondacks lying mysteriously below . . . He derailed this train of thought. Anticipation might be amusing and enjoyable, but as Galbraith was constantly saying, *The future is the province of soothsayers, Gary. We mere mortals have to make do with the moment.*

Epishev said, "Your superiors don't have much power, if the killing of three insignificant people causes them such worry."

"Oh, they have power, Colonel. But they also believe that discretion is one sure way of holding on to it."

"Why do dirty work if they can get somebody else to do it for them?"

Iverson nodded. "You were given an order from your own superior, Colonel. As far as I understand it, your mandate was to eliminate any threat to the plan. That's all you've come to America to do. Your duty. Plain and simple. Everything you need will be supplied to you. Immediately after the success of your undertaking, you'll be flown from New York to Germany. You'll re-enter Russia, your orders will have been carried out, people will be pleased on both sides. You'll have all the help we can place at your disposal. You can even have the use of our personnel – up to a point."

"And what point is that?"

"The point where their culpability might be established."

"By the ghosts you fear so much?"

"Exactly," Iverson said.

Epishev watched the old tug boat vanish from his sight. Then the yellowy river was empty and the sun hung behind factory stacks on the opposite bank. Greshko's face floated up before him, the smell of the sick-room, the aroma of death that clung to the walls with the certainty of dampness.

"I have guarantees?" he asked.

"Cast-iron," Iverson replied. "Remember. If General Greshko trusted us enough to enter into this partnership, well . . ."

Epishev considered this. If Greshko had trusted these people, then Epishev had no reason to feel otherwise. Greshko's trust, as he well knew, was given only sparingly, and then never completely – but if he'd made an important compact with the Americans, then it was because the advantages in it for him were too attractive to refuse. There was a long silence in the room, broken finally by Iverson, who looked solemn as he said, "You can count on our backing all the way."

"You have Pagan and the girl under surveillance?" Epishev asked.

"Constantly," Iverson answered. "We never sleep."

Moscow

"Tea, General?" Volovich asked, but his tongue was heavy in his mouth. He watched Stefan Olsky cross the floor to one of the armchairs, where he sat, crossing his legs and removing his cap.

"I don't think so," Olsky said.

"It's no trouble – "

Olsky held one hand up, palm outward. "I said no, Dimitri."

Volovich hovered in the doorway to the kitchen. Pain throbbed behind his eyes.

Olsky said, "I like this apartment. I imagine you're fond of it too. Convenient location. Pleasant rooms."

"It's comfortable, General."

Stefan Olsky was quiet a moment. "You were going somewhere when I arrived."

Volovich, whose mind suddenly had the texture of an ice-skating rink, a thing of slippery surfaces and frozen depths, nodded his head imperceptibly. "A stroll, a late-night stroll," he forced himself to say.

Olsky said nothing for a moment. "You took a call from Viktor Epishev a few minutes ago. The call was patched here through a KGB switchboard in East Berlin. It originated in the United States. My listeners are located in the basement of this building – does that surprise you?"

A tapped telephone. It was a nightmare and Volovich was hurled into it and, as in all nightmares, no immediate escape was apparent, no relief forthcoming.

Olsky said, "Viktor Epishev mentioned a threat to the plan, Dimitri. What is the nature of the plan?"

"Plan?"

"Don't play games with me. I hate games."

Volovich shook his head. Being stubborn would finally prove futile, but there were old loyalties and they would sustain him, if only briefly. "I don't understand what you're talking about, General."

"I know you and Epishev visited Greshko last Saturday. I know Epishev left the country the next day. I know you're all involved in some kind of Baltic conspiracy – don't waste my time or insult my intelligence, Lieutenant."

"I have nothing to say."

Stefan Olsky stood up and strolled around the apartment. "You have a comfortable life here, Dimitri. A good apartment, a car, a job that isn't terribly taxing. And yet you risk throwing it all away – for what? Why do you feel you have to protect Greshko and Epishev? Do you imagine they'd protect you if the situation were reversed?"

Volovich, who saw the logic of the question, didn't answer it. He looked down at the floor like a scolded schoolboy. He heard General Olsky move around the apartment, but he didn't look. Once, Olsky passed just behind him, so close Volovich could feel the General's breath on the back of his neck and smell his sweet aftershave lotion.

"I admire your loyalty, Dimitri. I understand your need to protect your superiors."

Volovich still didn't speak.

"But sometimes old loyalties have to give way to new ones, Dimitri. Just as old systems have to yield to new ones, if there's going to be progress." Olsky was quiet a moment. "I don't approve of some of the methods used by my predecessor. I admit they got quick results, but the cellars of Lubianka are damp and they don't feel quite right to me any more. Too medieval. Too crude. This is the late 20th century and Greshko's barbarism is outmoded. I much prefer the idea of solving this business between us in a civilised way . . ."

Stefan Olsky sat down again. He looked at the darkness upon the window, the slight light cast there by a streetlamp. A faint wind rustled the thin young trees outside. He turned his eyes back to the wretched Volovich. He felt an odd little sense of pity for the man.

"Tell me the nature of this plot."

"I don't know," Volovich said, raising his face to look at the General.

"Nobody told you, Dimitri? Am I to believe that?"

"Nobody told me. Correct."

Olsky said, "I understand you have a mother, Dimitri."

"Yes."

"You were able to use your influence to have her admitted to a KGB-operated rest home on the Black Sea."

"I only did what a great many people do."

"I'm not quibbling with that. But you used your influence in the wrong way, didn't you? Some people might construe it as misuse of privilege. Even a form of bribery.''

''Bribery?''

''In which case your mother would be obliged to move.''

''She's sick, General.''

''There are hospitals.''

''If she were in a hospital, she'd be dead now.''

Volovich glanced inside the kitchen where a kettle had begun to boil. He pictured his mother, who suffered from incurable emphysema, being moved from her light, airy room in the sanitarium and taken to some dreary state hospital in a small drab suburban town, where care would be minimal and medication unavailable and nurses rude.

''Make your tea, Dimitri. You need it.''

With hands that wouldn't stop shaking, Dimitri brewed tea, then stood inside the living-room and sipped it. He was quiet for a very long time, struggling with himself, seeing the sheer hopelessness of his situation. He said, ''I don't want her moved, General. She's comfortable where she is.''

''I imagine she is,'' Olsky said.

Volovich swallowed hard. He might have had a pebble in his throat. ''I'd tell you if I knew, General. But I don't know. They kept me in the dark.''

''You must have some knowledge.''

''I understood Romanenko was delivering a message to a contact in Britain. Then Romanenko was shot, the delivery didn't happen and Epishev was sent to make sure nothing else would go wrong.''

Olsky felt a little flicker of fatigue go through him. All afternoon long and throughout the evening, he'd been dispatching KGB agents to the major cities in the Baltic countries, to Riga, and Vilnius, and Tallinn, hundreds of agents, under strict orders to act with stealth and the appropriate discretion in their inquiries. Dissidents, refuseniks, political deviants – these had been rounded up quietly and taken from their homes and questioned, then returned as swiftly as possible. Apartments were ransacked, files removed, documents studied. The operation brought forth a number of unexpected prizes, although none of them was related to the Baltic plot. A musician in Vilnius had an illegal mimeograph machine, a Jewish writer in Tallinn was in possession of a large amount of foreign currency, a cache of heroin had been discovered in the apartment of a physician in Riga, and in the Latvian city of Valmiera a professor of physics had a collection of several hundred precious icons. At any other time, Olsky would have been pleased with these results, but not now. They brought him no closer to the truth he really wanted.

"You must have gathered *some* impressions, Lieutenant."

Greshko and Epishev, who sometimes seemed to share a common language Volovich couldn't penetrate, had never really made him an intimate part of the plan. "A few," Volovich said. "The truth is, *I really didn't want to know*."

"A conspiracy against your country, and you didn't want to *know*?"

"I worked with Colonel Epishev for twenty years – "

"And you're close friends – "

"Yes, we are – "

"And you couldn't let him down – "

"Correct, General."

Olsky sighed. "Tell me your impressions."

Volovich put his tea-cup down. "I understood the plot's aim was an act of terrorist aggression inside the Soviet Union."

"But not in the Baltic republics?"

"I don't think so, General."

Olsky asked, "Where in the Soviet Union? And when?"

"I don't know."

"Moscow? Leningrad? Kiev?"

"I swear I don't know – "

"And what kind of terrorism? Bombs? Assassinations?"

"My impression is that there's a plane involved. The attack will come from the air – but I'm guessing now."

"From the air?"

"Yes, General."

"But that's impossible," Olsky said, just a little too quickly. Ever since a foolish West German teenager had contrived to fly a small aeroplane directly into Red Square two years ago – to the general humiliation of the authorities – defences had been strengthened. It was boasted now that they were impregnable, even if Olsky knew that 'impregnable' was one of those illusory words of which the military was so fond.

"One would have thought so," Volovich said. "I just wish I knew more."

Volovich lapsed into an uncomfortable silence. General Olsky walked around the room, examining books and phonograph records. He picked up a copy of *Trud* from the table and flipped through the pages. He believed Volovich because he understood that a minion like Dimitri would not be made privy to essential information. He'd drive cars, and carry messages, and act as liaison, and he'd pick up information here and there, but his role would never be very significant. Greshko, even more possessive in old age than he'd ever been, more like a sharp-clawed cat than before, would have seen to that.

"What happens to me, General?" Volovich asked.

"Until I decide, you're under house arrest. You'll answer your telephone as you usually do, and if anybody calls from your office you'll say you're sick with cold, whatever. Apart from having this very severe chill, you'll sound otherwise perfectly normal."

"And when my cold is cured?"

Olsky didn't answer the question. He stepped out of the apartment and stood on the landing. He looked down the stairwell, seeing through pale lamps the shadow of Colonel Chebrikov waiting in the foyer. Olsky descended, nagged by the realisation that he'd been looking for the sources of this Baltic business in all the wrong places. Common dissidents, writers, dreamers, Jews, applicants for exit visas – he had reached into the predictable areas for suspects, when he should have been looking elsewhere. *An aeroplane.* What kind of people were in a position to help an aeroplane carry out an act of aggression, an act of terrorism, against the Soviet Union? The answer was obvious, and yet painful because it involved powerful men who were sensitive when it came to their domain, which was nothing less than the air defences of the country.

He crossed the lobby to where Chebrikov was standing. The young Colonel, who stood at attention whenever Olsky was within his line of vision, said, "There was a call for you on the car radio, General. From the Kremlin. The General Secretary wants to see you. Urgently, sir."

Manhattan

"I'm sorry, I didn't know you had company, Frank," Max Klein said when he stepped inside the hotel room and heard the sound of Kristina singing in the bathroom. He fidgeted with his bow-tie, a polka-dot affair that drooped, then sat down in one of the two easy-chairs in the place. He had a way of entering rooms, softly on sandals, that suggested the movements of a retired cat-burglar a little embarrassed by his habitual stealth. Even his feathery hair seemed stealthy on his skull, as though it would whisper secretively were a breeze to blow through it.

"It doesn't matter," Pagan said. He didn't have time for explanations of Kristina. He might have told a narrative of Soviet repression, the story of a man whose family had been destroyed years ago, and how Norbert Vaska was imprisoned in Siberia, but Pagan had no real urge to familiarise Klein with all this background, nor with how Kristina Vaska had swept into his world. The sound of the shower stopped, but Kristina didn't emerge and there was only silence from the bathroom for a long time.

Klein stared at the bathroom door a moment, then took some papers out of his jacket. Like everything else that found its way into his pockets, the papers were crumpled and creased, and he had to spread them on the table and smooth them before they were manageable. "Do you know how easy it is to set up a corporation in this country, Frank?" he asked. "It doesn't take much, I'll tell you. A lawyer draws up articles of incorporation, you pay the guy his fee – anything from three hundred to a thousand dollars – and you file the articles with the Corporation Commission, and that's it. Unless you're a known felon, you're the President of your own company within a matter of moments. A piece of cake."

Pagan leaned across the table to look at the papers Klein had spread out. Klein said, "These documents represent a triumph of corporate maze-making, Frank," and he pushed some photostat sheets toward Pagan, who was hoping only to hear a bottom line, not a digression on the illusory nature of corporate structures.

"Carl Sundbach operated a company called Rikkad Inc."

"Then *he* was responsible for hiring the Jaguar?"

"Not quite," Klein said. "He turned ownership of Rikkad over to another company named Piper Industries – they make belts for vacuum cleaners – but he stayed on as Chairman of the Rikkad board. Rikkad, incidentally, supply paper products to hotels. Not only was he Chairman of Rikkad, he was also CEO of Piper, so he'd sold his company to himself. High finance baffles me, so don't ask questions about tax strategies, because I don't have answers."

"Where is this going, Max?"

"I'm getting there, I'm getting there." Klein turned

over some more sheets of paper. "Look at this. Piper Industries, in turn, is a subsidiary of something called – drum rolls, please – Sundbach Enterprises, which was sold five years ago to none other than Rikkad Inc. The snake swallows its own tail and Carl was lying when he said he'd sold his company to another outfit. When you look at the names of the corporate officers in each case, only two names reappear. Carl's, and somebody called Mikhail Kiss, who is apparently the financial VP of all three companies."

"But who the hell leased the bloody Jaguar?" Pagan asked.

"To find the answer to that baby, we have to ask Kiss, don't we? If he's financial Vice President, he's got to have some kind of information about what flows in and out. And since it costs approximately eight grand a year to lease a Jag with insurance from the company on Long Island – I checked it, Frank – it's the kind of expense he's not exactly going to overlook."

Corporate mazes, funny paperwork, networks that swallowed themselves. Pagan gazed at the papers just as Kristina stepped out of the bathroom. Affected by slight awkwardness, Pagan made the introduction. Kristina, with a social charm he hadn't noticed about her before, shook Klein's hand and showered him with attention, as if he were suddenly the most important thing in her world – it was quite a knack and the small man looked as if he'd had an encounter with an angel. Pagan marvelled at the easy way she made small talk with Max Klein, then the grace with which she apologised for interrupting. She drifted to the window, turned her back on the two men, saying she hadn't meant to disrupt them. Max Klein protested – *her kind of interruption, hey, he could stand that any day of the week*.

Pagan watched her, saw the way her shirt tapered into the narrow belt of her blue cotton pants, and how her damp hair glistened in the fading sunlight. He was struck by wonder at the way she commanded his attention, by her grace and quiet elegance, and how the sunlight made a soft outline of her at the window.

"I've got an address for Kiss," Klein answered. He opened his notebook and found the page he needed. He showed it to Pagan, to whom the address meant absolutely nothing.

"He lives in Glen Cove, on the Island," Klein said. "The phone's unlisted. I could get it if you needed it."

"I don't," Pagan said. "I'd rather go in person."

"Now?" Klein asked.

"Why not?"

Kristina moved directly behind Pagan, one hand laid on his shoulder with a proprietary intimacy he enjoyed. She said, "I'll wait for you here if you like, Frank."

Pagan stood up. He looked directly into the woman's dark eyes, seeing sympathy in them, and insight, and he realised nobody had looked at him in quite that way since Roxanne. He was moving in other dimensions here, and enjoying them, even if he wasn't sure where they were ultimately taking him. She kissed him lightly on the side of his face.

"Take care," she said.

Moscow

The office of the General Secretary of the Communist Party of the Soviet Union was located in the Palace of Congresses at the Kremlin. It was painted in shades of brown and lit by concealed spotlights, each of which played quietly and artfully on the man's large desk, creating the impression that the Secretary was on a stage, the central player in an unfolding drama. The room, though vast, was stark in its furnishings. Thick brown curtains hung day and night at the window and the outer edges of the room were forever in gloomy shadow, and impenetrable. The General Secretary was middle-aged, the youngest leader of the Soviet Union since the Revolution, and wore no medals upon his chest in the fashion favoured by his bombastic predecessors. His style of governing was relaxed, at least in public, and low-key, and he enjoyed the rapport he'd established with the ordinary people. He took frequently to the streets, plunging among the workers, shaking hands until his flesh was bruised, listening to complaints and disappointments and promising to put things right. His was a new Russia, a different kind of Soviet society which, while forging ahead into unmapped regions, had to take pains not to offend and isolate the old – a difficult and rather delicate balancing-act, and a conundrum whose solution would take many years.

But the General Secretary was a determined man, and steely, and he'd been playing Party games for most of his adult life and so knew how to bend Party opinion in his direction, at least much of the time. He knew how to use patience to work the older members, those quietly sullen men who remembered Lenin and had survived the ravages of Stalin's ways. He knew how to use charm when he encountered stubbornness, and when charm failed him he knew the best way to be rid of the 'ideologically backward' was to send them to distant *oblasti* where they assumed grand titles and exercised absolutely no power. He knew how to use persuasion when it came to slowing down those of his own followers who wanted to hurry everything, men of excess and unbounded impatience, whose qualities of dedication were needed but whose temperaments were not.

Now, raising his face from the sheets of paper that contained the working draft of the speech he intended to deliver to the Praesidium in twelve hours' time at the Palace of Congresses, he capped his fountain-pen and looked at the figure of General Olsky, who sat facing him.

"This speech, Stefan, which may be the most audacious I've made," – and here the General Secretary tapped the papers with his pen – "is going to be called incautious by some, bold by others, and heresy by all the rest. The hardline Marxists are going to say I'm soft on Western capitalism, which is anathema to Communism. The so-called democrats among us are going to say I've bent over backwards to appease the Marxists and leftover Stalinists who got our economy into a mess in the first place. I want to make unemployment a fact of Soviet life, for example. A bad worker should be fired. Others should compete for his job. Isn't that perfectly natural? And the old men will nag me and say there can be no official unemployment in a socialist society. And the military – I see apoplectic generals when I announce my intention to cut military spending by twenty per cent over two years. I take a little from some, give a little to others, and hope it balances in the end."

The General Secretary took off his glasses. It was two a.m. and he was weary. He surveyed the banks of telephones on his desk. Directly below his office was the main auditorium of the Palace where Communist Party Congresses had been held ever since 1961, when the Palace had been constructed. It was an impressive building, containing eight hundred rooms and a banqueting hall that could seat a couple of thousand people, but it wasn't the General Secretary's favourite building at the Kremlin by any means. He much preferred the sumptuous halls that housed the possessions of the Royal Family – the Regalia Hall with its extraordinary thrones and crowns, or the Hall of Russian Gold and Silver where there were elaborate candlesticks, goblets, rings, earrings and likenesses of saints. These displays stimulated a quiet yearning for Russia's past that most people might have found strange in a progressive General Secretary, but he'd read widely in Russian history, and perceived his own roots in these readings, as well as his own designs for the future. This great sluggish bear that was Russia, bogged down in its own muddy past, had to be set free to survive.

Olsky, always awed in the presence of the General Secretary, gazed across the massive desk. Socially, he was comfortable with the Secretary when they met for drinks, or once in a great while to play cards, but when it was a matter of official business he could never bring himself to feel easy.

The General Secretary said, "About an hour ago, I spoke with Nikolai Bragin. At his insistence, let me add. He was most anxious." He opened a drawer in his desk and drew out some photocopied sheets of paper, which he slid toward Olsky, who read them slowly, once, twice, three times. He tried to keep his hand from shaking.

"I'm obliged to show them to you, Stefan."

"They're forgeries, of course," Olsky said calmly. "Where did you get them?"

"Would it surprise you to know they came from Greshko, who tried to interest Bragin in a story of scandal and corruption inside the Politburo?"

Olsky sighed. "I'm not surprised."

"According to Greshko, there's some kind of plot against the State going on. He told Bragin there are Baltic factions involved and he claims . . ." And here the General Secretary paused, searching for the right phrase. "He claims that you're part of the whole thing, Stefan. He also claims that a certain KGB Colonel, Viktor Epishev, has been sent abroad under your express orders to participate in the scheme."

"Do I *have* to answer these ridiculous charges against me?"

The General Secretary smiled. It was one of the most famous, most frequently-photographed smiles in the world. "I'm not satisfied there's any need for official action, Stefan. Do you know the exact nature of the so-called plot?"

"Not yet. But I'm close to knowing."

The General Secretary picked up the documents and arranged them in one neat pile. "Greshko's like a wild boar. Insane when wounded," he said. "I've always had a grudging admiration for the old fellow. I suppose that's a terrible admission to make, but he used to tell some entertaining stories."

"A dinosaur's charm," Olsky said.

The General Secretary made his chair swivel. "I wonder about his life these days. I wonder what it's like to be completely stripped of power and sent out to pasture."

Olsky said, "His mind wanders. He can't tell reality from fantasy. The old Greshko wouldn't have done anything as ludicrous as running to the press with forgeries. He's slipping."

"Slipping or not, he claims to have copies of these documents, Stefan. What worries me is the idea that he may have distributed them to people less scrupulous and more gullible than Bragin. A foreign journalist, for instance. Somebody in a foreign embassy, perhaps. You might make inquiries."

The General Secretary was quiet for a second. "I don't like the idea of Greshko shooting his mouth off to people about these documents, whether they're forgeries or not. My whole administration has advocated exposure of corruption. How does it look if articles appear in foreign newspapers about the Chairman of the KGB dabbling in capitalist money markets? The fact that the stories are false is irrelevant. People believe what they read, Stefan. And then the news comes back into this country over the Voice of America, or through Scandinavian radio, and before you know it we're discredited in front of our own people by rumours. It goes well beyond malice on Greshko's part, Stefan. It affects us all. It affects our standing in this country, all the way up from the smallest workers' soviet to the Central Committee itself – and we need all the support we can get these days. Any kind of weakness, any suggestion of corruption from within – I don't have to spell out the possible damage to us."

Olsky didn't know what to say. He'd underestimated Greshko, but he wasn't the first man ever to do that. He'd been humiliated by the old man, and his position placed in jeopardy. He felt a quickening of anger, a warm flush spreading across his face. The idea that his reputation had been attacked, and in the most questionable way, enraged him. But he maintained the appearance of control, if only because a display of emotion in front of the General Secretary would have been unseemly.

He said, "His physicians expected him to die months ago. I read their reports. Nobody expected him to live this long."

"He was bred into a tough generation," the General Secretary said. "The fact remains, he's still alive and doing damage. The problem for you, Stefan, is to make sure the damage isn't fatal."

"And how do I achieve that?"

The General Secretary took the cap from his fountain-pen and began to edit his speech. It was as if Olsky had ceased to exist in the room. After a moment, the General Secretary stopped writing, and looked across the desk at the Chairman of the KGB.

"You have to deal with it as you think fit, Stefan."

Olsky wasn't quite sure what the General Secretary was saying to him.

"There are a great many people in this country, Stefan, who want to hurt us. Greshko happens to be in the vanguard of our enemies. They are also the enemies of progress. Therefore, they are acting against the Party's interests. But you're the Chairman of the KGB. Why ask me for advice?"

Olsky stood up. He turned his cap around between his hands. As he moved his face, he was struck directly by one of the concealed spotlights. He blinked.

"And this alleged plot?" the General Secretary asked. "Can the Chairman of the KGB deal with that also?"

Olsky moved out of the light and stood in shadow. Was there something quietly mocking now in the General Secretary's voice? He wasn't altogether sure.

"I can deal with Greshko and his damned plot," Olsky

said, sounding all the more angry for the fact that he didn't raise his voice.

"Spirit!" the General Secretary said. "That's why you got this job in the first place, Stefan. Spirit."

Olsky moved toward the door. He understood he'd just discovered a use for Lieutenant Volovich. Yes, and it was appropriate, something the wretched Volovich was schooled to do. It pleased Olsky on one level, even as it dismayed him to think he'd reduced himself to the level of his predecessor, but it was a game of cunning now, and survival, and all the rules of decency were suspended.

"A question, Stefan."

Olsky stopped, turned around, listened.

"They *are* forgeries, aren't they?"

"Yes," Olsky said.

The General Secretary looked at the photocopied documents. "Clever ones, though," he remarked.

17

Near Tallinn, Estonia

Somewhere in the hours of darkness the girl called Erma came into the small room Marcus occupied at the top of the house and slid inside his sleeping-bag and put her arms round him, teasing him gently out of a sleep that hadn't been deep to begin with, a dreamless state, a dark floating. She curled her fingertips beneath his testicles and touched him, feeling him stir. She enjoyed the ease of her own power.

Marcus woke. He'd been expecting the girl to come to him for some time, and so he wasn't altogether surprised to find her beside him. He touched her breasts, which were soft, weightless, adolescent. He ran the palm of one hand – his skin was rough and this shamed him because he felt the girl flinch very slightly – down her flat hard belly to her groin, where the pubic hair grew light and shapeless. He moved a finger softly back and forth until she'd become very moist. She straddled him, rocking above him, invisible in the complete dark of the room. Blind like this, Marcus was conscious of how his other senses were extended – the slight milky smell of the girl, the unbearable softness of her flesh beneath his fingertips. It had been a long time since Marcus had been with a woman, and the girl could tell. He came quickly and she with him, shuddering, biting her lip to be silent because other people slept in this house, and she felt his sperm explode through the dark spaces of her body, thinking of it as a series of coloured lights popping deep inside her.

Then she rolled off him and lay beside him, holding his hand. She said, "I'm scared, Marcus. If you want the truth, I'm terrified."

"We're all scared," Marcus whispered. "We all pretend we're not because we have to. But deep down . . . You'll find you're no different from the others."

"Are we going to die?" she asked.

Marcus was quiet, listening to the dark, the sound of insects, the occasional flutter of a bird in a nearby tree, the light wind that blew from time to time upon the old shutters. He looked at the luminous dial of his watch. It was almost two a.m. This was the day, and he didn't want it to be, he wanted to stall for another day, perhaps find time to enjoy this girl a little longer. But there was no changing the calendar of events. Here in Estonia, and in Lithuania, in Latvia, in Moscow – this was the day they'd planned and worked for, through years of secrecy and fear, through euphoria and gloom, trust and paranoia. He listened to the tick of his old watch, then turned the dial away so that the sharp green light wouldn't annoy him. He put his hand around the girl's shoulder. She trembled.

He gazed at the window and saw a thin moon sailing behind a garland of clouds. Tonight he was more tense than usual. But so were all the others who occupied this old house. Erma, the young man who called himself Anarhist, and the old fellow named Bruno, who occupied the attic and snored deliriously in his sleep and who'd been fighting the Russians one way or another since 1945 – they were all anxious in this damp, silent place.

What made Marcus more uneasy than the others was the fact that he'd gone to Tallinn earlier in the day for some food, and he'd sensed it at once in the streets, a change, a poisoned atmosphere – and then he'd seen the number of KGB cars in the city centre, and the officers who moved through side-streets and alleyways, and it became apparent to him that the KGB was conducting one of its periodic assaults on the city, ferreting out names on one of its notorious lists of 'hooligans' and suspected criminals. They moved on this occasion with unusual stealth, Marcus had thought, and he saw nobody handcuffed, nobody harried or pressed unwillingly inside automobiles – almost as if the order had come down from Moscow to do things quietly and with the least possible fuss. But the timing was bad for him. A concentration of KGB officers in the city was the very last thing he needed, and he couldn't help wondering if their presence had anything to do with the plan.

Fear, Marcus thought. And he listened to the night, to the sounds that grew in the dark.

"I want to fight, but I don't want to die," the girl said.

"Nobody wants to die." He could see her small face by moonlight and thought how beautiful it was in silver and how tragic the world was that this young girl, brutalised by the Russians, was ready to take up arms – when in another reality she might have been falling peacefully in love. An ordinary existence, a husband, children. "Listen to me. You could leave now. Nobody would think badly of you. You've got a long life ahead of you."

"What kind of life, Marcus?"

It was a good question, and Marcus had no answer. A life of repression, a life of careful utterances, of never knowing who was watching you, who was saying things behind your back – he might have mentioned all this but he didn't. He slid out of the sleeping bag and went to the window and looked down into the courtyard.

"Not much of one," she said, answering her own question. "If I could keep my big mouth shut, and go about my business and notice nothing – but that would be like death."

Marcus gazed at the outbuilding where the vehicles were parked. He saw it then, or thought he did, the cold hard disc of a flashlight, something that burned brief and yellow in the dark before vanishing, something alien that shouldn't have been there. He turned to the girl and said *Ssshhh*, then he dressed very quickly and told her to do the same thing. After that she should go wake the others immediately and tell them to move around with no noise. Armed, he said. They must be armed.

"What did you see?" she asked.

Marcus picked up his automatic rifle, his Uzi, and made a gesture with his hand, a swift, chopping motion that meant the girl was to hurry. She scampered quietly out of the room and Marcus went back to the window, where he looked out cautiously, seeing once again the glow of a flashlight and hearing the noise of the tarpaulin that covered the vehicles being moved slowly aside. Now there were shapes that came to him in the thin moonlight – three men, maybe four, but he couldn't see clearly. He heard the attic floor creak, then the noise of Bruno on the narrow staircase, followed by the sharp sound of the boy's voice as he was awakened from sleep by the girl. *What?* he asked, but the girl must have silenced him then.

Marcus turned when the old man came in the room. He had a pistol in one hand and a Browning Magnum rifle in the other, and he carried himself with his chest thrust forward, his shoulders back, the stance of an old fighter ready to renew hostilities with an eternal enemy.

"In the yard," Marcus whispered. "Three, maybe four. I can't tell."

Bruno approached the window, peered down. He was licking his lips nervously, dehydrated by the possibility of gunplay. Marcus studied the darkness, seeing a figure emerge from the outbuilding with a flashlight, and immediately behind him two others, both illuminated briefly by the moon, young men, boys, dressed in KGB uniforms.

"Do we fire from here?" Marcus asked. He could smell liniment from the old man, which he habitually rubbed into his muscles every night, believing it kept him young and supple.

"Mida rutem seda parem," Bruno said. *The sooner the better.*

The three figures below were coming towards the front

door of the house now. They would knock first, Marcus knew, but only once, and then they'd force their way in. They had grounds for forced entry, even though they needed none. Four vehicles concealed under tarpaulin, highly unusual, even suspicious. It was enough.

Erma and the young man came into the bedroom. Anarhist had his M-16 strapped to his shoulder, the barrel slung forward. Erma carried a Uzi pistol, which seemed too large for her to hold. Tucked in the waistband of her pants was her other weapon, the Colt automatic. She looked fierce suddenly, no longer the scared girl who'd made love to Marcus moments before. Anarhist looked down from the window and Marcus could sense it in the young man, the urgency to fire his gun, the desire that drove him.

"Not yet," Marcus whispered. "There might be others in the vicinity. We need to be sure."

"Wait? Screw it." Anarhist raised the barrel of his rifle and Marcus gripped it with his hand. The angle was narrow now, because the men below were clustered around the front door and the boy would need to hang from the window to get a decent aim, and then he'd be exposed.

"Go to the top of the stairs," Marcus said. "When they come in, fire. You'll have a better chance."

The boy went out of the room, followed by Bruno, whose anxiety was as sharp as the young man's. Marcus stayed at the window, watching, thinking that sounds of gunfire would bring others to the scene – if there were others nearby. And if they came, they'd enter this courtyard, and he could fire down on them. He smiled at the girl, who crossed the room and stood at his side.

"I'm ready," she said.

Marcus touched the side of her face. It came to this moment, he thought, all the years of longing, the years of hatred, they came to a point in time when they couldn't be contained any longer. He seemed not to exist, or if he did it was in some form he couldn't recognise, shapeless, out of his body, an entity floating in the scant light. He held his breath, heard the sound of something hard on the door below, perhaps the barrel of a weapon – and then the door was forced open and the intruders were inside the house.

Marcus heard the gunfire, the terrible roar of it, and he saw through the open bedroom doorway the boy and the old man firing down into the entranceway, and the old man was saying *Kaunis! Kaunis!*, meaning, *beautiful, beautiful*. The fire was returned from below in a brief outburst, and Marcus saw the boy hit in the skull and thrown backwards against the wall. And then somebody was running from the house. Marcus, standing in the window, fired into the courtyard and the running figure stumbled, ran a few more paces, fell, crawled, and Marcus fired again.

The silence that flooded the dark was immense, oceanic. Marcus stepped out of the bedroom, glanced at the dead boy, then at the white face of the old man. The girl was making an odd little whimpering noise, her sleeve drawn up to her face like a mask. Below, at the foot of the stairs, lay two KGB men, one atop the other as if in death a strange intimacy had been imposed. Marcus went down the stairs, stepped into the courtyard, walked to where the third KGB man lay. The side of his skull was gone and his face, beneath the glare of Marcus's flashlight, had about it an unreality, like something left only half-created. He killed the flashlight, listening to the dark, concentrating. There was still only silence. He went out of the courtyard and walked until he came to the rutted track, and there he paused. A car was parked to the side of the track. He approached it cautiously. There was nobody in it, and no sign of any other vehicles. He sat down on the ground, his back to the front tyre of the car. He was shaking. He stuffed his hands in his pockets but the trembling went on, even after he'd risen and walked back to the house and climbed the stairs to look at Anarhist, who lay slumped against the wall.

Marcus reached down to close the boy's eyelids, conscious of the girl watching him, and of the old man standing nearby, clearing his throat in the manner of somebody about to make a speech. But Bruno thankfully said nothing.

"I don't know if they came here purely by chance or if somebody tipped them off, but we leave here now," Marcus said. "We'll go elsewhere until it's time."

Nobody disagreed.

Fredericksburg, Virginia

Galbraith had been furious – and his unleashed fury was like a mad panther loose in a room of fine china – when he learned of the risk Andres Kiss had taken by going to Carl Sundbach's apartment and unexpectedly killing the old man. The carnival in the street, the water display and the battered cop car, hadn't exactly delighted him either. It often seemed to him that the Clowns took their in-house name too seriously, and had some adolescent need to perform acrobatics and gravity-defying stunts in cars and the like, which Galbraith found distasteful altogether. True, they'd managed to divert Pagan from Andres Kiss, creating a triumph out of the almost disastrous coincidence of Kiss and Pagan being in the same area at the same time, but *still* . . . The whole situation need not have happened. *And it had arisen because Gary Iverson had failed to fathom young Kiss's killing potential.* He'd failed to read the man with any accuracy, and Galbraith was annoyed by the fact that his own trusted servant, the loyal Iverson, *his right fucking hand*, had proved less than perspicacious in an important matter.

Dressed in his robe, Galbraith was lounging in his basement, gazing at his consoles, tapping into the vast data banks of the planet. The grimness of his mood was caused as much by Andres Kiss's unnecessary risk as by his own apprehension, his tangible sense of anticipation.

The clock was running down, and Frank Pagan was out there – and he still had the potential to do damage.

Galbraith studied the consoles, albeit in an absent way, because he was thinking of Epishev. Listening to Gary's conversation with the Russian in New York a couple of hours ago, Galbraith had been struck by a chill note in Epishev's voice, and a curious reticence on the man's part – as if he suspected some kind of trap. Perhaps his long association with Greshko had made Epishev just as paranoid as his superior. It was only because of Greshko's suspicions that Epishev had become involved in the first place – and since Galbraith hated waste, it occurred to him that Epishev's talents should be put to the best possible use. It was one of Galbraith's most important gifts. He knew how to use the talents of other people to perform tasks he'd never undertake himself.

He looked at the consoles. There was a message from the US Embassy in Moscow, destined for the State Department, but picked up by Galbraith's technology just as it plucked everything out of the sky.

The General Secretary will address the thirty-eight member Presidium of the Supreme Soviet at approximately 1600 hours Moscow time. He is expected to push through a progressive programme on both social and economic matters although there is likely to be strong criticism from certain elements in the Party, who consider his innovations too drastic. It is thought that he has sufficient support, although the outcome will be close. End end end.

End end end – but of what? The world as he knew it? Galbraith wondered. He checked his wristwatch. It was almost seven. In three hours time Andres Kiss would be catching his plane to Norway. Three hours. Galbraith picked up one of his telephones, the white slimline one which looked incongruous amid the other five receivers, all of them standard US government issue. He punched in eleven digits, and almost immediately heard Gary Iverson's voice.

"Where are we, Gary?" Galbraith asked.

"On the Long Island Expressway," Iverson replied. His tone was muted, a little remorseful. He clearly felt he'd failed Galbraith, and Iverson was a man who rarely failed at anything. Except, Galbraith thought, simple human understanding.

"And where's Pagan?"

"Pagan and Max Klein are about four cars ahead on the outside lane, sir. The girl is not travelling with them."

"Their destination is Glen Cove?"

"Apparently," Iverson said across a connection that was remarkably clear. "I imagine Max Klein's researches at the Corporation Commission provided him with Mikhail Kiss's name. I guess they tracked down the number of Andres's Jag, and that got Klein rolling." A pause. "I'm sorry about that one, sir. I had no idea Andres would do what he did. If I'd known . . ."

Sorry, Galbraith thought. Being sorry wasn't going to cut it. Being sorry was a dead-end street. This was where the miscalculations had led. This was what Iverson's illiteracy in reading the human heart came down to. This panic, this last-minute crap, this needless pursuit and the inevitable slaughter. "Call the Kisses. Tell them to leave for the airport."

"My information is they've already gone, sir."

"Fine. Where's Epishev?"

"He's directly behind me in a van."

"And the MO?"

"It's his own idea and I think effective. It dispenses with both men at once."

Galbraith said, "I don't want you anywhere near it, Gary. Is that understood?"

"Understood. What about the girl?"

"I'm not interested in her in the meantime. When Pagan's no longer . . . well, *around*, we'll keep her under surveillance for a while to see what she does. Not that it's going to matter, because it's after the fact by then, Gary. Keep me posted. And no fuck-ups. No near misses. No collisions. No calamities. Are you receiving me?"

Galbraith hung up. He chewed on a fingernail. There was at least no caloric intake in this kind of oral activity. He was still nervous, and there were phonecalls to return from Senators Holly and Crowe, that fretful Tweedledum and Tweedledee. He lay down on the sofa, thinking how unfortunate it was that a man like Frank Pagan, whose file he'd pulled from the Scotland Yard interface, whose attributes he admired, was doomed to die because he'd been in the wrong goddam place at the wrong goddam time.

The fat man shut his eyes. He contemplated the design of White Light, the mosaic which, despite the unwillingness of certain pieces to fit, was nevertheless a fairly attractive thing to behold. He was pleased in general with the pattern, and the fact that neither he nor his department was even remotely involved in events which by tomorrow night would have echoed around the world. He even liked the sound of the very name White Light – which had about it a certain shimmering intensity, a mysterious quality, something that raised it above the mundane manner in which clandestine projects were normally christened. He thought of Operation Mongoose, and Operation Overlord, and Project Bluebird, and he decided that White Light was superior to all of them.

He opened his eyes when he heard the sound of somebody knocking on the basement door. He called out *Entrez* and saw the ugly little woman known rather cruelly around the building as Madame Avoidable.

"The papers you asked for," she said. She wore a green wool cardigan and matching skirt and her glasses kept slipping to the end of her nose, causing her to make constant adjustments.

Galbraith took the documents and thanked her.

She said, "These are in the system."

"And the genuine ones?"

"Expunged as per your request."

"Mmm mmm mmm, a million kisses of gratitude," Galbraith said. He flipped through the pages, about six or seven in all. He watched Madame Avoidable leave, then he spread the sheets on his table and gazed at them. They were very good, very convincing. It was Andres Kiss's military record, and it read like a case-study in schizophrenia. He absorbed such phrases as 'delusions of grandeur', 'failure to accept any authority other than his own', 'a sense of a personal mission against the Soviet Union', and 'unwillingness to comply with Air Force regulations'. At the bottom of the page was the signature of a military psychiatrist (since deceased) and the stamped legend DISHONORABLY DISCHARGED. It was a nice little piece of fabrication and it would go down well with the gentlemen of the press, when the time came.

Long Island

Max Klein had replaced the battered Dodge with another Department car, a tan Ford of unsurpassed anonymity, the kind of vehicle used by narcotics officers making undercover buys. Pagan noticed scratchmarks across the back seat where handcuffed suspects had presumably scuffled around vigorously. Klein, who hadn't said much all the way from Manhattan, was curious about the woman in Pagan's room, but reluctant to ask questions. He had the feeling the Englishman wasn't exactly a man who opened up for you. Likeable, tough, the kind of guy to have with you in a crisis, Pagan gave the impression of a *closed* person, difficult to know, hard to reach.

As the Ford passed an exit for Flushing, Klein decided to take a chance. He said, "I thought you came to New York on your own, Frank."

"I did."

"Don't think I'm prying. The woman, I mean."

"I don't." Pagan enjoyed the friendliness he found in Americans, the quick camaraderie, the casual way first-name relationships were formed, all of which made a bright contrast to the taciturn English, whose hearts you had to drill open as if they were safes containing something too precious to touch. The down side of this easy manner was the way certain Americans thought they had the freedom to go rummaging around in your life, which was what Klein was edging towards now. But Pagan was going to be firmly polite.

"I don't want to go into it, Max. I don't want to complicate your life."

"Complicate my life?" Max Klein laughed. "My life's already complicated. I'm thirty-seven years old and instead of hanging in the Museum of Modern Art I'm driving a goddam cop car on the Long Island Expressway. You think that's a simple transition?"

Withered ambitions, Pagan thought. He stared at the highway before him and the way the sinking sun glinted from passing cars. Did he want to hear about Klein's life? Apparently he had no choice because Klein was talking about his paintings, his days in art school, the months he spent dragging a portfolio of his stuff around midtown galleries, only to encounter the severity of rejection. At least it steered the subject away from Kristina, Pagan thought, half-listening to Klein's good-natured banter about the rebuffs he'd received at the hands of gallery owners and art critics. Max had developed a shell of self-mockery, referring to his paintings as the work of a quick-sketch artist with delusions of mediocrity. Pagan, smiling, looked in the mirror on the passenger side, seeing the flow of traffic behind.

"I used to be in demand with my sketches," Klein said as he deftly changed lanes. "Give me a witness, a half-assed description, and I'd whip out a picture of a suspect in no time flat. Nowadays, they can use computers or a pre-made ID kit. They don't need my particular skills. So they push me here and there, one

371

department to another. Fraud last month. Juvenile the month before. Before that it was missing persons. You want an insight into sheer misery, Frank, missing persons is the cream."

Pagan made a noise of sympathy. He saw the exit for Great Neck. "How much further?" he asked.

"A few miles," Klein replied.

Pagan glanced once more in the side mirror. A large cement-mixer rattled behind, and then tucked at an angle in the rear of this monster was a dark blue van whose windshield glowed golden in the sun. He looked at the greenery along the edge of the expressway, imagining simple pleasures, walking with Kristina Vaska through a meadow or along a sandy shore or lazing by the bank of some stream. *Sweet Jesus, Frank* – had it come to this so soon, these little halcyon pictures, these banal images of romance? He was almost embarrassed by the direction of his own mind. *You've been too lonely too long.*

Klein swung the car off the expressway now. Pagan saw the exit sign for Glen Cove and then the greenery that had bordered the expressway became suddenly more dense and leafy, and white houses appeared to float half-hidden in the trees. Klein slid from his pocket the piece of paper with Mikhail Kiss's address on it, and looked at it as he braked the Ford at a red light. Since he didn't know where Brentwood Drive was located, he said he'd have to stop at a gas-station and ask.

Pagan turned his head, seeing the same cumbersome cement-mixer and the dark blue van behind him, and suddenly, without quite knowing why, he was uneasy, perhaps because he remembered the van outside Sundbach's building, which had been the same make as the one behind him now, perhaps it was because the van hadn't attempted to overtake the slow-moving cement-mixer for the last twenty miles. *It's in the air, Frank,* he thought, this general wariness, this low-level fear that you'll go a step too far and upset somebody to the point of madness – something you might have done already.

He tried to relax, rolling his window down and smelling the perfume of new-mown grass float across the evening. He had a sudden glimpse of water, a narrow inlet that penetrated the land from Long Island Sound, and then the water vanished behind trees. Klein pulled the Ford into a gas-station and Pagan saw both the cement-mixer and the dark blue van go past, and he felt a quick surge of relief because he'd already begun to construct unpleasant possibilities in his mind.

Pagan took the slip of paper from Max Klein. "I'll get directions," he said, and he stepped out of the car, glad to stretch his legs. He walked toward the glass booth where the cashier sat. He pushed the paper towards the woman, who was middle-aged and wore her hair in a slick black bun. She had the slightly flamboyant look of a retired flamenco dancer. She started to give directions, then interrupted herself to answer the telephone.

Pagan, staring across the forecourt, past the pumps, past Max Klein in the tan Ford, folded his arms. He could hear the distant drone of a lawn-mower, a summery sound, lulling and comforting, as if the very essence of the suburb was encapsulated in that single familiar noise. There was nothing alien here, nothing extraordinary, just this unchanging placidity.

He shut his eyes a moment, caught unaware by a sudden tiredness, then he shook himself, opened his eyes, saw the dark blue van come back along the road, moving slowly, the windshield still burnished by sunlight. It came to a halt on the side of the street opposite the station. Pagan felt curiously tense as he watched the vehicle.

The van moved again, but slowly still, making an arc in the direction of the gas-station. Pagan put his hand behind him, reaching for his gun in the holster, but not yet withdrawing the weapon because this might be nothing, an absolutely innocent situation, a van driver deciding he needed gasoline and turning back to get it, nothing more than that. Frank Pagan fingered the butt of the Bernardelli, watched the van cruise toward the pumps, and he realised how jumpy he'd become. He saw Klein behind the wheel of the Ford, his head tilted against the back of his seat in a weary manner.

The van kept rolling forward. It was about twenty feet from the station now. It stopped again, hidden somewhat from Pagan's view by the thicket of gas-pumps. The cashier hung up the telephone and said, "Now where was I? Oh, yeah, you take a left at the second light," but Pagan wasn't really listening. He saw a hand emerge from the blue van and something dark flew through the air, crossing the bright disc of the evening sun a moment, flying, spinning, falling, and it was a second before Pagan realised what it was, a second before he opened his mouth and shouted *Max!*

He saw Klein's face turn towards him even as the van hurried away and the driver was briefly visible. Then the Ford exploded and a streak of flame burst upwards, blue and yellow and red fusing into one indescribable tint, and he heard the sound of glass shattering into something less than fragments, something as fine as powder, then a second explosion which caused Klein's burning car to rock to one side. For a moment all light seemed to have been sucked out of the sky, as if the sun had dimmed. Pagan wasn't sure, but he thought he heard Max Klein scream from behind the flames that seared through the car, the burning upholstery, the black smoke that billowed from under the wrecked hood. He rushed forward, thinking he might have a chance to haul Max out, but the intensity of heat and the choking smoke drove him back, scorching his face and hair, blackening his lips. He saw Klein through flame, burning like a straw man, one fiery hand feebly uplifted, as if he might still find his way out of this furnace – and then the flames engulfed him. Pagan, drawing a hand over his face, was forced to step back. The air was unbreathable and the smoke that rose furiously out of the car stung his eyes and blinded him. A mechanic rushed out with an extinguisher but he couldn't get close to the car because of the heat. Besides, it was far too late to help Max Klein. Inside the glass booth the cashier was calling the fire department, also far too late for Max Klein.

Pagan moved back from the sight of the burning car and sat down against the wall of the gas-station, paralysed by utter dismay. He hadn't acted quickly enough, hadn't drawn his gun when the van had first aroused his interest, hadn't done a goddam thing to alert Klein. He listened to the sound of the car flaring and he turned his face to the side because he could still feel the awful blast. The cashier came out of the glass booth and touched him on the shoulder and asked if he was hurt. Pagan shook his head. He hadn't even suffered a superficial burn. The woman pressed a wet cloth into his hand and he covered his face with it. Poor fucking Max Klein, the department handyman. Whoever had tossed the grenade hadn't meant it to be for Klein alone, he was sure of that.

Whoever. He rose, threw the damp cloth away, drew his sleeve across his forehead. For an instant, just before the blast, before the rich, deathly smoke had covered everything, he'd seen the face of the van driver with striking clarity, and he remembered the last time he'd seen that face on a London street. Viktor Epishev, impassive behind the wheel of the van, his expression one of complete concentration, like that of a man who loved control. Pagan wondered bitterly if Uncle Viktor had ever done anything in a spontaneous way. Had he ever seduced a girl? Fallen hopelessly in love? Yielded to a casual whim like rolling up the cuffs of his pants to walk the edge of a tide or gone out and bought a brightly-coloured shirt just for the sheer hell of it?

Control and violence.

Pagan, shocked by the suddenness of things, numbed by his last image of Max Klein behind the screen of fire, wandered inside the men's room and filled the wash-basin with cold water and plunged his head into it, holding it there until he thought his lungs might explode. Gasping, he raised his face up from the water, and grabbed a handful of paper towels, then he walked back out to where the Ford was burning like some awful pyre whose colours kept changing. He shook his head from side to side, wondering if Epishev had mistakenly thought both Pagan and Klein had been in the Ford. Perhaps, blinded by sunlight, he hadn't seen clearly. Perhaps even now Epishev imagined that Pagan was dead in the ruined car. Whatever, it was painfully clear that Pagan was to be prevented at any cost from visiting the house of Mikhail Kiss – whose address he held, scribbled on a piece of creased paper by Max Klein, a name and a number surrounded by half-sketched faces and interlocking circles and three-dimensional squares, the work of the failed artist.

Throat parched, Pagan watched as a bright red fire-engine drew into the gas-station, a flurry of sirens and dark hoses unrolling and men who worked at a speed that suggested the whole gasoline station was going to blow up at any moment. In silence Pagan watched them blast the blazing car with their high-pressure sprays, but then he walked away because he didn't want to be anywhere nearby when they doused the flames sufficiently to pull the remains of Max Klein from the crematorium.

Kennedy Airport, New York

Mikhail Kiss found the bright lights of the terminal painful to his eyes, and he blinked a great deal, although sometimes he wasn't sure if it was the harsh light or the prospect of tears he was struggling against. He watched Andres at the Scandinavian Airlines desk, the check-in procedure, the way the female clerks fawned around him. He didn't have a suitcase, only an overnight bag. There was no luggage to go on board. Andres returned to the place where Mikhail sat and took the seat next to him, saying nothing, just tapping his fingertips on his knees or every so often checking his boarding-pass.

Mikhail Kiss lit a cigarette and for the first time in many years inhaled the smoke deeply into his lungs. He took his eyes from Andres and looked across the terminal floor, seeing two security cops move side by side with vacant looks on their faces. They passed through the glass doors and out into the failing light. Mikhail Kiss examined the departures board. Soon they'd begin boarding the plane that would take Andres to Norway. Mikhail stubbed out the cigarette and sighed. Why was there nothing to say? Why, at the very point he'd worked so long and hard to reach, were words so reluctant to form in his mouth? He laid his hand on his nephew's sleeve, a gentle gesture, perhaps more meaningful than any words could be. But it was a small thing, and it didn't go very far to dispel the feeling of estrangement from the young man that Mikhail Kiss experienced.

Something was wrong, and he couldn't define it. It was more than the goddam dream that kept coming back at him like a bad taste. The face of Norbert Vaska. The music in that white restaurant. *They don't go away*, he thought. *They come back to haunt you, no matter what you do.* What did he feel? he wondered. Was it sorrow? Or resentment at the tenacity of ghosts? But it was more than just the persistent image of Norbert Vaska that troubled him, and he searched his mind fruitlessly.

A bad feeling. Like the one he'd had that night in Edinburgh. That was close to the sensation.

Andres Kiss smiled. For a second Mikhail thought he detected a slight tension in the expression, and he was caught in a memory of when Andres had been a young boy, ten, maybe eleven, stepping into a boxing-ring for the first time, his face hidden behind a protective head-piece too large for him, his hands dwarfed by enormous gloves. He remembered how Andres had turned to him at the last moment and how frightened he'd looked and Mikhail, touched by this vulnerability, had felt needed then – but the moment passed and Andres went inside the ring and demolished his opponent with fierce speed and Mikhail realised that night he'd never *really* be needed in this young man's life, that Andres could achieve everything he wanted on his own, without help. And so it was now.

There was an announcement that the flight to Oslo had begun to board. Mikhail looked at his watch. 9:30. Andres examined his ticket and boarding-pass again, saying, "Round-trip. I appreciate your optimism, Mikhail."

Was this meant to be a small joke? "I wouldn't send you anywhere one-way, Andres," and he reached out to embrace the young man, whose body was stiff and unyielding, as if human contact distressed him. It was then Mikhail noticed a scratch on his nephew's forehead, which had apparently been covered by some kind of makeup, a powder of the kind women use, and he was going to ask about it. But now there wasn't time. And he didn't want to know anyhow.

Andres Kiss stood up. "I guess this is it," he said.

Mikhail Kiss felt moisture forming behind his eyes, but he blinked it away. It was a time for strength, not for useless sentimentality. He wished Carl Sundbach could have been here, because there was a sense of incompleteness, of somebody missing from the circle. Maybe he'd call Carl later, tell him that Andres was on his way to Norway, keep him informed. And maybe by this time Carl would be over his weird paranoia that somebody was following him through the streets and watching his apartment. Old age, Kiss thought, feeling the phantom of it move through him. It rendered men absurd, magnified their fears, expanded their anxieties.

Andres said, "The day after tomorrow, Mikhail. Until then."

"Until then," Mikhail Kiss said quietly. He watched Andres walk to the gate, then pass through without looking back. Mikhail had an attack of sudden panic and was filled with the urge to go after his nephew and call him back and tell him that everything was cancelled, there was no need to fly. Even if he'd done so, it would have been a futile gesture because the scheme had a life of its own now, a force that couldn't be halted, not even by the man who'd first set the whole thing in motion. It had grown, and matured, like a child over whom you no longer have dominion.

His work was finished. He walked out of the terminal. He stepped under lamps and signs and moved between taxis and buses. He felt his age again, a decay, a sense of internal slippage. And his memory was surely going. He'd forgotten to say to Andres at the last moment the words *Vabadus Eestile* – freedom for Estonia. But it was too late now even if the unspoken words seemed very important to him. He walked into the parking garage and took the stairs up to the second level, where he'd parked his Mercedes.

It was time to go home and wait.

18

Without waiting to answer awkward questions from investigators, Frank Pagan, sickened by the stench of fire that clung to him, had walked away from the burning Ford and moved through narrow streets, following the general directions the cashier had given him. These were impressive streets where branches of old trees interlocked overhead, creating barriers against the sky. The houses here were large, built on enormous green lots. These were streets in which money didn't speak, it hummed tastefully. Pagan paused when he reached the corner of Brentwood Drive, where the greenery was even more dense and the houses virtually invisible behind crowded stands of trees and thick hedges.

There was something secretive about the street, the impenetrable shadows, the way the houses were concealed from view. People here wanted to live private lives, and so they'd created their own wilderness in the suburbs of Long Island. A pedestrian in this place stood a pretty good chance of being arrested, because it was the kind of area where walking was something only criminals and cranks ever did.

He looked at the driveways of homes as he passed them. Numbers were so discreetly displayed you had to search for them among shrubbery. He found number fourteen. A hedgerow grew around the property and a gravel driveway disappeared among foliage. The only part of the house that could be seen was the red-tiled roof. Pagan took a few steps along the driveway, which curved suddenly and the house came in view, an ornate turreted construction set just beyond a well-kept lawn. A green awning hung above the columned porch. There were no cars in the driveway, no signs of life. He glanced at the windows, noticed nothing, no face behind glass, no curtain shivering.

He walked up on to the porch. The doorbell was one of those old-fashioned brass affairs that you pulled toward you. He could hear the bell echo within the house, but nobody came to answer. He moved slowly around the back of the house where an impressive rose garden was located. The flowers grew in lavish, meticulous beds.

Pagan looked through the glass walls of a sun room, which had been added to the original structure. But he saw nothing, only the vague outlines of furniture. Then he stared across the rose beds for a time, where there was a white-latticed gazebo draped by willows, and beyond that a thick stand of oleander. None of the surrounding houses was visible because of the dense foliage, which gave this particular dwelling a sense of isolation, of loneliness – as if nobody had ever lived here.

Some of this isolation touched him. He had an urge to sit down and sleep and withdraw, making himself numb to the death of Max Klein, numb to the question that had begun to nag at him ever since he'd strolled away from the gas-station – *how had Epishev known he was in the United States?*

Maybe it was no great mystery. He imagined how it might have happened that Epishev came across his information. John Downey, for instance, who was known to have connections in Fleet Street, and who was often the so-called 'reliable source' in newspaper stories about the Yard, might have run into an intrepid reporter anxious to get some eyewitness details about events in Edinburgh – and Downey, after a few of the Newcastle Brown Ales he so enjoyed, might have let slip the fact that Frank Pagan was off on some junket to New York City. As soon as the scribbler had his information, it would then travel along the Street, passed from the mouth of one crime reporter to the next, from one pub to another, where sooner or later the item would reach the ears of one of those accredited, if vaguely shadowy, journalists who gathered information for the Soviet press. From there it was a cinch that the knowledge of Pagan's trip would find its way back, sooner or later, to a source at the Soviet Embassy. A whisper in the ear of Epishev, and there it was . . .

Pagan could imagine this sequence, which was less one of malicious exposure than of bloody careless talk loosely bruited about in places where cops and reporters met to sink a few jars.

Epishev, Pagan thought. Everywhere Uncle Viktor went there was death in the vicinity. Everything he touched shrivelled and turned black. It was quite a knack to go through life laying things to waste all around you.

His head still filled with the memory of flames, Pagan peered once again through the glass walls of the sunroom. Then he tried the door, which yielded. Whoever owned this house, whoever Mikhail Kiss might be, he clearly felt he had nothing to fear from burglars, that the quiet authority, the rich seclusion of the street, was enough of a deterrent in itself. Pagan pushed the door, entered the room quietly, stood motionless. There was a strong smell of cut flowers in the air.

He stepped out into the hallway. To his left a flight of stairs rose up into darkness. Ahead of him, across the entranceway, were other rooms. Doors lay open and the half-darkened surfaces of wooden furniture gleamed quietly. The silence here was deep and impressive and the dying sunlight that managed to find its way inside rooms, squeezing through drawn-down blinds, was slightly unreal, like light from another planet.

Pagan went to the foot of the stairs, looked up a moment, then walked inside the room just ahead of him, a dining-room with an oval table and rather spare contemporary prints on the walls, a room with a certain sterile quality that suggested meals were never actually eaten here, nobody sat down to dine. It reminded Pagan of a window display in a furniture shop. Unlike the home of Carl Sundbach, with its clutter and disorder and a sense of an unarranged life being lived in its rooms, the house of Mikhail Kiss was imbued with absences and silences.

Pagan entered another room, a sitting-room, expensively done, white leather sofa, matching chairs, chrome, and again the same spacious emptiness. He walked to the stairs, climbed quietly, reached the landing. Two bedrooms, an office, a bathroom. The first bedroom was large and uninteresting, the bed made up, a book open and face down on the bedside table, an easy chair under the bay window. Pagan glanced at the book, which was in a language he didn't understand, then he noticed a photograph of a woman on the mantelpiece across the room. He didn't pick up the framed picture. The woman wore her hair in the style of the late 1930s. It was a good face, probably beautiful if you liked the gaunt, rather haunted look. Written on the picture, and barely legible, was an inscription – again in a language Pagan couldn't read – and the signature *Ingrida, 1938*. For a reason he couldn't begin to explain, Pagan was touched by a momentary sadness, perhaps caused by the look in the woman's eyes, or the sense he suddenly had that he was gazing upon a picture of the dead. Why did some photographs create the impression that the subject of the picture was dead?

He stepped out of the bedroom, then into the adjoining one. A narrow room, a single bed, prints depicting a variety of aircraft, and trophies – shelves of silver cups and medallions and plaques, awards decorated by miniature figures, a boxer, a runner, a javelin-thrower. It was quite a collection. Pagan picked up a statue of a boxer and read *To Andres Kiss, First Prize in the Junior Boys Section, Long Island Boxing Association, 1969*. All the awards here were to the same Andres Kiss, and there were scores of them, attesting to a disciplined, athletic life, an achiever's life, the kind of existence defined by very definite goals. Did Andres ever have time for fucking around? Pagan wondered. Presumably not, if he spent all his adolescent years training for competitions and winning trophies.

Andres Kiss. Was he Mikhail's son? Pagan replaced the trophy, crossed the room, looking for photographs of the boy wonder. Trophies galore, but no pictures, no casual snapshots. He looked at the posters of aircraft. They were all US and British fighter planes from World War II. So Andres liked athletics and aeroplanes – what did this tell you, Holmes?

Pagan went to the window, looked out across the garden at the back of the house, seeing how darkness, almost complete now, robbed the roses of their colours. He let the curtain fall back in place and was about to turn out of Andres Kiss's room when he noticed some framed papers on the wall above the bed. He had to turn on the bedside lamp to read them. Interesting stuff. A certificate issued by the United States Air Force to Captain Andres Kiss on the occasion of his promotion. An award from the USAF to Captain Andres Kiss for compiling one thousand hours of flying time. An honourable discharge to Major Kiss, dated September 1985. So young Andres went from being a juvenile terror in the boxing-ring to a wizard of the airways, a high-flyer. Pagan turned off the bedside lamp and stepped out of the bedroom to the darkened landing.

He was about to go inside the room that was clearly an office when he heard the front door opening and the sound of a key being tugged out of a lock, then the *chink-chink* of a chain in the palm of a hand. Frank Pagan stood very still at the top of the stairs, watching as a light was turned on in the hallway, illuminating the big man who stood in full view for only a moment before he stepped out of Pagan's vision.

Pagan held his breath. He heard water running inside

a glass, then the rattle of ice-cubes, the sound of liquid being stirred. He descended slowly, quietly, watching the square of yellow light falling out of the kitchen and into the hallway. The big man's shadow appeared briefly, then was gone, and a door closed somewhere. The sun-room, Pagan thought. *He makes himself a drink, takes it to the sun-room, sits down, relaxes.*

Pagan reached the foot of the stairs, where he paused. Through an open door he could see the man sitting on a wicker sofa, his legs crossed, his head tilted back, a drink held slackly in one hand. Pagan, taking his gun from its holster, moved into the doorway that led to the glass-walled room.

The man stared at him in surprise. Ice-cubes made faint knocking sounds inside his glass.

"Don't bother to get up," Pagan said. It was the man in the photograph, the one who'd been snapped beside Romanenko and Sundbach. Altered by time, his hair white, his body rearranged by the years, but it was undeniably the same man.

"Mikhail Kiss?" Pagan asked.

"Who wants to know?"

Pagan flashed his ID in front of the man's face. Mikhail Kiss, who had looked alarmed, seemed to relax now, reassured by Pagan's identity card.

"I thought you were, I don't know, a burglar," he said. "I'm Kiss."

"You left your side door open, Mr Kiss."

Mikhail Kiss stood up, sipped his drink, smiled. "I grow careless with age, Mr Pagan. Do me a small favour. Put the gun away."

Pagan returned the Bernardelli to his holster. "A precaution," he said.

"Sure. I might have pulled a gun and fired on you. After all, we live in an age of guns," Kiss remarked, still smiling, running one large hand through his white hair.

Pagan glanced a moment through the glass walls, seeing the ghostly shape of the gazebo out there in the darkness. Then he turned to look back at Mikhail Kiss, who seemed completely at ease now, and hostlike, as if he were wondering what kind of treats he could find to force upon his visitor.

Pagan had an uncomfortable moment suddenly, a light-headed sensation, a flashback to the sight of Max Klein in the burning car, and he wondered if this image was going to recur, if it was going to come into his head when he didn't want it, or enter his sleep when he didn't need nightmares. He pushed the picture from his mind and looked at Kiss, wondering if the big man had noticed his discomfort.

"You've come a long way," Kiss said. "What can I possibly do for a man from Scotland Yard?"

Pagan needed to sit down. He moved to one of the wicker chairs. He studied Kiss's face, thinking it was good-natured, and cheerful, the face of a man who doesn't come to subterfuge easily. Where to begin? Where to make the first incision? Start with the car. Start with something simple. Go slowly at first.

"I'm trying to trace the driver of a certain Jaguar," Pagan said.

"A Jaguar?" Mikhail Kiss asked.

"The car was leased to a company called Rikkad, of which you're the financial Vice President."

"Rikkad," and Kiss looked like a man ransacking his memory, a man who hears a faint bell ring at the end of a long corridor.

"Rikkad is one of your business ventures with Carl Sundbach," Pagan said in the manner of a theatrical prompter. There was an act going on here, and Kiss had slipped into some kind of amnesiac role, but Pagan wasn't in the mood to be a gullible onlooker in the balcony.

Mikhail Kiss drained his scotch, set his empty glass down. "We've had so many business ventures, sometimes I forget," he said. Why in the name of God was an English cop interested in the Jaguar? Only Andres ever drove it, and he'd returned it to the offices of the leasing company late that afternoon, so why was Pagan asking questions about it?

"But you remember now," Pagan said. "And you remember the Jaguar."

"Yes, of course, it comes back to me."

"Did you drive it?"

Mikhail Kiss shook his head. "Too sporty for me, Mr Pagan."

"Who used it then?"

"My nephew mostly. Andres Kiss."

Pagan sat back in his chair, and the wicker creaked under his weight. *Andres Kiss, Superboy.* "I'd like to talk to him."

"Unfortunately, that isn't going to be possible."

"Why not?"

"He just left on vacation."

"When?"

"Tonight," Kiss said.

"Where did he go?"

Mikhail Kiss shrugged. "Europe," he answered.

That, Pagan thought, was fucking useful information. "Where exactly?" he asked.

"He said he was touring. You know the young, Mr Pagan. They don't make plans."

"He flew, did he?"

Mikhail Kiss nodded. He had a tight, claustrophobic feeling, and it made his chest ache. What did an English policeman want with Andres, for Christ's sake?

"Where did he fly to?" Pagan asked.

Kiss laughed. "I'm only the boy's uncle, Mr Pagan. He tells me nothing." He lit a cigarette. "Why are you asking these questions about Andres?"

Pagan didn't answer at once. He liked the silence, the way it built, the suspense that lay at the heart of quietness. He got out of the wicker chair and looked across the darkened gardens. The gazebo was no longer visible, the sky moonless.

"Carl Sundbach was murdered this afternoon," Pagan said, and he turned to look at Mikhail Kiss's reaction.

Kiss was waxy suddenly, and pale. "Murdered?"

Pagan nodded. It was obvious that Kiss, unless he was more talented an actor than Pagan imagined, hadn't heard this news before.

"And you suspect my nephew? Is that why you're here?" Kiss asked. He had to fight the blackness that was inside him now, the sense of inner control receding, the wave of nausea that rolled through him. He remembered the unexpected way Andres had gone out, the moodiness of the boy later at the airport, he remembered aloofness and ice.

Pagan said, "A young man drove a Jaguar to Sundbach's street. He parked it, went up to Sundbach's apartment. Twenty minutes later Sundbach was found murdered. The young man and the Jaguar had gone."

Kiss asked his question again. *And you suspect my nephew?*

"Yes," Pagan said.

"Why would he kill Sundbach, for God's sake?"

Pagan had a small enjoyable moment, like the kind a conjurer might savour before pulling a multitude of things out of a hat he has shown the audience to be empty. Silks, rabbits, doves, pineapples, an unexpected world.

"My guess is he learned that Sundbach had arranged the murder of Aleksis Romanenko," and here Pagan took one of the photographs from his pocket and tossed it into Kiss's lap. It was done with flair and great aplomb and the timing was a joy. Three faces stared up from the photograph – Sundbach, Romanenko and Mikhail Kiss, three young warriors fighting on behalf of a lost cause.

Kiss shut his eyes and laid one hand over the picture and he thought *You old fool, Carl.* Of course there had been pictures, and he remembered the bravado of the day when they'd been taken, and how they'd gone out that morning – four of them, the nucleus of the group – and ambushed a Russian patrol, a successful enterprise, and how Sundbach, who was never without his pre-war Kodak, had insisted on photographs. Souvenirs, he'd said. *Mälestusesemed*, things of remembrance. Something to show our grandchildren, he'd said. Now, after all this time, the pictures, which Kiss had told him several times to destroy, had resurfaced and a prying Englishman had seen them. It was strange, almost mystical, the way the past clung to the present. And it was there in the old photo, a connection that couldn't be denied.

Mikhail Kiss looked down at the picture. He could smell the dampness of the forest, he could feel the wet earth against his face as he lay in a hollow while the *tiblad* patrolled nearby. Now what was this Englishman telling him? what nonsense was this about Sundbach arranging the death of Romanenko? and Andres killing old Carl?

"I think you're mistaken, Mr Pagan. I can't believe Sundbach would have anything to do with the death of Romanenko."

Pagan, glad that Kiss wasn't going to dispute the authenticity of the photograph and deny it was his own younger image there, reached down, picked the photograph up, looked at it. "Quite the opposite. I think there's a strong possibility Sundbach arranged it because he discovered Romanenko was controlled by a certain faction within the KGB."

"Controlled by the *KGB*? You're out of your mind."

"I don't think there's any doubt, Kiss. The KGB knew what Aleksis was carrying to Edinburgh, but they didn't stop him leaving the Soviet Union. And you want to know why they didn't? Because they *want* the Brotherhood's plan to work."

The Brotherhood. Mikhail Kiss, who had a stricken look on his face, walked quickly into the kitchen. Pagan followed, watching the big man make himself a second drink. Ice-cubes slid from his hand and fell to the tiled floor and cracked like glass. Kiss kicked the broken cubes aside and looked at Frank Pagan and wondered how this Englishman had heard about the Brotherhood.

He sipped his drink and tried to remain calm. He said, "I think you've made a grave error. Especially in your suspicion about Andres."

Pagan admired Kiss's control, even though he sensed it was superficial. The man's manner was cool, smooth, and there was something of perplexed innocence in his expression.

Pagan said, "I suppose I could always put the matter beyond any doubt by looking at a picture of your nephew. Do you have a photo?"

Mikhail Kiss stared at the Englishman, who had one of those faces that can be deceptive, a mask drawn across true feelings. But Kiss saw it in Frank Pagan's eyes, a core of conviction that what the Englishman was saying was the truth. Kiss turned away, fighting a chill he felt. He heard himself ask how Carl had been murdered, and Pagan replied with the single word *strangulation* and Kiss remembered the cut on Andres's forehead, which perhaps Carl, the old fighter, the *vöitleja*, had managed to inflict at the end of his life. Something dark raced across Kiss's heart when he thought of this boy he'd raised, this killer of old men. He shut his eyes tightly. He wondered if he could deny the boy's existence, if he could deny the very thing he'd created.

"I don't have a photograph," he said.

"I didn't think you would." Pagan poured himself a glass of water from the faucet and drank it quickly. He could still taste smoke in his mouth. "What is the Brotherhood's plan, Mikhail?"

Kiss turned to the Englishman. "Plan? What plan?"

"The one the KGB seems to like," Pagan replied. "The one the KGB has found some use for."

Mikhail Kiss shook his head. There were edges here, boundaries he couldn't chart, as if the landscape Pagan described were too chaotic to grasp. There was no way in the world that the KGB could have controlled Romanenko. There was no way the KGB would encourage the scheme. They'd destroy it, not use it. Everyone connected with it, himself included, would have been disposed of in some way.

"When you talk about the Brotherhood, you seem to ascribe to it a sinister quality it doesn't have. I admit we're a group of loosely-organised patriots who regret the seizure of our country – but we're not planning anything, you understand. And if we did, it wouldn't be anything the KGB would approve of, I can tell you."

Pagan folded his arms, leaned against the sink. There was a flatness in the way Kiss talked, a lack of vigour. It was as if his understanding of his nephew's crime had diminished him in an important way, and now he was simply going through the motions of concealing the Brotherhood's scheme.

"Too many people have died," Pagan said. "Too many people have died for me to buy your bullshit. Is it terrorism? Is it political assassination? What the hell is it?"

Mikhail Kiss walked out of the kitchen and back into the sun-room, the glass walls of which were pitch black now. Pagan followed him, frustrated by the big man's evasiveness. What was he supposed to do? Pull a gun and force Kiss to tell the truth? Pagan had the distinct feeling that guns wouldn't convince Mikhail Kiss to do anything he didn't want to do.

"How do you feel, Kiss, about the fact that your plan is being put to use by the KGB? How do you feel about serving up something useful for your enemies?"

Mikhail Kiss sat down, looked sadly at Frank Pagan. "Please, Mr Pagan. No more. No more questions. I'm tired now."

Goading wasn't much of a strategy either, Pagan decided. He moved a little closer to Kiss and said, "Romanenko is dead. Carl Sundbach is dead. Two London policemen are dead. A young English diplomat was killed. And tonight a New York cop was burned to death inside his car. This plan of yours is running up quite a total, Kiss. Somebody gets in the way of it and whoops – the fucking KGB makes sure they're not around to do any more interference. You make a great team. The Brotherhood and the KGB."

Kiss said nothing. He wasn't really listening to Pagan. He was thinking of Andres Kiss killing Carl Sundbach. He was trying to imagine that, seeing pictures, Sundbach perhaps rolling on the floor while Andres tied the cord tighter and tighter still, the old man struggling, fighting, gasping at the end of it all.

Pagan brought his face close to Kiss's ear. "Is Andres part of it, Mikhail? I understand he's a hot-shot flyer. Is he part of the scheme? Is he going to fly a plane for you? Is that it? A bomb, Mikhail? Is he going to drop a bomb?"

"*For God's sake.*"

Pagan was trying to come in from all angles here, as if this buckshot approach might confuse Kiss, might draw an answer out of him that he didn't want to give, but Kiss was too quick for this tactic.

Kiss rose from his chair, brushing Pagan aside. "You bark up the wrong tree, Pagan. Go home. Go back to London. Let it be. It doesn't concern you. Countries you know nothing about, countries occupied by the Soviets, why should you interfere with them? The British had their chance in the 1940s, Pagan, and sold the Baltic cheaply to Stalin. I'm telling you now, it's too late to sit up and take a fresh interest in my people. Forget it. Go home. Leave it to people who care, people who understand. What the hell do you understand about it? Mind your own damned business."

"It's become my fucking business, Kiss!"

Kiss stepped into the hallway, and Pagan went after him. There, under the hall light, Mikhail Kiss stopped moving, and stood very still. Pagan, surprised to the point of silence, felt an odd tension at the back of his throat.

She was standing by the front door. She wore a plain white t-shirt and blue jeans and her shoulderbag hung at her side. There was very little make-up on her face. When she smiled at Pagan she did so in a thin way, and he thought she looked beautiful, but in some way changed, except he couldn't define it.

"Frank Pagan's right," Kristina Vaska said. "This whole thing *has* become his business, Mr Kiss."

Moscow

General Olsky went to the window of his office and parted the slats of the blind, seeing a strange red sun in the morning sky which, in a theatrical manner, lit the old women sweeping the street below, so that they had the appearance of a Greek chorus keeping itself busy. Then he closed the slats and turned to look at Deputy Minister Tikunov, who sat on the other side of the desk.

Ever since the meeting with the General Secretary, Olsky had despatched hundreds of additional agents into the field, in Moscow and Leningrad and Kiev. He'd ordered them to enter the offices of the Defence Ministry and examine the files of personnel deployed in sensitive positions at radar installations, which he considered a logical place to start if Greshko's scheme involved the flight of a plane into Soviet airspace. It wasn't a decision Olsky had taken lightly, and it infuriated Tikunov.

Tikunov, Deputy Minister of Defence, was also Commander-in-Chief of the Soviet Air Defence Forces. He was a squat man who bore an uncanny resemblance to the late Nikita Khrushchev. To Tikunov's way of thinking, the KGB had too much influence, both in civilian and military life, and he frequently found himself hoping that if genuine reforms were to be made in the Soviet Union they would first of all be applied to the kind of authority commanded by the organs of State Security.

Tikunov said, "I assume, comrade General, you can explain the *swarms* of your men in my headquarters? I assume you can explain the nature of your business?"

Olsky regarded Tikunov's large red face, a peasant face given to Slavic volatility, extremes of emotion not easily hidden. His face was an accurate barometer of his feelings at all times. Olsky didn't feel obliged to give an immediate explanation. There were delicate and rather ambiguous questions of rank at issue here, and Olsky was conscious of the fact that Tikunov had been Commander-in-Chief of Air Defences for a longer time than he, Olsky, had run the KGB. Olsky, though, was a candidate member of the Politburo, and closer to the General Secretary than Tikunov, which compensated for the matter of longevity.

"I'm operating with the full authority of the General Secretary," Olsky said, which was stretching a truth slightly. The General Secretary had simply said *Deal with it as you think fit, Stefan.*

Deputy Minister Tikunov wondered if he should ask to see some kind of written authorisation. He had every right to do so, of course, but the Chairman of the KGB, no matter who occupied the position, was never a man one questioned lightly. And so he hesitated a moment, considering his options and trying to bring his temper under control.

"Let me ask you a question, Minister," Olsky said. "How difficult is it these days for an aeroplane to penetrate our airspace undetected, Minister?"

"What the hell kind of question is that?" Tikunov asked.

"A simple one."

Tikunov bristled a little. He hadn't come here to discuss hypothetical matters with the Chairman of the KGB. He simply wanted all those bloody snoops, those supercilious upstarts, those fucking *gangsters*, out of his buildings and out of his domain. "It's possible. Hardly likely."

"In what circumstances is it possible, Minister?"

Tikunov raised a hand and counted on his fingers. "One, if the plane flies beneath our radar. And two, if the radar is malfunctioning. In the former circumstances visual contact would be made sooner or later."

"Are any of your radar installations malfunctioning?"

"To my knowledge, absolutely not. If such a thing happened I'd know about it."

"Automatically?"

Tikunov nodded. He wondered where this was leading. He had the feeling he'd allowed Olsky to take control, and he didn't like it.

"Are there circumstances, aside from malfunctions, when a radar installation would be inoperative?" Olsky asked.

"During routine maintenance, of course."

"And is there any such maintenance presently going on?"

"There's nothing scheduled."

"Could maintenance take place without your knowledge?"

"Hardly. Only the smallest of jobs could be done without my permission. Anything that affected the grid as a whole would need my approval."

"Let's say, for the sake of argument, that certain men under your command decided to render radar inoperable and didn't want you to know? Is that possible?"

Tikunov, who liked to think he treated his officers with respect and believed he was respected by them in turn, was shocked by the suggestion. "I'd have such men shot, General. Are you *questioning* the loyalty of my officers?"

Olsky nodded. "I think there's a possibility your system may have been tampered with, Minister."

"Unthinkable," Tikunov said.

"To you, perhaps. But I insist you check the status of all the radar installations in the Baltic sector."

Tikunov felt he had to assert himself here. This whole conversation had begun to sound like an extended personal insult to him. "I'll be perfectly happy to check the status of my radar and investigate possible disloyalty among my officers – just as soon as you show me a written order from the General Secretary, Comrade Chairman." Tikunov, his face growing more red, his cheeks quivering, was adamant. What he really despised about the KGB was the way they eroded one's sphere of influence. They could strut in and take over your whole life. "I'd also like to get a grasp on the reason behind your questions, General. Do you know something I don't know? Have you heard of an unauthorised plane intending to violate Soviet airspace?"

Olsky moved round his office in a restless way. "I've received information that leads me to believe an aircraft is planning an attack on the Soviet Union."

"What kind of aircraft?"

"I don't know."

"Perhaps you know where it might be coming from?" Tikunov asked in what he thought was the tone of voice used to humour people, but it was a clumsy effort made by a humourless man.

Olsky shook his head.

"By God, General, you're an encyclopaedia of information," Tikunov said. "Just the same you think you have enough to send your agents into my province and cause all kinds of mischief. Where did you get this so-called information from anyhow?"

"I can't answer that," Olsky said. "And you know better than to ask."

"The only possible enemy aircraft in this region capable of delivering any kind of strike against us would be from NATO," Tikunov said. "Are you saying that we can expect a plane from NATO to attack us? One plane? One little plane, General?"

"I'm not saying that," Olsky answered.

"Then what the hell are you saying, Olsky?"

Olsky wished he had answers to Tikunov's questions, but all he had to go on was Volovich's vague information, and that wasn't enough. A plane, but what kind of plane? and from where? He picked up a pencil and tapped the surface of his desk with it, conscious of how he might have appeared to Tikunov – as a man coming apart slowly under the pressures of office.

"I can't take chances, Minister," he said. "Which is why I ordered my men to search the quarters of every member of your staff in any kind of sensitive position, and not only in Moscow."

Tikunov spluttered and his red hands – which despite their colour suggested iciness – became welded together. "I'm goddamned appalled, General! First your thugs ransack my personnel files and tamper with my computers – "

"Hardly thugs, Minister," Olsky said. "They know what they're looking for. They're interested only in those officers whose positions might allow them to interfere with radar operations – "

Tikunov ignored this. "Then I find they've been given carte blanche to rummage through the accommodations of my officers. The whole situation's gone beyond intolerable." He walked to the door and made a gesture of exasperation. "I'll communicate my displeasure to the General Secretary at once, of course."

"Your prerogative," Olsky said. "But I still suggest you check the status of your installations before you start making angry phonecalls, Minister."

"Don't tell me what to do, General," Tikunov said. "I quite understand that the business of the KGB is other people's business, but keep your nose as far out of mine as humanly possible."

Olsky watched the Deputy Minister slam the door as he rushed from the office. After a few moments, Colonel Chebrikov came into the room, carrying some papers in his hand.

"There's something here that will interest you, sir," the Colonel said. "Three KGB officers were found murdered twenty miles from Tallinn."

"Murdered?" Olsky slumped back in his chair. It was going to be one of those days, he thought, when bad news creates a force all its own, and keeps rolling, accumulating more and more unfortunate items like some great black snowball turning to an avalanche.

"They were apparently suspicious of an abandoned farmhouse about twenty miles from the city, and they went to investigate – acting under your general orders to locate dissidents and apprehend them. The farmhouse, it seems, was used by itinerants from time to time. When the officers didn't re-establish contact with Tallinn HQ, a search of the area was made. All three of them were found wrapped in tarpaulin and stuffed inside an old well. They'd been shot. The farmhouse had recently been occupied – signs of food, a couple of sleeping-bags. A vehicle was left behind, an old Moskvich. The ownership hasn't been traced."

Olsky leaned across his desk. "Could there be a connection? Could there be some kind of link between the assassins and this alleged conspiracy?"

"Perhaps, General. On the other hand, you always find extremists in the Baltic countries. They come with the territory. Every now and then we pick somebody up because he's been distributing anti-social documents and we find he's got an old gun tucked away someplace. A war souvenir, usually. Maybe the occupants of the farmhouse come into that category, loonies who happened to have guns. They're not necessarily linked with a major conspiracy."

Not necessarily. It was the kind of vague response Olsky didn't want to hear. He needed definite information, hard facts. He was suddenly restless. There was an architecture to all of this, a blueprint he couldn't read, a design he couldn't grasp, a logic that eluded him. A plan, a widespread plan, something carefully contrived, years in the making, years of patience and the kind of singleminded determination that is the legitimate child of obsessive hatred. The Balts hated the Russians – a fact of life, something that didn't diminish with each new generation of Balts, no matter how many Lithuanian children were pressured into joining the Komsomol or how many young Latvians were members of the Party or how many youthful Estonians learned Russian in schools. The hatred went on and on, seemingly without end. Olsky, who would gladly have found some suitable accommodation with the nationalists in the Baltic if the choice had been his to make, was depressed. Three dead officers in Estonia, a terrorist conspiracy within the Soviet Union, Viktor Epishev in the United States, Greshko cruising Moscow in the hours of darkness and spreading rumours – these things impinged upon him all at once, creating a knot in his brain.

And then there was Dimitri Volovich.

Poughkeepsie, New York

The airfield had once belonged to a private flying club that had gone bankrupt, amid rumours of embezzlement and some public scandal, a few years ago. Now the hangar doors flapped in the breeze and the perimeter fence had rusted and kids sometimes played baseball on the old runway. The runway was cracked and weeds came up through the concrete here and there, irregularities that caused the single prop Cessna to bounce and shudder as it came down to land.

Iverson, feeling a slight chill creep through the dark, drew up the collar of his lightweight overcoat and glanced at Epishev as the plane bumped and taxied toward the place where they stood.

"Unseasonable cold," Iverson remarked.

Epishev said nothing. He gazed at the plane, which was smaller than he'd expected. He'd arrived first-class and now, with his work done, he was leaving through the back door, being flown from Poughkeepsie – which was God knows where – to Canada, and then back to the Soviet Union. He would have preferred to depart in more comfort, as befitted a man who had completed an important task.

Iverson saw the little craft come shivering toward them and he reached out, touching the back of Epishev's arm.

"You did very well," he said. "My people are pleased. I hear General Greshko is delighted."

Epishev listened to the dark wind make rustling sounds as it slithered through the broken fence. A light went on in the cockpit of the Cessna and the silhouette of the pilot became visible.

"Who flies the plane?" Epishev asked.

"One of our own pilots," Iverson answered.

"Is he good?"

"Are you nervous, Colonel?"

"Small planes . . ." Epishev didn't finish his sentence. The plane, which bore a false registration number, was moving nearer.

"He's a good man," Gary Iverson said. "The best."

The Cessna had come to a stop now. Epishev took a step towards it, hearing the propeller turn slowly. He was unhappy with this. The small airfield, the ridiculous plane, the way he was leaving the United States. He felt he deserved better.

"You'll be comfortable, Colonel," Iverson said. "I promise you that." He took a small flask from his pocket and poured a shot into the silver cap, which he passed to Epishev. "A short toast to the friendship between our countries, Colonel. To cooperation."

Iverson raised the flask to his lips.

"What are we drinking?" Epishev asked.

"What else? Vodka."

Epishev tossed the shot back, returning the cap to Iverson, who immediately stuck it back on the flask.

"The girl," Epishev said. "What will you do with the girl?"

"Our general feeling is that without Frank Pagan she's been rendered ineffective."

"That's all? You see no danger?"

"She'll be kept under surveillance for a while," Iverson said. Now that the toast had been drunk, he was impatient to be gone from this dreary place. "But she's no danger to our plan now."

Epishev shrugged, then walked toward the Cessna and climbed up into the cockpit. He waved at Iverson, who returned the gesture, even if Epishev couldn't see it in the darkness. The plane made a circle, bouncing back onto the runway, and then it was racing along, up and down, wobbling, finally rising just before the runway ended. Up and up, slow and noisy, vanishing into the blackness. Iverson watched until the wing-lights were no longer visible, and then he walked to his car.

He used the car telephone to make a connection with the house in Fredericksburg. When Galbraith came on the line, Iverson said, "He's gone, sir."

"He drank the toast, I trust?"

"Of course."

"I think it's better like that, don't you? Are you going to spend the night in New York? Or are you headed back down here?"

"I'll stay in the city," Iverson said. "I'm tired."

"Sleep well, Gary."

Galbraith hung up. Iverson replaced the telephone and sat in the darkness of the abandoned airfield and thought he could still hear the distant thrumming of the small plane. He turned the key in the ignition, looked at the dashboard clock.

Approximately thirty minutes from now the tasteless sedative in the vodka would send Epishev into a sound sleep. The pilot would parachute from the Cessna at a prearranged spot close to the town of Troy, and the craft, with the comatose Epishev on board, would crash in the Adirondacks, quite possibly in the sparsely-populated region beyond Lake Luzerne, where it might lie undiscovered for many years.

Without a trace, Iverson thought. And he was filled with renewed admiration for Galbraith, who had seen this whole scheme in one flash in the yellow house in Virginia Beach, one blinding insight, the way a grandmaster will see checkmating possibilities twelve devious moves ahead. *Use outside talent whenever you possibly can, Gary. Just make sure it never gossips about you. People who tell you a dog is man's best friend are wrong. Man's best friend is silence.*

19

Glen Cove, Long Island

The question that formed on Mikhail Kiss's lips was one he didn't have to voice aloud. He knew the answer anyway, because the family resemblance was too forceful, too striking. He knew who this young woman was even before she said, "*Küll siis Kalev jõuab koju . . .*" with that thin, misleadingly playful smile on her face.

She stepped past Kiss and Pagan and entered the glass-walled room, where she stood in the middle of the floor. There was something just a little arrogant in the way she stood, Pagan thought, a quality he hadn't seen in her before – but then she was apparently full of surprises, and one more shouldn't have troubled him. He had a depressing sense suddenly of being caught up in a drama whose first two acts he'd missed or, at best, had seen only obliquely from the corner of his eye. He was very aware of an unresolved conflict between Kiss and Kristina, a situation he couldn't bring into sharp perspective. He was standing outside, his face pressed against the glass, and the room into which he tried to look was out of focus.

Mikhail Kiss said, "I used to wonder what had become of Norbert's daughter. I tried to stop thinking about her, and sometimes I succeeded."

"It's taken me a long time to find you," Kristina said.

Mikhail Kiss's mouth was very dry. "I think I've been expecting you for years, one way or another. I had a dream about Norbert last night."

There was a strange crossfire here, and Pagan knew he

didn't belong in it. He'd gatecrashed. Shadows moved on the edge of his mind, and he didn't want them to take recognisable shape, because he didn't want to see what they really were when they emerged into the light. There was one unmistakable conclusion, and he needed to avoid it.

Kristina moved closer to Mikhail Kiss and asked, "Do you know the last thing Norbert Vaska ever said to me?"

Kiss shook his head slowly.

"*They've betrayed me,*" Kristina said. Her voice trembled. "*The Brotherhood betrayed me.*"

"Betrayal's an easy word," Kiss said. "It's too simple."

"What would you call it?"

"I would call it sacrifice."

"Sacrificed by his old comrades. His friends. His own Brotherhood."

Kiss ran the palm of his hand across his eyes. "You have to understand the circumstances," he said quietly.

"Why? Would they justify everything?"

"They may help you understand, Kristina."

"I doubt it," and she was fierce, unrelenting, her expression more intense than Pagan had ever seen it. She was talking to Kiss as if Pagan – having served his purpose in leading the way to the heart of the Brotherhood, a feat she apparently couldn't achieve on her own, a goal obscured by the passage of time and the pseudonyms the Brotherhood had assumed, old trails that had faded, old pathways too weatherbeaten to follow – had ceased to exist. Gone. Shoved aside. Used. Just like that. He didn't know whether to be outraged or bewildered by his own negligent heart. He didn't know whether to admire this woman's tenacity of pursuit. This talk of betrayal and sacrifice – was it vengeance she wanted? He moved his hand very slightly, letting it hover behind him, concealed from view but close to the location of his gun.

"Briefly, it comes down to the fact that Romanenko was in serious difficulties some years ago," Kiss said.

"He occupied, as you may know, a position that created problems for him. He led two lives. And sometimes they came in conflict with each other. You understand this much, of course."

Kiss paused. Was the story worth telling now? It was fading, because that was how he wanted it, a threadbare memory, something whose shame was no longer so bright and blinding. He glanced at Pagan, aware of the *inglane*'s look of confusion, and what was apparent to Kiss was that Pagan and Kristina had enjoyed some kind of relationship, perhaps they'd even been lovers – but Pagan hadn't expected the woman to turn up here in this house, of all places. And there was a shadow of hurt on Pagan's face, an imprint of anxiety on those features that were so used to concealment.

"I'm listening," Kristina Vaska said. Now she did look at Pagan, and offered him a brief smile, nothing of consequence. Frank Pagan wondered if he was going to be fobbed off with this trifle. He put out a hand towards her, laying the palm on her arm, but she appeared not to feel his touch. She was concentrating on Kiss.

Kiss went on, "There was a time, when our plan was in its earliest stages, when Aleksis realised he was coming under suspicion from certain factions in the Party. And the KGB had begun a particularly tough campaign in Tallinn. Aleksis's loyalties were in question. There were rumours about his life. Questions he couldn't afford, Kristina. A man in his position had to be above any kind of suspicion, because he was important to the cause."

Kiss paused. This was the tough part. This was the part he didn't want to utter aloud. But ghosts were pressing against him, forcing him to speak. "It was decided that he had to prove his loyalty to the Party. He had to stop the questions, the whispers. What good would he be if he were arrested and imprisoned? How could he contribute to the cause from a jail cell? Therefore, whatever he was going to do would have to be drastic."

"I can guess the rest," Kristina said.

"Maybe, maybe not. Romanenko and I had a meeting in 1971 in Helsinki. Our meetings, you understand, were difficult to arrange and often held hurriedly in strange places. This particular meeting – and I don't remember it with any pleasure, believe me – took place on the ferry to Suomenlinna. I remember the day – it was cold and rainy. Fitting weather for what we had to do. Aleksis outlined a plan to protect his reputation and I agreed to it. Between us, we decided to give Norbert Vaska to the KGB. Everything. His participation in a democratic society. His part in running an underground newspaper. Aleksis gave the information to a certain Colonel Epishev, who then arrested your father."

There was silence in the room for a long time.

"You did a terrific job," Kristina said eventually. "You must have been very proud of yourselves."

"We did what we had to do to save the plan. You must try to understand that, Kristina. It was a matter of survival. It was either your father or the death of everything we had ever hoped for and worked for."

"You made the wrong choice," Kristina said.

"Choice isn't the word. The solution was forced on us. Dear God, do you think what we did was easy for us?"

Pagan thought how painful it was to see a man obliged to speak a truth he'd clearly contrived to keep from himself for years, the forced words, the pauses, sentences dragged up from a place deep inside. He was filled with a sense of anticipation now, wondering what Kristina would do next. There was an air of unpredictability about her.

Kiss said, "There. I've told you. I owed you that."

"What do you want now?" Kristina asked. "Absolution?"

"I sometimes think that if he knew, Norbert would understand why we did what we did. But I don't expect forgiveness from you."

"Forgiveness is the last goddam thing I could give you even if I wanted to," Kristina said. "I didn't come here to do you favours, Kiss. I came here to look at you. I came here to see what kind of man betrayed my father."

Mikhail Kiss stared uncomfortably at the floor. He said, "I'd do it again if I had to, Kristina."

Kristina Vaska walked across the room and looked out at the darkness. She said, "You ruined my family, Kiss. It wasn't Epishev who wrecked it. What did he care? He was only doing his fucking rotten job. But you and Romanenko, you gave my father away, you practically made a donation of him to the Russians. And my mother . . ." She paused here and there was a slight catch in her voice and Pagan had the urge to go towards her and comfort her, but he didn't move. The space between himself and Kristina had filled up with unexpected obstacles.

"My mother sits in a forlorn little house upstate and she writes letters, Kiss. She writes letters to the Kremlin and the White House and Number Ten Downing Street. Begging letters. *Please help me get my husband released from Siberia.* Year after year she sends off the same letters and it's deadening to go through the same process endlessly – petitions, forms, the whole dumb rigmarole that you know in advance isn't going to work, but you do it anyway because you don't have any other channels . . ."

Kiss sighed. His mind had drifted away from this room, this house, this girl who had opened the door for ghosts. He was thinking of Andres high above the Atlantic. The journey, the arrival.

Kristina Vaska opened her purse, took out a pistol, turned it on Mikhail Kiss. Pagan stepped toward her, and she waved him away, gesturing with the gun. Her expression was hard and uncompromising, as if whatever beauty she had was destroyed by her murderous intention. Kiss looked at the pistol, watched the way the woman came forward, saw how she held the barrel of the gun towards his head, then he felt the pressure of metal against the side of his face. She pushed it hard into his flesh.

"Kristina," Pagan said.

"I looked for a long time, Frank. Ever since I first came to this country, I've been looking. Sometimes I thought I was getting close, then it would slip away. I'd get only so far before I'd run into blank walls," she said. "When I was running out of options, I found you. And you found Kiss."

Pagan wanted to reach for her and take the weapon away. He saw Kiss's flesh fold like paper where the barrel of the gun made a deep impression in his face. Kiss had his eyes shut. There was the sound of the safety being released and it echoed inside Kiss's skull like the noise of somebody shouting in a tunnel.

"Kristina," Pagan said. "He's the only link I've got with the Brotherhood's plan. If you shoot him . . ."

She stared at Pagan. "What do you think I care about that, Frank? What are they going to do? Say boo to the Russians? The Russians will squash them the way they squash everything." She pushed the gun harder and Kiss, flinching, moaned at the way metal cut into his flesh.

"Let me at least talk to him," Pagan said.

Kiss, moving his face away from the gun, tapped the side of his skull. "Talk until you're blue in the face, Pagan. The plan is locked in here, and that's exactly where it stays."

Pagan stepped closer to the old man. "Stay away, Frank," she said. "Keep out of this. It's got absolutely nothing to do with you."

"People keep telling me that. And I don't seem to hear them properly."

"You better start listening," Kristina said. She tightened her finger on the trigger, conscious of the vulnerability of Kiss's flesh, the veins at the side of the skull, the fragile arrangement of bone and flesh and tissue she could blow away in a fraction of time. And then it wasn't Mikhail Kiss she was seeing, suddenly it was her father, it was Norbert Vaska, and she envisioned him in his white wasteland

and wondered if he'd died there, or whether he was alive and still remembered his daughter, if he remembered love and all the things that had been taken from him. She imagined him with his eyes shut in death and then she had an image of gravediggers spading half-frozen ground, not yet thawed after winter but softening in the growing warmth of spring, and then they laid Norbert Vaska into this chilly earth. She shut her eyes a second. These pictures were more than she could bear. The frozen white hands, crystals of ice clinging to eyelashes, the lips silent and blue, the eyes – perhaps open – staring into an arctic nothingness. She thought she heard his voice say *The Brotherhood betrayed me.* Is this what you want me to do, father? she wondered. Do you want me to pull this goddam trigger? To avenge you? Or would you tell me now that Kiss and Romanenko did what they had to, that in any war – even a lost one like this, even a pathetic little struggle like this – all useful tactics are justifiable? Confused suddenly, enraged by her own bewilderment, Kristina Vaska stared at the side of Kiss's face, seeing one expressionless blue eye, a faint shadow of white hair on the damp upper lip. *Kiss and Romanenko riding a ferry in the rain, and planning Norbert Vaska's death* – how plain, how straightforward, how civilised. Would you have agreed with them, Norbert Vaska? If it had been you and Romanenko on that ferry discussing Mikhail Kiss, how would you have behaved? There was madness here, the madness of patriotism, of men fighting for a totally hopeless cause, creating their little make-believe reality in which they see themselves bravely evicting the Soviets, pitchforks against submachine guns, Molotov cocktails against tanks, sorry dreams. Anger went through her, a dark red rage filling her brain. It was uncontrollable.

"*Kristina,*" Pagan said.

She saw him reach for the gun and she said, "Get the fuck away, Frank."

"Kristina," he said again.

"Goddam you!" Her eyes were moist and she couldn't

quite see Kiss clearly now, but enough. She said, *"You piece of shit, you useless piece of shit,"* and she understood she couldn't shoot him. She couldn't do it. She smacked him across the lips with the pistol and as his head tilted away from her she struck him again, bringing the barrel of the gun down upon his forehead, and his whole face swung back, blood pouring from his brow, from his split lip. She raised her hand up and started to bring it down a third time in a violent arc, a mindless movement, but Pagan caught her hand in the air and took the gun from her, and all her terrible fury collapsed and she slid to the floor where she sat cross-legged, staring at Mikhail Kiss, who had his face covered with his hands. She thought *A worthless piece of shit, and I can't even shoot him*, and she closed her eyes and imagined she felt the misty rain fall across the Suomenlinna ferry where two men planned her father's betrayal. And she had the thought that even though he was absent, even though he knew nothing about the plot against him, just the same Norbert Vaska *would have agreed, he would have given his consent to his own condemnation because he lived with the taste of the Brotherhood in his mouth, he lived in the past, when the enemy was somebody you could see at the end of your rifle and your native land hadn't altogether yielded to the Russians . . .*

Mikhail Kiss, his hands covered in his own blood, sat down in a chair. He was breathing hard. Pagan bent over him.

"When is it going to happen?" Pagan asked.

"Go fuck yourself," Kiss replied quietly.

"When and where, Mikhail?"

"Vabadus Eestile," Mikhail Kiss whispered.

Moscow

In her apartment near Izmailova Park, Valentina Uvarova hurriedly packed clothing. She'd been told to travel lightly which was no great problem because there wasn't much she wanted to bring along with her in any event, there was nothing here worth remembering, or keeping, except for a couple of toys – sentimental favourites of the two children – and a few necessary items of clothing. She was a small woman with a tiny oval face and cheekbones so high her eyes seemed deeply recessed into her head. People who knew her spoke most often of her determination. *Valentina's such a determined person*, they'd say, as if grit were a fault. But her determination concealed something else, a basic discontentment with the barren prospects of her life.

She stuffed the case, closed it, noticed how nervous she was. She sat on the bed and smoked a cigarette, listening to the sounds of the children in the kitchen. They knew they were going on a trip, she simply hadn't told them where. They knew Daddy would be joining them wherever it was, and this made them happy. Valentina touched the small crucifix she wore round her neck and said quietly to herself *Dear Jesus, help us now*. She let her hands fall into her lap and she pressed them together.

We're going away, we're going away, we're going away!

This was the girl's voice, shrill and penetrating. Valentina Uvarova had warned the children to say nothing to anybody. Not to their friends, their relatives, not even to their grandmother. They were to keep completely silent, but for a kid secrets were impossible to maintain. She walked into the kitchen and silenced the children. The boy, who looked like a miniature of his father Yevgenni, was easy. The girl was the spirited one.

"We must keep very quiet," Valentina said.

The girl asked, "When are we leaving?"

"In a couple of hours."

"Why can't we go now? Right now?"

"Why? Do you want to wait in the railway station?"

"Yes," the girl said. "I like stations."

Valentina considered the prospect, but she didn't want to hang around a station, passing hours before the train arrived. If she stayed here, at least there were still things to keep her occupied. There were dishes to clean. There was rubbish to be removed. Even though she might be leaving this apartment forever, she couldn't possibly leave it in disarray. They'd talk about her after she'd gone, and they'd say *She left the place like a pigsty*, but what can you expect from a traitor's wife anyway? She wouldn't leave the place dirty. Not Valentina Uvarova. She couldn't stand the idea of the women in the neighbourhood saying bad things about her.

She went to the sink, turned the faucet, and lukewarm water spluttered out, and the old gas-heater wheezed on the wall above her.

We're going away, the girl said in a whisper. *We're going to see Daddy*.

Valentina shushed the child again. She ran some dirty plates under the water, wiped them with a cloth, set them aside to dry. A new life, she thought. The phrase kept running through her head like an inescapable melody. A new life.

She dried her hands on a towel. And that was when she heard the heavy knock on the front door. She felt it then, blood draining from her face, from her hands, her heart turning a somersault in her chest.

Somebody's at the door, the boy said.

She looked at her son's small upturned face, the eyes that were suddenly wary, and then she stepped along the hallway. She opened the door slowly. It was not one visitor, but two, and they wore uniforms that filled her with dread.

Glen Cove, Long Island

If there was any evidence of what the Brotherhood planned to do, Pagan thought the logical place to find it was in the only room he hadn't so far explored, the office on the second floor. He switched on a light, surveyed the room. It was the desk that interested him primarily, and he walked towards it, scanning the papers spread across the surface. He began to flick them, beset by a sense of urgency. A need to keep busy, that was it. Keep going. Don't stop. He was aware of Kristina Vaska entering the room and he thought, *Ignore the woman.*

He didn't look up. He heard her cross the floor, felt her hands on his shoulders. He didn't move. Her touch stirred him and he resented his own response.

"You must accept one thing, Frank."

"Tell me about it," Pagan said.

"I care about you. I didn't want to, but it happened. And that hasn't changed. At first, I just thought you were going to be useful to me, you had resources I could use. But it changed. It became something else, Frank."

"Terrific," Pagan said.

"I've hurt you."

"You're an insightful sort of person. I like that."

Pagan shuffled the papers around. They were written in Estonian. What else could he have expected? He kept shuffling them anyway, looking for something he might understand.

"Frank, listen to me. I never intended to cause you any harm."

"I'm not harmed," he said sharply. "Disappointed, yes. Up to here with you, yes. Disgusted with the idea you used me, absolutely. But harmed? No, love. Not harmed. It's like having something in my eye. It smarts for a few minutes, but a little water flushes it away."

"I want to talk to you. Look at me."

He did, but only briefly, then went back to the papers. There were bills, credit card vouchers, letters, but nothing that yielded up the kind of information he could have used.

"I admit," she said. "I wanted to kill him. Or I thought I did. But when it came right down to it, Frank . . ." She touched his arm. "I thought I wanted to kill Romanenko too, but I don't know if I would have been able to do

413

that either. Circumstances prevented me from finding out anyway."

He said, "Look, you drift into my life. We spend a couple of pleasant hours passionately fucking – "

"It was more than that, and you know it – "

Pagan shook his head. Taken for a ride, he thought. The careless heart. The alchemy of attraction that transmuted blatant lies into shining truths, changed dross into lovely little gems. He remembered one of the first things she'd ever said to him. *I don't have any concealed motives, Frank. I heard about the killing on TV, I thought you might need information you weren't going to get anywhere else. Here I am. That's it.* And you bought it, Frank. You laid your money out and you bought the whole gooseberry patch. She's been working you from the very start, twisting you and shaping you, oiling you so you'd run smoothly along the right tracks. And, boy, didn't you ever? Wind my clockwork, sweetie, see how I run.

He looked at the typewriter on the desk, scanned a sheet of paper in it. That damned language again. He swivelled the chair around, turning his face away from Kristina Vaska.

She said, "It doesn't have to end like this, Frank. We could walk away. We could leave this place right now. What goddam difference does the Brotherhood's plan make to us? Does it matter if it succeeds or fails? Who cares?"

"I care," he said.

Mikhail Kiss appeared in the doorway, a blood-stained towel clutched against his face. When he spoke he did so through swollen lips and a mouth that no longer felt associated with his face. "Feel free," he said. "Papers, letters, documents – look at anything you like, Pagan. I'm a hospitable man, but you'll find absolutely nothing." And then Kiss turned and went into his own bedroom, where he sat on the edge of the bed with his eyes closed and the towel pressed to his lips.

Pagan watched him go. There was something smug in

the way Kiss had spoken and Pagan wondered if there was a bluff going on. *Ransack my office all you like, you won't find a goddam thing.* No, it wasn't a simple bluff. If Kiss had kept anything important in this house he wouldn't have gone out and left the place unlocked, and he wouldn't be allowing Pagan easy access to this office. He tore the sheet of paper from the typewriter and handed it to Kristina and asked her to translate it. She looked at the paper a moment before she said it was a recipe for a dish called *mulgikapsad*. She looked at the other papers that lay across the desk, the ones Pagan had leafed through, and they were all recipes, every single one of them.

"He must be compiling a cookbook," she said.

Pagan got up and walked to the window. *A cookbook. A bloody hobby.* He parted the curtains and looked down into the darkness of the garden. *Think. Just think. You're supposed to have some kind of knack for hunches, little flashes of intuition. They served you beautifully when it came to Kristina Vaska, didn't they?* He heard the woman come up behind him and lay her hands on his shoulders and he loved the way she touched him, despite himself.

"Forgive me, Frank."

Forgiveness was hard. There was always the spectre of deceit. *My little actress,* he thought. *But it couldn't all have been an act. There must have been moments of truthfulness.* He wanted to think that the lovemaking – at least that – had been real. Besides, what had she done but harbour the desire to avenge her father's betrayal? It wasn't as if she'd found in herself the capacity to kill anybody, was it? Pagan turned to look at her, but gazing into her face was as difficult as finding forgiveness. He'd been fooled, and that was a tough one to digest.

"How long is it going to take?" she asked.

He raised a hand and lightly touched the side of her face a moment. "If you'd been straight with me from the start – "

"And you would have helped me, Frank? You would

415

have gone out of your way to help a crazy lady with vengeance on her mind? I thought my way was better. The anxious daughter worried sick about her father's health – I figured that was the one most likely to succeed. And if it sounds calculated, you're absolutely right. It *was* calculated. I could have used a goddam slide-rule."

Calculated, he thought. He walked back to the desk. Through the open door and across the landing he could see inside Kiss's bedroom. Kiss still sat motionless on the edge of the bed, the red towel pressed to his mouth, his eyes shut. He seemed absurdly calm, removed from the situation, secure in the knowledge that Pagan would find nothing in any of the rooms of this house.

Pagan sat on the edge of the desk. *Think, Frank. Relax, and think.* Kiss doesn't want to tell you where Andres went. Why not? Answer: because he's up to something and Kiss doesn't want you to know. Such as? Such as? Answer: he has to be part of the plot. Unavoidable conclusion. What part, though? What role? Pagan walked out of the office and went inside Andres's bedroom and Kristina followed.

Pagan sat on the edge of the bed. On the bedside table there lay a couple of books, a paperback novel detailing the exploits of a deformed avenger in post-holocaust America, a daily meditation book, and a world atlas. Frank Pagan glanced at the paperback and read *Bosco kicked the door down and fired his machine-gun, splattering the hooded figures until the room turned red with blood and spilled brains*. Pagan set the book down, flipped through the meditation book and saw underlined the sentence *How many of the world's prayers have gone unanswered because those who prayed did not endure to the end?* Pagan put the book aside, then glanced at the atlas. On the map of Europe somebody had drawn thin red lines seemingly at random, inscribing them over Britain, then across the North Sea, where they ended in Scandinavia, a whole meaningless tangle of lines. He closed the atlas, stood up. The clues to

Andres Kiss, he felt, were all here, except that he couldn't read them.

And when you couldn't find inspiration, you fell back on that other policeman's tool which, though blunted from constant repetition, was still a useful device. You fell back on that old standby – the sheer doggedness of inquiry. He returned to Kiss's office and dragged the telephone directory out of a drawer and turned to the section marked Airlines, dismayed when he saw how many there were. He'd start with the As and just keep working until he could locate the airline on which Andres Kiss had left the country – provided he *had* flown overseas, as Mikhail had said. Provided, too, that he was travelling on an authentic passport under his own name. Long shots, long odds.

Pagan picked up the telephone. He glanced through the open door and across the landing, seeing Mikhail Kiss observe him with mild interest as he dialled.

Tallinn, Estonia

The man known as Marcus drove the Red Army truck along Gagarini Street in the direction of the harbour. He saw KGB agents everywhere he went. He saw them milling around the railway station, some of them in uniform, others trying to look inconspicuous in plain clothes. By now, of course, the murders of the KGB officers would have been discovered, and consequently more men would be poured into the streets. By mid-afternoon Tallinn would have the atmosphere of a convention city accommodating a thousand or so KGB. It was not a festive thought.

He checked his wristwatch. Four more hours. He thought of his comrades in Latvia and Lithuania and wondered how many of them were presently looking at their watches and counting minutes away into hours and feeling the same apprehension as he.

He drove the army vehicle in the direction of the harbour. The rendezvous was to take place in an old warehouse close to the docks. He entered the narrow street where nothing moved but plump pigeons flying out from the protection of eaves. Nothing out of the ordinary. He passed the building, a dilapidated brick structure. He slowed the vehicle, swung it round, went back the way he'd come. When he reached the warehouse again, he parked the truck, making sure the engine was still running. He approached the large door of the warehouse, pushed it open, then drove the truck inside the building.

There was a score of people inside already. Among them, Marcus saw Erma and the old man Bruno, who had made their way to this place separately. Marcus opened the tarpaulin that covered the back of the truck. The three boxes contained rifles and handguns. He passed them out quickly and quietly, thinking how there was nothing left to say because everything had been said already, the speeches had been made, the toasts drunk. He looked at the faces of those present, and he saw grim expectation in the expressions, and a certain fatalism. What they were going to do in a few short hours was inevitable – and so was the outcome.

Glen Cove, Long Island

It was dawn when Frank Pagan, who had spent hours having airline personnel wakened from their sleep, finally received the information he wanted. He put the receiver down and rubbed the back of his neck wearily. He looked at Kristina Vaska, who was curled in a chair, half asleep. Mikhail Kiss stood in the doorway of the office.

"You're a persistent man, Pagan," he said.

"Sometimes."

418

"What good will it do you to know where Andres has gone?"

"I don't know yet," Pagan said. He picked up the telephone again. "I'll have the answer to your question as soon as I've called the police in Oslo."

Mikhail Kiss stepped closer to the desk. "And they'll stop him?"

"They'll hold him," Pagan replied.

Kiss, alarmed, put his hand over the telephone, firmly pressing the cradle down. "No," he said. "I can't allow you to do this."

Pagan looked into the big man's bruised face and what he saw there was desperation. "You can't stop me, Kiss."

Kiss, who was strong, tried to yank the telephone from the wall. Pagan caught him by the wrist. For a moment neither man made an impression on the other, neither man budged because there was an equivalence of strength, a balance. It might have remained this way for many minutes except for the fact that Kristina Vaska got up from her chair and struck Kiss on the elbow with her gun – a quick blow, delivered sharply and with admirable economy, which made the big man shudder and loosen his grip. He sunk into a chair, clutching the bone at the place where he'd been struck. Then he immediately rose again and reached out for Pagan, but Kristina Vaska pointed her gun directly at him and shook her head from side to side.

Kiss saw the determination in her face and stood very still. His blood-stained hands hung at his side. He was beset by a sense of futility, of having built the last twenty years of his life on an edifice that was quivering under him now, shaken by the Englishman, by the young woman with the gun, by the ghost of Norbert Vaska.

Pagan drew the telephone towards him. He dialled the number for the international operator.

"Say thanks or something," Kristina Vaska said. "I just helped you out."

"Thanks or something," Pagan replied.

"Smartass."

Olso, Norway

Andres Kiss was met at the airport in Oslo by a dark blue Volvo, whose driver barely glanced at him.

"You'll find a suit in the back seat," the driver said. "When we're out of the city I'll stop in some quiet place and you can put it on."

Andres Kiss placed his hands flat on his knees. He settled back in his seat, hearing the driver talk about the recent heatwave that had afflicted Oslo, but he wasn't really listening. He had other things on his mind.

"You'll have a clear afternoon for flying," the driver said.

Andres nodded absently. "Good," was all he said, and his voice was strong and confident. It was a fine thing to go out to and meet your destiny untroubled by any hint of fear.

20

Mossheim, Norway

Andres Kiss thought the plane looked beautiful on the ramp. He approached the craft with the awe of a man who is as close to perfection as he is ever going to get in his lifetime. There was a magnificent austerity about the F-16 B, its vicious potential concealed in smooth, aerodynamic lines. If you narrowed your eyes and looked at the plane sideways, you might think it a sharp-beaked hawk. Andres, who wore a fire-retardant Nomex suit, a G-suit, and a survival vest, strolled round the aircraft, almost hesitant to go up the ladder and into the cockpit, as if he wanted to prolong the joy of anticipation.

He sniffed the sweet morning air into his lungs. It had been three years, three long years, since he'd been in this place. Three years since he'd flown an F-16 on missions in the Baltic, when his squadron, based at Luke Air Force Base in Arizona, had been deployed by NATO to participate in routine tactical manoeuvres.

The man who had picked him up in Oslo stood with the shadow of a wing falling across his face. He appeared very anxious to Kiss, in a hurry to get the bird off the ground. Andres, on the other hand, felt no such urgency. He'd climb into the plane, and he'd put on the helmet, attach the harness, and go through all the necessary steps before takeoff, all those logical little moves you made prior to flight. Andres adored the checklist, the jargon, the sense of belonging to an elite group of men who knew how these birds worked. When he spoke the secret language of flyers, he felt eloquent. It was as if he were a member of a select freemasonry, privy to all kinds of arcane information.

"Here," and the man handed Andres a set of charts.

Andres Kiss took them, studied them briefly. The flight plan, but he knew it already. Besides, it wasn't a directive he intended to follow. Not all the way. Only up to the point where he would digress radically from it.

"Let's move," the man said.

Andres was still unhurried. He stared across the runway, seeing other planes sitting motionless here and there on the base, each casting elongated shadows. He saw the barbed-wire fence beyond the hangars, and the security checkpoint, through which he and his companion had passed without any difficulty. It was a good feeling, Andres reflected, to know that Iverson's promises had all been kept, that his part in the scheme was working perfectly.

He followed the other man around the plane, wondering how much his companion knew, if he was part of the whole tapestry or simply somebody following an order that had come down from Iverson in the United States, an unquestionable command that, although irregular, he had to execute.

They moved together to the forward fuselage on the lefthand side of the plane, checking the canopy, the external jettison handles, the Side Winder missile on the leftwing tip. They went next to the nose wheel, and circled to the righthand side of the craft and the outboard station on the wing that housed the second Side Winder. Andres Kiss looked automatically for leaks, for any kind of fluids that might have dripped from the craft, but he saw none. Then the fusing of the Mark 82 bombs was checked on the underside of the plane. After that it was time to go to the cockpit. Andres felt the first little shiver of the day, a slight tremor of anticipation.

He climbed the ladder and squeezed himself inside the cockpit. He stared at the instrument panel, the radar display panel, the vertical velocity indicator, the airspeed mach indicator, the autopilot switch. On the left console was the G-suit hose connection, the fuel master switch, the throttle. On the right was the oxygen and communications hook-up, the oxygen regulator panel, the stick. Andres stared at the dials with an expression of intensity. There were so many of them, each dedicated to the perfect functions of the craft, each related to the other in a sequence of irrefutable logic, and he knew them all, and they made him feel comfortable.

The other man, who had given Andres no name but who was obviously employed at this base in the capacity of crew chief, reached inside the cockpit and attached the fittings that linked Andres to the ejection system. Then, still working in silence, he plugged Andres into the oxygen system and handed him his helmet, which Andres put on.

Cockpit check. Andres studied all the switches to make sure they were in the off position. *Verify fuel master on guard down. Engine feed knob normal. External power unit switch normal. Fuel control in primary position. Throttle off. Brakes locked. Landing gear handle down. Master armament switch off. Air source knob normal.* Andres went through this procedure, realising that what had been missing from his life was this sense of well-defined purpose – and now here he was following all the old rules rigorously.

The other man climbed down the ladder from the cockpit. He didn't give Andres the customary thumbs up OK sign, as if he wanted no further part in the whole affair. Andres looked down at him, still smiling. He turned the main power switch to battery. The batteries discharged, the invertor output was good. Everything was fine.

Andres spoke to clearance delivery in the control tower. "Mossheim Clearance. Louisiana Alpha 07, IFR Round Robin, clearance on request."

There was a brief pause before Andres heard the response. "Louisiana Alpha 07 Mossheim Clearance, clearance on request. Forty-five past the hour. Stand by this frequency."

"Louisiana Alpha 07, roger." Andres placed the jet fuel switch to Start 1. He checked the back-up fuel control caution light, which registered OFF. Then he stared at the RPM gauge. Throttle advance to idle. The hydraulic oil pressure lights went off, and RPM stabilised at normal ground idle. Functioning, Andres thought. Everything in position. The sweet integrity of the plane.

The voice in the tower said, "07 you are cleared by the Mossheim One departure direct to the Stockholm 140 at 50 climb and maintain flight level 250, squawk 2545, departure control frequency will be 345.5."

Andres repeated this and the voice in the tower said, "Read back correct. Contact ground for taxi."

Andres contacted ground control and was told to taxi to runway 03. He felt the rumble of the craft vibrate through him as he looked from the cockpit and gave the wheels out signal. The man on the ramp alongside the craft hurriedly removed the chocks and Andres increased the throttle slightly and released the parking brake. He taxied to the arming area, conscious of the muted power of the plane, the way its ferocity was held momentarily in check. In the arming area he let his hands hang from the cockpit as the ordnance crew chief attached a variety of electrical leads to the bombs, the missiles and the 20-millimetre cannon, which made the weaponry operational. The ordnance chief gave the thumbs-up sign, indicating proper configuration.

Andres thought, *Let's go. Let's just fucking go.*

He taxied to the edge of runway 03, where he initiated the automatic on-board test system, which checked fifty-seven separate functions of the craft. It was all beautiful. He checked the flaps. Normal. Trim centre, both ailerons, horizontal trim and rudder. Fuel control in the primary position. Speed brakes closed, canopy closed. He checked the harness, the attachment of the G-suit to the console. Verified that external fuel tanks were feeding the main tanks. Ejection safety lever, oil pressure, warning and caution lights.

"Mossheim Tower, Louisiana Alpha 07 takeoff one with clearance."

"Louisiana Alpha 07, Mossheim Tower, taxi into position and hold runway 03 right."

The moment, Andres thought. The final check. "Roger. Posit and hold." He verified engine oil-pressure and saw that the generator lights were out. Ready to go.

"Louisiana Alpha 07, Mossheim Tower cleared for takeoff, runway 03 right contact departure."

Andres accelerated the engine through 80% and released the brakes. The aircraft accelerated to one hundred and fifty knots and he eased back on the side stick to establish an 8 to 12 degree takeoff attitude. At approximately one hundred and fifty-six knots, the plane was airborne. It was a rush, a great surge of adrenaline. Andres felt his stomach tighten and his heart leap. He was home at last.

He said, "Mossheim Departure, Louisiana Alpha 07 airborne, passing 7,000 feet for flight level 250."

The message came back, "Roger 07, Mossheim Departure, right turn now direct to Stockholm. Maintain flight level 250." The F-16 was climbing at a speed of 10,000 feet a minute. Andres Kiss, in complete control of the craft and himself – if indeed there was any distinction between the two at this moment – looked down on a diminishing landscape turning yellow in the early afternoon sun. So far as anyone on the ground was concerned, this flight was just another exercise carried out by an American fighter plane attached to NATO. Routine, simple – drop a few bombs and fire the cannons at targets on the uninhabited little Baltic island that was used for target practice, then return to base. That's what all the paperwork would say.

Andres, climbing still, soaring, knew otherwise. This exercise was in no way routine. When he reached Russian territorial waters, when he arrived at the place where he could go no further without violating Soviet airspace, he wasn't going to turn back. Nor had he any intention of squandering his weapons on some uninhabited little island. No way.

Glen Cove, Long Island

The speech of the police inspector in Oslo had a curious kind of formality to it, as if he'd learned the English language from teachers in tuxedos. He apologised profusely, perhaps with more politeness than the situation warranted, saying that Andres Kiss had been picked up at the airport by a man in a Volvo, prior to the arrival of the Oslo police, and taken elsewhere. And, according to a reliable female eyewitness taken by Kiss's striking good looks and thinking him a rock star, the car that had picked Kiss up was registered to a certain Flight Sergeant at Mossheim Air Base, which was a North Atlantic Treaty Organisation base – and, perhaps Mr Pagan would understand, the Oslo police had no real desire to enter the base unless Norwegian security was 'indisputably' at stake. There were, ah yes, ah-hum, *political* considerations involved as well, and surely Mr Pagan would also understand that much too. Frank Pagan thanked the inspector and hung up.

He went inside Andres Kiss's bedroom and looked at the world atlas. He found a map of Norway and Sweden, discovered Mossheim about twenty miles from Oslo, close to the Swedish border – and two hundred miles from the Swedish border was the Baltic Sea.

He closed the atlas, thinking it was no distance at all from Norway to the Baltic, and from there to the coast of the Soviet Union. In the kind of plane Andres Kiss was presumably accustomed to flying it was a distance that could be covered in thirty minutes. Another thirty minutes across the Baltic, and you were practically in Leningrad. If you chose to enter the Baltic through Latvia, then it was only a matter of about an hour's flying time until you reached Moscow from Riga.

Pagan went back to the office. Mikhail Kiss was looking out of the window, his back to the room. Below, in the early light of day, the roses had begun to assume their colours again, bold, almost defiant in the dawn.

"Are you going to tell me?" Pagan asked. "Or am I going to have to guess?"

Mikhail Kiss turned. It was hard to see him in the softly-lit room because the sun hadn't yet penetrated it. "What do you think, Pagan?"

"Life would be easier if you told me," Pagan said.

Kiss was quiet a moment. "I put it all together from nothing. It would only be fair to see you reconstruct it from nothing."

Pagan shut his eyes, rubbed the lids. "Andres is going to fly a plane from Mossheim. He's going to enter Soviet airspace somehow. Then, presumably, he'll deliver some kind of bomb or rocket. Is that close enough?"

Kiss smiled. "You expect an answer to that?"

Pagan went on, "My guess is that he's going to strike a symbolic target, something that's going to displease the Soviets no end. I think he's more interested in damaging Soviet prestige than anything else."

Soviet prestige, Kiss thought. He was thinking now of the fighters waiting in the Baltic cities, the men and women ready to rise up and do battle. He smiled. "You're still cold, Pagan." And he remembered Pagan's story about how Romanenko had been used by the KGB, which now struck him as a preposterous bluff on the Englishman's part, a ploy to lure Kiss's secrets out of him. Well, if Pagan could play games, then so could he!

"You wouldn't tell me if I was warm anyway," Pagan said. He gazed across the room at Kristina Vaska, who sat huddled and shivering, because there was a chill in

427

the air at this time of day. She was pale and tired, as if all her energy had evaporated during that one moment of fury against Kiss. But it was more than a moment, Pagan thought. She'd carried it with her for years.

"How does he get an aeroplane? How does he manage to do that? Does he steal one?" Pagan asked these questions in the manner of a man thinking aloud. "How does he get inside a NATO base and steal a bloody plane, for Christ's sake?"

Mikhail Kiss shook his head. "You work it out, Pagan."

"Inside help is the only way."

"You're sure of that?"

"I'm not sure of anything. Especially the target."

"Maybe there's no target," Kiss said.

Pagan sat behind the desk, shut his eyes. He'd forgotten the last time he'd slept, the last time he'd lain down – and then it came back to him. It must have been the hours spent with Kristina.

He said, "No more games, Kiss. No more guessing games."

"You're out of stamina, Pagan?"

"I've got stamina," Pagan said. "At least enough to make another phonecall."

"You've already called half the civilised world," Kiss said. "Where this time? What's left?"

Frank Pagan reached for the receiver and called Directory Assistance. Without taking his eyes from Mikhail Kiss's face, he asked for the number of the Pentagon.

The Baltic

Andres Kiss, who had refuelled in the air over Gotland Island, a tricky manoeuvre he handled deftly, looked down on the grey-green waters of the Baltic. The F-16 carried 13,500 pounds of fuel, and he'd need every last pound of it if he was to get in and out again according to plan. As soon as he'd disengaged the F-16 from the airborne tanker, and seen the amber disconnect light on his panel, he suddenly pulled the nose of his aircraft up, simulating an out-of-control situation.

The plan called for him to broadcast an emergency message, which he now did. "Mayday, Mayday, LA Alpha 07, I've got a fire light." And he continued his rapid rate of descent, plummeting to 10,000 feet, then 5,000, then 2,000. Down and down, rolling, swooping through cloud banks and seeing vapours disperse as he plunged.

"LA Alpha 07, state your position."

Andres Kiss didn't reply to the voice in his headphones.

The request came again, and Andres ignored it a second time. He turned off the IFF switch, which would indicate to any radar probe that he'd hit the water below and was beyond any possibility of communication. Radar operators would assume that the emergency bleeper hadn't gone off because he hadn't ejected before the craft struck water.

So far, Andres thought, so good.

The plane was now about a hundred and twenty miles from the city of Riga in Latvia and travelling at six miles a minute. He kept descending, stabilising the craft when he was a mere hundred feet above the surface of the Baltic in Russian territorial waters. He could feel the effect of the water, a series of vibrations that disturbed the flight path of the craft. Using the Inertial Navigation Set, he flew east. As a back-up he had charts which would allow him to make visual verification of the information provided by the INS.

The island of Saaremaa, which the Soviets had seized from Estonia, loomed up to his left. A faint early morning haze hung around it. Andres Kiss thought of Mikhail now, and wondered what he was doing at this precise moment. He might be sitting in his sun-room, looking out into the garden. Or he might be pacing nervously, counting down the minutes.

Andres smiled, glanced down at the water, watched spray churn up from the surface. At this height he was flying below the point at which he might be picked up by the Soviet radar – provided the radar systems were operating. If the plan was running smoothly, they would not be. By flying this low, Andres wasn't taking any chances. If something had gone wrong inside the Soviet Union and the air defence systems *were* functioning normally, he'd still evade detection by radar.

Sun burned on the water, broken by the disturbed surface into millions of little sparkling lights. Andres checked the instrument panels again. He was travelling at three hundred and sixty knots per hour, a speed that conserved fuel. He was already far beyond the reach of any NATO aircraft that might have picked up his mayday signal. It was about ten minutes now to the Soviet mainland. Ten minutes through the Gulf of Riga – and then on, inevitably, towards Moscow.

Fredericksburg, Virginia

Galbraith had one of those numb moments of bewilderment, a time in which all brain activity seems suspended. What he was hearing made no immediate sense to him and might have been uttered in a foreign tongue. He opened his eyes – he'd been snoozing, dreaming of tropical places, sand dunes and palms and free-flying parrots and great date clusters – and heard the sound of Gary Iverson's voice coming through the telephone speaker on the bedside table.

"Name of God," Galbraith muttered sleepily. "Tell me again."

Iverson repeated what he'd said a moment ago, when Galbraith had first been stirred from his all-consuming slumber by the buzzing telephone.

"Fucking Epishev," Galbraith said, tossing back the bed covers. "God damn his soul."

"He erred, sir," Iverson said, his voice made hollow by the echo in the speaker. "He must have assumed there were two men in the car. But the man who used Mikhail Kiss's telephone to reach the Pentagon was Frank Pagan – "

"Assume! We assume nothing in this business, Gary," and Galbraith, stark naked, stepped out of bed. "We never assume. Assume is not in our vocabulary. Assume is a word for goddam politicians and priests. Assume is a word for people who have faith in things that cannot be seen, Gary. For example, you assumed Andres Kiss would obey Mikhail and leave Carl Sundbach untouched, did you not?"

"Yes, sir."

"You see my point." Galbraith, breathing hard and vowing anew to diet, climbed into a vast pair of pants with a waist wide enough to encompass two, perhaps three, slender adults. "What will we do now, Gary? What will we do?"

"A dark deed," Iverson suggested quietly.

"It's a frightful thought," Galbraith replied, though without much conviction. "There has been a traditional alliance, Gary, which I don't have to point out to you, between our two nations and their law-enforcement agencies. There has been shared information, even if in recent years there has been a falling-out between clandestine services in the two countries. Nobody trusts the Brits, do they? Well-intentioned men whose security has had the integrity of a colander. Nevertheless, Gary, the idea of *my* agency doing a dark deed on Frank Pagan . . ." Here Galbraith pulled on a tent-like white shirt. "I think I'll speak with this tenacious fellow and see if I can make him see sense, and if I can't do that, then perhaps – Well, I daresay the Clowns can have him, but only if they dine with discretion. We can't leave the man free to walk about, can we?"

"No," Iverson said. "We can't do that."

Galbraith, looking sorrowful, forced his feet into a

pair of black leather pumps. He was hugely unhappy that Epishev had failed, because the onus was squarely back on him, and he didn't like that at all. He stood up, stamped his feet inside his shoes, and suddenly remembered the mention of something in the dossier he had on Colonel Epishev. Of course, the silly bastard was far-sighted and had to wear glasses, which he was seemingly too vain to do! Idiot vanity! Galbraith thought. If Epishev had worn his glasses as he was supposed to, then perhaps Frank Pagan wouldn't be around right now, doing damage, threatening the outcome of White Light.

Iverson said, "I took the liberty of arranging to meet Pagan at Grand Central Station, sir, an hour from now."

Galbraith thought of the fast chopper that would hurl him through space at a speed of some two hundred miles an hour. He hated the deafening roar of the blades and the headache that always gripped him and the miserable sense of being tossed around in midair. But he knew of no faster way to Manhattan from Fredericksburg. His flying time would be approximately one hour and twenty minutes.

"I'll be there as quickly as I can," he said.

Moscow

General Olsky handled the contents of the envelope as if they were fish that might or might not be dead. What he had in his hand were three American passports and fifty thousand American dollars. He flicked one of the passports open, stared inside it, then set it down. He tossed the bundle of money on to his desk in a dismissive fashion. He looked at Colonel Chebrikov.

"The woman actually *denies* knowing how the passports and the money came to be hidden under her floorboards?" Olsky asked.

"Yes," said the Colonel.

"Even after it was pointed out to her that the passports bear photographs of herself and her two children?"

"She claims it's a malicious practical joke, General."

"I don't see the joke at all," Olsky remarked. "Perhaps Mrs Uvarova has a strange sense of humour. What about her husband, Colonel?"

"He's going to be brought in for questioning, General."

"Has Deputy Minister Tikunov been informed that the family of one of his 'trusted' officers has foreign money and foreign passports in its possession?"

Chebrikov said, "I imagined you'd prefer to make that call yourself, General."

Olsky smiled. "How right you are," he said.

New York City

It was five-thirty a.m. when Frank Pagan entered Grand Central Station. When he'd finally reached the Pentagon by telephone and had been put through to a duty officer there, he'd been told to hang up and wait. Somebody would call him back. What Pagan detected in this procedure was the kind of paranoia patented by the military mind. Ten minutes later, the telephone had rung in the kitchen of Mikhail Kiss's house and a voice that did not belong to the first duty officer asked Pagan for details.

It wasn't a situation in which details were exactly plentiful and Pagan's narrative, he realised, had about it a demented tone. Was he being relegated to that category of nuts who call the Pentagon or the CIA in Langley with schizoid tales to tell of dark plots? Was he just another lonely loony calling to hear himself speak?

Apparently he was taken with some seriousness, enough at least for the listener to suggest a rendezvous in a mutually suitable place, which turned out to be, at the suggestion of the listener, Grand Central Station. It wasn't altogether convenient to drive from Glen Cove back to Manhattan, but Pagan – forced by old habits

– broke the speed limit all the way, using Kiss's large Mercedes instead of Kristina Vaska's Pacer, which reminded him of a fishbowl equipped with wheels. Whether Kristina was still in Glen Cove, or whether she'd gone by now, Pagan had no way of knowing. She'd wanted to come with him to Grand Central, an offer he flatly refused. He kept insisting, for his own benefit, that he didn't give a damn anyhow. Seal it and bury it, he told himself. Inter the whole bastard thing. *Put it in a coffin and deep-six it*.

He moved across the concourse, seeing a sparse gathering of early morning travellers, a couple of derelicts, a few drunks wondering what fibs to tell their wives who'd been waiting up all night in the suburbs. He'd been told to look for a man carrying a copy of *The Cleveland Plain Dealer*, a clandestine touch he found amusing. He stood outside a shuttered news-stand, which was the appointed place, and there he waited.

He gazed across the station, impatiently tapping a foot on the ground. He thought, *It began in a railway station and it may end in one, among the litter and the discarded tickets and muffled voices out of loudspeakers and the air that's dry and hard to breathe*. And then he was thinking of Edinburgh and a trail that had begun with the assassination of Romanenko. But it had begun long before that in a forgotten guerilla war in countries which, to all intents and purposes, had been erased forever from the minds of mapmakers.

He moved along the front of the news-stand, hearing the shunting of a locomotive nearby. Then he saw his contact, a tall stiff-backed man with a copy of *The Plain Dealer* held against his side. Pagan stepped forward to greet him. The man looked at Pagan, smiled. He had a pleasantly bland face and fair hair that was cut very short across his skull.

"Frank Pagan?"

Pagan nodded. The man, who had very pale blue eyes, studied Pagan's face a moment, as if he were searching for visible signs of lunacy. The man started to walk, and Pagan followed, thinking it apt that no name had been given, no handshake, no rank, no affiliation. Secrecy was a way of life in military circles. And when it was impossible to keep something secret, you did the next best thing, you stifled it in incomprehensible jargon.

They walked together towards a bar, which was closed. The man peered through the windows and said, "Your story's fascinating."

"I'm happy you think so," Pagan said.

"Goddam fascinating." The man turned and clapped one firm hand on Pagan's shoulder. "And unfortunately vague. A plane flies out of Norway. What kind of plane? And who authorised it to fly? Or was the plane stolen? You got any idea how difficult it is to steal a military aircraft? It's all pretty damn thin, but it gets worse, doesn't it? You don't know the specific target, you don't know the nature of the alleged strike. Boil it down, Frank – mind if I call you that? – and you're not left with much, are you? Just a few guesses, basically. And to be perfectly candid, if you hadn't been affiliated with Scotland Yard – I checked you out, by the way – your story would be in the slush pile already. NFA – no further action."

Pagan wondered if he was supposed to have documentary evidence of his story, if it had to be suitably notarised. He said, "It shouldn't be beyond your resources to find out if a plane has been stolen from the base at Mossheim."

The man shrugged. "There are always NATO exercises around the Baltic, and they involve scores of aircraft. It's not as simple as you might imagine to locate one particular craft, especially since we don't know exactly what we're looking for."

Pagan was disappointed by the man's lack of enthusiasm. He struggled to be patient and calm. "I understand it might be difficult, but in the circumstances don't you think you should be making some kind of bloody effort? Don't you have a computer tracking system?"

The man's smile seemed an immutable thing, living a separate life from his face. "Don't get me wrong, Frank. I'm not going to dismiss your story. I'll look into it. I promise you that. But it's going to take a little time."

"Look, I have a feeling we don't have time. This character Andres Kiss is already on the base at Mossheim. He might even have flown by this time – "

"Frank, Frank, Frank. We checked Andres Kiss out and he used to be a USAF Major, just as you said. But why do you make the assumption he's gone to Mossheim to steal a plane, for heaven's sake? Some of his old squadron members are based there right now, the guy could be paying a visit, a vacation. It doesn't have to be anything nefarious. Like I said, Frank, if you had just a little documentary evidence, well, it would make a hell of a difference."

Pagan said, "I'm beginning to get the impression that my narrative isn't quite setting you on fire. If I were a suspicious man, I'd say you weren't exactly interested in it."

"Of course I'm interested in it," the man said.

"Then why aren't you doing something about it?"

The man laid his hand on Pagan's shoulder again. "Here's what I suggest, Frank. You trot on back to your hotel and leave it all to me. Don't worry about a thing. It's in good hands."

"I'm not about to trot anywhere," Pagan said. Especially not at the suggestion of someone as patronising as you, Blue Eyes, he thought. There was an insincere quality to this nameless man, and Pagan didn't like it, didn't trust it. He didn't like the way he was being stalled either.

"Jesus, you're a hard man to convince, Frank. You imagine I'm going to *ignore* the whole goddam thing? You imagine I don't believe you? I'll take the appropriate steps, I promise you that."

"When?"

"Frank, let me give you the simple ABCs of it. This

is a military matter. We're all goddam grateful you brought it to our attention, believe me. But it's out of your hands now."

"I don't think so," Pagan said, and he stared at a row of phonebooths a hundred yards away. What was the time in London? he wondered. Martin Burr would be at his desk and if Pagan couldn't get this supercilious bozo to do something quickly, he'd cheerfully call the Commissioner, who would most certainly contact the NATO command in Europe. But why in the name of Christ was there such reluctance here?

He said, "If you don't want to follow up on my story – and I mean *now*, sunshine – I'll make a phonecall to somebody who will. That way, if I'm completely off the wall, if I'm suffering from a brainstorm, then at least I'll have the benefit of relief."

The man followed Pagan's line of vision in the direction of the phones. "I wouldn't," he said, and the smile finally was gone.

"Give me a damn good reason not to," Pagan said.

"We've got a communications problem here, Frank, and it bothers me. What I'm trying to say is that as far as you're concerned, those phones are off limits."

"Off limits?"

"Precisely."

"If I want to make a call, you stop me, is that it?"

The man said nothing.

Pagan briefly closed his eyes, hearing the sound of something he should have caught minutes ago, something that echoed in his head and throbbed. Realisation, a cold dawning, the noise of a frozen penny dropping inside his brain. He looked into the man's face, which had all the animation of a stiff mask.

"You *want* it to fly," Pagan said quietly. "You *want* the fucking plane to make it!"

The man continued to be silent.

Pagan could still hear the coin tumbling down the chutes of his mind, gathering momentum as it moved, and he was reminded of a game he used to play at carnivals as a kid, when you stuck a penny in a slot and watched it roll towards a variety of possible destinations – some of which returned your coin, most of which kept it. Christ, what had he stumbled into? Where was the rolling coin destined to go? You call the Pentagon, you report the possibility of a stolen plane, an impending disaster, and the duty officer turns you over to Blue Eyes, who's seemingly in no great hurry to prevent destruction. What the hell was going on here?

"Let me see if I can guess it," Pagan said. "Are you and Andres Kiss working together? Is that it? With a little help from some friends inside the Pentagon? Am I right? Is it some kind of elaborate military conspiracy?"

The man shook his head. "That's too simple, Frank. There's no military conspiracy. There's no vast involvement at the Pentagon."

"What is it then? Just a chosen few? A helping hand here, a little support there? Why don't you spell it out for me, friend?"

"I want you to meet somebody, Frank. Somebody who can give you a better perspective on this whole matter. He's waiting outside. He doesn't like public places."

Pagan hesitantly followed as the man began to walk across the concourse in the direction of the exit. Outside the station a long black limousine was parked in defiance of No Parking signs. Pagan understood he was to move towards it. The back door was opened from inside. Pagan hesitated.

Blue Eyes said, "You'll be fine, Frank. Go ahead."

Pagan looked inside the car. A fat man, his face in shade, occupied most of the back seat. There were two televisions, a couple of phones, decanters of scotch and sherry.

"Go ahead," Blue Eyes said again.

Pagan concentrated on the fat man's face, the eyes that were hardly more than two very narrow gashes, the cheeks that appeared to be stuffed with food – as if the man were a hibernating animal preparing himself for the long sleep of winter.

"Frank Pagan," the fat man said, and patted the space on the seat alongside him. "I've been looking forward to meeting you. But we can hardly talk like reasonable men if you insist on standing in the street, while I sit in the comfort of this car. What's it to be?"

"You step out," Pagan said.

"Humbug. It's more comfortable in here."

Pagan shook his head. The fat man sighed and emerged from the limousine, looking just a little testy but forcing a smile anyhow. Blue Eyes moved some distance away, browsing through newspapers at a news-stand.

"Stubborn, Pagan," the fat man said.

"So I've been told."

They walked a few paces. The fat man asked, "How is Scotland Yard?"

"Is this going to be small talk? I already told your man out there that I had a situation I thought should be checked out. He appeared completely reluctant."

"He's a good man. Don't be hard on him. He takes orders well."

"From you?"

The fat man nodded. "I understand you want to stop a certain plane flying to the Soviet Union, Frank."

"I had a notion," Pagan said. He was suddenly very impatient.

"Question, Frank. How much do you know? How much have you glued together?"

Pagan studied the man's face. He had a small mouth and rather tiny teeth. Pagan thought for a moment before he said, "Why should I tell you what I know? I don't even know who you are, for Christ's sake."

"My dear fellow, I'm a great fan of Scotland Yard. You and I, old man, we're on the same team. Nobody's going to hurt you, Frank. We're friends here. My affiliation is a wee bit difficult to explain."

"I bet it is."

"National security."

"Whose national security?"

"The whole Western world, Frank. I'm not speaking only of our own backyard, my friend."

Pagan started to move away. He was tired of obfuscation, weary of allusion, sick to his heart with mystification. All he wanted to do was to go back inside the station and call the Commissioner. The fat man caught the sleeve of his jacket and held it.

"Don't rush away, Frank. Tell me what you know. Besides, you've got nothing to worry about, have you? You're armed. I'm not. I've read your dossier and I know you carry a Bernardelli in a rear holster. And I wouldn't be seen dead near a gun. All I'm interested in is your version of the situation."

Pagan assembled his thoughts, which raced here and there like doomed summer butterflies eluding a net. He said, "The KGB found some use for a group of Baltic freedom fighters. At least certain factions in the KGB and their friends did. The Balts don't seem to have a clue they're being used by the very people they despise most. I assume the KGB motive is related to a power-struggle inside the Soviet Union – old against new. That's my best guess. I can't see any other reason for the support of the Balts. But now I get the distinct impression from your friend over there that there's more to this than I imagined. Now it appears that the Balts aren't only getting help from the Soviets, they're also getting assistance from certain Americans as well, some of whom have military connections."

The fat man shrugged. His small eyes were very bright and hard like two polished brown stones. He appeared to be just a little amused now.

Pagan said, "American and Soviet collusion. It explains some things. Such as how Epishev knew I'd come to the United States. The Americans told him. How Andres Kiss could steal a NATO plane and fly it inside Soviet territory. The Americans could provide the aircraft, the Soviets the means of entry."

"Ingenious," said the fat man. He pressed his chubby fingers to his mouth.

"What I don't entirely understand is American involvement," Pagan remarked.

"Think about it, Frank," the fat man said. "I'm sure it's on the tip of your tongue."

Pagan was quiet a moment. Traffic chugged past the entrance to the station, taxicabs honking at the black limousine that impeded their movement. Pagan observed that the limo wasn't equipped with the usual licence plates. Instead, it had the kind of temporary plates used by car dealers.

He said, "My best bet would be that some Americans would like to see the new Soviet regime replaced. I'm naive enough to wonder why."

"Replaced is understatement. Try removed and forgotten, Frank. Buried with all its manifestos of good intentions. Interred with all its spurious nonsense about democracy and freedom. That's closer to the mark. It's a matter of protecting our civilisation, for want of a better word."

"So Andres Kiss flies an aeroplane inside the Soviet Union and *that* act of terrorism protects our civilisation?" Pagan asked.

The fat man grinned and his eyes vanished off the planet of his face. "You know, Frank, some of us long for the old days when we knew who the Russians were. We had a set of rules, and we could get along with the Soviets because they were predictable. We understood how they operated. We knew their level of incompetence. Government by geriatrics. What do old men love more than anything else, Frank? I'll tell you. They adore the status fucking quo, that's what. But all these goddam changes have upset things more than a little. When the old farts started dying off, we always assumed other old farts would take their places. We thought the Soviets had an endless supply of old farts. We didn't see a new breed rising, did we? We didn't think ahead. Now we don't know where they stand these days. And worse than that, we don't know where *we* stand either."

Pagan said nothing. He felt restless. Was the fat man trying to stall him? Detecting Pagan's restlessness, the fat man raised his voice.

"When they talk about reforms, and how they're going to change the Soviet Union from top to bottom, that really troubles me. Ye gods! who knows what they're going to release? Vast reservoirs of untapped talent lying around, skills that have gone unused because nobody gave a fiddler's fuck about a system that disregarded basic human rights. But give people a sense of dignity, give them some comforts, make them think they're really important, and we might see a goddam Russian renaissance in technology, science, energy. *And then what?*"

The fat man took a handkerchief out now and blew his nose in short, trumpeting sounds. "The big question is, can this fragile globe stand a *really* powerful Russia? Will the old power pendulum swing over to the red zone? What kind of world would it be if the Russians dominated it? I get chills up and down my spine. You see, I liked things the way they were, Frank. I think what we're doing can help us keep the upper hand. We're not discussing some lunatic right-wing bullshit here, Frank. Let's just say a few people, with different motives but a common goal, put their resources together. Certain Americans don't like this new Russia. More importantly, a good number of Russians don't like it either. Change, they say. Screw change. We want things the way they were. Let's have it back the way it used to be. What a nice coincidence, don't you think? Here's something the Americans and the Soviets can get together on finally. A joint Soviet-American venture to destroy all this unwanted *newness* in Soviet society. A collaboration, Frank, between ourselves and some sympathetic Russians. Fraternity and cooperation."

"With the Balts playing the fools," Pagan said.

"That's your choice of description, Frank."

"When you say *ourselves*, who are you referring to?"

The fat man fell silent now. Pagan knew his question was going to go unanswered. The fat man was something within something within something, connected to the US government, but tucked away, and well-hidden, and finally beyond the pale of the federal bureaucracy.

"And this plane?"

"It's going to cause a commotion, Frank. And we're gambling that it will bring down the present Politburo – leaving a nice empty space for some reliable old faces."

"If I might use an Americanism – the whole thing sucks."

"Pray tell."

"It's a volatile plan. You don't know the precise consequences of it. If you attack the Soviet Union, if a NATO plane violates Soviet airspace and drops a bomb – how can you tell there won't be retaliation of some kind? Even if that doesn't happen, I don't like the idea of people needlessly dying, which I imagine will happen if this plane flies."

"Needlessly, Frank?"

"I don't want to argue with you. Your outlook's unreal. The world changes, and you can't stop it. You can't interfere."

"Oh dear," the fat man said. "I thought you might reach a more balanced judgement than that, which is why I gave you the benefit of this nice little chat. Think again, Frank. I do wish you'd keep in mind the fact that an arthritic Russia is a containable one. Anything else is, well, a little too unpredictable."

Pagan shook his head. There was nothing in the world so astonishing to him as the compulsion of organisations and fraternities and secret societies that think they can alter history, nothing that reduced him quite so quickly to speechlessness. Partly it was the conceit of it all, the terrible arrogance. Partly it was the desperation of these men, and their obsessions, which lay beyond reason. For Kiss and Romanenko it had been vengeance. For the fat man and his Russian cronies it was nothing less ambitious than trying to preserve a Russia to which they'd become complacently attached for their own reasons. Anything new, anything that might bring about a different Soviet Union, even a progressive one – God help us all – was not remotely acceptable.

"You think you can get away with it?" Pagan asked.

"Get away with it? We can get away with anything. Shuffling paperwork so that a plane can be taken without authority – by a former pilot who's utterly deranged, of course, as all the records will show – that's child's play. Don't worry about us."

Pagan was quiet a moment. "I don't walk away from here, do I?"

"Frank, really. Step out of my life. I never met you. You never met me. And you never will again. Simple. I love Scotland Yard, and I wouldn't dream of harming one of its people. But I do wish you'd stay a little longer and chat some more with me. I'd like to talk about more pleasant things. London, for example. Tea at the Ritz. Dinner at the Connaught. The South Coast. I have so many fond memories. There's a small town in the West Country, Bideford, and I recall – "

"Some other time," Pagan said.

The fat man smiled, looked at his watch. Then he shrugged. "Goodbye . . ." He snapped his fingers in frustration. "Christ, I've already forgotten your name."

Pagan stepped away from the man. He felt tense, dehydrated. The fat man returned to the big black car, stepped inside along with Blue Eyes. The car pulled away, vanished. Pagan moved back in the direction of the station entrance. Back to the telephones.

But he knew he wasn't going to be allowed. He wasn't going to make it that far. He sensed it. Even the morning air around him was charged suddenly with the electricity of fear. He moved slowly towards the station, passing under the shadows of the building, turning his face from side to side, seeing nothing, but knowing, just *knowing* that somebody was about to prevent him from reaching the phones.

He didn't see the sniper on the roof of the station. He didn't know he was being closely observed through a telescopic lens by a sharpshooter, a former Marine champion, who held a Weatherby auto rifle. Pagan only knew that as he walked towards the entrance he was exposed and vulnerable, but at the same time didn't want to break into a run, he wanted to look totally calm. Halfway towards the station entrance he paused, looked from left to right, saw nothing unusual, nothing concealed in shadows, nobody seated in parked cars. Just the same, *he still knew*.

He kept moving. He didn't see the glint of the rifle as the early sun struck the walnut stock, or the way the sharpshooter took out a pair of dark glasses and pulled them over his eyes. Pagan had to stop because several cars blocked his way into the station. But he didn't think to look up, he was concentrating on the station entrance, the idea of making it as far as the telephones. When the traffic passed, he stepped off the pavement. He had perhaps fifty yards to go. He hurried now for the first time, unaware of the fact he was trapped in the dead centre of a lens, a moving target neatly bisected by crosslines.

And then something, an inexplicable impulse, made him raise his face and look up, and he saw the way the sunlight caught the weapon, although for a second he wasn't absolutely sure of what it was that glinted high above him, and he thought of a bird carrying a piece of silverfoil, or a sliver of broken glass. When he understood what it was he knew the realisation had come a little too late for him.

He barely heard the voice from behind.

"Frank!"

He did the only thing he could think of. He threw

himself forward, hearing the noise of a gun, realising it was too loud to have come from the roof, that it originated from a point just behind him. It was followed by a second shot, then a third, and the sound echoed around him. He raised his face and gazed up at the roof, but the gunman was gone, scrambling out of view, leaving behind him only an expensively modified weapon that bore no registration number, no marks of ownership, and no clue to the identity of the person who'd altered the weapon.

Pagan rose slowly to his feet, aware of cars crowding around him, irate drivers, delayed commuters, the screaming of horns. And there, standing alongside her idiotic little car, her Pacer, stood Kristina Vaska, looking very solemn and quite lovely in a pale, tired way, one hand on her hip, the other wrapped loosely around her pistol, a tiny smile on her face – enigmatic, and quite unfamiliar to Pagan, but nevertheless at that moment the most welcome gesture he'd ever received from another human being.

He returned the smile and then he went inside the station and walked towards the telephones.

Moscow

Deputy Minister Tikunov, who hated to admit he was ever wrong about anything, and who thought crow the most disgusting taste a man could carry in his mouth, spoke into the telephone. "It appears that your information is genuine, General. An F-16 was stolen from a NATO base in Norway. It's heading for Russia."

"Stolen?" Olsky asked.

"That's the official NATO statement. I've just had their Commander on the line from Brussels."

"Then do what you have to do," Olsky said. "But do it quickly."

Tikunov flicked a switch on a communications console on his desk. He ordered a top priority check of every radar installation between Moscow and the Baltic. He also ordered squadrons of MIG-29s and MIG-25 Foxbats to fly immediately on a seek and destroy mission.

21

Saaremma Island, the Baltic

When he saw the F-16 go flying past in the far distance, Colonel Yevgenni Uvarov hurried in the direction of the beach. The falsified maintenance order he'd issued meant that any radar sightings, which would normally have been relayed to his control centre and from there to Moscow, were effectively contained inside the computers under Uvarov's command. Because technicians worked on the computers, the line of communication from Saaremaa Island to Moscow was severed for the hours of their labour. Uvarov had short-circuited the system, and since no sightings could be reported to the Ministry in Moscow, no order could be given to destroy the intruder. Only the Minister, or the Deputy Minister, or somebody authorised by them, could issue such an order.

Uvarov reached the beach and ran towards the stone jetty, looking for the launch. There was no sign of the vessel. Panicked, he raced to the end of the jetty and scanned the water. There was a faint haze rising off the sea. He thought he could still hear the roar of the F-16 as it raced – barely above sea-level – towards the coast, but he couldn't tell since the plane was out of sight.

Where was the damned launch? Uvarov anxiously scanned the water. Nothing. No sight of anything. What if he'd been tricked? What if there was no such vessel? What if Aleksis had been lying all along? Uvarov, so panicked he could barely breathe, peered out into the haze, his eyes stinging from salt spray. He looked back the length of the jetty, seeing the barbed-wire strung around the control centre and the radar dishes that turned ceaselessly, probing the sea and the sky. *Where was the fucking launch?*

And then he heard it. He heard it! It appeared through the haze, a small vessel that churned up an enormous wake as it speeded towards the jetty. Uvarov raised his hand, waved impatiently. Hurry, he thought. Dear God, hurry. He glanced back at the control centre once more. There was another sound now, and one he couldn't altogether identify because he was concentrating on the launch, which had cut its engine and was drifting towards the quay. *Hurry, hurry.* Uvarov started down the steps, seeing two figures on board the small green craft. One of them was preparing to toss a rope towards Uvarov, uncoiling it. And then Uvarov felt it, the turbulent passage of air, the breeze that swept his face and ruffled his hair, and he looked upwards, drawn to the great turning blades of the helicopter. The rope came towards him and he clutched it hastily as the launch drifted nearer to him – ten feet, seven, five – dear Christ, he'd have to leap. He braced himself, jumped, clutched the side of the launch and was hauled on board even as the helicopter descended like some predatory creature and the man who appeared in the open doorway of the chopper started firing at the launch with a machine-gun. On and on and on, blitzing the deck of the small craft, a crazy kind of firing that seemed to have no end to it. Uvarov fell, conscious of a wound in his side – a distant awareness, beyond any immediate pain. What he felt more than anything was sadness and regret.

He shut his eyes and even though he didn't see them he experienced the heat of the flames that had begun to billow out of the launch's fuel system, which had caught fire during the machine-gun assault. The launch smoked and smouldered before it finally exploded, sending debris up and up into the salt air.

Tallinn, Estonia

In the middle of the afternoon, the man known as Marcus met three other men, each of them carrying a concealed weapon, outside the Hotel Viru. At the same time another three men assembled near the Tallinn Department Store on Lomonossovi Street. The Viru Hotel, a modern twenty-two storey construction on Viru Square, could be seen from the department store. Marcus and his companions crossed Estonia Boulevard where the afternoon traffic was dense and the pedestrians, swollen by hundreds of tourists, created a slow-moving crowd that made progress along the pavement difficult. Marcus looked once at his watch as he reached the corner of Lomonossovi Street. Thirty minutes.

The three men who had gathered outside the department store were following some yards behind. Marcus had the thought that they all looked suspicious, that anyone observing them would notice that they all carried hidden weapons, but this was the result of his own tension and fear. In fact they looked just like anyone else strolling through the afternoon sunshine under a blue Tallinn sky.

Marcus paused, lit a cigarette, caught the eye of a pretty girl moving past. Her ash-coloured hair, tugged by an ocean breeze, blew playfully up around her cheeks and she pushed it aside in a gesture Marcus found unbearably sweet. In thirty minutes he'd probably be dead. In thirty minutes, simple things, beautiful things like the girl's hand caressing her own hair, would be beyond his experience.

He thought of the girl Erma and the old man Bruno, who were part of a second group forming on Suur-Karja Street, some distance from the old Town Hall. This unit, consisting of twenty people, would enter the Central Post Office and order the clerks to close the doors for the rest of the day. In Latvia and Lithuania similar insurrections were taking place simultaneously. In Riga, groups were scheduled to seize the Post Office on Lenin Street, the Latvian State radio offices, and the TV tower located on one of the islands on the Daugava River. In Vilnius, the targets were the Central Post Office on Lenin Prospekt, the State Television studio, and the railway station. From the post offices in all three cities, telegrams would be sent to a variety of cities in the West – including Stockholm, Paris, London and New York. These messages would be the same in every case – a declaration of Baltic independence, evidenced by this robust resistance, no longer passive, no longer a matter of mere flag-waving, to Soviet occupation – and by the daring flight of a patriot into the heart of Russia itself. A message was being delivered to the world, and it was one of freedom.

Marcus stopped on Lomonossovi Street. He checked his watch again. Synchronisation was important. He would deliver his own message at precisely the same time as the aeroplane launched its attack. There was impressive power in such orchestration. Chaos would convince nobody. Who would respond to a disorganised rabble? If there was to be a general revolt throughout the Baltic countries, those who decided to participate in it had to be convinced that the leaders were proficient as well as patriotic. They had to have confidence in the organisation. Everything had to be done the way Aleksis had planned it, with attention to detail, to timing. Aleksis had once said that revolutions often failed because they weren't punctual, a statement Marcus had thought amusing at the time. Not now . . .

Marcus continued to walk. Up ahead was the building that housed the Estonian Radio and Television studios. He lit another cigarette, glanced at his companions, noticed how they bantered among themselves like working-men going home at the end of a long day, men who perhaps had stopped at a café for vodka or beer. Marcus put a hand inside the pocket of his overcoat. The gun felt very good to him. He was aware of crowds jostling him, the smells of colognes, bread from a bakery, gasoline fumes, so many scents. Was it like this when you knew your life was almost over? Were you suddenly sharper, keener, more receptive to the world you were leaving?

He put his hand around his gun. He looked back at the men following him. He smiled, a tense little movement of his lips. Now, he thought. It was almost time.

The Soviet Union

Andres Kiss flew low over marshy countryside, noticing here and there small rounded hills and the occasional river, now and then a farmhouse. He avoided towns and villages. He was still flying at a speed of six miles a minute. He set the radar on 'range only', which permitted him to look approximately eighty miles ahead and thirty thousand feet above, then he placed the master arm in the ON position, so that he was armed and ready in the event of an attack – if there had been a visual sighting of his F-16, and he prayed that there hadn't. He continued to fly between the low hills and through shallow valleys, keeping to the shadows where the sun didn't penetrate. If he hugged the landscape this way, the chance of any high-altitude craft spotting him was severely limited. He saw nothing above him in his radar, and ahead the landscape was dreary. His luck, so far, had held. But luck, he knew, was a fickle bitch, and could change her mind at any time.

Not today, Andres Kiss thought. He had a feeling that fortune was with him.

He was heading due east now. He was approximately 180 miles – thirty minutes' flying time – from Moscow. And the Kremlin.

He studied the landscape around him, seeing it flash past at the kind of speed he loved. Blurs, brown-greens, a landscape that suggested spilled paint. Cattle whizzed past, and grain silos, and houses, and the stacks of the occasional factory. Reservoirs, dams, electricity pylons. It was crazed speed and impressions came at him faster than his senses could truly register them.

This, Andres thought, was power.

Tallinn, Estonia

The first casualty was the uniformed guard who stepped from behind his desk to question Marcus.

"You need a pass, comrade," the guard said. "And an appointment."

Marcus said, "*Ya ne panimayu parooski*," which meant he didn't speak Russian, which was a lie. He asked the guard to speak in Estonian. The guard, a surly young man from Minsk who loathed the Baltic, and who was homesick for his native city, said he didn't speak Estonian. He did, but only to a small degree. Today, though, he didn't feel like wrapping his tongue round those strange sounds, and he didn't like the look of this fellow who'd just strutted inside the building. The young man put his hand on his holster.

Marcus shot him then. The guard fell backwards and a girl began to scream at the end of the hallway. Marcus turned, saw his companions enter the building with their guns drawn. He hadn't expected to kill the young man, but this was too important for scruples now, too important for hesitation. He hurried along the corridor, seeing doors open on either side, the troubled faces of men and women, employees of the State Radio and Television Company which regularly flooded the air with Soviet-approved trash and which took its editorial direction from the Ministry of Communications in Moscow. The girl who'd been screaming before was silent now, covering her face with her hands and kneeling on the floor.

"You're not going to be hurt," Marcus said. "Direct me to the broadcasting studio."

The girl pointed towards a staircase. "Up there. Studio Two is radio. Studios One and Three TV."

Marcus moved toward the stairs, leaving five of his men posted in the hallway. He took the stairs quickly, followed by two men who were brothers from the district of Tallinn called Mustamae, a place of monstrous Soviet apartment houses. He checked his watch again as he moved.

Ahead, a second guard stepped out of an office into the corridor. He had a pistol in one hand and he fired it directly at Marcus. The shot struck one of the brothers, who fell silently. The guard didn't get the chance to fire again before Marcus had shot him in the forehead. And then he was hurrying along the hallway, looking for the door of the studio he wanted. He didn't want TV, he preferred radio because he believed more people listened to music on the radio in the afternoons than watched the tedious graveyard that was Tallinn television.

More people were filing out of their offices. Marcus didn't know how long he had. Sooner or later somebody was going to pick up a telephone and call the militiamen and then the building would be invaded by cops. The five men posted in the hallway below could hold them off for quite some time, although Marcus wasn't sure how long that might be. He took the prepared message from his pocket as he rushed along the corridor. Studio One. Three. What had the hysterical girl said? Studio Two? Marcus noticed a red light above the door of Studio Two. He pushed the door open, stepped inside the soundproofed room.

Two women were seated round a microphone discussing how best to pickle herring. In a glass booth beyond the women sat three technicians. The women stared at Marcus as he entered, then – utterly perplexed by this unscripted occurrence, this intrusion into their domestic programme – looked at the technicians for guidance.

Marcus waved his gun and made his way to the control booth, shoving the door open.

"I want to read a statement," he said.

The technicians didn't know how to behave. One, muscular and bearded, asked, "On whose behalf?"

"The Movement for Baltic Independence."

The bearded man smiled. "Be my guest," and he gestured towards the microphones where the two silent women sat.

The Soviet Union

Fifty-four miles from Moscow. His predetermined initial point. Nine minutes of flying time. And so far it was working, everything, working like a goddam charm. Even the landscape seemed welcoming to him, a carpet laid out for him to fly over. Magic, Andres thought. Pure magic.

And then he was tense. Flying low over a flat landscape was one thing. Flying between stunted hills, that was a piece of cake. But Moscow was looming up, and Moscow was going to be something else.

He punched the on-board clock, starting from zero and counting up to eight and a half minutes. He pushed a small white button which armed the station where the three Mark 82s were located. Weapons live. Bombs live.

Now, he thought. The last lap. The big city.

Counting up. Still counting up. Five minutes. Six. Seven. But then time was becoming meaningless to Andres now, because he felt he was beyond such measurements. He was in a place without clocks. He was airborne and free and time was a ball and chain you tossed down through the clouds.

When eight minutes had elapsed, he began to climb rapidly, creating an angle of eventual descent. Three hundred feet. Five hundred. One thousand. Fifteen hundred.

Andres's face sweated in his helmet. He could see Moscow – *Matushka Moskva* – spread before him in the afternoon light. He could see towers and apartment buildings and spires and a gleaming stretch of the Moskva River and the movement of traffic on the streets. As he climbed, he said in a soft voice the Estonian version of the Lord's Prayer, which he'd learned from Mikhail Kiss in childhood. *Mei isa, kes sa oled taevas . . .*

Tallinn, Estonia

Marcus looked at his watch. It was time to read his statement. He sat nervously at the microphone and spread the sheet of paper out on the table before him. For a second he couldn't quite make out the words. He rubbed his eyes, cleared his throat, stared at the technicians in the glass booth. Two were expressionless, but the bearded man looked encouraging.

"Any time you like." The bearded man's voice was loud inside Marcus's earphones.

Marcus took a sip from a glass of water and began to read. His statement, carefully composed by Romanenko many months ago, concerned the travesty of international justice that was the Soviet occupation. It concerned the rights of nations to self-determination. It concerned old non-invasion treaties, compacts made between the Russians and the Baltic countries, that had been cynically disregarded by the Kremlin. It concerned the revolutionary movements in Latvia and Lithuania that even now were broadcasting to their own people in Riga and Vilnius. And finally it concerned the daring flight of a young pilot into Moscow and how that single act of unselfish bravery was the standard against which all patriotic acts had to be judged, the spearhead of a new movement towards freedom, the call to liberty, the ultimate symbol.

Marcus stopped reading. He didn't realise that his

speech hadn't been broadcast, that the transmitter had been rendered inoperative by technicians after he'd read the opening three sentences, and that the five men left to guard the downstairs hallway had been shot and killed by an invasion of militiamen. He had no way of knowing that the young man from Mustamae, who had been standing guard outside the door to Studio Two, lay dead in the corridor, shot by militiamen. Nor could he know that the group that had seized the Post Office at number 20 Suur-Karja had been killed in a thirty-minute gun battle with the KGB.

Marcus raised the water glass to his lips and looked at the bearded man, who winked at him through the glass. Marcus ran a hand over his face. He set down his glass just as the studio door opened. He reached at once for his gun as two militiamen, armed with automatic rifles, entered the room with their weapons already firing.

Marcus slumped across the table, spilling his water glass. A stream of water slithered across the paper on which his speech had been written, causing the ink to run in indecipherable lines, as if a bird with dark blue claws had alighted on the paper.

Moscow

At two thousand five hundred feet Andres could see Red Square, and the Kremlin – and there was the Palace of Congresses, where the Communist Party conferences were held.

Andres Kiss's target. Mikhail Kiss's target. The target of the Brotherhood. The place where destinies were decided, the malignant heart of the system the Brotherhood had despised. Andres Kiss could see the great columns that surrounded the building and he thought of how, within its vast auditorium and spacious offices, men decreed the fates of people within all the Soviet Republics, how decisions taken here filtered down into everyday life in the countries of the Baltic, and affected the way people lived. Here the party bigshots planned to bury the Baltic nations. Here they planned to turn Balts into third-class citizens in their own countries. Here the party engine functioned, pumping out poisons that had to be swallowed by people who had absolutely no desire to feed on Russian lies or to embrace a system that was alien to them, one that killed the spirit and demolished the soul.

It was Andres's intention to drop the first bomb at one end of the building, the second in the middle, the third at the other end, and then turn the aircraft in the direction of Leningrad and the Gulf of Finland, which was his one chance of getting out of the Soviet Union before he was attacked.

That was his intention.

He was about three miles from the Kremlin when he nosed the F-16 downwards, conscious now of the way the city tilted through his cockpit, as if the buildings all listed impossibly to one side. Down and down now. Fifteen hundred feet above ground level, twelve hundred. That was when he saw three MIG-29s in the eastern sky, perhaps no more than two miles from him. That was when he realised, with a start that made his heart shudder, that something had gone wrong with the plan.

Without thinking, operating entirely on old instincts and training, he manoeuvred the F-16 into firing position and released one of the forward quarter heat-seeking Side Winders. It exploded on contact with the MIG-29 nearest to him: a flash, a violent plume of smoke, and the Soviet aircraft was gone. Andres fired the second missile and made a direct hit on another of the MIGs, destroying the plane with startling immediacy. The afternoon, so placid before, was filled with trails of smoke and turbulence and destruction.

The third Russian plane zoomed above him and attacked him with cannon. The F-16 trembled and vibrated in the storm of fire but didn't receive a hit.

Andres, still believing in luck, still believing that the angels were on his side, rolled back into his dive on the Palace of Congresses as the remaining MIG-29, the Fulcrum, fired down on him from above. Let him catch me, Andres thought. Let the fucker do his worst. He'd already brought two of them down and he wasn't about to be stopped by some goddam Ivanovich shooting at him. He was about two miles from his target now and he had his hand poised over the bomb button, and when the bombs fell upon the Palace they'd explode after a fifteen-second delay.

At one thousand feet two SA-11 missiles, fired from a site three miles beyond Moscow, came screaming towards him, disintegrating the fuselage of the F-16 and turning the aircraft into a mass of fiery debris that splintered in the sky and fell, like the tail of the most glorious firework that had ever lit the air above Moscow. Andres Kiss, harnessed to his seat, helmeted, still saying the closing lines of the Lord's Prayer, his hand reaching for the bomb button, felt nothing save a very brief moment of burning discomfort before he was falling and falling, along with the flaming remains of his aeroplane, into an empty soccer stadium a mere two miles from the Palace of Congresses.

Zavidovo, the Soviet Union

It was almost midnight when Dimitri Volovich arrived at Greshko's cottage in Zavidovo. The Yakut nurse opened the door for him. Without waiting for any response from her, he stepped inside. "I'll need a glass of water," he said.

"Of course." The nurse fetched him the glass. He didn't drink from it. Instead, he pushed open the door to Greshko's bedroom.

Curtains had been drawn against the windows. The only source of illumination was a tiny reading lamp affixed to the wall above Greshko's pillows, but this was barely more than a pinpoint of electricity.

Greshko, who had been lying with his eyes shut, opened them when he heard Volovich enter the room. Because of the bad light, he could barely make out the Lieutenant's face. He propped himself up on his elbows, rubbed his eyes. He saw a glass of water in Dimitri's right hand.

"Come closer, Dimitri."

Volovich did so. Obedience to the old man, he thought, was a hard habit to break. But General Olsky said it had to be broken. It was the only way.

Greshko frowned. There was something here that wasn't quite right, something askew. Perhaps it was the flat tone in Volovich's voice, an edge, barely noticeable, which sounded abrasive.

He sat upright now, expecting pain, which had gone through him all day long like a blade, but surprisingly there was none. When there was no pain he imagined he'd held death in abeyance once again, that he'd overcome his oldest adversary – but why did he feel no sense of exaltation, no joy, no triumph?

Volovich approached the bed. Greshko stared at the glass of water. "You have a message from Viktor?"

Volovich sat on the edge of the bed, crossing his legs. "No message, General."

"No message?"

"None."

Greshko gestured toward the stereo. "Put some music on, Dimitri."

Volovich shook his head. In this small act of disobedience, Greshko suddenly saw the limits of his power. So this was it. After all these years, this was the moment. Losing wasn't the thing that troubled him, because a gamble was a gamble after all. It was the way they'd changed the rules of the game that irritated him. He imagined Olsky and Nikolai Bragin, a cosy little chat, a handshake, a secretive smile. Perhaps even Birthmark

Billy had been involved. Of course he should have foreseen such collusion against him, he should have known that the rules would be altered – but what was life if you didn't take bloody risks? A toss of the dice, a turn of the cards. But the dice had been loaded, the cards unfairly marked.

"How did they get to you, Dimitri?"

"It doesn't matter."

"Money? No, I doubt that. Threats, then. They threatened you."

Volovich nodded.

Greshko smiled. "And if you kill me, you'll be protected."

"Yes."

Greshko uttered a hoarse laugh. "And you believe this? You believe your protectors are honourable men, Dimitri? You believe they'll let you keep your job, your perks, your nice uniform?"

"I have no choice."

"How is it to be?" Greshko asked. "Does the General commit suicide while depressed over his incurable physical condition?"

"No suicide."

Greshko watched Dimitri Volovich raise the glass of water.

"Something to drink, is that it?" he asked.

"Yes," Volovich said.

"Ah," Greshko said. "A heart attack. Cardiac arrest. Weakened by his long illness, the General succumbed peacefully at midnight."

Volovich removed his wallet, opened it, shook a small capsule out. He cracked the plastic casing, dropped white powder into the water, and swirled the glass around in his hand.

"Mix it well," Greshko said.

Volovich looked at the clouded water. He held the glass to Greshko's lips. The old man didn't drink immediately. He smiled over the rim of the glass.

461

"Drink," Volovich said.

Greshko sipped the liquid. It tasted slightly bitter. He felt it burn at the back of his throat, but then the sensation passed.

"I wish Olsky had administered this himself," Greshko said. "But he's such a gutless little shit. He wouldn't have the courage to come here."

Greshko closed his eyes, smiled. Then, through the fluttering of his eyelids, he saw Dimitri Volovich, who appeared to be floating a very long way off. Fading. Darkness. Sweat. It was like falling through water whose temperature increased the deeper you sank. He raised a hand in the air, a weightless thing of skin and bone. This sense of life closing down, of blinds being drawn, wasn't so bad except for the terrible heat that had begun to burn inside him.

"And what becomes of Russia, my dear Volovich?" Greshko asked.

He lay very still. Dimitri Volovich stood up and left the bedroom. He told the Yakut nurse that the old man was sleeping, and then he stepped outside into the darkness, hearing the trees rustle and night creatures foraging in the forest, sounds that filled him, for some reason, with an odd sense of fear.

Epilogue

Sussex, England

Frank Pagan stretched out in a deckchair and stared up into the sunlight of the early afternoon. It was one of those brilliant mid-September days that condescend to visit England infrequently, warm and yet with a hint of the autumn still to come, that glorious time before the leaves change and drift in a brittle dance to the ground, and the landscape turns melancholy. He enjoyed the feel of sunlight on his eyelids, the drone of insects, the sound of a cricket-bat colliding with a leather ball, a timeless click, placid and unthreatening and peculiarly English.

He looked across the playing-field at the white-suited figures who stood motionless on the rich grass. It was one of those games you didn't have to pay attention to, because very little ever happened. Occasionally a batsman was out, and occasionally some daring soul would swing his bat at the ball and send it flying over the boundary, but attention wasn't a necessary condition of enjoyment. Serenity was the soul of all village-green cricket games. Peace and detachment, idleness, a glass or two of beer, a suggestion of unimportant pageantry. He edged himself up in his striped deckchair and watched the bowler approach the wicket and make his delivery, and he followed the leisurely flight of the red ball as it spun towards the batsman. The ball went harmlessly past the batsman, and the wickets, into the enormous gloves of the wicket-keeper.

Pagan reached for his beer, which had turned warm under the sun, and he sipped it slowly. He stared beyond the playing-field to the oak trees on the other side, where the scoreboard was located, and a small ramshackle pavilion stood. The score, to Pagan, was utterly irrelevant. There were some animated old men in chairs around the pavilion, and here and there an interested youngster, but in general the event was observed with nonchalance and the kind of patience required by any cricket spectator. Nothing mattered here. Nothing that happened here would change the course of the world in any way. And he liked that sensation. He liked the notion of being removed from anything that was hectic, and he liked the peacefulness of doing absolutely nothing.

And watching cricket. And drinking flat beer. And not thinking about Kristina Vaska, whom he hadn't seen or heard from since the events at Grand Central Station. He owed her his life, he understood that much. And he was grateful. But he had the feeling that other possibilities had slipped away, that other conceivable futures had cancelled themselves, and this thought – try valiantly as he might to ignore it – left him depressed.

He looked along the row of deckchairs that stretched on either side of him, shielding his eyes from the sun and seeing Martin Burr – who carried two glasses of beer – come towards him from the striped marquee where beverages were sold. Pagan had come here at Burr's invitation, an invitation he'd accepted gladly because for the six days since he'd returned from the United States he'd done very little but make a report and linger aimlessly in his apartment. He cleaned the place up, but that took only a day and a half. He shuffled pictures on the wall, made some minor changes, moved furniture around, dusted his record albums, and that took another day. Coming down here to Martin Burr's little corner of the world was a break from the dreariness of London.

Burr looked out at the cricket players. A batsman had just been declared out and there was a smattering of subdued applause from the pavilion area. The Commissioner made an adjustment to his eyepatch and turned towards Pagan.

"I have some news that may interest you, Frank."

Pagan didn't want to hear what it was. He wanted to lose himself in laziness and detachment. He wanted to believe that Burr had invited him down here for rest and relaxation, that the Commissioner had no ulterior motive. Life had to be simple, for God's sake.

"I mention it in passing, Frank," Burr said. "If you're interested in loose ends."

Pagan looked at the Commissioner. Martin Burr sipped his beer, leaving a ring of foam on his upper lip, which he made no attempt to wipe away.

"It's from Witherspoon. Thought you might be curious, that's all," and Martin Burr looked rather sly all at once.

"All right. I'm curious."

Burr leaned a little closer. There was something mysterious about the Commissioner, Pagan decided, as if this cricket game were just a front, an excuse, for something else. He wasn't sure what.

"We keep getting news about revolts all over the place. In Latvia. Lithuania. Estonia. It seems that armed bands rose up and were quickly put down again. There's nothing very firm, you understand. Some eyewitness accounts, some diplomatic reports. A couple of telegrams purporting to be from the Movement for Baltic Independence were received in Paris and Stockholm. And the BBC monitored a speech on Estonian radio about the fight for freedom, but the speaker was cut off in the middle of it. That's all. The Soviets are officially saying nothing, of course. But it appears that these rebellions were timed to coincide with the attack of that plane. One massive display of defiance and courage. One huge cry for independence."

"Which didn't quite make it," Pagan said. It would have been quite a symphony, he thought. Quite an arrangement, everything succeeding at the same time. He remembered Aleksis and he thought of the bravery, the effort, the sheer damned ambition of Romanenko and Mikhail Kiss. He thought of their commitment, that zealous attachment to their cause that overwhelmed everything else in their lives – even such things as simple loyalty to an old comrade like Norbert Vaska. Commitment and vengeance. And betrayal. There was a level on which Frank Pagan admired that kind of courage even if he didn't agree with its ultimate chaotic aim, a bloody war all across the Baltic nations, a war that could have only one outcome. But finally he felt a certain ambivalence toward the Brotherhood and if there was a sensation he hated in himself, that was the one.

"Damned good effort, though." Burr was quiet. "The Americans are saying the pilot was a complete schizophrenic. History of mental illness. To be expected."

Pagan nodded. "Of course." He was remembering Mikhail Kiss and the big house in Glen Cove and the empty rooms. He wondered if Andres's trophies were still in place, his certificates still hanging on the walls.

Burr watched the game a moment. "Perhaps even more mysterious is the way Epishev has simply vanished from the face of the earth. My feeling is that the Russians are playing that one really close to their chests. They probably took him out and shot him for his role in this subversive drama." Burr sipped his beer. "Tommy also says there's an unpublicised shake-up going on in air-defence personnel, which is to be expected, of course. According to his sources, about a score of officers have been arrested already and more are expected. Most of them were in possession of large sums of American money and false passports. Presumably these came courtesy of that Brotherhood of yours, Frank, which must have spread more than a few dollars around the place."

Martin Burr set his glass in his lap. He was silent for a time. "And General Greshko is dead. A timely sort of death, wouldn't you say – given the role he's supposed to have played in this failed revolution. Heart-attack. Naturally, it would be. Unless it was a car crash. Prominent Soviets usually only succumb to those things."

Pagan smiled. Burr drained his beer and added, "One of the last chaps to see him was one of our own, a fellow called McLaren at the Embassy. Greshko told him the most outrageous story of financial skulduggery and sedition on the part of the new Chairman of the KGB. There were documents too."

"Documents?"

"Apparently. The PM doesn't want them bruited about. Can't embarrass our Soviet friends. We're allies these days. Expect you've heard that, Frank. We're like that with the Bolsheviks." Martin Burr closed his index and middle fingers together, then belched in a restrained way. "As for your fat man – well, no trace, absolutely no trace at all. He just doesn't exist, it seems. A spooky thought, Frank. Somewhere in the hidden government of the United States, in one of those subterranean outfits that really run the show over in America, there lurk figures prepared to plan the future direction of the human race, without regard to reality. Makes you think, Frank."

Pagan watched him for a time because he couldn't escape the uncomfortable sensation that Burr was withholding something else, a topic he didn't want to mention, words he couldn't quite get right. He had the look of a man rehearsing in his head. Pagan knew it would come out eventually. It always did where the Commissioner was concerned.

"Lovely day," Burr said.

The weather. But that wasn't what was on Martin Burr's mind, Pagan was certain. Burr stood up, prodded the ground with his cane, surveyed the field of play a moment.

"I feel like something to eat," Burr said. "A sandwich perhaps."

"I'm not hungry," Pagan remarked.

"Walk with me anyway, Frank. Keep me company."

Pagan rose from the deckchair and followed Martin Burr in the direction of the marquee, making his way past people who dozed in chairs, or who lay indolently in the grass, past toddlers and young lovers, and others who were simply sunning themselves on this rare day. The marquee, pitched on the edge of the green, was a colourful affair of red and white striped canvas. Pagan could see people milling around inside, cluttered at the drinks table or buying sandwiches and pork pies.

He followed Burr into the large tent. The light here was muted, filtered through heavy canvas. He had an impression of beer kegs and sandwiches under glass trays and a muddiness underfoot where beer had been spilled. He had another impression too, and he couldn't quite define it, but for no good reason a slight sense of expectation went through him, as if this were the place where Martin Burr intended to reveal the thing he'd so obviously been reluctant to mention. He walked behind Burr to the food table and the Commissioner, after surveying an unappetising array of tomato and cucumber sandwiches, turned with a serious look on his face.

"I'm not sure how you're going to feel about this, Frank," he said.

"Feel about what?"

The Commissioner gestured to the far side of the marquee. For a second, Pagan hesitated, didn't follow the Commissioner's direction. He stood very still, not wanting to look, and yet knowing beyond any doubt what he'd see when he did turn his face. He felt strange, just a little disoriented, and all the sounds inside the tent became magnified in his head and echoed there.

"You may consider it unfair of me," Burr said. "Or you may think it's presumption on my part to interfere in your life, Frank. But there you are. I was tired of seeing you moon about. I think you need to give the girl and yourself a break."

Frank Pagan turned his face slowly.

468

She was wearing a plain lemon dress and a wide-brimmed hat that cast a shadow over her features. She was looking directly at him and there was the slightest suggestion of a smile on her lips, but he couldn't be sure of that. She was motionless, and lovely, and he felt odd, out of touch with himself, all the pulses in his body unsynchronised. And then his attention was drawn to the figure who stood just behind her, a man of indeterminate age, slightly stooped but clear-eyed, a man who held himself erect as if only with enormous effort.

Even if he'd never seen the man's photograph before, Pagan would have known that it was Norbert Vaska.

Pagan didn't move. He heard Martin Burr say, "She's on her way back to the States, Frank." Burr paused. "Just came to collect her father in Berlin. And I thought, why not? I'm not, you understand, playing bloody Cupid."

Pagan returned his gaze to Kristina Vaska, wanting to go towards her but not moving even though every urge in his body commanded him to cross the space that separated him from her.

She stepped towards him. She said, "We didn't say goodbye before." She moved her hand, laying it on the back of his wrist and this touch, so casual, reminded Pagan of what had been lost along the way.

"You got your father out, I see," he said.

"It all happened very quickly. I received a phonecall telling me to meet him in West Germany."

"I'm glad."

"I owe it to you, Frank."

"Me?"

"It seems the Soviets were happy that you warned them about Andres Kiss. That's what I gather. My father's a kind of gratitude present."

"You saved my life. So that makes us equal."

Kristina Vaska nodded her head. She looked, Pagan thought, almost unbearably beautiful.

"I guess so," she said.

Pagan stared at Norbert Vaska. He was white, withered, but there was a spirited quality in the eyes. It was the same determination he'd seen in Kristina many times, that grim sense of focus, of purpose.

She took his hand and shook it. It was a prosaic gesture that made him ache.

"Frank," she said. "Is there a chance for us?"

What a question, Pagan thought. He wasn't sure how to answer.

"It's just that I'd like to think so," she said.

"We'll see," was all he could find to say. "Let's give it some time."

He turned and walked out of the marquee into the bright afternoon sun and he moved, somewhat blindly, back in the direction of his chair.

Burr appeared, settling himself into the chair beside Pagan. "Have I missed anything?" he asked, gazing out across the cricket field.

Pagan smiled. "I've never known you to miss a thing, Commissioner."